THE GIFTING

by

J. D. Cosh

First published in Australia by Aurora House
www.aurorahouse.com.au

This edition published 2023

Typesetting and e-book design: Cognition Technology |
www.cognition-technology.com
Cover Designer: Linda Westmoreland | www.lindawestmoreland.com

ISBN number: 978-1-922913-25-8 (paperback)

A catalogue record for this book is available from the National Library of Australia

Distributed by: *Ingram Content*: www.ingramcontent.com

Australia: *Phone*: +613 9765 4800 |
Email: lsiaustralia@ingramcontent.com

Milton Keynes UK: *Phone*: +44 (0)845 121 4567 |
Email: enquiries@ingramcontent.com

La Vergne, TN USA: *Phone*: +1 800 509 4156 |
Email: inquiry@lightningsource.com

Dedication

This story is dedicated to my sister,

Claire.

A woman who, very much, lived her life.

I would also like to thank Dorothy Hillis and Fiona Duggan for their much-appreciated help and guidance.

Also, my friend Linda Westmoreland for her inspirational art work, which kept me going and pointed in the right direction; telling me I paint better pictures with words than I do with paint or photographs.

Finally, but not least, much thanks go to my friend Christine Porter, who, through the years, corrected my many dyslexic and grammatical faux pas, along with thoughtful structural suggestions. This, I have always, very much appreciated.

For me, being dyslexic has never meant I was dumb, it just meant I had to find a different way of learning. My brain doesn't see words the way most people's brains do, but I persevered, and have come to terms with the vagaries of the English language because I like telling stories.

Over the years, I've found many people like reading my stories.

I hope you do.

CONTENTS

Map of the Main Landmass on the Planet of Meglian

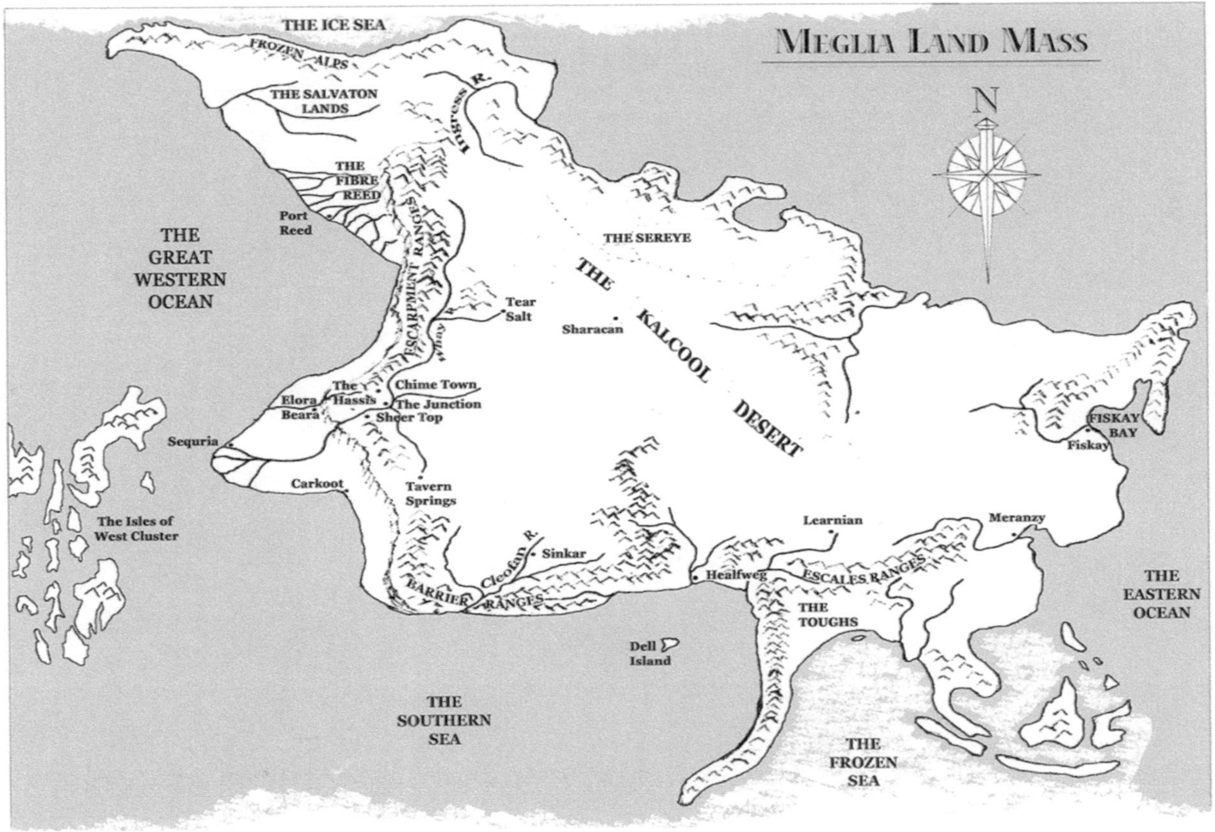

PART I
THE UNFOLDING SAND

INTRODUCTION

From a low rise on the southern side of the gap, Gaywin looked out at the small desert village—all that now remained of the once vibrant city of Sharacan. On all other sides of the once mighty metropolis, rocky hills rose to shelter it from the worst of the desert storms. Yet not even this barrier had saved it from the College's wrath.

From his vantage point, it seemed as though time and the persistence of the desert had continued the College's destruction. The stone buildings that had once been the pride of the ancient city were now just piles of rubble jutting from the sand, and the thousands of mud-brick structures Gaywin had read about were already dust.

He hated this place. He always had, even though this was the first time he'd actually seen it. He also despised its people, for he held them to blame. Like Sharacan itself, even in this diminished state, they too still survived. The fact that he had been sent here was testament to that.

In sending him here, the College Hierarchy were sending him a message. They were telling him not to get above himself—that his family was still in disgrace. It was here, at Sharacan, that his family's honour had been shattered, and so it was here that the Hierarchy had sent him, to remind him of this fact.

Because of the actions of one ancestor, none of his family would ever again be welcomed into the College elite, and he would forever be marked as lower-classed. He wore the black robes of the College, but could never hope to hold any meaningful rank.

Two hundred years ago, Gaywin's ancestor and the elite squad of Black Robes he'd commanded had deserted their post during the battle for Sharacan, never to be seen again. Word of their desertion had destabilised the entire might of the College's force. After all, if the army's most elite squadron could no longer withstand the Comcree, what chance did the rest of them have?

Despite eventually winning the battle, this one act of betrayal had caused the College to lose their advantage. They'd been forced to abandon their hope for supremacy and instead negotiate a truce.

After Sharacan, the Black Robed forces never again won a battle. The taking of the city had ruined everything for the College, and so Sharacan was made to pay the price. For two hundred years, the Black Robes had occupied the city and imposed their laws of subjugation.

Looking down now at what remained of Sharacan, Gaywin, became aware for the first time of the large, circular hillock in the very centre of the depression that cradled the city. To him, it seemed oddly out of place within the landscape.

He now turned his attention to the obelisk. With its almost translucent crystal tip, it stood in contrast to the mound, and he knew its purpose. Through his research, he knew that the location of the great tower was supposed to mark the site of Sharacan's once magnificent temple—a temple that no longer existed. It had been destroyed by the College after the battle, in an attempt to obliterate the Comcree and their gods from the city. It had been his ancestor's squad that had been put in charge here, and it was from here that they had vanished. The obelisk, however, had been allowed to remain. Not because of the myths and legends surrounding it, but rather because it served as a reminder of the College's dominance.

Scowling, Gaywin wished he had been there to assist in the temple's destruction. He would have had no hesitation in obliterating the place where his ancestor had betrayed the College and doomed his descendants. In fact, if he had been there, he would have ensured that the disgrace had never happened in the first place.

He was almost smiling now as another thought came to him. He could never change the past, but he could change the future. By placing him here, the hierarchy had given him the perfect opportunity to remove this last vestige of Sharacan's famous temple. In his mind's eye, he saw the obelisk fall. Nothing would be left to remind anyone that the temple had ever existed. There would be nothing to remind people of his family's shame.

In just two hundred years, Sharacan had shrunk to become just a minor outpost of the College, but it hadn't disappeared entirely. The ancient legends stated that if Sharacan no longer existed, neither would the world, but these were just stories—tales that the ancient priestesses of the temple had shared alongside stories about gods who hadn't been seen in thousands of years. Like all Black Robes, Gaywin's schooling had taught him that there were no gods, and that there never had been.

Only the Comcree, guardians of the gods, were said to still exist. But even they hadn't been seen since just after the great battle for Sharacan. After binding the College to its domain with the treaty they'd exacted, the Comcree, too, had vanished from the world, just like the gods they were said to represent. They were now no more than wraiths on the wind in the minds of the people.

But with Sharacan gone, even those memories would eventually die. The College could once more grow strong, and it would be his doing. His family's honour would be restored.

Halfway between the obelisk and the village, the sight of a group of elderly women—walking freely and unsupervised—broke Gaywin's thoughts. He would put a stop to that as well.

He now studied the well-pond, with its encircling ring of batter-palms. Long ago, every ninth tree—the number nine being symbolic of the gods—had been cut away by the Black Robes to signify the College's domination. But looking at it now, he could see that the repetitive gaps might be thought to symbolise the gods too. All the trees would need to go.

He sensed his hatred gathering within him. Like all Black Robes, he knew that the concept of the gods had really just been a way for the Comcree to control the masses. Only the superstitious and weak-minded truly still believed in them.

He would prevail here. Even the Hierarchy would finally have to accept him for doing what they'd neglected to do.

The shrow moved impatiently beneath him, causing Gaywin's scowl to deepen. Shrows were always difficult beasts to control, but they were necessary for venturing out into the wasteland that was the Kalcool Desert. They were the only animal that could survive in such a harsh environment.

Gaywin lifted his last waterskin and drained it before splashing the remaining drops across his face. He returned the receptacle to the saddle-hook and dug his heels into the shrow's sides, urging the animal forward. He decided in this moment that he also hated shrows.

As with nearly everyone else alive on Meglian, Gaywin didn't know the truth of Sharacan. He didn't know that his ancestor's squad hadn't in fact deserted. He didn't know that they had all been killed in a battle that no one knew about because there had been no one left alive to tell its tale. He didn't know all this because his ancestor's squad had lost that forgotten battle, and now other events were awakening to exert their influence. Gaywin also did not know that his own dreams would be shattered in this place by someone he was soon to meet; unknown to him, he would still turn out to be no more than a bit player in someone else's story.

1

One turning of the moons had passed since Hestean first saw the young Robe riding into the village on a shrow he could barely control. She had wondered then how he'd survived such a journey. He seemed to have little knowledge of the desert, but must have come all the way from Learnian, as that was the only place the Black Robes ever came from. It was said to be their stronghold; their place of learning, far to the south in the mountains.

Keeping her face blank, Hestean smiled inwardly, knowing that she was probably the only Sharacanese to have ever seen those mountains, even if only in a painting.

Since his arrival, she'd seen him many times, observing the villagers and hiding in the shadows, away from the desert heat—just as all Black Robes did when they first arrived. But even from the start, she had thought there was something different about this one. From within the open keffiyeh scarf that draped down over his head and shoulders, held there by a pakol cap, he seemed always to be expressing unpleasantness. Even when mixing with other Robes, his facial expressions never seemed to vary much.

Occasionally, though, when he was reprimanding someone, she had noticed his eyes brighten. It suggested he enjoyed inflicting College law on the people of the village. "Zealot" was the word her mother had used. Her mother had said that all Black Robes of the College were like this when they first arrived, yet the desert had a way of changing even them.

And yet, Hestean still felt there was something more sinister about this one.

The image of the Black Robes' citadel returned to her more fully now. She recalled her curiosity after being told that mountains were hills a thousand times bigger than those surrounding her village. At first, she'd tried to imagine them, but knew she never could. How could anyone imagine something they'd never seen and would never be allowed to see?

The Sharacanese were not allowed to travel to Learnian. In fact, as far as she knew, nobody from Sharacan had ever been allowed to travel anywhere, and even less so if they were female.

She had never understood the Black Robes' dislike for women. Even with her ignorance of the wider world, she still knew the laws of nature; the bonding that was necessary between men and women if generations were to replenish themselves. Why would anyone continually throw scorn on such a necessary part of their being? Under the Black Robes, women were hardly allowed to do anything without permission.

And that was exactly why the newcomer was confronting her now.

'Are you mocking me, woman? You don't even appear to be listening to me,' she heard him say, her mind quickly returning to the present.

It was strange that her mind had wandered; usually, she had her excuses all lined up and ready to go. Maybe it was because, this time, she actually hadn't done anything wrong. Or, more to the point, she hadn't had time to do what she was now being accused of. Again, she almost smiled, but didn't. She knew better than to incite him further. This accusation would be a foolish thing to die for when there had been other things—worse incursions against the Black Robes' laws of which she was actually guilty.

Things like breaking into their meeting hall. No one had ever managed that apart from her, as far as she knew. Not without being caught, anyway. That was where she had seen the painted image hanging on the wall, of the mountains and the Black Robes' citadel of Learnian. That was also when she had discovered, as she'd already suspected, that all the Black Robes' books were written in the modern tongue and therefore undecipherable to her.

She knew there was only one way to solve this problem. She had to find a way of learning to read the language the Black Robes used.

She didn't know why the painting had flashed into her mind now, with the Black Robe before her. Was she actually afraid? She knew that she was still too young to receive a full punishment, but maybe she had accumulated too many warnings, and now, she would be dragged into the Black Robes' meeting house to receive their justice.

She saw movement from behind the Black Robe's shoulder and was astonished to feel a glimmer of hope. Hope was never something she would normally feel when catching sight of a second Black Robe coming towards her.

The elderly Robe stopped beside them, and immediately asked, 'Gaywin, what is it you do here? I could hear you at the other end of the square.'

'I caught this woman here reading a book, but she continues to deny it.'

The elderly Robe now turned to look upon her, suspicion rising. 'Daughter of Sharn?'

Hestean lifted her head to look directly into the elderly Robe's eyes, while simultaneously committing the younger Robe's name—Gaywin—to memory. This was the first time she'd actually heard it. And now, again, she knew all the Robes by name .

Still wishing she had actually been able to do what she was being accused of, Hestean said, 'The book was just there, Robe Elless. I was not reading it because, as you know, we are not taught how to read your words. So how could I have been reading this book?'

'But I saw the pages turning!' said Gaywin.

'It was the breeze that turned the pages, Robe Elless, not me!'

'She was looking at the pages! I saw her!' insisted Gaywin furiously.

'Were you looking at the pages, daughter of Sharn?' asked the elderly Robe.

'I was just wondering who left the book there. That was all. I thought it a foolish thing to leave a book on the edge of a water well.'

Hestean never saw the slap that knocked her to the ground, but she did feel it. Dazed, she lay sprawled on the sand as Gaywin yelled, 'Don't ever call me a fool, woman.'

'So, the book is yours, is it, Gaywin?' asked Robe Elless. A puzzled look now spread across his face as he turned his attention back to the younger Robe. 'You should know better than to leave a book where it could so easily be damaged. Why did you do such a thing?'

Gaywin reddened. He flustered to find some words. 'There was a disturbance that needed attending to, and I forgot the book when I went to attend to it.'

'I heard no other disturbance, and I have been in the square myself now for some time. The only thing that has come to my attention is you and this girl.'

Gaywin's scowl deepened. 'But this woman was reading the pages—I saw her. She needs to be punished for that.'

'Gaywin, how long have you been in the village now? One cycle of the moons? And still it seems you have not learned the colour-coding of Sharacan dress. She wears a red sash around her waist, not black. The sash is there for a reason. It shows that she is not yet an adult, and until she is, under our law, she must be reprimanded by her parents, not by you. If they do not do this, then they will be the ones we punish. You were told this when you arrived, were you not? I know this is not normally the way with College law, but it is here?'

Robe Elless again turned his attention to Hestean, then bent down to grab her forearm. He pulled her to her feet, and she could see that he was somewhat annoyed by the younger Robe's behaviour.

After a moment, he said, 'Come, daughter of Sharn. You've caused enough trouble for one day. I'll take you home.'

'But my mother sent me to fill the waterskin!'

'Well, then, she will now have to come and fill it herself, won't she?' said the elderly Robe.

'You had better never lie to me again, girl,' spat Gaywin as Robe Elless towed her past him.

Without warning, Hestean found herself being swung round as the elderly Robe spun on the spot to face the younger man. 'Enough, Gaywin,' he said. 'Do you think I was in the square by accident? Every new Robe that comes to Sharacan is scrutinised. This is Sharacan, and within Sharacan the rules are different from elsewhere under College law. For a start, yes, you are right, this girl can read—just as all the women here can. You were told about this. But she cannot read your book, just as you were also told! Here, unlike in other parts of College territory, women are permitted to read and write, but only in the ancient tongue, because nowhere else in the world is that language still used. It is a compromise, for under the Treaty of Truce, the women of Sharacan must be allowed to read and write.

'In addition to the administrative staff, there is only one squad of Black Robes here, Gaywin. One squad to maintain order in this whole village. That may sound like a comfortable number until you consider that this is Sharacan. The women here may not be the warriors of legend, but they are still Sharacanese, and would be the equal of any man if it came to a fight. They are born with that instinct to survive, Gaywin. All who are born with Sharacan blood carry that in-built ability, and in that, the Sharacanese women are no different from their men. The Sharacanese game of stones may have been outlawed to all except children, in order to blunt their edge, but it does not fully negate that edge. Unbelievable as it might sound, this one squad of Robes survive here because the Sharacanese allow us to survive.'

Elless let a moment pass for this to sink in. Then he went on. 'It takes ten days for a message to be sent to Learnian and that time again for reinforcements to arrive. You young Robes think you know everything, but you do not. Sharacan is different from everywhere else under College rule, and you had better start learning that. The only thing that holds these Sharacanese villagers in check is the knowledge that if the College was forced to return here *en masse*, then none of them would be allowed to live.

'By then, though, Gaywin, you and I would be dead. Do you understand now? Ruling Sharacan is a balancing act that you do not want to unbalance, because if you do, you might just topple the whole world.' He lowered his voice. 'Do you really want to start another war, Gaywin?'

Just for an instant, Hestean thought she saw a strange expression on the young Robe's face, expressing that this might be exactly what he wanted. But then the expression vanished, replaced by the ever-present scowl.

As if realising that he had gone too far, Robe Elless turned to hide his regret from the younger Robe. But Hestean saw it.

After a moment, the older Robe stiffened and stretched to his full height before striding off, Hestean's arm once more gripped tightly in his hand.

She would have to be wary of this Gaywin, Hestean decided. He may need to be watched and followed more closely before she set out on any more of her questionable adventures. Not that she would be set free for a while, as she already knew what her father would demand.

Walking towards her house, something Robe Elless had said began to pin-prick its way into Hestean's thoughts. Like a trap, her mind caught everything. And in time, she would be able to make sense of these new grains of information.

Claiming this as a victory, she smiled.

* * *

In the years since her status had changed from child to adult-in-learning, Hestean had contrived a habit of climbing onto the flat roof of her family's stone and mud-brick dwelling to look out upon her village, as she was now.

Yesterday had been a disaster.

As a child, she had been unaware of the world and the limited freedom of the adult women. Now, though, she knew that there were consequences to everything. The encounter with Gaywin had once more shown her that. Yet again, her dreams had been stifled.

She was fortunate in the positioning of her family's home on the higher side of the square, and from her hiding spot behind her rooftop parapet, Hestean surveyed her surroundings. She could see the low hills and their jagged outcrops of rock, the few isolated fields of green, and the great sea of sand beyond the hills, which spread out in all directions. It was as if the desert itself had incarcerated Sharacan, and in response, Sharacan had imprisoned her.

In the light of predawn, whenever she could, she had always observed her village and wondered about the ancient ruins that surrounded it. She had once even started to count all the remnant buildings until she abandoned the idea, realising she could never count them all. Most lay collapsed and lost in time beneath the encroaching desert.

Now, lying flat and wrapped in her cloak for warmth—the day's heat still far from its inevitable thick shimmer—her eyes were drawn out past the well-pond. This was the moment she had been waiting for.

When the sun's rays first touched the crystalline top of the obelisk, she smiled. This had become one of the few joyous fragments that made up her life. She wasn't quite sure why. Perhaps because it was predictable and beautiful; or maybe it was how the obelisk seemed to come alive, absorbing the sun's magnificence.

Hestean, too, wished that she could soak up the sun like that, taking in the entire world. If only she was as free.

She turned her gaze back to the well-pond and the broken ring of batter-palms that surrounded it. Looking at them now, she wondered if they were the only full-grown trees she'd ever see.

Beneath the white glare of the obelisk, Hestean turned to the central mound, and began to speculate about the true history of this place—something she entertained often. She had been told once that the mound had always existed, but looking at it now, bulging up from the shallow valley's emptiness, she wondered if this was true. She also pondered why the Black Robes forbade anything being built close to the obelisk or the great mound.

She tried to piece together what she really knew of Sharacan, but all she could manage were disjointed tales of fantasy. Open discussion about Sharacan's past was frowned upon by the Black Robes, even though it did still happen occasionally. When it did, she had always been an attentive listener, despite the scantness on detail. Armed with these stories, she had worked out that long ago the well-pond had supplied the entire water needs of the city. But how could this one well-pond have been enough when all it could sustain now was the remnant village?

Sharacan had done what it could to sustain water. Underground channels had been dug to lessen evaporation, which had once fanned out in all directions and ducted water to not only urban wells, but the fields and farms that had once existed beyond. Most of these were now collapsed, having succumbed to generations of neglect. Only the most integral tunnels remained tended, and only a few crop fields remained in use.

Breathing in, Hestean could almost taste and smell the flutter-weed, matoze, and towtowee that grew in these fields. Her mouth threatened to salivate at the thought of rows upon rows of lush-melons soon to be ripe. Since the age of nine, Hestean had been forbidden from running between the gardened rows. That was seven years ago now, and she still failed to understand how the women here managed to endure the entrapment of their gender. There was a strength to them that she still did not yet understand.

Hestean knew her eighteenth birthday would drive her life in one of three directions. Like some, the knowledge she'd gained would slowly wither her away and send her into an expanding sense of hopelessness. Or her life may be cut short after lashing out against the Black Robes. Hopefully, like most, she would gain the strength to endure and accept her place in the world.

But Hestean was not optimistic. Unless her nature drastically changed, she knew which of the three was most likely to be her destiny. She'd never been good at keeping quiet.

'Can I truly survive here?' she mouthed to herself. 'Can I truly stand to be imprisoned within this dull emptiness for the rest of my life?'

She pulled herself into a ball, becoming smaller and less visible upon the pillows of her nest. She stayed that way, wishing she could vanish. She had watched the Robes try to drain the hope from other women's lives, yet many persisted. Why? Would it not be simply better to die than to have your life shackled forever?

It wasn't as though she could escape; she had nowhere else to go. If she ran from here, the desert would claim her in days. Her investigations had shown her that much. Unable to take more than the water she could carry, the sun would crack and burn her skin until she died slowly from dehydration.

Yet, despite everything, she also recognised a love for this place within herself. She was part of this village. Maybe, eventually, she would realise what gave these women their strength, and it would be worth waiting for. Worth staying alive for.

Hestean wore the yellow clothes of a woman, but she was not, as yet, an adult. The red sash around her waist showed everyone that. Only when she was fully matured would she be endowed with the secrets that enabled the women here to survive.

She sighed and stretched, turning onto her back to look up at the brightening sky. Her mind once more shifted to yesterday. All she wanted was to know and understand her world, and for that, the Black Robes had punished her. And they would keep punishing her simply because she was a woman. In her mind, she had done nothing wrong. The book had just been there; her eyes had just fallen upon it. She had surmised that the key to possibly understanding this place was in the written language of the Black Robes, but she had failed in that endeavour.

However, she had learned something.

Robe Elless had told Gaywin that ruling Sharacan was a balancing act, which if unbalanced could topple the world. What had he meant by that? Had he meant his world, or the world of the College? Or had he really meant the *whole* world?

Hestean heard the front door open and close beneath her, and she moved to look out over the roof. She saw her father with his hoe over his shoulder, walking off to join the other men in the fields. He was not good with animals; he never had been. He much preferred to toil in his gardens and barter for the meat they ate. Hestean loved her father and knew he was only surviving the best way he could. He might not be so bound as the women of the village, but he too was shackled.

‘Hestean, are you up there?’ called a female voice.

Hestean frowned, then reluctantly began her descent towards what would surely be a tedious day.

* * *

‘He has warned you, Hestean,’ stated Hestean’s mother, Sathea, as she stepped off the ladder.

‘Oh, don’t worry, Mother,’ said Hestean. ‘I can handle Father! In a few days he will have forgiven me, the way he always does.’

‘You little fool. You know we all have to live within the laws of these Robes, don’t you? One day you will push your father too far. Hestean, you will give him no choice!’

Looking out through the window, Hestean’s thoughts drifted for a moment to the fields where her father spent most of his days, and where she would never again walk freely.

‘Are you not listening to me?’ demanded Sathea, jerking her from her daydream. ‘Don’t you understand the foolishness of these constant irritations to the Robes? They are not playing a game, Hestean! The Black Robes don’t play games, nor do they forget.’

‘How long this time, Mother?’

Sathea turned from her daughter to the pile of dough in front of her. She thumped at it, breathed, then again began to knead at the mixture of bean flour and water. ‘For once, he would not say,’ she said. ‘You are to remain bound to this house until he decides. He wants to truly see your repentance this time before making a final judgment.’

‘He will,’ said Hestean. She picked up a tarrawomb—a type of desert fruit—and took a bite out of its ripe flesh.

‘Do you not see, Hestean?’ said Sathea, whirling round to stare at her daughter. ‘You make him visible, too! You make us all visible! The Black Robes rule here! In order to survive, you must understand that. Yes, they tolerate the exuberance of the young, but when you are older there will be no tolerance. You have only two years left, Hestean. Two years in which to grow up and learn. Or you will die. They are the only options. You are my only child—don’t you understand that? Our family will either live on or die with you. When your father and I are gone, you will be the last of the Descee lineage in this village.’

Hestean retreated to the other side of the table, seeking to find the words that might quiet her mother’s assault.

'How do you stand it, Mother? Tell me that,' she said.

As if afraid to move a single muscle in case she struck out at her daughter, Sathea just eyed the young woman looking back at her from the other side of the room. She put down her tray.

Still looking directly into Hestean's eyes, she said, 'I submit, child, so that I can walk out into the sun on my own and feel the breeze upon my face. I decided long ago that I would never allow these Robes to take that from me. It is enough when you know there is nothing else you can have. Not if you want to protect the world.'

Hestean stilled. She knew, instinctively, that she had just heard something important—something profound. In just two days, two different people had mentioned "the world". She knew better than to think her mother would reveal more to her, but she finally had confirmation that there was something truly hidden within the history of Sharacan. Like all the women here, and all those who had come before her, Hestean would have to wait to find out what it was. The "adult-in-learning" stage was a cultural practice unique to the Sharacanese, practised nowhere else. It was a time of testing, and like all young females here, Hestean needed to pass that test.

There were secrets here that the women guarded, and carrying forward those secrets was what gave them purpose.

Hestean noticed her mother looking at her strangely, and heard her say quietly, 'Have you seen it, Hestean? Have you just seen how we survive here? I think you have, haven't you?'

'I think I'm beginning to, but …'

'No *buts*, Hestean. I think you have just uncovered something that most girls don't find out about until their eighteenth birthday. Am I right, Hestean? Because for some girls, it is never enough, and they still fade. This is the way we survive here, but you have to be able to hold it. The strength comes naturally to some who grasp it early, but have you that strength? You will have to decide if it is enough for you, and you will have to be prepared to wait.'

'Does Father know?'

'Your father is a man, and he will always be able to survive in a world that is ruled *by* and *for* men. What we hold was given to a woman, and here in Sharacan it has become strictly women's business.'

'You mean that elsewhere men can hold it, too?'

'I believe that there are some men who can, yes.'

'In the last two days, I have more than once heard Sharacan likened to 'the world', mother. So, can the gods truly destroy the world?'

'If the gods really do exist, Hestean, then they could never destroy the world, for they exist in order to protect it and guide us forward. The College, however, has decreed that the gods do not exist, and this is important to them. They cannot stop us from believing, and while they tolerate it, they don't like it. The rituals are no longer performed, and the stories no longer told aloud, but we remember them, Hestean. They are carried forward by the women of this village. And one day, they will all be told to you. Only then will you understand for yourself.'

'How?'

'Most women here find out on their eighteenth birthday, as I have said. You need to try to limit your disobedience, so that you, too, can one day know all the stories. The tellings, they are called. And we need you to survive, Hestean. We need all the women of this village to survive. It is what we were brought into this world to do. We are all that remains of the Temple, Hestean. We are the priestesses. We are the last, and the Black Robes must never know we still exist, or they will kill us all. One of the reasons why the Black Robes of the College hate all women is because it was women who ran the Great Temple. It's one of the reasons why they destroyed it.'

Dumbfounded, Hestean went to sit down, almost missing the stool she was aiming for. 'Priestesses, history … I cannot just be still, Mother, it is not who I am! You know it is not who I am. I have always hated what the Robes are doing to this place, and you have just explained why I *should* hate it. I am Sharacanese!'

'But you must, Hestean. Can you at least try? If you don't, then you will not last long into your adulthood, and that would be a waste.'

'I can try, I suppose.'

'I hope so, Hestean. I hope you can, because we need you. The gods need you.' Sathea walked around the table and pulled Hestean close to her. 'But for now, you had better take over here, because after your foolishness of yesterday I'll have to go and get the water this morning. You do remember how to make flatbread, don't you?'

'Of course I do, Mother.' Pulling away, Hestean shot Sathea a derisive glare.

'Hestean,' said Sathea. 'I'm only going to say this once, so listen. You are an exact copy of who I once was, so if I can do it, so can you.

You have to. Do you understand me? Do you understand what I am saying?'

'You were never like me, Mother.'

'Trust me, Hestean. What you will learn will change you forever, so start now and learn to survive. I was once *exactly* like you. Why do you think your father lets you get away with so much? He knew me when I was young. He saw me change and he has hope for you, too. He loves you, Hestean; you should think about that. You should think about what you could bring down upon all of us by being too visible.'

2

The days of Hestean's penance continued, and despite what she now knew, her life stagnated in the confinement of her home. The only relief was on her rooftop, from which she continued to observe the village. Knowing now why the women here tolerated their existence didn't make things any easier, but at least now she felt closer to them.

However, there was still the cleaning and the washing, the collecting of dung and its everyday turning and drying so that it could be burned as fuel for cooking. Without her excursions, it was this everyday repetition—and the mindless boredom of it—that stifled her.

Late one afternoon, though, she watched with interest as a traveller arrived, leading four silver shrows. As a child, she'd marvelled at these large, slim animals, which could rise up on their four back legs to scavenge high foliage from amongst the crown of a well-pond batter-palm. They were able to forage with their long tongues and two front paws, while using their bulbous tails for balance. They were beautifully trimmed with colour; this stranger's shrows captured her anew with their large red and orange frills tipped with blue, which fluttered rhythmically along the undersides of their necks.

She had first seen the young man and his caravan as a shimmer to the east, at the entrance to their shallow valley, and had watched as their ghostly shapes solidified into more recognisable forms. Now in the village square, he had stopped to speak to some of the village men, who in turn pointed him towards the Black Robes' House of Authority. Compared to the blue-black of Hestean's people, his skin looked pale—more like the colouring of the Black Robes, but not quite so bland. The Black Robes' hair was usually black or brown, whereas this stranger's hair was a real red—almost the same colour as a shrow's frill. She had never seen a person with red hair before. He also seemed slightly taller than the men around him, although perhaps this impression came from the courtesy he seemed to show towards the men for their helpfulness. His slim, young body seemed to carry firmness and strength despite his dishevelled and travel-worn appearance.

Her eyes again examined his caravan. She noted the many empty waterskins, along with shovels and picks, packed against the shrows' sides. She realised with a rush that this stranger had come a great distance. Had he, too, come all the way from Learnian as the Robes had?

Later, unable to sleep, she lay wondering about the young stranger. Who was he? Where had he come from? Her first thought—Learnian—had been a presumption, but his manner of dress had quickly changed her mind. His clothes were colourful, seeming to match the colours of his shrows. He'd also entered through the eastern opening from the north side, whereas the Robes always entered from the south.

This stranger was something else, and from somewhere else. So what did he want with the Black Robes, and why had he come here?

Whenever she could in the following days, Hestean searched for the young man from her rooftop, generally finding him walking amongst the ancient ruins of Sharacan. She noticed he'd cleaned himself up, shaved his face, and now looked rather handsome. Then one day, she saw him with the Village Chairman of the Robes, pointing out parts of the surrounding landscape.

Their gestures and other mannerisms showed their conversation to be intense, even heated, although when it concluded they seemed to agree on something, grasping each other's forearms in acknowledgement of the fact.

The next day, she looked on as a big tent was erected to the east, out past the well-pond and obelisk. The young man had employed some of the village men, setting them to digging up the earth. Hestean was curious, and pondered what he would find; what he was seeking. She wondered, too, if it was the same thing that had always pulled her eyes in that direction. Her thoughts drifted to the gleaming white stone of the obelisk for a moment. Did he also want to know the past—the unknown history of this place about which she herself also desperately wanted to find?

She knew that with herself as a daughter, her father always felt a need to show his house's willingness to participate in any extra village labour. She had made them too visible for him not to. So, it was no real surprise that night to hear him suggest to Sathea that she should offer her employment to the stranger as one of the women needed to supply water.

'It can only be for the mornings, though,' he said, 'for you will still have to accompany Hestean in the afternoons to help with the outside chores. As of yet, I am still not ready to put aside her confinement.'

'I suppose I could ask Amri if she wants to do half a day?' said her mother. 'I hear the crosslander is paying in coin? Even the gods must know that the house of Amri's bind-mate could do with some extra income.'

'The young crosslander's coins were guildens, I was told. He's converted them into College constantiams at a rate of about one for two. It was Fhean himself who told me. He saw the crosslander walk into the Robes' House of Authority with one bag and walk out with two, so it seems true enough. Fhean has never been one to distort what he sees.'

'Are you sure? Guildens haven't been used here since the gods' Guardians left Sharacan.'

'Maybe the gods are on their way back, because it seems odd that one guilden is worth two constantiams.'

'Perhaps they are!'

'Perhaps they are what?' said Sharn, stopping his eating to look at his bind-mate.

'Perhaps the gods are on their way back, and perhaps one guilden is worth two constantiams.'

'Don't be silly, woman. Sharacan is not what it once was! Why would the gods come back here?'

'Well, you brought the subject up, not me. And if I am to carry water tomorrow, I had better go and find another waterskin to fill; it will have to be soaked overnight. I'll have to go and talk to Amri as well.'

The following day Sathea and Amri offered themselves for work as water carriers, and the young crosslander accepted. Every afternoon, Hestean bombarded her mother with hundreds of questions, but Sathea could tell nothing of value as far as Hestean was concerned. No more than the young man's name: Jarrak.

* * *

After sixteen days, Hestean could stand it no longer. Her inquisitive personality was bursting free again as her stimulated mind overpowered the stillness her mother had hoped for.

When her mother left the next morning, Hestean climbed again onto the roof of her home and watched as the workers set to their tasks.

Once she deemed it safe to follow, she ventured down to gather up the empty waterskin she'd selected and soaked the night before.

She looked towards the closed front door, and then, with a deep breath, decided the gods alone would be her judges. She stepped forward and opened the door just enough to glance out, then opened it further and stepped hesitantly through into the village square.

She was nervous at first, but soon she was walking quickly towards the excavations. Until she was employed, she knew she could be stopped and sent home at any moment. A light, dry dust puffed up from around her feet as she scurried past the closed doors of the houses, and she made sure not to look at any men who glanced in her direction.

As she headed for the well-pond, her vision seemed to narrow and yet broaden at the same time. Luckily, she saw none of the Black Robes who could scuttle her plan. She'd chosen her moment, hoping that most of the Robes would be at their daily meeting where they espoused the righteousness of their beliefs to each other.

'Daughter of Sharn.'

A quiver vibrated through her, and she instantly stopped and turned towards the voice. It was the Robe named Gaywin who had caught her looking at the book. A slight grin of triumph rested on his face. Immediately she knew that her adventure had been thwarted.

'Are you not bound still, daughter of Sharn?'

Hestean hesitated, but her mind was exploding. Was he again trying to trap her into something more than a misdemeanour, as he had tried to do last time? Why was he like this? Why were all the Robes like this? Surely they knew that, without women, none of them would have ever been born. But maybe that was it. Maybe they felt inferior somehow, and this compounded their dislike for the priestesses, too. There was something deeper, though. There had to be.

From the corner of her eye, she noticed movement near the blacksmith's. She looked to see a figure she knew step out into the sun's brightness.

Although Dillane was strong—he had arms almost the thickness of a normal man's leg—he was a placid man, and usually kept to himself. Like Hestean, she'd noticed he was an observer. Unlike her, though, he'd never done anything out of place that she knew of. He must have heard the Black Robe call out to her and come to see what trouble she'd gotten herself into this time.

She looked back to the Robe and saw that the young man's presence had blunted the triumph he'd only moments ago displayed. With Dillane watching, she realised that the Robe was trapped by the laws and rules of the College. Dillane would have heard him initiate the conversation.

'Yes,' she said instantly, speaking the truth, knowing that in this moment she had to. But then she followed it up quickly with her well-rehearsed lie: 'My mother … She has taken the wrong waterskin. I gave her the wrong one. It will be leaking. I didn't realise until just now when I went to mend it. There is no one else, so I had to come, or my father would be disgraced for supplying worn equipment.'

'You are bound,' the Black Robe said, his scowl deepening further at her lack of cold fear. Biting his lip, he turned towards the young man who had spoilt his sport. 'Boy, do you know this girl?'

Dillane lifted his head a little to stare at the Robe. 'Yes,' he said, with a coldness that made Hestean gasp. His eyes revealed the mistake he knew he had just made in stepping out of the shadows.

'Then you know her father and his woman?'

'I know them; I make Sharn's hoe heads!'

'Then you will not want him disparaged, for it will also belittle you through association,' said the Black Robe, threatening. 'Take the waterskin to his woman and I will take his daughter back to her confinement, so that he can deal with her there.'

'It will need filling,' said Hestean hurriedly.

Dillane glared at her inferred insult. It had hit home, just as she'd hoped. Then, abruptly, as she had also hoped, she saw his expression change. Her words had been meant as a plea, and not just the statement of derision that the Robe would have heard. A few years older than her, Dillane had already been an adult-in-learning when Hestean was a child. Back then, she knew he'd watched her play the stone game and seen that misdirection was her trademark. She'd learnt to feign weakness and simplicity, all while remaining perfectly at ease.

He looked to her more intensely now, as if considering her—judging what he remembered of her. Then he turned back to the Black Robe.

'That is women's work,' he said. 'Let her take it; her father will deal with her this evening, as you have said. I will make sure of that myself now!'

The Black Robe momentarily seethed at the young man's rebuff before smiling slightly.

Gaywin rubbed his chin, considering the young man's words as he looked across to the Robes' House of Authority, where his compatriots were already gathered, and where he should now also be. 'Very well. But make sure her father's discipline is seen to. That is your duty now.'

Hestean saw that Dillane had trapped himself into sticking to his word; he would have to tell her father.

Both Hestean and Dillane watched Gaywin quicken his gait towards the meeting hall.

'I think you have been lucky,' said Dillane once Gaywin had entered the building. 'I don't think he likes you very much, Hestean Descee, but he obviously had somewhere he needed to be.'

It took a moment before Hestean realised that Dillane was speaking to her. Still cautious, she spoke quietly. 'I am a woman. That is all he needs.'

'No, I don't think so. I was watching him hurry towards their hall when he first saw you. In a way I think you frighten him, Hestean Descee! He can see that you resent their doctrine and beliefs. You allowed him to see that. With him, you would be wiser to hide instead of stand out.'

With some bewilderment, Hestean took in Dillane, amazed to find such frankness coming from someone she had mingled with only infrequently as a child. 'Why do you tell me this?' she asked.

'Women may be nothing here, but men are equally trapped within this world of the Robes. Not many men bother to see this, but we are! He called me *boy* … I am no longer a boy. You may think he has let you go, but he has not. If I don't see your father this evening, he will have us both, for it is no longer just you he has taken a dislike to.'

'They call him Gaywin.'

Dillane chuckled. 'I've heard him called that. It's ironic, don't you think? But whether it is his name or just a play on his personality, tell your father I will call on him this evening. I'll have to, now. This Gaywin will know if I don't.'

Dillane stood in silence for a moment, looking across to the Meeting Hall. Then, without saying another word, he turned and walked back to his forge. He began again to work its bellows with his foot, and Hestean's eyes watched him as she thought about what he'd said. His words had reached her more than her father's or mother's ever had.

Was she finally growing up? She felt that she was not only seeing the truth within her mother, but within others. Her father had always seemed different from other men, but maybe, like Dillane, there were other men who were also different. Now she knew that her actions would always have consequences for others, and as a result, her vision of this world had broadened.

At the well-pond, she filled her waterskin, then she heaved it up by its strap and placed it over her shoulder. She looked back to the forge for a moment, then turned and continued on towards the young crosslander's excavations.

Out past the giant obelisk and on towards the mound, she observed her surroundings more carefully. It had been years since she'd been this far from the village centre—above ground, anyway—and no matter what happened, she was determined to soak in what she could today.

With her head turned down to avoid her mother's notice, Hestean's eyes searched for the red-haired young man from across the desert. Although she knew she would have to explain herself later, she rationalised that if she was employed here first her mother might go easier on her. She would, after all, be serving the men of the village here instead of clandestinely flouting the laws of the College.

* * *

'My most gracious interruptions to you, Maskee,' said a female voice nervously. Jarrak turned abruptly to find himself looking at a dark, slender girl with a red sash around her waist, which he knew designated her as an adult-in-learning. 'I understand you are seeking water women?'

Contriving to appear uninterested, Jarrak nevertheless listened. He knew that the Black Robes of the College looked down on women, and he had done well with his negotiation. To upset those arrangements for any reason would be unwise, and so he did his best to emulate them. He knew that there would be no remuneration given directly to this girl. Women here worked only by the will of their households, not for themselves. He knew also that it was only the conditions of work she would bargain upon, as she must have already been permitted to attend him.

'I can give the whole day, if you require it,' said the girl, not quite meeting his eyes. He noted that she seemed genuinely willing, as did the other women who had come to him, which was strange for a College enclave. Still, at first glance she appeared capable.

'It will not be a full day today, as this is late morning,' he corrected, hoping the sternness in his voice would carry.

'I had chores to attend to.'

'Then what of tomorrow and the next day, and the day after that?'

He saw her swallow, before saying with determination, 'If I am employed here, my chores will be put aside.'

Jarrak looked at her a little more closely, wondering how long it would take for him to understand these people. 'What's your name?'

'Descee. Hestean Descee.'

He observed her for a moment longer, before bending down to pick up his script-hold and jot down the name she'd spoken.

'House?'

'House of Sharn Descee.'

He turned back a few pages to see if she had kinship ties to any of the men working for him. He noticed that one of the other water women was from the same house.

'Is it your mother that works for me already?'

'As of tomorrow, I will be taking her place full-time.'

'And the other woman that works in the afternoon? What of her?'

'Have you not another place for her?'

'I do, if she can find someone else to pair with.'

'She will keep her position, then?'

'If she meets the conditions I have stated, then yes.'

Jarrak looked on as the girl pondered this. Her face set firm with decision as she said, 'We are agreed, then.'

'*If* the conditions are met,' repeated Jarrak. He raised his arm to point out a small rise. 'For today, and then maybe from tomorrow onwards, you can take a position up there.'

Before turning back to his tasks, he took one final look at her. There was clearly a determination within her. He found himself observing her, although now surreptitiously. He saw a momentary explosion of exhilaration appear on her face as she hungrily looked about before some inner shadow changed her expression. Her eyes locked onto something, and then—still looking in that direction—she walked off towards the spot he'd indicated.

He watched her for a moment, puzzled by her initial elation and then the tension that arose. He wondered at the oddities of this village. If he didn't know better, he would think that maybe the College didn't really rule here. He shook his head to dislodge the stupid thought, but before he returned to his work, he glanced in the direction that the girl had fixated on. He noticed nothing untoward; all he saw was another woman watching the men to whom she supplied water.

* * *

A little after midday, Sathea had been relieved by Amri, and she was now crossing the chasm that had separated mother and daughter since earlier that morning. They had discovered each other just after Hestean's arrival at the dig, and at first she had been surprised and then irritated to see Hestean talking to Jarrak. But then the inevitability of the moment had dawned on her. Hestean would always be Hestean.

She climbed the next slight rise towards her daughter. By now, Sathea had resigned herself to her daughter's wilfulness. She sat down beside the girl, and for a silent moment they looked at each other, determination reflected in Hestean's eyes.

'Why are you always such a trouble to me, daughter?' Sathea finally sighed.

'Because I have never believed in what these Robes impose upon us, Mother. That's why, and you know it!'

'*Shush*,' said Sathea. She swivelled to see if anyone else had heard these unguarded words. 'You are never to say that aloud. Not here, not anywhere. Do you hear me?'

Sighing again, Sathea peered into Hestean's soul, acknowledging the utterance for the wisdom it truly contained. 'Two years, Hestean. Just two more years and we will no longer be able to protect you from yourself. Have you thought of your father? What do we tell him? Have you worked that out?'

'Out here, the Robes can see me, Mother. Here, I will always be seen.'

'And is that what you want?'

'No. What I really want is to be the one doing the seeing.'

Sathea shook her head and then slowly started to chuckle. 'I don't know if you'll be able to achieve much of that—not from here. That is not what you really want though, is it? You want to understand this place. You want to see beyond what the Robes allow. That is what you really want, isn't it?' She observed her daughter for a moment, catching the non-verbal confirmation of what she had just said. Then she added, 'I will have to talk to Amri. You know that, don't you? So we shall see.'

'I've already sorted that. If she wants, she can find someone else to do the day with her, or do the full day herself.'

Sathea snorted. 'And you think it is as easy as that, do you?'

Seeing a worried look spread across Hestean's face, Sathea relented a little, and said, 'It is at least something to see you now trying to think of others, so don't worry. I'll fix it properly for you! Things need to be done in a certain way if they are to be successful, as you will hopefully find out one day.'

'Then you had better hear the rest of it,' said Hestean, a little hesitantly. She continued on to tell her mother what had happened before she reached the dig.

'You certainly do have a way of making life exciting, don't you?' said Sathea, as she too began to search for a solution to this problem. 'You really *do* want to be here.'

'Yes!'

'Very well, then, but I think this may be your last chance. Your father is reaching his limit with you and this little stunt will not help things at all.' Sathea looked around, then added, 'At least out here, the Robes can see that you are sustaining the men for a change instead of disobeying College law.'

A slight smile crossed Hestean's lips.

'This is not something to smile about, Hestean! You do have a full day here, I suppose?'

'I signed on for a full day!'

'Of course, you did,' said Sathea, peering deeply into her daughter's eyes. 'Well, enjoy it. This might still be your only day here. It might be your last day anywhere, if I can't persuade your father and sort something out for Amri. You *do* know I'll have to work twice as hard at home without you?'

'Yes, Mother!'

'That is not something you'd really thought about, is it?'

'No, Mother.'

'It is your wilfulness that is the problem. You do understand that?'

'Yes, Mother.'

Sathea got to her feet. 'Well, then. With the gods' will, I shall see you this evening, for there is one thing in your favour. I have noticed that this dig is like the inside of a giant dwelling, and like all dwellings, the man Jarrak is its master under College law—not the Black Robes themselves.' She turned to walk away, the seriousness of the moment welling up inside her. But then she stopped and looked back. 'Why I was blessed with a child like you, I will never know.'

Hestean smiled. 'Maybe it is because you wanted a daughter like yourself.'

Sathea snorted. 'No,' she said. 'I think now that you have far surpassed me! I was never as wilful or questioning as you are, and my wilfulness has been subdued. This is not a world for women, Hestean, and I only hope that you can survive yourself as I did, for if you can, you will most definitely be a contender for the *cwen*!'

* * *

Hestean hadn't expected to be dealt with so softly. There was a comprehension within her mother—something that made her love Hestean for the way she was, and this place despite the way it was. But this comprehension was something that Hestean herself, as of yet, had not fully grasped. She knew this, but she'd learnt not to ask about the unsaid. As always with her mother, she'd felt there had been something brushed upon but not fully disclosed.

With a jolt, Hestean recalled a word Sathea had mentioned. Her mother had used the Fem word, *cwen*, instead of "queen". She knew that the two words held slightly different meanings, and now began to wonder if her mother had indeed said something important. More intently now, from her position on the low rise, her eyes followed her mother all the way from the dig to the village. She saw Sathea turn and walk towards the dwelling of the oldest women in the village, who was never spoken of with too much affection. Was this also a ruse? The elder was something, or in this case *someone*, also kept hidden. Despite her ordinariness, all the women seemed to turn to Reglean when they needed advice. 'Why am I seeing this now when I've seen it so many times before?' Hestean asked herself quietly. She realised she had said the words aloud and looked around to see if anyone had heard her.

It had been a word mentioned here and a phrase mentioned there. Even the word "matrefem" had been used once in relation to Reglean, and this now flashed through her mind. For the first time, she began to see the old woman for what she was. *Matrefem* meant "female leader", but Hestean had at the time thought this was a joke. It was certainly made out to be a joke by the woman who had said it.

So many questions. So many unseen answers. Was this really what came to the women here as they approached their adulthood? Why did everything just seem to suddenly make sense, somehow? Hestean began now to wonder why the Black Robes and the men of the village had never seen Reglean properly, either. Then it hit her with a thud. For the first time, she realised the power that could be attributed to words if they were spoken at just the right moment, in just the right way. Had her mother intended to make her see this, or was it an accident?

'If you aren't looking for something, or are looking for it in the wrong place, then you very rarely find it,' she said to herself, smiling as she wondered what Reglean—or rather, the village's matrefem—would have to say about her most recent of escapades.

3

The door to Reglean's dwelling rattled as Sathea knocked, and a moment later it was opened from within. Standing dominantly in the doorway, Reglean studied Sathea.

'Can I speak with you?' Sathea asked. 'If you have the time, that is. I noticed Manea leaving as I crossed the square.'

'Manea has brought me one of her worries,' the old woman replied. 'Unlike you, though, she has many, so yours will be a pleasant change.'

'What was Manea's worry?'

'Like you, this time it is her daughter also.'

'How did you know I needed to see you about Hestean?'

Reglean smiled. 'Hestean is the only reason you ever seek my advice, Sathea. Unlike Manea, and some others, all else you seem capable of sorting out for yourself. I think perhaps that with Hestean, you are too close—too much the same! I remember when you were young and the trouble you caused my predecessor.'

'I no longer think I was ever like Hestean!'

Again, Reglean smiled. 'Have it your own way, but I remember it as I saw it, even if you don't.'

Since those earlier days, Reglean's respect for Sathea had strengthened as she'd seen how capable the younger woman had become. As she ushered Sathea through to a small communal room at the centre of the building, which she shared with a couple of other elderly women, Reglean said quite deliberately, 'Manea is worried about Blinnie and the man she has been tied to. Apparently, he has become more hierarchical in his beliefs. He has started going to the Black Robes' meetings. When Blinnie was first tied to him, the man's mother had just died, and he needed a woman to talk to other women that came into his shop. But he has recently stopped Blinnie from seeing to their needs, and his business is suffering. Blinnie's father only saw the bind-price the man paid and didn't consider the man himself.'

Reglean sat down, leaving what she had said to bubble away in Sathea's mind. She changed subjects, bringing the conversation back to Sathea's own problem. She listened patiently to Sathea's story, pushing her towards the past in order to find the answer for today's quandary. Reglean had always known that Sathea could find her own answers when nudged in the right direction.

'As you survived, so will your daughter,' she said, once Sathea had finished speaking.

'There were many times when I didn't think I would survive, Reglean. That's just it; I was lucky. My inquisitiveness started when I was a lot closer to my adulthood than Hestean is. Even as a child, she was aware of this place. But luckily, back then, she didn't know it. It is only recently that things have started to become clearer to her. Since the day her adult-in-learning started, she has been asking questions. I have been reluctant to answer, yet she sees those answers already, Reglean. She now knows who we are, and sometimes I even think she knows about you. I am afraid luck will not be with my daughter as it was with me, or even yourself! She already asks questions that are far beyond those I asked.'

Sathea paused as tears began to well in her eyes. Reglean felt her anguish. Eventually, Sathea's eyes dried and she continued. 'If we cannot find a way to circumvent their wrath and remove her from their gaze, the Robes will have the sun claim her, like they did my sister. Only after she becomes an adult will the fullness of our secret allow her to survive. If she allows herself to survive, that is.'

'Maybe Hestean is what we survive for?'

'You are joking, I hope?' Sathea choked back another sob. 'She endangers not only herself but everyone around her. You have seen that for yourself, surely!'

'I only meant that even despite her wilfulness, all the women think well of her. She embodies that part of ourselves we must all give up in order to maintain ourselves here. She is like a flutter of freedom, and it reminds us of who we are.'

Sathea sniffed. 'Even though she now knows some of it, she does not fully know why we must survive. Without that, I fear she is doomed. Why are there these rules we must follow, Reglean? This morning, she even pulled one of the village men into her web.'

Reglean's brows rose, and Sathea told her of Hestean's encounter with the Black Robe and Dillane.

'Do you have a solution to Dillane's visit this evening?' asked Reglean.

'I think so,' said Sathea, having calmed herself. 'But she is my only child, Reglean, and I need your opinion of it.'

'Of what?' asked Reglean, when Sathea hesitated.

'Well … I think we should give her what she wants. Put her out there on the dig and under this Jarrak's protection. We can make it seem like the punishment that Dillane will inform us is necessary.'

'And what of yourself?'

'I will have to return to the normality of my days. That creates a problem for Amri, but hearing Manea's concerns has given me an idea there, too. If Blinnie's bind-mate is truly drifting toward the Robes, then he would want his woman to be seen to serve the village, too, wouldn't he?'

'A well-thought idea!' said Reglean with a smile. 'I'll see Manea later, and she can put it to Blinnie.'

'Blinnie's husband is still a merchant, isn't he? And to the Robes, women are thought of as just another commodity, so hopefully he'll see its merit if he can be made to believe it was his conception!'

Inwardly, Reglean continued to smile. Even with her own deep worries, Sathea had still fully considered the plight of someone else; a far cry from how she'd been as a child.

'Go on,' said Reglean, affirming her approval of Sathea's statement so far.

'Well, I was also thinking that if Blinnie's husband truly is leaning towards the College, and if his business is failing, and if he is still enough of a merchant, he might be willing to give Blinnie up for a lesser amount than the bind-price he originally paid.'

'Who do you have in mind?'

'I recall that Dillane was also interested in Blinnie, but he didn't have the funds at the time. Now that he's taken over his father's forge, he may be in a better position, and he might still be interested. What do you think?'

Reglean considered Sathea's solution for a moment. Then she got up. 'Bring the subject up this evening and let the wind blow where it may. Also, do what you think should be done with Hestean. I agree with you there, too. It is a risk, but one that could work out well for all of us if she can tame herself.'

* * *

The following morning, all Hestean's father could do was glare at her from across the table. For a long time, he sat in silence before finally deciding to speak. The night before, he'd listened to Dillane and then Sathea's proposal. He'd fumed at first, but then he'd melted into a confused state of indecision. He'd been remembering the night when Hestean was born—the unexpected joy he'd felt when he'd planted her birth tree. Even with Hestean the way she was, he was still looking forward to her eighteenth birthday when he could cut the tree down and announce her fully grown, just as his own father had done on his eighteenth birthday.

He knew that in the eyes of the Robes, he was not supposed to feel what his heart felt towards his daughter. It was his wife's spirit that had first attracted him to Sathea, and he had seen this same spirit bloom within Hestean. Yet he knew, also, that too much spirit could be fatal for a woman. Having found no other solution, he shared Sathea's hope that out at the dig, Hestean would be separated from her suicidal attempts to understand what the Black Robes didn't want any woman to understand.

'I cannot have you disobeying me anymore, daughter,' he finally said. 'You went out to your mother yesterday when you knew you were bound to this house. I think, though, that your mother may have been right in letting you stay there. However, you will now use your time to think! The time has come for you to decide whether you want a long life or an extremely short one. You will, of course, still have to help your mother with whatever she requires of you when you return home of an evening. You do understand this?'

'I do, Father, yes,' said Hestean, glancing quickly towards her mother.

'The Robes' rules of obligation, which dictate that women are bound to the man of a household, hold true for these new excavations too, I understand. So, out there, this Jarrak will be you master. Try not to rile him as you do me. He may not allow you to indulge yourself, as I have. This is a punishment—not a reward. You are *my* daughter, not his. The gods alone will judge you now, Hestean, for there will be no more leniency. Today I am drawing a line.'

Hestean nodded earnestly, but inside her heart was soaring.

4

Hestean's finger traced through the sand, sketching out the village, the well-pond, the obelisk, Jarrak's tent, and the large mound at the most westerly point. She looked up once more to survey her surroundings. She had mapped them all now.

Her expectations had been high, at first, but had yet again been stifled. As always, boredom irritated her. At home, she could have talked to anyone at any time, whether it was her mother, her father, or even just herself. Out here, it was not quite as her mother had hinted. It was true that, like within a dwelling, the man Jarrak was in charge. Yet the laws of the College were also in place, limiting her movement and conversation. Like elsewhere in the village, she couldn't speak to the men unless first spoken to or directed to do so by another man.

And so, to compensate, she had taken to drawing mindless doodles in the sand. She was seldom allowed to move, only standing occasionally to stretch out her muscles. The only times she could actually walk anywhere were when she was summoned by a man, who required water to quench his thirst.

Despite this, however, or maybe because of it, her eyes sought out anything and everything around her in an attempt to stifle the tedium that had begun to fill her soul. She observed Jarrak as he walked around, checking on the progress of his men. She watched, too, as he decided where to dig and where digging seemed to have become fruitless. She also watched as he instructed the men, storing it all away in her memory. The mattocks, shovels, trowels, small brushes, and little finger picks all needed to be used in particular ways to lessen the risk of damaging the hidden mysteries found below the sand. She watched every retrieval she could, significant or not, and noted always the care that was taken. She observed as the objects were first sketched by Jarrak while half-submerged, and then followed their progress as they were removed and carried to his large tent. At times, too, she observed sand-shakers being used; large boxes in cradles, which were rocked back and forth in order to allow the sand to fall out of the bottom, revealing any larger items.

Since Hestean wasn't able to talk with anyone but the women, she still had little understanding of the excavation. She had worked out only that Jarrak was looking for something specific. He'd already closed down certain areas in spite of the abundant treasures and trinkets they produced, since they were not the kind he was looking for.

During the many evenings that followed, Hestean watched from her rooftop as the two moons, Glemman and Wraith, twirled around each other in their slow dance of twenty-eight-and-a-half days. She felt frustrated that Jarrak's purpose still eluded her. She looked out longingly at the dig and found her eyes lingering upon the strange, unflickering lantern that illuminated the big tent's interior. She had never before seen a lantern that didn't need filling with lard or oil, and Jarrak was very particular about placing this one out in the sun every morning before setting off to work for the day. This, too, was just one more thing to puzzle over.

Most evenings she could make out his form seated at his writing desk, and later she would watch as the light moved to his sleeping quarters, where it was soon extinguished. The questions that had drawn her to the dig still remained; knowledge of the past, and of the great city that had once existed, were still things that filled her mind.

These curiosities were what drove her towards another of her potentially dangerous decisions.

It was in the afternoon, just before the day turned too hot for the labourers to work, when the water-walker struggled up the slight rise towards her.

'It looks as if you've had enough for the day?' said Hestean.

'That I have, girl! I could do with your job for a while. In fact, quite a while, I think.' The woman wiped sweat from her brow. 'The warmer season is coming, and it's already getting too hot in the afternoons. I think this year is going to be brutal.'

Hestean studied the exhaustion on the woman's face, and despite this observation, initiated her decision. 'All right, I'll swap you.'

The woman looked at her. 'And just how long do you think you'll last, girl? You're a thimble.'

'I'll do your job for as long as I can, whether that is only a day or until this crosslander leaves. And you can sit here and watch me. Deal?'

The woman eyed Hestean, clearly wondering for a moment what might be coiling within her head. Everyone knew Hestean, and everyone knew of her long list of misdemeanours.

'I promise you won't suffer for it!' said Hestean, already knowing what the woman was thinking.

The woman's expression slowly changed into a thoughtful grin. 'Very well then, girl, but I think you'll be back sooner than you think.' She lifted the waterskin from her shoulder, clearly still wondering whether she was perhaps facilitating something she should have no part in.

'It won't bite you, I promise,' said Hestean. 'But you will be tethered here until this work is done, and I will be out there, walking around through all of it,' She refastened her hat into a better position for walking, then hoisted her own waterskin up onto her shoulder.

The woman seated herself, collapsing onto the sand with relief. Her eyes then following Hestean as she began to walk off, proceeding from one water-woman to the next.

One after the other, and then eventually collectively, Hestean felt their eyes drift after her.

* * *

To the surprise of the women, including her mother, Hestean continued with the task of water-walker all through the next day, without any visible signs of fatigue. Sathea had hastily arranged to relieve both Amri and Blinnie for the day, contriving an illness that both of them could suffer from, so that she could observe her daughter. She watched on now with the other women, wondering what her daughter was up to. Hestean only ever conformed to the rules when she had a hidden reason to.

As she arrived beside each water-woman, Hestean asked them lightly about what they had seen, and shared news and observations from other parts of the dig. Sathea saw that Hestean was trying to build a mental map of the site. She observed, too, that the other women were starting to look forward to their next encounter with Hestean, and they, too, were beginning to take a greater interest in what was happening around them.

During the following cycles of the moons, Hestean's activity began to have another effect. She developed a much larger appetite, and her frame subtly strengthened into one of extreme physical fitness.

Because of this, Sathea began to see—outwardly at least—a benefit to her daughter's exercise. Slowly, she found her motherly anxieties starting to dissipate.

As work progressed, and the ground filled with many more trenches, objects dug from the ground began to crowd the tables that had been set up under the heavy canvas tent. The same delicate care was taken here, too, with most of the pieces laid out on soft cloth.

Whenever Hestean walked past, she studied the items, which were both strange and familiar. She saw plain, unadorned pots and utensils, like the ones used in her village. There were also broken pieces of decorative items, such as small statues and parts of wall sculptures or floor tiles. These objects showed the great wealth that had once existed in the ancient city, but amongst them were rare and unknown things she couldn't understand.

In spite of her observations, she could comprehend none of the written pages held down by stone weights on the tables. She had discovered that, as with all things in this male-dominated world, this man's writing was unintelligible to her. Even though the snippets of information she'd collected from the women were useful, she decided she would still need to be smart, and patient, if she were to discover anything in this man's writing.

* * *

'Hey, you there. *Waeter*!' called Jarrak, using the female vernacular. He had never before heard the words of the ancients spoken, but here, in this outpost of civilisation, he had come to notice that some of the old words were still used in the whisperings of women.

He watched the young water-walker stop. With the waterskin slung full over her shoulder, she looked around to pinpoint where the male voice had come from.

He was leaning back against a large rock, sitting in its shade with his constant companion—his script-hold—rested lightly in his hand. Once again, he had forgotten his hat today. So when he saw the water-girl, he paused his meandering over abstractions and motioned a make-believe cup to his mouth.

She started towards him, her long dark hair swaying down her back. He watched the vivid whites of her light green eyes, which contrasted against the blackness of her skin. Her large straw hat, woven from the leaves of a batter-palm, covered her head to the width of her shoulders and was held in place by a string beneath her chin. Like all the women here, this girl was covered in sandy yellow cloth from neck to ankle, although unlike the older women she also wore a red sash. Her long-sleeved blouse hung loosely from her shoulders, tucked into the lightweight skirt that draped almost to the ground. As with the other village women, a unique red-and-blue pattern trimmed the bottom of the skirt, denoting her clan and family. Jarrak looked from the large waterskin hanging at her side to the strap that crossed between her breasts. Two metal cups hung from it on a strand and clattered against her leg as she walked. As she crossed the dry, light sand, he noticed little puffs of dust rise from beneath the soft soles of her moccasins. *How dry this place is*, he thought, remembering the greenery of his homeland. He noticed that her eyes were more alive than most and observed how colourful her movements were as she strode purposefully towards him.

Pulling up on the strand, Hestean grabbed a cup and rinsed it with a splash of water. She then poured a full cup, and Jarrak reached out his hand. 'Thank you,' he said. 'I needed that.'

Hestean nodded and prepared to walk away, then paused. She took off her hat, turned back, and threw it to him. Her aim was good. The hat first hit his chest and then fell into his lap. 'I'll take your hat,' she said. 'You have no respect for it. Maybe you will have better respect for mine.'

Bemused, Jarrak sat watching as she turned and walked towards the tent housing the dig collection and his sleeping quarters. He saw her walk inside and stroll slowly around the display, before walking out again with his hat upon her head. How had she known exactly where it was hanging? Without another glance towards him, she continued on with her task of supplying water to the other women and whoever else asked for it. He smiled, then became self-conscious, as if feeling the weight of many eyes upon him. He looked around to see if any of the other women had noticed the encounter, but if they had, they'd already turned from him. All the men seemed still to be hard at their work.

The incident stayed with him, though, flashing again through his head when he went to leave his tent later that day. He sought the girl's name in his notations, which evoked the memory of their first encounter. Looking down at the page, he noticed that he had, even then, written a note against her name: *Hestean Descee—Gumption.*

She had taken a big risk in throwing her hat to him, he now realised. It was not something that could have been dared with any of the men from her own village. He found himself thinking of it as an off-handed compliment; out of respect for her bravery—or was it foolishness?—he vowed never again to be found without her shade. From this day on, he told himself, Hestean Descee's hat was to be placed on his head whenever he ventured out into the sun.

5

Jarrak turned to look down the slope he had just climbed, and then sat down to observe the valley and its surrounding hills. From here, he could see it all—the obelisk, the well-pond, the village itself, and all the hills that, in the shape of a short-handled spoon, made this valley a refuge from the open desert. Directly east, he could see straight down the handle of the spoon towards the opening which gave access to the desert beyond.

Although the obelisk was taller, the mound dominated this place, and would have even when the ancient city of Sharacan was still at its most spectacular. So, was the mound also part of the old religion? There were no signs that it had ever been fortified, so what could it have been if not something ceremonial? The thought had gone through Jarrak's mind often since he'd come to Sharacan, and here it was again, tickling at his imagination.

The two moons had cycled through their lunar dance seven times since he'd arrived. Occasionally since then, sometimes for several days at a time, he'd called a halt to the excavations so that he could assess his progress. It was what he was doing now.

Sighing, he removed his hat, which he had recently taken back from the girl, and wiped his brow. He had procured the hat in Elora-Bearer especially for this expedition, and having experienced the Sharacan sun, he knew it had been a purchase well-made. He thought of Hestean and her chastisement; he missed the girl's hat, which he'd preferred to his own, but she needed it as much as he did. He lifted the brim to his nose and sniffed. Her scent still lingered on the fabric, and maybe that's why he had preferred hers. It smelt of her and this place and its history. He looked at his own again for a moment, then placed it onto his head, remembering something his professor had once said: *Everyone is knowledgeable, and there is something to learn in everything.*

He recalled something else now, too.

Despite having secured backing from the Guild itself, Professor Bornn Sageling's eccentric beliefs were still scoffed at by some of his contemporaries. This, Jarrak knew, was why he alone had been sent on this expedition. He was an unknown, and the Museum would lose none of its status if he failed. He'd made a vow back then not to fail, and to validate Bornn's judgment. He had been given three years to come up with something, and so here he was, almost six months through with no real discovery to date.

The truth, my boy, is always staring you in the face, but it is also the hardest to see. You must always be looking for it. His professor had said this many times during his training, and it was these words that came to Jarrak now as he again wondered what he was doing here. What was he looking for? Was it still what he had come here to find?

Below the sand lay the past. Yet over the days and nights that had followed his encounter with the girl, Hestean, he had begun to speculate more broadly about whether there was indeed more to be found here than just a forgotten legend—a legend about a female warrior. Was there still knowledge of the old city itself, and the ancients who had built it? He had only been permitted to dig by the Black Robes because he had stated that he was seeking proof that the College had a legitimate right to rule here. That had been a lie. Maybe, though, that was the very excuse he needed to enlarge the dig. Beneath the tenet of the Black Robes—and largely because of the girl—he had begun to notice a subdued covertness that separated this place from other College enclaves. He wondered anew if this was really a glimpse into what he was truly seeking. Despite the College's control, he was now sure that something elusive lingered here; something ancient and Sharacanese that dwelled only in the hearts of the women.

Back in the city of Elora-Bearer, in his and Bornn's favourite tavern, he and his professor had put together their revolutionary theories over tankards of ferment. It was here, too, that they had come across the story that pointed to the once-great city of Sharacan. Sharacan, they knew, had been the hub of commerce in the old world. All the desert caravans had to follow water, and Sharacan had water. That was one of the mysteries of the city—it's well-pond. It was thought that the well-pond had been constructed long before the great city itself, but by whom no one really knew. Its origins were now lost in time. It was because of the well-pond alone that all northern trade had been forced to travel through Sharacan, and it was the well-pond that had once made the city great.

These caravans no longer came to Sharacan, though. Giant sky-ships now plied the skies, and they had stolen away the city's importance. Yet Jarrak and his professor had concluded that what they really sought might still be found in Sharacan's remains.

Through the Black Robes, like all enclaves under College rule, the new Sharacan had become excessively male-orientated. Women were banned from the fields and places of business, and were only allowed to maintain their households. Just stepping outside their front doors brought the women of the village into the full servitude of the College. Jarrak and his professor knew that some incident in history had driven the College towards these extremes, but exactly what, Jarrak still didn't know. Had it happened here? Had something actually happened in Sharacan far back in history? They knew that the College could not stand for Sharacanese women to triumph, and the reasons for Sharacan's demise might contain the secret as to why. It could all be linked.

It was rumoured that one of the Comcree, a warrior guardian by the name of Andreena, had almost triumphed in her defence of Sharacan before she'd suddenly vanished, allowing the College to take control of the city. To the College, the tales of Andreena's close success could not be permitted, and so they'd sought to eradicate all traces of her name. Now, the truth of her existence had almost completely slipped from history.

Here, though, in this birthplace of her story, the College had still not been fully successful in expunging the influence of Sharacan's true history. It seemed to Jarrak—maybe because of the terms set out in the Treaty of Truce—that College law here was tainted. There was a softness to the way it was enforced. How much of Andreena's legend still existed here, he didn't know, but he was now sure that at least part of it lived on. If her influence still maintained itself here, then perhaps she had once really existed. The Deserteers—the merchant couriers of the Kalcool—certainly believed she did.

Jarrak stared out over his excavations. Where was Andreena now, though? Inflaming the Black Robes was a betrayal he could not afford, so for now he still had no choice than to observe this place passively, while searching for something that would point him in her direction. History had recorded one version of what might have happened here, but now, in this wasteland of sand, perhaps he could discover proof of a truer version. Sighing, he leaned back, resting his head on his hands. The temple would be the obvious place to start, but where was that, exactly? Almost all records of its position had also been eradicated.

His mind drifted to the girl again, and in his imagination she was still wearing his hat. Every time he reissued his call for workers, he had noticed his hat appear at the back of the crowd, alongside those of the other female water-bearers. It was because of his hat that he had been able to keep track of the girl. He'd noticed how she always worked her way slowly forward to join the front of the women's crowd. It was also because of his hat that he'd become aware of something else, too. He smiled, now, just as he had on the day he finally saw it.

The women were each allotted to their own sections of the excavation site, and only ever serviced their own sections with water. However, his hat alone could be seen wandering throughout the entire excavation, from section to section. He wondered how he hadn't seen it before. He had only just become aware of it when a Black Robe had asked Hestean why it was always she who did the walking. She had simply told the man it was more efficient, and that it was a logical choice to have the youngest amongst them do the walking. The matter was a trivial one, but it seemed the Robes would question even this.

Jarrak had been intrigued. In spare moments, he found himself watching his hat float through the excavations. He saw and heard nothing unusual, until one day he heard her voice whipped towards him on a gust of wind. 'I think in this context, "avenue" just means a wide street.'

He recalled having used the word "avenue" earlier in another section of the dig, and he turned to see her topping up a woman's waterskin at the crest of a rise.

At first, he'd thought she seemed quick to understand things that, before his arrival, she would never have had the chance to understand. Then he'd thought that she was good—surreptitiously good—in her judgment. The third thought to strike him was that in every society there were sub-societies, groups, and alliances, and now he knew that he had found one here.

If it hadn't been for his hat, and the girl who wore it, he might never have come to understand this subgrouping. As far as the men were concerned, the women were at the dig simply to supply water. But the women, he now realised, were exploiting this perception of their servitude. While the men formed themselves into families and clans, knowing only their patch of the dig, the women—who were already at the bottom and knew that they would always be so—had unbound themselves from the rigid hierarchical structure in the hope of creating something new. Or was it something old? Something as ancient as Sharacan …

There was only one water source in the village—the well-pond. If only one of the women fetched the water and did the walking, then she was their common means of communicating. He recalled hearing more brief and general conversations by other women that, on their own, had seemed to mean nothing. Only one person heard everything, and she had been wearing his hat. If he was right in his musings, Hestean probably knew this dig almost as well as Jarrak did.

As long as the women did as they were told to do, the men had no reason to see anything else. The skill of these women in hiding what they had really begun to do was a revelation to Jarrak, and he knew now that this marked him even more as an outsider. He now knew something that no other man here knew, and as a result he felt himself once again grateful for this girl.

When Jarrak had summoned Hestean again and taken back his hat, he'd said to her only: 'To be truly a ghost, you must be hidden by normality.'

She had looked at him, puzzled at first by his words. Then, as she'd walked away, she'd turned back and smiled at him knowingly.

Jarrak sighed now and sat up, examining the place where he was thinking about putting in a new trench. He would move his planned location a little to the left, and bring it into line with the mound and the obelisk. He would get the workers back tomorrow.

6

Glemman and Wraith had danced their dance twice more before Jarrak heard Hestean Descee's voice again. She said four words that stopped the entire dig dead in its tracks.

'Not like that! *Stop*!'

He turned just in time to see her waterskin hit the ground, its contents spilling into the sand. She herself was in mid-air, having launched herself from the edge of a trench, skirt billowing and hat tie pulling tight under her chin.

Bewildered, he stood for a moment. Then his script-hold dropped from his hand as he grasped what was occurring. He accelerated into a run, reaching the trench in time to see a male labourer lying on his side, his shovel cast from his hand. Hestean pulled a long pin from her hair and began to ever so gently use it to scrape at the face of the excavation.

The man was clearly incensed. He scrambled to his feet, but Jarrak found himself ignoring the man's outrage as he locked onto what the girl was doing. He slid down the side of the trench and crawled quickly over to her. 'What is it?' he asked.

'I don't know yet, but it's something large,' she said, engrossed in what she was doing.

The rise of voices around him finally brought the communal unease to Jarrak's attention. The significance of the incident and its dual meanings hit him. The girl knew exactly what she was doing, which was a revelation in itself, but at the same time, Jarrak grasped the fact that she was a woman. And here, what she had done was forbidden under the rule of the Robes.

With sudden clarity, he saw that he needed to create some time to think. If he pulled her away now, her fate would be sealed by Robe law. However, this was his dig. He was in charge here, and with that came some autonomy. He would let her continue while he thought, making it look as though she was working to his instructions.

'Round here, girl. There, clear that away!' He concluded, perhaps unwisely, that he would find a way later to deal with the Black Robes and argue her case. But for now, he was just amazed by her care and skill. 'That's right, good.'

He would allow her this moment, he decided. It could be her last chance at brilliance.

'Now here! There, that's right.' The strange S-shaped form below the earth started to reveal itself. 'You're a little fool, aren't you?' he said in a soft whisper.

In a hushed tone, Hestean replied, 'Yes, Maskee. I think that maybe this time I truly have been.'

Jarrak sighed and said, 'Just keep working, while I see if I can find a way to get you out of these shambles. What made you do such a thing?'

'I don't know!' Hestean said. 'It just happened. I saw the labourer talking to his friend, distracted and careless, while still digging into the sand. A moment sooner and I may not have noticed anything, but the position of the sun made a part of this thing glint at me. At that same moment, a fall of sand told me that something lay just there, within the wall of the trench. He raised his shovel blindly for another strike, and so I … I just reacted!'

'It was foolish! You know that, right? But it's a good thing you did react—at least for me. I think it's just what I've been looking for.' Once more, Jarrak raised his voice so that the men around him would hear clearly. 'Round here! There! Remove that!' He turned to one of the other men and held out his hand. 'Brush!'

The man lent forward. He was frowning, but he passed over his coarse-haired brush anyway.

Jarrak started to tickle away the loosened sand. 'What do you think it is?' Hestean asked.

'You mean you don't know?'

'No! I've never seen such a thing before.'

Jarrak started to smile, then said, 'This might just be your lucky day, too. I think it's a woke horn—an instrument of the gods. I think we've found the temple … And if we have, then your village law has no legal standing here. It might be a ruin, but it's still holy, and under the Treaty of Truce, in this place, temple law will hold above any other.' Jarrak paused to look around for a moment. Now might not be the best time to discuss the College's nemesis, he realised. 'Even the Black Robes will be reticent to anger the gods in their own house,' he finished.

Hestean's grinned brazenly. Then she said, 'And why is that?'

Jarrak looked at her for a moment and then said aloud, for everyone to hear, 'Dig, girl! Just dig.' In that moment, he knew he was looking at a slightly younger version of himself. Was that what he'd seen in her all along? Hestean started again with the excavation, picking carefully through the sand.

Sweat started to drip from Jarrak's face and sink into the earth as, once again, the day's heat battered him. He wiped his forehead, then looked around in search of a water-woman, 'Hey, you. *Waeter,*' he said.

Descending from her vantage point, where she must have seen the entire scandal unfold, the woman came to kneel beside him, her face fearful. Just for a moment, she glanced at Hestean.

Noticing this, Jarrak took the proffered cup from the woman, then allowed it to be filled again before handing it to Hestean. The woman gasped and grabbed for the other cup tied to her waist, but it was too late; Hestean had already swallowed without realising the cup's gender. A dull whisper went through the men around them. Jarrak turned back to the woman; she looked horrified, and he tried to convey his sympathy through his eyes.

Choosing his words carefully, he raised his voice and said, 'This girl stays here when we're finished! Right here.' He pointed at the ground. 'Find someone to bring her a blanket and food, and that person is also to stay by her side until I say differently. If anyone else tries to override these instructions, then I must be informed immediately. Do you all understand this?'

The woman again looked to Hestean, then back to him, nodded her understanding with a weak smile before rising to do as he'd asked.

* * *

When the find had been recovered, Jarrak closed the dig and sent everyone home. He made a show and a big fuss about Hestean, again insisting loudly that she was not to move until he said so. He noticed, then, that it was the woman he knew to be Hestean's mother who had been sent for. She seated herself down with two blankets and some food next to the girl, clearly preparing to stay through the night if need be.

Later, the full consequences of the event started to play out just as Jarrak had suspected they would. When he arrived at the House of Authority, having been summoned by the village chairman, the displaced labourer was still simmering. He obviously wanted to justify himself in front of the Black Robes.

'She should be driven from the site—cast-off from our village and sent out into the desert to be made subject to its elements,' he said as Jarrak walked in.

Jarrak knew that the Council would always be driven by law and a strict adherence to rank, subjugation, and the fear of deviation. But he'd discovered even before arriving in the village that their laws had complications. He'd made a study of them, so he would be better able to negotiate control over his excavations. So maybe now, he decided, their law could also be the girl's best salvation.

He had been granted an invitation to stay and work in this village, so he also had rights. He had selected areas where he wanted to dig, and he had been given permission to occupy those areas. He now unrolled the special permit given to him by the Council and began to read it aloud.

'For the period of time in which the crosslander, Jarrak Hammill, is to carry out his excavations, and as long as there are no permanent structures built, he will have full tenure and control over his granted site.' He cleared his throat. 'Because of this, and because the girl is employed by me, she is subject to me first. Therefore, I hold the right of punishment. It is for me alone to punish her insolence, which I have already begun to do.'

He didn't mention the temple. He kept that silent, hoping secretly that it may indeed be the starting point he was seeking.

It was well into the night when he emerged from the House of Authority with Hestean's punishment specified to his liking. The Council's chairman had been amazed by Jarrak's knowledge of College law. Although he knew that Jarrak was not a follower of their doctrine, he'd noticed that the young man hadn't just used their laws blindly against them. His arguments had been constructed correctly, showing a genuine understanding of their concepts, and showed Jarrak truly to be a knowledgeable person. This had endeared Jarrak to the elderly patriarch, as under College doctrine, knowledge gave status. The Council had decided in favour of Jarrak's case, ruling that for as long as his work continued, the girl would be his personal property to do with as he saw fit. The wronged man, while unhappy, had to concede that Jarrak was above his station here.

Several of the younger Robes were also put out. Finally, the most aggrieved of these young Robes spoke with a sneer on his face. 'I see that this punishment serves to remind all the women of their status. It will be a warning to them. But I will write to Learnian myself, and ask for a higher judgment on this.'

Gaywin was his name, and as Jarrak watched him go, several other young Robes fell in behind him. Jarrak knew now that he would need to watch this man in future. In Gaywin, he saw a fanatic, without the rounded mindset brought about by age or experience.

Later still, walking back to his own camp, Jarrak's hand curled around the scroll. He was glad he'd remembered that the proceedings needed to be written down to make them truly binding.

He slept sparingly that night, wondering why he had done this to himself. His resistance had pushed him almost to the edge of the Council's tolerance; it would have been easier to abandon the girl. But a sense of obligation had set his path, and the choice had seemed obvious. Hestean had revealed herself to be more than just bold, but also skilful and knowledgeable about how a dig should operate. During his brief dreams, he found himself hoping that she would be worth the effort. In her, he saw passion—the same passion that raced within his own soul. She harboured a desire to understand this world.

Still, there was something else that he couldn't quite place. It was as though his decision had been necessary; completely and utterly necessary.

7

After sitting vigil with her daughter all night, Sathea roused Hestean to watch the tip of the obelisk gleam—perhaps for the last time—with the light of dawn.

But from their spot in the trench, they also saw that Hestean had been banished from the village. All of her clothes and other possessions were laid at the entrance to the dig, and Hestean's tree of birth had been cut during the night and now lay dying on top of them. Tears began to well in Sathea's eyes. She held Hestean tight to her chest, grasping at her familiarity. She knew that Hestean had finally pushed her father too far, and that now to him she was dead.

Hestean's mind was churning. She looked to her mother, grasping at the waterskin that had given her such an adventure. 'Am I truly dead to him, do you think?' she asked.

Before her mother could answer, another voice said, 'You, girl, put that down. It is no longer yours to use.'

Hestean turned to see Jarrak walking towards her and flinched at his coldness. Yesterday he had been warm, but now his blue eyes were glazed over with an iciness such as she had never seen before. She wondered what the Council had decided. Was she going to live? She knew that, from this moment on, it was not going to be the life she'd always wanted. For once, she really wished she'd been able to restrain herself.

Jarrak glanced towards the dying tree that had been placed on top of Hestean's clothes, and a look of puzzlement crossed his face. Then he returned his attention to Sathea, and said, 'You are to find someone else to do this girl's work. She has been permanently extracted from her duties.'

There was now a depth in Sathea's eyes that Hestean had seen before. She knew that her mother was considering this young man's nature. She looked to Hestean and then back to Jarrak before softening. She nodded once in compliance.

'It has already been done, Maskee,' said Sathea. A great weight seemed to lift from her shoulders, and Jarrak winced, buckling slightly, as if that weight had now been passed to him.

'Mother?' said Hestean, confused.

But before her mother could reply, Jarrak nodded uncomfortably to Sathea and turned to Hestean, handing her his script-hold. 'Come, girl,' he said. 'You can get your things later.'

He started to walk off in the direction of his tent. Bewildered, Hestean glanced at the book now in her hand. She looked to her mother again and saw a smile cross Sathea's face. Sathea trusted Jarrak, she realised.

A moment later, Sathea looked towards the pile of clothes and the tree, then stepped back as tears became visible in her eyes. With a jolt, Hestean saw the truth. Her mother couldn't say anything in so public a place, for Hestean had really been banished. She was no longer part of the village.

Understanding became sadness, and then the tears came. A series of images flickered through Hestean's mind as she recalled all the things her mother had talked about during the night. Suddenly she understood them better. She was not dead to her mother, but for the time being she had to appear to be. So, sniffing back her tears, Hestean smiled weakly and turned to follow Jarrak.

Upon reaching the big tent, he ushered her through the entrance and into the living quarters. He pointed, saying, 'You can sleep over there, and if you're hungry there's food through that flap.' She looked at the place on the floor that had been cleared for her, then looked to where she knew he slept. It was no better or worse; just a spot on the floor like hers, but with a mattress and bedroll. Her bedding was still near the entrance to the dig.

He had spoken to her as if she were a servant, but here she saw something different. Here, hidden from the outside world, was equality. To the village, she would seem his slave, but for some reason she would not be. She glanced at his eyes and saw that the coldness was gone. Instead, she saw uncertainty—the same uncertainty that was now flowing through her.

'For the rest of today, you are to follow me and listen. Help when you know what to do, but only after I give permission. You are also to see to the welfare of my shrows every day. Do you understand me?'

'I think I am beginning to, yes.'

'Good, then we shall begin.' Jarrak turned and walked back out into the sun, and Hestean followed. But when she went to say something, he rounded on her quickly. 'Quiet! I said to listen, not to talk.' After a moment of bewilderment, reality dawned on her. She was not to speak to him outside.

So, for the rest of the day, she conformed, doing only what she was told. Later that afternoon, when the rest of the workers had gone home to shelter from the desert heat, Jarrak sent her to retrieve her belongings. He watched as she collected them and brought them into the tent. The small tree was the only thing she left behind. She knew better than to take it; she'd observed earlier that the Black Robes were still watching. Maybe later, she would get a chance to cut a thin cross-section from its trunk.

* * *

Jarrak observed quietly as Hestean reverently stood beside her fallen tree. The tree had no meaning within College law, as far as he knew, so it must be unique to Sharacan society. He wanted to ask her about it, but when she'd brought the last of her possessions in, there'd been fresh tears in her eyes. So, he decided to stay away from the subject for now. He could ask someone else about the tree's significance later.

All day, Jarrak had issued instructions and orders to Hestean, but he'd not been able to shake the look of gratitude and hope in her mother's eyes when she'd looked at him that morning. Hestean had already been able to help him more than he had expected, and an idea had begun to form in his head.

When she approached after unrolling her bedding, he spoke to her. 'Sit down, Hat.'

'What?' she asked.

'I said *sit down*.'

'No, you called me *Hat*.'

'Did I? Sorry! It's a name I gave you after you took my hat that day, so in my head it's become a habit, I suppose. But please sit, would you, Hestean? I have something I want to talk to you about.'

'What?'

'Let's not start that again just yet! Please, sit down.' He took a seat himself, just outside of the tent's entrance. He crossed his legs and leaned back against the remnants of an ancient stone wall, which had once been part of a rather large building. In the afternoon, it provided quite a reasonable amount of shade, and he had taken to sitting there regularly to think.

Hestean looked down at him for a moment, then sat opposite him, tucking her feet neatly beneath her knees. 'Well?' she prompted, when he said nothing further.

He looked towards her, still thinking. Studying her, he said, 'I thought, originally, that you would have to be just a servant, helping with the mundane tasks to give me more time to concentrate on the parts of my work that only I can do. But it's not going to be that way. The outcome of yesterday is that you no longer have a life outside this dig, and I feel, partly at least, responsible. A lot of what you already appear to know about this dig came about because I didn't put a stop to what you were doing when I first saw it.'

'You knew what I was doing?'

'I'm not blind. I came here to find something, and my training has equipped me to see what is hidden. Just listen for a moment, will you? You will have no place here when I leave, so to repay my debt, I am going to equip you with a set of skills that will allow you to have a place somewhere else in this world. I have decided to teach you, a woman of this village, everything I know of the wider world in payment for the disturbance I have brought to your life.'

'But I did this to myself,' said Hestean. 'My mother and even my father have warned me many times, so it cannot be your fault. Do you really mean what you have just said?'

'It seems so, yes.'

There was silence between them, until Hestean said, 'I am more than halfway grown from child to adult, and I had thought I would be dead this morning. No matter where I go, my life will be short, for I will always want to know beyond that of which I am allowed to know. That will always be my problem, for it *has* always been my problem.'

'All the world is not as it is here, Hestean. The College does not govern it all!'

'They don't?'

'No, they don't! Where I come from, there are also women who do as I do.'

Hestean's eyebrows lifted sceptically, and she stared at him for a long moment. 'Even though I am still not an adult, under the law of these Robes I should have been banished from this village and sent out into the desert to die. Instead, I am sitting here, and you are giving me a chance at adulthood. You are telling me that the world is not all like the one I've grown up in. It is I who should be grateful! Do you really mean it? Are you really going to allow me to understand these holes you are digging?'

'Only when we cannot be overheard, yes. Unfortunately, the Robes do rule this part of the world, so here we must at least appear to be living by their directives. It is true that it's their law that would have taken your life, but it's also their law that saved it. Under their law, all of this dig site is my domain, and so it is I who has the right of punishment. As long as you are here, you are bound to me.'

'How bound?'

'As bound as any servant should be! You will do what I say when I say it, but you will also listen, and you will learn. They must see and believe what we are showing them. Do you understand?'

Hestean was again silent for a long moment. Then she said, 'If you saw what I was doing, why didn't the Robes?'

Jarrak just smiled and chuckled lightly to himself. 'Have you heard any of what I have said?'

'Yes! But why didn't they?'

Breathing in, Jarrak accommodated her question. 'Even though I am here every day, Hat, it still took me a long time. They, on the other hand, have this whole village to administer and are more concerned with me, an outsider, than you. They simply weren't looking at you.'

'Are you sure they don't know, though?'

'It wasn't brought up last night, so I don't think so, no. The other women are safe, if that's what you're worried about.'

'It is. I may have escaped the Robes, but the others would not be treated as I have been. They are adults and would be treated as such.'

'You should have thought of that beforehand.'

'Yes, I know I should have.'

'So why do you think they followed you so willingly?'

Hestean shook her head. 'I don't know.'

'Well, I think that, in a way, they all wished they were you. So, perhaps it's a good thing you have been punished for something that did not involve them. Occasionally, you can be lucky enough for a dust storm to blow away from its beginnings. Are you any good at cooking, by the way?'

'Not the best, no. Why?'

'Then already, we are equals in one way,' said Jarrak, getting up. 'Burnt offerings it will have to be, but I think I am getting better. I was so hoping you could cook, though.'

Slowly, Hestean smiled.

* * *

Just a few days later, Jarrak saw the young woman who had taken Hestean's place as water-walker. She made her way towards a newly uncovered water shaft just beyond the Obelisk, which had been discovered about a moon previously by a group of men digging one of his trenches. Once cleaned out, its bottom had begun to fill with water from one of the old underground channels. Hestean had also begun using it to fetch water for Jarrak and herself, as she could no longer go to the well-pond.

He went to his water jug now and emptied it out into a basin. Holding it out to Hestean, he said, 'Hey, Hat! Go and get some more water, will you? This is empty.'

At least once a day over the next few days, whenever he saw the other young woman walking towards the newly discovered well, he tipped out the jug and called to Hestean. It didn't take her long to catch on. Jarrak felt a hidden smile grow within him the first time she picked up the water jug and headed off to meet the young woman, seemingly on her own initiative. He had seen how this hidden alliance of water-women she had created could become his eyes and ears, too. But it was Hestean herself he was smiling about.

'Hey, Hat,' he called out, making her turn back to him. 'See, I knew you were smart.'

His young prodigy smiled, and despite her circumstances—still very much isolated from the rest of the village—her eyes seemed to sparkle. She brought her hand first to her forehead, then to her mouth, and then to her chest before she bowed mockingly.

She then turned to walk with the other young woman to the water-well.

Jarrak pondered the flippant gestures Hestean had made. He'd never seen this performed before. It must be a Sharacanese thing; it wasn't something he'd seen elsewhere in the world and he knew that it wasn't part of College society, either.

He watched her go and again began to smile. This village did indeed seem to hold many secrets, and this was just one more he'd have to add to the list.

He was starting to like this village very much.

8

The morning sun had still to fully extinguish the freshness of the night when Jarrak leaned back against the stone wall in front of his tent. His eyes closed, and his mind began to recall the twists and turns that had brought him to Sharacan. A light breeze tickled his skin.

The previous afternoon, he'd once again sent away his workers while he re-evaluated his decisions. His objective was still proving elusive, even though he was now sure he'd found the right place to start. He'd decided trenches were no longer enough; the sand would have to be stripped back from what he believed to be the entire temple complex beneath.

Drifting further, he recalled a bright, clear day like this, while on a visit to his maternal grandparents, when his father and mother had first taken him to the great Hassis Museum Historical. It had been his sixth birthday and his first glimpse of the wider world, which would one day become his passion.

Drowsily, he opened his eyes again and looked out across the sand. He needed to sort out once and for all what he was doing here. Was what he had come to find really what he was looking for? Had it just been the truth behind Andreena's story, or had he and Bornn always been looking for something bigger? Was Hestean finally the piece of the puzzle that would break open the past?

In a way, he was starting to suspect that she was, because he wasn't finding quite what had been expected. The women were broken in other College enclaves he'd visited, accepting of their fate as little more than slaves. But here, the women still retained a kind of strength. Only the deepest and strongest of roots could hold such a tree upright against the ever-demoralising wind of the College.

A picture of the batter-palms around the well-pond flashed through his mind. He smiled, having moons ago realised what they represented.

But even the Robes, it seemed, had been hesitant to chop them all down. Perhaps it was the shade and the coolness they gave, which was a rarity in the desert. But then again, maybe not. There was more likely to be another reason, like a story that told of doom for all the world if the batter-palms were ever to disappear completely. Superstition was just as much a part of the College as it was anywhere else.

As his mind returned to thoughts of a large tree, his eyes sought out Hestean. At that moment, she came out of the tent and sat herself down beside him.

'I've finished cleaning those two vases. Anything else?'

'No, that will do for now. I know I should get back to it, but not yet. Later this afternoon, I'll need your help to mark out the new border, though.'

'Why did you want those vases cleaned? They're nothing special as far as I can see.'

'You're right about that. They're nothing special at all, but did you notice the decoration on them?'

'You mean the male figures and the weapons?'

'They'll make a nice display for when the chairman and his robed entourage make their next visits, don't you think?'

'I'll put them near the front, then, will I?'

'That's what I was thinking, yes.'

She tilted her head. 'You looked deep in thought as I came across just now.'

'I was!'

'You also seemed far away.'

'I was that, too. I was just thinking how strange and unexpected the things that determine our path in life are at times.'

'They can certainly be that,' said Hestean.

'Yes,' said Jarrak, realising what he'd just said. He brought his thoughts back to himself. 'It's my birthday today, and it was on my birthday while still a child that my path was set.'

Hestean smiled. 'Really? I didn't know old men remembered their birthdays.'

'I'm not that much older than you,' said Jarrak, looking at her once more. 'Do I look old to you?'

'You look ancient.'

'I'm just tired, Hat! Responsibility can do that to a person.'

'So why are you here, really?'

'What makes you think that the reason I'm here—and the reason I say I'm here for—are two different things?'

Hestean pointed to the two vases she'd just cleaned. 'They do, for one!'

Jarrak's eyes twisted towards the tent. He smiled as he realised it was only fair for her to know at least some of the truth he had so far kept to himself. After all, he was now putting her in danger, too. 'All right,' he said, gathering his thoughts. 'I suppose it was my father, firstly. We were visiting Elora-Bearer, which is a huge city on the coastal plain to the west of here. While we were there, my father showed me through the great Museum Historical. It was my mother's idea to go, but she was caught up in her own fascination for the exhibits, so it was my father who told me about the stories behind the displays.'

'That's the place you now work for, isn't it? You called it the *Hassis*.'

'Yes,' said Jarrak, lifting his hands and placing them behind his head. Closing his eyes again, he remembered the next main event in his life. 'I was eight when my father died. He was a merchant and ran a business in Chime Town, on the eastern edge of the great plateau. I think I've told you that, haven't I? Anyway, his death hit me hard, but it hit my mother harder. Heartbroken, she decided to move back to Elora-Bearer, where her parents were still living. It was from that time on when the giant building that houses the Hassis Museum Historical really came into my life. I might have become a merchant like my father if he hadn't died. But then Chime Town isn't what it once was. Since the Kalcool expanded, there are only a few outer settlements that it now re-supplies. My father was only there because he inherited the business from his father, who inherited it from his father before him.'

Saddened, Jarrak became silent as thoughts of his ancestry consumed him. But a moment later, he returned to the tale of his life. 'I recall that, at the age of only fifteen, I talked my way onto a local excavation site, gaining work as a navvy, and then—when I was sixteen—I persuaded my mother to let me attend lectures at the Hassis, under the professorship of one Bornn Sageling. I don't think I was looking for a new father, but I found one anyway. Bornn has taught me a lot since then.'

'He taught you, and now in a way he is teaching me,' Hestean said.

Jarrak opened his eyes and looked at Hestean. 'You could put it that way, yes. Anyway, it was just three years later that I accompanied Bornn north as his assistant, into a part of the world called the Salvation

Lands. We were tracking down another piece of his favourite puzzle—a puzzle that has now also become mine. And that's why I'm here, Hat.'

'The gods, you mean?'

'The gods, yes.'

'Do you really think they once existed?'

'I'm here, aren't I?'

'That's not an answer,' said Hestean. 'What do you know of them, really? I mean, I've been told about the gods all my life, but I'm no longer sure if I really believe in them. Why would they trap women here like this if they were really as egalitarian as you say they're supposed to be? That *is* the right word, isn't it? Egalitarian?'

'It's one word, yes. And I don't know,' said Jarrak. 'All I know is that once they were supposed to have ruled this world. Whether they were gods or just people is unknown, because the stories are thousands of years old, and since then, reality has become myth. The Comcree—the ones we call the guardians—are supposed to be guides that were sent to us by them. But even they haven't been seen for more than two hundred years. We have better records of them where I come from, and the word "warrior" is used more often as a title for them.'

'I've heard of the Comcree, but I've never heard them called warriors before.'

'That doesn't surprise me. It was my father who first told me this. Every night after our visit to the Hassis, he would tell me stories. As guides, the Comcree's path has always been in one direction—that of equality and advancement. Each time the Comcree have appeared, it is thought that the world has grown a little stronger in all forms of knowledge. The College, on the other hand, have always thought themselves superior to most other clans because of their own so-called advancements—in agriculture, mostly.

'But then the world's climate changed, and they changed, too. The Kalcool's expansion towards the mountains meant that their crops failed, and instead of admitting they might need help, the Robes of the College began to impose tariffs on any commodities that passed through their territory. They increased those tariffs, and increased their territory, also. Eventually, the other regions of the world had had enough. They found a way to move trade north using Sharacan as a hub. The merchants of the world began to employ a group of desert tribes, who had always—in a small way—been traders. It is these tribes—today called Deserteers—that now control trade in the world, as they alone can transport it across the Kalcool. They have always had a code of respect; the desert taught them that. To survive in the Kalcool, you have to be respectful of its desolation, because one day it might be you who needs help.'

'I've never heard of these Deserteers.'

'The College didn't like it when the Deserteers began to move goods they'd previously controlled. Eventually, they forced their borders north to cut off this new trade route, effectively cutting the world in half. Again, they imposed their tariffs, but this time they truly miscalculated. Their actions brought the Comcree back into the world to restore the equilibrium. With the Comcree's help, the Deserteers forged themselves into a fighting force that rivalled that of the College. The resulting conflict eventually came to an end when the Treaty of Truce was signed. There are rumours that the Deserteers could have won outright, but for some reason the Treaty of Truce was signed instead.'

'So neither side actually won?'

'The Deserteers hold the advantage in trade, but the College was never forced to give back the territory they had taken. So yes, neither side won.'

'So where are these Deserteers, then, if they control trade? Why have I never seen or heard of them?'

'They are not allowed into College territory. These days, they no longer walk the desert; they fly over it in giant sky-ships. I have a book which describes how they do this. I'll show you later.'

'And the Comcree? What became of them when the fighting was over?'

'I myself have never had the opportunity to meet one, so your guess is as good as mine. The real truth about the Comcree is what Bornn and I would like to find out. Where they come from, and where they go, is a mystery. Whether or not they are actually real is also a mystery. Have you ever heard of the Shadow Shire, sometimes called "the Shirey"?'

'No.'

'Well, the Shirey are supposed to be the close kin of the Comcree; the only ones who know who the Comcree really are. They, too, are only spoken of in a few story fragments.'

'But the Comcree are called the guardians of the gods!'

'Somehow, they have always been seen as this. The stories tell us that they always held great knowledge and appear to be looking after this world in the same way that the gods once did. They seem to ensure that the world doesn't bend too far this way or that. This is why they're linked to the gods. Gods think in the long term, though. Maybe there is something that needs to happen, or that we need to do, before we see them again.'

'It was the Comcree, then, who brought you here. Not your father or the gods!'

'A story brought me here, Hat. Just another story. That's what Bornn and I do. We chase stories and see where they lead us. Every story holds an element of truth, and that's what I'm looking for here. The truth.'

They sat in companionable silence for a moment before he changed the subject. 'How are you going with you own learning, by the way? You seem to have grasped the ability to read very quickly. Are you sure you've never had lessons before?'

'No woman here has ever been taught to read the Black Robes' books,' Hestean said. 'I can see now why I was never able to work it out on my own. But it's starting to get easier.'

'That's because it's a bastardised language that we speak today. It comes from all over the world. To speak it is one thing, but to read it and understand its written form—as you have said—is another. However, you're picking it up quicker than I thought.' Jarrak sighed, knowing he had to get back to work. 'You should practise your reading for a while; I'll come in shortly and see how you're going. Then we'll mark out that new border.'

Hestean frowned, ignoring this last part. 'But you and the College both use a form of this modern writing. Why is that?'

'It was written into the Treaty of Truce that all the tribes and clans must use the same language. The trading tongue of the Deserteers was selected because its origins belong to no one group of people. Learn to read it, Hat, and you'll be able to answer all your own questions, no matter where you are in the world. With it, you will gain the ability to unravel all the other languages. All except one, that is. There are only about five people I know of in the world who can completely unravel the *lingua antiquitas*, the ancient language. I still need a book to help me, so if you want to someday learn it, you will have to find someone else to teach you.'

'But …'

'No more *buts*. That's enough about the world for now. Go and practise your reading, so that one day you can answer your own questions.'

Reluctantly Hestean got to her feet and walked back to the tent. Watching her, Jarrak thought to himself, *I'll run out of books, soon. Then what will I do? Get her to read them again? If it wasn't that she still gets the letters mixed up, I'd almost swear I'm just teaching her something she already knows*. His eyes closed, and his thoughts faded as, finally, sleep found him.

9

Later, Jarrak opened his eyes again. He noticed that the sun had moved higher into the sky. He knew he should get up and find his hat, but as he'd said to Hestean, this was his birthday. He'd turned twenty-two today; young by his reckoning, but old by Hestean's.

As he gazed sleepily out at the dig, he found himself challenged now by thoughts of his professor, and deliberated on why he'd travelled out into the desert on his own. He knew why, of course, and it wasn't just because of the Museum's doubts. He knew that if Bornn Sageling had strolled into the desert, the College of Learnian would have immediately known what he was seeking: a history they refused to countenance. As a result, they would never have permitted the professor to enter their domain.

Over the last four years, Jarrak had allowed himself to be swallowed up by the Museum. He'd worked across all sections of the Hassis in order to round out his knowledge, which looked to observers like he was trying to separate himself from the professor's side. He had spent a whole season just collating in archives, and two more studying the juxtaposition between Guild alliance lore and Learnian College law. It had only been in the evenings, during long philosophical conversations, that he had been able to discuss with his mentor their mutual opinions on history and how wrong this world seemed. Jarrak had become an unknown—a minor historian without rank—and so stayed apart from the Museum's reputation.

What would his professor truly think of this village now, if he were here?

Alone with this assignment, he was finally getting the chance to do what he had always wanted to do. In his soul, he felt the respect Bornn would be feeling towards him. Hestean was right; Bornn was also teaching her; his knowledge was spreading through Jarrak.

He yawned, and his thoughts continued.

He knew he had been privileged in another way, also. It had been one of the giants of the sky, the *Merysands*, that had transported him to Sharacan. The colossus exemplified the latest in sky-ship technology. Its crew of Guild Air Deserteers were the direct descendants of those trading tribes he'd told Hestean about. The *Merysands*' crew had only enhanced the reputation of all Deserteers in his eyes. Yet while the Deserteers had delivered Sharacan its greatness, he was aware that it was also the Deserteers who had brought about the city's demise. Not because they had wanted to, but through a consequence of necessity; they had fought hard to overthrow the tariffs that the College increasingly extracted.

Jarrak recalled more fully the first day he'd stepped aboard the *Merysands*.

The captain had looked at Jarrak's orders, knowing even before he'd opened them that this was to be no ordinary flight. The sanctioning deviation had been issued within one of the rarely used Blue Certificates; a certificate only ever dispensed by the very centre of the Guild. One had to have great authority to reroute a sky-ship from its determined path, and so the captain had come to realise the importance of the young man seated in front of him. He had looked closely at Jarrak as he pondered the blue wax seal. He'd carefully opened the document, taking special notice of the seal's markings—the six-sided polygon with its six spokes linked to a central hub. It was a symbol that meant much to the Deserteers, representing the six original tribes from which they were descended. It was an ancestry much older than most realised, now shrouded in myth and legend.

'Tell me, Maskee,' the captain had said, lifting his head to look directly into Jarrak's eyes. 'What is so important that you have been given the authority to disturb our trade? The certificate doesn't say.'

Jarrak's face hinted at a knowing smile. 'And I don't believe it has to, captain. You are aware of that. It is a Blue Certificate, and that in itself is a reason.'

Jarrak had felt the full weight of the obligation that had come with his charter; even though he was no worldlier than other ordinary men, he knew he had to seem it. He knew that his next words would cause further disturbance to the captain.

'But you're right,' he said. 'There is a reason, and it is important. I was told to use my own judgment on this matter, so if I cannot trust you, the captain of the *Merysands*, who can I? It is the Comcree, Captain! We are seeking to uncover the truth about one of the last known guardians of the gods.'

The captain's eyes had widened as he examined Jarrak closely. 'The last Comcree lived nearly two hundred years ago, Maskee, at the time of Sharacan's relinquishment. What makes you think there is still some truth to be found in the ruins of that city?'

'It is the warrior, Andreena herself, that we are seeking.'

The captain spluttered out a cough. 'You have found her ghost, you think? Or her resting place? She is supposed to have vanished without a trace. What has changed?'

'I have found that few in the world today know of Andreena, Captain.'

The captain mapped Jarrak's face closely. 'I am a Deserteer, Maskee, and our history has always interested me.'

Nodding, Jarrak continued. 'We have come across new information.'

The captain had lifted himself out of his chair and walked around his desk to lean against its edge. He'd looked intently towards Jarrak, and said, 'Can you elaborate on this new information?'

Jarrak had sat back deeper into his chair, cocooning himself in the luxurious leather. 'I'm afraid not, Captain. Not because I don't want to, but because the Museum doesn't want to look foolish if we are wrong.'

'I see. If this is indeed who you're looking for, then I can see why they are being cautious. Her disappearance almost unglued the Guild, and the College's lies have left even her very existence in doubt. To lose two of the Comcree one after the other the way we did … Well, it was a calamity. I am as sure of that as every Deserteer. Can you imagine what would have happened if the College had won control, back then? What this world would be like now? Their dogma would have stifled the very fabric of this world to an even greater extent than it has already. She was no ghost, Maskee. I truly believe this. And it is probably why it is my ship that was assigned for you to commandeer.'

Jarrak had been told that the captain was a true Deserteer, with beliefs and convictions that were strong within the Guild. But his manner was softer than he'd imagined. The crest of the Deserteers—hanging prominently on the wall of the cabin behind the captain's writing desk—was the only clear example of his beliefs and chosen profession. The elderly man had a rough exterior, yes, but he was obviously a perceptive person with a strong knowledge of his people's history. Jarrak decided he liked him.

'When together,' the captain went on, 'Elora and Andreena were as two halves of the same person. My great, great, great grandfather was there when we lost the Comcree Elora. He saw her fall, and the Comcree Andreena erupt in fury. He wrote in his journal that Andreena had howled as if she herself were broken. She should not have had her story warped the way the College has done. Andreena was no imposter, Maskee. Unless she can be pulled from fiction, and proof of her existence found, then belief in the gods will continue to wane. Those women were two of the greatest minds, and to lose them both was a tragedy.'

In researching the story of Andreena, Jarrak and Bornn had also come across this Deserteer record of history. Jarrak found himself entranced by the captain's personal rendition, and he settled back further into the chair to listen.

'If their two young apprentices hadn't taken over the way they had,' the captain continued, 'the Comcree Hexagon would have lost the advantage Andreena had created. Those two women chose their successors well, I can tell you that! They had that same connection with each other as their mentors had; the deep connection of twins or lovers. Yes, they were young, and yes, they did bring about the Treaty of Truce, but not because they were cowards or could not lead. My great grandfather suggested on his deathbed that there was another reason they couldn't go further; a brick wall they could not pass.' The captain's eyes deepened for a moment, as if distracted. Then he said, 'What makes you think you can find what happened to Andreena at Sharacan? Not in these two hundred years has anyone been able to discover where she rests.'

Jarrak looked down at his clasped hands, then rubbed his thumbs together as he composed a response. He knew that all Deserteers had similar memories to the captain's. It was something every one of them claimed a link to. The Comcree formed a mighty tale of strength and enlightenment, and it was their legend, along with Deserteer lore, that bound the Deserteers to each other and their Guild.

Jarrak never tired of hearing such stories. They were all slightly different, but one thread rang true in all of them—the events had occurred at the very time when the gods were reborn into the world. It was this reality that had driven the College into their rage. This was what Bornn and he had concluded. The College had realised that there would be no attainment of power for them if the gods were allowed to return and thrive. The knowledge that the gods passed on through the Comcree was vast, and it was for everyone. Once shared, it could not be controlled as the College desired. But the College had never been able to obtain the Comcree's knowledge for themselves, as the Comcree had vanished.

Jarrak unfolded his legs and leaned forward. 'Andreena was thought to be Sharacanese, as you know. But what we now think is that she may have also had a sister, and not just brothers. The evidence here is fragmentary. The sister seems to have been much older and married. We don't know how close they were as sisters, but as you can ascertain yourself, blood is blood. We now suspect that Andreena's direct lineage is from one of the oldest blood-lines. As I said, there are several obscure hints, but in every known depiction of her, she has been placed to the left of the matrefem. This suggests she was next in line to become the Matrefem Ze Hub Comcree, and for that, we believe she had to be of blood.

'As you have stated, the College had control of Sharacan at the time. When Andreena disappeared, the thought is that she may have been trying to get her sister out, or at the very least, her sister's children. There would have been a need to preserve the female line of her house, and the closest direct lineage to her may have been in Sharacan. It's an assumption, but one Professor Sageling and I feel is worthy of investigation. We believe the generational line of the Comcree is not passed directly from parent to child, as it seems sometimes to take steps backwards. It seems her apprentice at that time was not of her house, and so could not take on her rank. Maybe that's the brick wall your great grandfather spoke of. There is still much we do not know about the Comcree, but we are starting to think it's true that they're historically descended from the time of the Danannee! Maybe I shouldn't have told you this, Captain, but I have.'

The captain absorbed the young man's words. The room was silent as he raised a hand to his chin. 'It is rare to see the fanaticism of the College these days, as they're restricted by the Treaty of Truce. But back then, they were trying to cut off trade routes. That's why the College took Sharacan.'

'Are you sure, Captain?'

The captain gently tapped the top of his desk. 'Although they still hold Sharacan, their plan has rebounded on them. The *Merysands* is the latest in a progression of sky-ships. The first small blockade runners were born from the need to keep trade flowing past Sharacan. Did you know that, Maskee? It is not widely known outside the Guild, but as I have said, Deserteer history is something in which I have always taken an interest. It would appear you yourself have a great capacity for the learning of history. Back then, just as is the case now, all trade flowed because of the Guild. If the College hadn't taken Sharacan, the Deserteers may never have lifted into the sky, and this world may not be as it is today. That, my young friend, is something you should remember. Things often happen for a reason. The gods move slowly, Maskee, but there has always been a purpose in the acts attributed to them. Sometimes it's not obvious. The Comcree may well have had other motives for halting their advance, but what they did, lifted us into the air. The Comcree and the gods would not do something if it weren't for the betterment of this world. You may find that Sharacan holds a great many secrets; the Comcree Andreena may only be part of what you will discover there. Also, the College still hold a great anger against the Comcree. If I were you, I would hold my thoughts while in the company of the Black Robes. It may be safer.'

'You are right,' Jarrak said. 'Sharacan may indeed hold a great many secrets. It is a place mentioned far back into antiquity.'

'I take it, then, that you don't want us to set you down in Sharacan itself?'

Jarrak smiled. 'No, I think not, Captain. I would like to live past the first day of my arrival. I, too, fear that arriving in a Deserteer sky-ship would not set the right tone within an outpost of the College.'

'I thought not,' said the captain, removing himself from his desktop. 'Rather you than me! Let's get First Officer Petty in here, and we'll see if we can choose a landing site. I would never have objected to the authority of a Blue Certificate, but it is good to know I agree with the mission it enforces!'

* * *

The following morning, having reassured himself that all his supplies were loaded and stowed correctly, Jarrak made his way to the control deck, wrapped in his travelling cloak and sporting the insignia of his trade. He stood silently to watch the giant sky-ship be readied for flight. He followed the verbal dance of the command crew, and then, as the ship started to rise, noted everyone's voices go quiet. He'd been told of this moment.

The only sounds came from the ship itself. Until they had altitude, there would be no time to manoeuvre the giant sky-ship to safety if something went drastically wrong. They needed at least the airship's length beneath them before the danger passed. He found himself holding his breath.

The *Merysands* hovered steadily as it rose above its release point. The crew continued their work with the smoothness of a well-oiled machine. Mister Petty's eyes scanned the air, darting to the height meter with routine regularity. 'We have our quota, Captain,' he said finally. Jarrak saw the men visibly relax. But even though this was his first time aboard a sky-ship, he knew a ship in the air was never completely safe.

'Very good, Mister Petty,' said the captain. He looked out at the city sprawled below them. 'Give us an altitude of two marces, then a course nineteen fingers north of the rising!'

'Yes, Captain.'

'You also have command, Mister Petty. I'll be in my cabin if you need me. Let me know when we reach our altitude.'

'Yes, Captain.'

'And Mister Petty,' said the captain, 'it is good to have you aboard! It's been a long time since we shared the same ship.'

'It has been that, Captain. It's good to be under your command once again!'

Jarrak had thought the two men to be good friends who'd already spent much time together aboard the *Merysands*. Apparently, this was not so.

As the captain stepped onto the access stairs leading to the main deck of the ship, he said to Jarrak, 'Enjoy the view, Maskee. It is not one you will have seen too often, I suspect.'

'Indeed not, Captain!'

'I will show you around later when things are a little less unforgiving. See Mister Petty if you need anything in the meantime.'

'Thank you,' said Jarrak.

Nearby, Petty strolled to a window, a thoughtful expression on his face. He turned to face Jarrak for a moment before returning to his contemplations. Around the control deck, other men still busied themselves with their work.

Jarrak strolled across to Petty and said, 'You look far away, Mister Petty.'

Petty smiled. 'I was, Maskee. I haven't been home in a long time, and now here you are with orders that will take me there.'

'You're from Sharacan?'

'No, Maskee. I'm from the Sereye, just north of Sharacan, but it is close enough when you haven't been home for many years.'

'I didn't think the Sereye was still habitable.'

'Most of it isn't. These days, my people maintain themselves by living in just a few of the larger sinkholes—as you no doubt know, these are believed to once have been large underground lakes, collapsed into themselves. We survive on the water in subterranean caches, grow our food in terraced gardens protected by the depressions, and batter-palms line the bottoms to give us shade during the hottest parts of day. I used to spend a lot of time under those trees, just thinking about the wider world, and now here I am in it.'

'How many of your people are still there?'

'Just a few tribes now. Most of them scattered to all corners of the world when the Kalcool began to expand, just like everyone else.'

'Fascinating,' said Jarrak. 'I really didn't think anyone still lived there.'

'Why would you? We are an unimportant people, Maskee, and small in number. We also keep to ourselves, bothering no one.'

The helmsman approached, putting a stop to their conversation. 'We're approaching two marces, Mister Petty,' he said.

Petty glanced out of the window to see the escarpment, which was now well below them. 'Thank you, Gabes,' he said, before activating his sound receiver to speak to the captain. 'We are at two marces, Captain,' he said, once more focused on his tasks. 'Setting course nineteen fingers north of the rising, as you asked.'

* * *

Over the next few days, Jarrak found himself walking through the *Merysands*, making his own observations from the decks. On the third and last day, he found himself peering out over the distant landscape. This part of the plateau had been green once.

Petty stood by his side. Throughout the journey, he'd struck up a friendship with Mister Petty and the captain, and he knew that today was the last he'd have for a long while to discuss the College and their dogma. 'If the College had taken control back then, no one would have survived this changeling world when it decided to hiccup,' he said, almost in a whisper to Petty. 'The Black Robes don't have the historical knowledge. They have always been obsessed with control, but what this world has always needed is guidance. The Comcree do exist, Mister Petty, and they exist for a reason.'

'There is much the College has to answer for,' said Petty. 'But they have held to their bargains so far as we can see, so we must respect that. In more ways than one, it is a fragile world we live in, Maskee.'

Later, just as the sun was setting, the *Merysands* drifted low as they searched for a landing site. Through his optical lens, just visible as a shimmer in the distance, Jarrak observed the hills surrounding Sharacan.

Waterless, the Kalcool desert stretched for thousands of marces across the continent of Meglia, one of its tiny exceptions being Sharacan. He now knew that there were other watering places in the deep desert, after hearing Petty's story, but Petty had only told him about those because the captain had thought he might need to know if something ever went wrong.

A mighty temple had once stood within Sharacan, but all that now remained was an obelisk. He realised it was this obelisk he was seeing now, just visible above the low hills surrounding the ancient city.

There was a legend about the temple and the well-pond; one he would tell the Black Robes to explain his arrival. Although it was well-documented that priestesses ran the temple, the story spoke of the Danannee as masculine and the priestesses as no more than servants. He knew this would appeal to the Black Robes' sensibilities, and hopefully pave the road to permission for his excavations.

Petty decided that they would land downwind of the village. In this season, the wind only blew in from one direction. This meant Jarrak would have to circle widely round the hills and come in from the other side to make his story believable.

In the belly of the *Merysands*, three ports opened, and from within these harpoon guns were made ready to fire their darts deep into the sand. The rotating blades of the *Merysands* held steady against the breeze as the ship descended ever closer to the surface of the Kalcool. At the wrong moment, a strong gust of wind could injure the delicate craft, but this time Jarrak learned the sky-ship was to be tied securely and held firm for the night. It would spend two nights tethered to the ground in case his arrival was rebuffed, and then would rise into the sky and be gone.

So, early the next morning, with the night's lingering chill still gripping at his hands and face, Jarrak walked out onto the desert sand, leading his four silver shrows, which were loaded high with equipment and mostly empty waterskins, to better cement his fictional story of arrival. He turned back to look at the *Merysands* one last time, knowing that, from now on, he would have only himself to rely on. The Black Robes could not find out the true reasons for his excavations. If they did, they would destroy all that he found.

* * *

Jarrak felt his hat flop onto his head, and without opening his eyes he knew Hestean was back.

'You didn't come in, so I came out. You'll get burnt!' she said. She was fidgeting with something.

He yawned; eyes still closed. 'Not with you around, I won't.'

Wooooooooooooooooooook. Jarrak jerked to full wakefulness, his ears blasted by the sound. *Wooooooooooooooooooook.*

Hestean examined the instrument in her hands with curiosity, failing to see the expression on his face. Astonishment and puzzlement rotated though his brain as she said, 'I can make a sound with it, which I can change by manipulating this section here. But I can't sustain the sound …'

'Why would you want to?' Jarrak said.

'Because it's about time I showed it some respect!'

'Respect?'

'Yes! It was found where the gods reside. My mother has always said the gods only give you what you're capable of holding, and even though I told you I'm no longer sure they exist, and that what happens to people is just fate, this horn was shown to me.'

Jarrak looked at her, realising again just how often this girl could surprise him. 'So, you still believe in the gods, then, do you?'

'In a way, I guess so. We're not supposed to—the Robes don't like it—but they can't stop you from believing if you want to. They can stifle us women all they want, but we continue to believe. Even some of the men still believe. I know my father does!'

Jarrak found himself wondering about this. As he did, Hestean asked, 'I know I've asked you before, but do *you* really believe in the gods?'

He lifted his eyes. 'As I have told you, neither the gods nor their guardians have been seen in a long time. But I think there is some truth to the legends. The stories are so similar throughout the world that there has to be an origin of truth to them. So yes, I believe.'

'Do you really think the whole world once believed in the very same gods we do?'

'I believe so, yes.'

'The Black Robes have always said that we are the last. They scoff and ridicule us for refusing to forget, but I am wondering now if that's *why* we have refused to forget.'

Jarrak's forehead wrinkled as he realised the strength in Hestean's enlightenment. 'I think it would be best if you don't pass on what I have told you, Hat. I don't want to give the Black Robes another reason to revoke my tenure just yet.'

She turned and stared at him for a moment, as if seeing directly into his mind. He recalled her mother doing that very same thing. 'As if I would,' she said, then changed the subject of their discussion. 'Do you know how to play this horn?'

He grinned. 'I can't help you there, I'm afraid. I've seen woke horns in paintings, but I've never seen or heard one played. I don't know anyone who has. I think it's an ability that has been lost!'

Hestean sighed, fiddling with the instrument. 'I'll work it out somehow.'

'Is that necessary?'

'Of course!' She grinned cheekily. 'The gods have plans for me, I think.'

'I was afraid you were going to say that.'

'Come on, sleepy,' she said. 'Weren't we going to set out that new border today? I'll put this back inside.'

'I wasn't asleep! I was just thinking about what I came here to find.'

'Sure you were. I heard you snoring a little while ago!'

'I wasn't snoring!'

Hestean's grin deepened. She turned to step back into the tent, then paused. 'You know, you've not told me what it is you're really looking for, have you?'

'That's because I don't exactly know myself, Hat,' he said truthfully, getting to his feet. 'And I wasn't really snoring, was I?'

'No,' said Hestean, smiling again. 'But you shouldn't work so late into the night; it's wearing you out!'

'I have to. There's no one else.'

'There's me.'

'The Black Robes won't allow these men to be directed by a woman, you know that.'

'I could do more in the tent!'

'Unfortunately, Hat, you don't know enough yet. I'll just have to think of something else. Also, did I tell you it's my birthday today?'

Hestean smiled, then rolled her eyes. 'This is the second time.'

10

Silent and hiding from the world, Hestean sat on her bedroll with her blouse half buttoned so that it hung loose from one shoulder. The comb in her hand had been her grandmother's. She looked at it, running her finger along its pointed teeth. It was the last token from her mother's bloodline she would ever receive. Never again would she set foot in her family's home, and never again would she be allowed to cross the boundary between the dig and her village.

She still only knew what Jarrak had told her about the exterior world she'd been banished to. The only other person she spoke to now was Aswonnea, the young woman who came to the water-well. Over the three moon cycles since her banishment, she and her mother had only seen each other from a distance, as that was all that was possible now. Another tear ran down her cheek, and she lifted a finger to wipe it away.

'You awake yet?' Jarrak called. 'I could do with some help out here!'

She heard his stool creak, and a moment later he appeared at the opening to their living quarters, the object he had been examining still in his hand.

A look of concern crossed his face, and he asked, 'Are you alright?' It was then that he noticed a mark he'd never seen before scarred into her shoulder. 'What's that?'

'What's what?'

'That mark at the top of your arm.'

'Oh,' said Hestean pulling her blouse up. 'It's my mark of servitude.'

'Your *what*?'

She lifted her eyes and stared at him coldly. 'Don't you listen? It's my mark of servitude! All the women of my clan have it. It's carved into us at birth, to remind us that we are forever indentured to men.'

Jarrak stood for a moment, her explanation making him smile rather than carrying the bite she'd intended. Her eyes followed him as he moved to kneel beside her, and she watched as he drew three marks in the sand. He then left a space and drew two more marks.

'Have you ever seen these?' he asked.

'No, what are they?'

He drew the mark from her shoulder into the space he had left and underlined all of them with one quick stroke. 'These six marks are house marks.'

'What are house marks?'

'These house marks represent the six great houses of our world. We all belong to one of them. I belong to this one, and this,' he said, lightly touching her blouse where it now covered the mark on her shoulder. 'I presume this is the one that you belong to. It isn't a mark of servitude—it's a mark of belonging. If I were to guess, I would say someone wanted the women of your clan to never forget which house they truly belonged to.' He seemed to consider something for a moment and then stood up. 'I've never seen it carved into flesh before, though. Do the Black Robes do this to all the women here?'

'The Robes don't do it. A woman does it; usually our oldest.'

'The women do this to themselves, and you're told it's a slave mark?'

'Yes!'

'Believe me, Hat,' he said, beginning to chuckle, 'it's a house mark, and I bet your "wise woman" knows it, too!'

Hestean recalled telling him of the wise woman. In that conversation he had laughed like this, and she had come to realise since then that in moments of discovery he had a propensity for amusement. He turned and went back to his cataloguing while she remained seated on her bed, looking at the marks in the sand. She noted their similarities and differences, and wondered if he was just playing with her. She looked up to find him through the gap that connected the two parts of the tent and followed his movement as he walked to one of the display benches. Her sorrow was driven from her head and replaced with an intense wonder.

* * *

Three days later, Hestean entered the tent after having been to the water point. She was smiling for the first time in days.

'You look cheerful,' commented Jarrak.

'You were right!' she said as she put down the water jug.

He stopped his reading and turned on his stool. 'About what was I right, exactly?'

She squatted down and drew the six marks in the sand near her feet. 'I sent a message saying the Ze Hub was to be shown these. I didn't say why, just that she was to be shown, and today she has sent back a reply.'

'And what was this reply?' asked Jarrak, Hestean's infectious exhilaration capturing him now, too.

'She said, "tell the child to smile".' Hestean's eyes glowed as she looked at him. 'Your sand marks seem to have revealed a well-kept secret that even I didn't know.'

With the privilege of knowledge that Reglean had bestowed upon her, Hestean was once again feeling connected with her people. But then Jarrak said, 'You mentioned a word a moment ago—*Ze Hub*. What is that?'

Hestean realised the word had slipped from her mouth and instantly panicked. 'Oh … It's just a word I've heard some of the women call our matrefem. I think it's a nickname. I kind of like it, don't you? *Ze Hub*,' she said again, letting the term roll off her tongue.

'They must care for her a great deal,' said Jarrak.

Hestean wondered if he knew she was lying. From the corner of her eye, she caught sight of an old book open on his writing table. Still flustered, her mind retreated from his interrogating eyes.

'What have you been doing?' she asked, motioning to the book.

Jarrak's lips cracked into a smile as he lifted a plaque from his lap. 'I've been trying to work out what this means. One of the men brought it in while you were gone.'

Hestean took the object from him, looked at it, and still in her fluster, failed to realise when she started translating the inscription aloud.

'You can read this?' asked Jarrak, amazed.

'What?'

'The man who found it had no idea what it meant!'

'No, well … Well he wouldn't, would he?' said Hestean, resigning herself to the fact that she had let another secret flow from her mouth.

'What do you mean?'

'Well, it's written in Fem!'

'What do you mean, Fem? What is Fem?' asked Jarrak, having seen only the written language of the ancients scribed across the plaque.

Hestean was silent for a moment, gathering her thoughts. She decided, finally, to be truthful.

'It's the written language of women here,' she said with proud conviction. 'As you know, women in Sharacan aren't permitted to learn the written language of men, so we use this one. The Robes allow it because they say it's a dead and useless language, but it still works for us.'

'You mean … The women here can all read?'

'It's hidden,' said Hestean, 'but yes. It was only your words—the words of men—that I couldn't read.'

'So that's why you were able to pick up the modern tongue so easily …'

'Once you showed me the patterns, it turned out not to be so hard.'

'You never said.'

'No. We don't usually tell. It's not welcomed, even though the Robes must allow it.'

'Why is that?'

'I heard Robe Elless say once that it was written into the Treaty of Truce.'

'Is it?'

'That's just what I heard him say.'

Jarrak looked at her in silence for a moment. That amused expression she had come to know so well spread once more across his face. 'So why did you choose this moment to reveal that you could read this language you call "Fem"?'

'I didn't mean to! It was an accident. It just escaped my mouth, like *Ze Hub* did. I wasn't thinking properly!'

'Are there any more of these accidents you want to share?' When Hestean's body went stiff, he said, 'I'm sorry! I shouldn't have asked that.' She relaxed a little, and he leaned across his desk to pick up a small book. 'This afternoon, when it gets hot, you might like to read this,' he said, handing it to her. 'It's written in the language of the ancients. If you recall, I mentioned that I only know of a few people who can read it these days.'

Although by now she had read a lot of Jarrak's books, some many times over, she had not yet been allowed to read the ones he kept tucked into the back of his desk. Flipping slowly through its pages, her eyes widened. 'These are our words.'

Jarrak stood up from his stool, smiling fully now. 'Dead it might be, but useless it is not. I'm going to see where they found this plaque, and while I'm gone, you can clean up that bench like you should have been doing instead of telling me tales.'

He walked across to grab his hat, and then headed towards the exit. But before he reached it, Hestean dashed across to stand in front of him. 'What I said—it is a secret still, isn't it?'

He looked at her. Then he let his eyes fall to the book in her hand, and said, 'You know, I think there are a lot of secrets here.'

Hestean lowered her own eyes to the book, and after a moment said, 'Yes, I think so, too.'

'Then they will remain so until they are not meant to be secrets anymore.' He stepped past her, and as he did, he picked up a long, vibrantly coloured stake from the table next to him. He drew a six-sided polygon in the sand, then drew a circle in its middle. He then connected each face of the polygon to the circle with six lines. 'Do you know what this is?'

'No?'

'When the six houses of our world are written about as a whole, they are often drawn as a symbol, like this. A six-sided polygon. Each house is connected to the centre by a spoke. I wonder if you can tell me what the centre is called? I'll give you a hint; it's a Fem word I heard you mention a moment ago. No rush, but you're smart—you'll work it out. It will give your brain something to do while you tidy up.' He replaced the coloured stake back onto the table, and with a spring in his step, turned once more towards the exit.

'Sweep that bench off. We'll need it when I get back!' he called loudly from outside.

* * *

Jarrak's legs carried him through the dig as his mind pondered this newest insight. What else did Hestean have to reveal? Nowhere did the Black Robes teach their women to read, so he had assumed—stupidly, it now seemed—that the women here were also illiterate. How foolish of him to think that Hestean had just been quick at understanding when he'd started teaching her to read and write in the modern form. He realised now that the women of Sharacan kept this skill very secret, indeed. But why had it been written into the Treaty of Truce? In the wider world, Hestean would need to know the modern script, but he now realised that this skill of reading Fem, or the *lingua antiquas*, as he knew it, would give her a much-needed place in his world.

He realised, now, that there were two places the ancient text could still be useful. One was in this village, but why? And the other was at the Museum in Elora-Bearer. With her full and proper understanding of the ancient text, the insights Hestean might find in the ancient scripts of the Museum vaults would be enormous. How large was the circle of people who could understand the language? Were there other places on this world where it was still spoken? Unlike the scholars, he knew Hestean had grown up with Fem, so her knowledge of its syntax and grammar would be instinctive. With her knowledge, she could teach him these details, and as her understanding of the modern form grew, so could his knowledge of the old. There were nuances within the language that were placement and position specific. Not even the five scholars understood this properly, whereas Hestean perhaps could.

He came to a halt in front of the partially revealed form of the temple. Recalling the words on the plaque, he knew that this place was indeed beginning to yield up its story. He realised, too, that the captain of the *Merysands* had been right; he was indeed uncovering many unforeseen secrets.

11

Jarrak didn't hear the footsteps coming towards him as he scraped away at the small mosaic on the temple's courtyard floor. He had come across a number of them around the vaulted chamber, which had been recently unearthed, abutted with the obelisk on its western side. The large single room had only one entrance, which also faced west. Inside, directly opposite this opening, was a highly decorated altar attached to the wall, which was part of the obelisk itself. The chamber was also elaborately scribed with magnificent and intricate patterns.

'What have you discovered?' said a voice, which startled Jarrak completely. He jerked round to see boots followed by a black robe, then the face of Gaywin looking down at him.

As Jarrak rose to stand, he said, 'I'm not sure. They're different in style and rather unlike anything else I've come across. If you wet them, the colours change.'

'And is that significant?'

Maybe, maybe not. It could just be one particular artisan's preference. A joke, perhaps. But on the other hand, it could be quite significant. If you wet the mosaics, the female figures within them become male.'

'So, is this what you have been looking for?'

'No, not really. Not only this, anyway. It's just one more piece of the puzzle.'

'And have you found anything else?

'Oh, yes! Just look,' said Jarrak, pointing up at the obelisk. 'It's like a giant four-sided phallus, see? Here, the obelisk represents birth, life, and even death. And these mosaics, they seem to be paying homage to the obelisk.'

'But you have sent your workers home once more.'

'I need some time to sort out where to start the next phase of the excavation.'

'I see. And what's that you have in your hand?'

Jarrak looked down. 'I'm not sure of this, either. It's a broken piece of silicon tile, I think. I've found a few such fragments lately but haven't as yet found where they've come from. They're unusual, too; made up of layers. Each layer has been engraved before the next was added to it. These engravings form some sort of pattern, but without a whole tile, I have no way of working out just what it means. Would you like it?' He held the fragment out.

'I have no interest in souvenirs of this place,' said the Black Robe. He looked around, observing the ever-expanding excavations. 'And what of the girl. Where is she?'

'I sent her to get some more water.'

'And will you be finished here soon, do you think?'

'It depends on what else I find. I would like to get a few trenches into that mound there, as well.'

'Why would you want to dig up a hill?' Gaywin spat.

'Because I don't think it is a hill. I think it's a mound, and mounds are made by people, not nature. I am starting to think, also, that it is older than even the temple.'

'And why is that significant?'

'The oldest parts of this temple seem to be closest to the obelisk, which is clearly meant to be a symbol of masculinity. And if the mound is older, it could be a crude masculine form, inidicating still more directly that the Danannee were entirely of the male gender.'

Gaywin brought his hand to his face, his thumb and finger resting on his jaw. He then looked around at the temple once more, and said, 'You think this, do you? You think the people here first built the mound to venerate the gods, and then built the temple to do the same?'

'Yes, I do. Just look at it. The mound is due west of the temple, and the temple is due west of the well-pond. Nature doesn't build in straight lines—only people do.'

'So, you are now saying the well-pond is part of this, too?'

'Maybe, maybe not. The well-pond may just have been the original gathering place because of its sustenance. They might then have built the mound where it is because the well-pond was to its east, towards the rising sun that brings life and death in the desert. The well-pond to the east could have been an attempt to ensure that the sun always brought the former. The temple, a later addition, also links the mound and the well-pond to the sun.'

'So you are saying, in effect, that these first people worshiped the sun?'

'It is a theory, yes. And isn't the sun even today thought of as male, and the two moons as female? Isn't that why the College permits a man to have two wives if he wishes?'

'Then, for Sharacan's influence to be fully extinguished, you would have to remove all three—the mound, the temple, and the well-pond.'

A cold shiver went through Jarrak's body. 'No,' he said. 'You would also have to extinguish the sun to do that!'

In all the years that Jarrak had been alive, he had never seen a man exude such loathing as Gaywin did. A deep hatred of Sharacan seemed to waft from the man. Jarrak was glad that Gaywin was not the village chairman, and hoped he never would be.

Gaywin looked at the sun, then at the mound, and then his eyes surveyed the temple once more before he glanced towards the well-pond and the village beyond. 'I suggest that you get everything you want from this place while you still can,' he said, before walking away. At the edge of the temple's courtyard, he touched a hand to some of its fallen stones, running his palm across their surfaces. He again looked up at the sun, then back at Jarrak for a moment before he started briskly off towards the village.

There was a shuffling in the sand behind Jarrak as he continued to follow Gaywin's departure.

'What was that all about?' asked Hestean, coming up to stand beside him.

'You heard all that, did you?' he said, now turning to reach for the beaker of water she held out to him.

'I was just coming back from the water point when I saw him enter the courtyard, so I ducked through into the vault before he saw me. I hate that man. There is something wrong with him, even for a Robe.'

'Yes,' said Jarrak thoughtfully. 'For a few years now, there have been rumours of a split in the College. Of a younger, more radical group with no tolerance for anything other than their own beliefs. From what I understand, this new faction seems to be blind to the lessons of history. They have not lived through them, so they do not believe in them. They think they are just stories, and not teachings to take notice of. Until now, I hadn't realised that Gaywin might be one of them.'

'Should we be worried? I was watching his face when you mentioned the sun. It seemed to scare him a little ...'

'If Sharacan vanishes, so will the stars! It's probable that this story has crossed his mind. It was that story that stopped the College from completely destroying Sharacan two hundred years ago. Gaywin may have looked hesitant, but the arrogance he displays might just drive him to do such a thing. But for the moment, the old guard still runs Sharacan.'

'Our sun does not light the entire universe, though.'

'No, but what I said was enough to perhaps slow him down, which is all I think we can do.'

'You told me the mound was female, but you let him think it was male.'

'Do you think I should have told him the truth?'

'You also told him that the female figures turned male in the mosaics—not that the males turned female.'

'That's right, Hat. It's something no Black Robe would want to hear. And as you said, there is something not quite right with that man.'

12

It was just out from the obelisk's eastern face that most of the fragments now bothering Jarrak had been found. The piece in his hand had been found this morning. Jarrak had been working endlessly on little sleep, and now felt exhausted.

He looked up at the stars for a moment, then walked back inside, grabbed his stool, and placed it centrally between the tables holding his growing hoard of oddities. He sat down, placing his lantern on the bench in front of him. He focused on the small broken pieces of silicon tile in front of him. 'What are they?' he asked himself, leaning across to pick up another of the shards. 'They make no sense. The deeper I dig, the further back in time I should be going, but these seem to be telling me that I'm actually going *forward* in time. They're just too refined to have existed back then. Even today, I doubt that we could produce such sophisticated crafting ...'

Exhaling deeply, he stood, placing the fragments back with the others before again moving the stool and sitting at his desk. It seemed he needed to be in many places at once. The dig had evolved since his workers had begun shovelling sand from around the temple complex, and he was becoming aware that he could no longer control the whole site himself; not if he was to fully research and understand what he was finding. Every night now, he worked later into the evening, deciphering what was found. He could feel the mental load crushing him. He couldn't leave the work in the tent solely to Hestean, as she was still only an apprentice. And besides, the Black Robes wouldn't like to see her working unsupervised in anything but the most menial of roles. The men of the village wouldn't work to a woman's command, either, even if her accumulated knowledge could be useful. Jarrak folded his arms onto the desk and slumped forward, his eyelids closing.

When he woke, he found that Hestean had put a blanket over his shoulders, and he knew he had to find a solution to his fatigue.

The next afternoon, he dismissed all the workers, and that evening he wrote a letter. The following morning, he told Hestean that he needed time to think, and set off on a long walk into the hills surrounding Sharacan. Three days after that, when the two moons sat side by side in the night sky, he hooked his lantern to a pole just outside his tent and left it shining all night, as he had many times before.

* * *

When Hestean first heard the voices, she thought she was dreaming. She had become aware of them subliminally—they were faint and wistful in the air. Her mind awake, but her eyes still closed, she lay listening to the fragments of sound that wafted in on the breeze. 'They're real,' she said to herself.

Opening her eyes to the night, she found the moons illuminating her surroundings in a soft, shadowy grey. Since Jarrak had closed down the dig to concentrate on cataloguing his findings, the two lunar spheres had spun through their sky dance and once again sat together in the night sky. Jarrak had even started to get some sleep lately, and she turned over to look in the direction of his bedroll. Finding it empty, she twisted towards the whispered sounds outside, lifting the tent's outer wall slightly to see where the voices were coming from.

She saw Jarrak seated on the ground, facing away from her. Opposite him was a man, almost hidden. At first she thought he was one of the Black Robes, then she realised that the man's cloak and hood were almost the same colour as the sand he was sitting on. His cowl was folded back slightly, revealing the colour of his hair and face. His skin was a little darker than Jarrak's, but nowhere near her colouring, and in the dim light she thought the man seemed quite old, too. *A sand shepherd*, she heard her mind say, but didn't know why or where the word had come from. She couldn't remember having heard it before, but here it was in her head.

After folding back her bedroll, she got up and walked stealthily through to the outer tent, where she leant silently against one of its upright poles. The stranger was the one who noticed her first, and she watched him flick his gaze to Jarrak, warning him that they were now being observed. Turning towards the darkened tent, Jarrak stretched out his arm and beckoned Hestean forward.

Closer, she was better able to glimpse what the stranger was wearing beneath his cloak. His tunic was also sandy in colour, as were his trousers. He wore knee-high moccasin boots and a dull red belt circled his waist. Sitting down beside Jarrak, Hestean thought she also saw a scabbard attached to the belt, enveloping a red-handled dagger.

'We have a visitor,' Jarrak told her. 'A Mister Petty. Mister Petty, this is Hestean.'

'You have my greetings, Maskea,' said Petty.

A shiver ran down her back. It was only the second time in her life that a man had greeted her as an equal. To him, like Jarrak, she seemed a real person. Hearing his deep voice, which had an unusual note of serenity, she warmed to him instantly. She noticed it was the same warmth she now felt around Jarrak, but in Jarrak's case the warming had taken some time to establish itself. With this stranger, it was almost as though she had recognised a distant member of her own family.

'As she is awake,' said Jarrak, 'you may as well give it to her yourself.'

'Give me what?' asked Hestean, mimicking their softly spoken tones.

'Don't worry, Hat. I've got one too, see?' said Jarrak, lifting his hand from his lap. 'It's something Bornn thinks may help with our work.'

'What's it do?'

'Perhaps the best way to show you is to demonstrate,' said Petty, unfolding a piece of cloth sitting on the sand in front of him. 'This bit goes over your left ear, like this.' He lifted the smaller part and placed it around her ear before feeding a soft, flexible wire down her back. 'The rest can clip to your waist. Do you have a belt we could use? I doubt if your sash will be strong enough.'

For a moment, her eyes studied the apparatus he was holding, and then she nodded. 'Inside, I have.'

Petty placed the larger part of the device in her hand. 'Could you get it, do you think? I can fit it properly, then.'

Hestean studied the device for a moment longer, then lifted her eyes to study Petty. It seemed a long time before she nodded and stood up to return to the tent. After some rummaging, she found the belt she was looking for. Curious about the part that had been placed inside her ear, she picked up a mirror and examined herself. Having seen how it was fitted, she pulled it out to look at it more closely. 'I wonder what you're for,' she breathed into the device.

'By the gods, how do you turn this thing down?' said Jarrak, his words singing softly from the device in her hand. It slipped from her fingers, fell to her bedroll, and a moment later, still stunned, she heard his voice again. 'What do you think it's for, Hat?'

For an age, she sat staring at the device, then picked it up and placed it back into her ear. She lifted the tent's wall once more to check if Jarrak was really still seated where he had been. She looked out and saw Jarrak and Petty chuckling, their voices once more flowing from the small object in her ear.

She heard Petty say, 'It does appear they work, Maskee!'

'It would appear so, yes,' said Jarrak.

At first, Hestean didn't realise that a scowl had cemented itself onto her face, but then she felt the anger beginning to rise. She walked back out to confront the two men. 'So, men from the outer world *do* laugh at women,' she said, thumping Jarrak on the arm. She glared as she sat down beside them.

'*Ow.* No!' insisted Jarrak.

'Yes, we do,' said Petty. 'And at men, too, when the situation warrants it. But it's not so much laughing *at* someone. Rather, it's the moment in time itself that's amusing. You are the first in your village to see and hear this technology. It's quite new, so even to the Robes of Learnian, it is not yet known.'

'I see,' said Hestean, not quite believing him. 'So, you are a philosopher too, then?'

'No, just someone who has had time to look at this world.'

Taking in Petty's sage-like posture, she said, 'Can I really speak with Jarrak using these things?'

'That's the idea, Hat,' said Jarrak, still massaging his upper arm.

'Good … Then I may never shut up again.'

Petty broke into a hushed laugh, then turned to Jarrak. 'Do you still think they're a good idea, Maskee?'

Hestean almost smiled herself, then, but resisted as she observed Petty more closely.

She then noticed that Jarrak was looking at her. 'Do you want to hear what they're really for, Hat?' Her inner smile vanished, and she just nodded, trepidation unexpectedly filling her. Jarrak reached into his tunic's inner pocket and pulled out a letter, which Petty had earlier given him. Unfolding it, he read aloud:

'*My young Maskee, I have given your request some thought and have decided against sending you a new field tech. Because of the scepticism that still surrounds me here, and because of what you have told me, it seems to me that you already have the best field assistant you could hope for under these circumstances. The girl knows the site, she has learned how a dig should operate, and it would seem she is a quick learner.*

'*As to negotiating your little problem and furthering your need, I have sent two pieces of equipment. If the Black Robes think the girl is merely doing your bidding, and not initiating decisions or orders of her own, then your problem may resolve itself. It will fit with the College's hierarchical beliefs. Let me know how you get on; it would be a shame to waste talent when you have it on hand.*

'*I am sorry I cannot fulfil your request, but to do so might jeopardise both your safety and your goal.*'

Jarrak finished reading, then folded the letter and put it away.

'The Black Robes will never let me!' said Hestean, staring at him open-mouthed.

'We will see,' he said. 'I have an idea.'

'An idea! What you intend is to get us both banished into this desert!'

'She does have a point,' said Petty, starting to smile once more.

'See, even Mister Petty here agrees with me!'

'Petty doesn't know College law as I do. It can be turned on itself, if you know how.'

'And you know how?'

'As I have said, I have an idea.'

'Well, it had better be a really good idea, or we will both be bleached bones! But now there is something else I want to know.' She turned to Petty. 'Just who and what are you, exactly?'

'Who do you think?'

'Well … When I first saw you, one description popped into my head. "Sand shepherd". And I don't know why because I've never heard this term before. What is a sand shepherd?'

Petty huffed with mirth at the descriptive phrase, and then was silent for a long moment. 'You know,' he said eventually, 'I haven't heard those words for a long time.'

'You know what they mean, then?'

'Oh yes, I know what they mean. Every Deserteer knows of the sand shepherds. Only, the more current descriptor is "sand shadow". "Sand shepherd" is an ancient term, and possibly shows your Sharacan heritage. Sharacan is ancient too.'

'So, you're a Deserteer?'

'I'm the first officer and navigator aboard the sky-ship, *Merysands*.'

'But Jarrak said that Deserteers aren't allowed into College territory!'

'We're not! So, I'm not here, am I?'

'Like a sand shepherd's shadow …'

'Exactly! But the sand shadows were the best of us. They are, or rather were, the elite. They were the Deserteers assigned to protect each of the Comcree warriors when we went into battle against the College, so collectively they became known as the Protectorate.'

'So, are you a sand shadow or not?'

'There are no sand shadows any more, Maskea. There hasn't been a need for them in over two hundred years.'

'Pity.'

'Yes, it is! It's a great pity.'

'So, not a sand shepherd, then. But you did say that you were a navigator … What is a navigator and what does a navigator aboard a sky-ship do?'

'Now why would I want to bore you with that?'

'Because, as with Jarrak here, I've taken a liking to you. That's why. So, tell me about being a *plotter*.'

Petty grinned. 'Now there's another word I haven't heard in a long time. It appears you know a little about navigation.'

'I showed her a book about the ancient language, and she's picked up on some vocabulary,' said Jarrak, looking sidelong at Hestean.

'I can't help it if I like the words,' she said, eyeing Jarrak conspiratorially. She wondered why he didn't want Petty to know about the women's knowledge of Fem.

'They are fine words, I agree,' said Petty, looking from one to the other.

'You know the old language too, then?' she asked.

'No, but I was born in the Sereye. It's a part of the desert, and my people still use some of the old words.'

'You are desert-born like me, then?'

'I am. I was still a boy when I took my first flight in a sky-ship. I was a boy when I found out I'd been apprenticed to the Air Deserteers by my mother. Captain Hanjie of the *Merysands* had the same experience.'

'It was your mother who decided your path in life?'

'Well, it's more that she saw where my heart was leading me, and she helped me to achieve that dream.'

'The College would never allow my mother to do that … So, you and this captain have served on the same sky-ship since you were boys?'

'No, the *Merysands* is a new ship, only a few years old. The captain and I have spent many of our years serving on separate sky-ships.'

'So, why aren't you a captain, too? If you both started at the same time?'

Again, Petty chuckled as he brushed back his greying hair. He ran his finger back and forth across his lips, pondering the question. 'I never really wanted to be a captain. I would like to end my career with the man I started with, though. He was born to be a captain, whereas I enjoy the job I have. I like who I have become, Maskea.' He gazed up at the two moons. 'I should be going soon. But I'll say this first. I am pleased to have risen to my rank on one of the great sky-ships that first lured me from the desert as a boy. The adventure has cost me, though. When you first came aboard, Maskee, both the captain and I were at a loss as to why I was appointed to the *Merysands*. He had not asked for me, and I had not sought the posting.

'However, after having spoken with you, Jarrak, we understand that the Guild set my appointment specifically. I am one of only a few navigators who know this region of the Kalcool. These days, few sky-ships sail this part of the skies, but years ago I plotted aboard one that did.

'There have only ever been two ways into the fortress that is the Hassis Valley,' he went on. 'Although the College had blocked one, they could not control the other. The Comcree gave that dominion to the Deserteers, and the Deserteer alliance has held it until this very day. Once the Deserteers only governed trade across the sand, but from that point on we also dominated the sky. It was not just the sky-ships that defeated the College. It was knowledge, freely given.

'There are stories of weaponry that the Comcree once deployed—weapons that flung fear into the College, and led to their eventual fragmentation. A short time afterwards, the Comcree vanished, as if they had only ever been ghosts. But they are still here, Maskee. They took their weaponry and the knowledge they had yet to disclose to us and left the Guild Deserteers to watch over this world. Since then, the College has remained irrelevant, surviving only in pockets such as Sharacan. The College saw the true wrath of the gods back then, and because of that, even now, they hold those days firmly within their memory.

'I am now wondering, however, if the balance is once again being tested. Are the gods themselves setting something unseen in motion? You told me there seems to be a more radical sect in the College, Maskee. If the gods do exist, they won't like that. I know that the Guild does not assign Deserteers on a whim, and my mind chills at the thought of another great conflict. You told me that, five years ago, your professor came across the story that brought you here. Well, since I have been aboard the *Merysands*, Captain Hanjie has been telling me about the ship's history. As you know, the *Merysands* is the first in a new breed of sky-ships, and her plans were also delivered to the Guild in that same year. I have learned, too, that our loadmaster was reassigned to the *Merysands*, just as I was, and she is from one of the great Deserteer families. Since we first brought you here, Maskee, the captain and I have come to realise that our whole crew has been selected from across the entire Deserteer squadron. The *Merysands* is more than just a new sky-ship, Maskee; things are changing, and you—it now seems to me—will play a role in whatever is beginning to happen.'

'But I am an historian, Mister Petty, and not a Deserteer,' Jarrak said. 'I have no interest in the Guild.'

'True. But you do have an interest in the Comcree, don't you? And it now seems to me that the Comcree have an interest in the *Merysands*.'

'There are no Comcree anymore, Mister Petty.'

'Are you sure? Just because they haven't been seen, doesn't mean they don't still exist. There are men and women at the centre of the Guild who know a lot more than you or I will ever know.'

'Are you implying that the Museum works for the Deserteers?'

'No, Maskee. Only that maybe we all work for the gods.'

Hestean noticed that Jarrak seemed rattled by Petty's musings. From what Jarrak had told her, Petty's tale almost seemed plausible.

'I must go,' said Petty. 'The *Merysands* needs the sun. She must rise, hidden by its glare, if she is to stay hidden while we depart.'

'You're landing to the east now, then?'

'Winds change, and so must we, Maskee.'

'I wish you could stay longer,' said Hestean.

'There are some things that a person must learn for themselves, Maskea; things a person cannot be shown. One day, maybe you will see the *Merysands* for yourself, and the rest of the world too.'

'Maybe,' she said, 'but first I must survive what Jarrak has in mind for us.'

'I have a feeling you are meant to,' said Petty. 'Just as I was meant to be a plotter.'

Hestean smiled at his little joke, then watched as he disappeared into the night.

* * *

Hestean slept lightly for the rest of the night, constantly stirring as her mind filled with visions of the trading tribes of the desert. These Deserteers, whom she had once never even known about, filled her with dreams of freedom and authority. Petty's own mother had been the one to send him off to his destiny. That would never be allowed under the Robes.

The following morning, she erupted at Jarrak, saying, 'You're not going to tell me what to do anymore. I have never been your slave, and I have no intention of being so now.'

Jarrak's mouth opened and closed, and then he stared at her in complete silence.

'My family is lost to me; my village has banished me; and it would appear that now you want to put me back under the thumb of a man. You, of all men! My freedom within this dig has been my only sustenance. I have become who I am here, and I am not going to relinquish that.' She picked up a cup and threw it at him. He fell backwards onto the ground, his arms held out to protect his face. This was enough to rouse him, too.

'Will you be still and listen?' he said loudly.

'No!'

'Well, it's your choice, but I don't care if you switch the damn thing off the second you leave this tent. Just don't tell the Robes that!'

This time it was Hestean's mouth that opened and closed without words as she fell silent, staring at him with eyes that glowed hot with rage.

'I don't want to tell you what to do,' said Jarrak calmly, observing her fragility. 'I want them to *think* I'm telling you what to do. You're good enough to do this job on your own. I won't be able to see you, only hear you when you choose to tell me what you see. What you do, and what you tell them, is entirely up to you. The only way this will work, though, is if they think your words are mine. Truly, Hat! Isn't this the only way of it? I can't continue on my own—it's wearing me out—so we have to find a way for you to do more.'

It was fear that had driven her outcry. She knew this. She saw now that she had reacted how she'd always wanted to react whenever a man of her village had condescended to her. In the past, she would never have objected or talked back, even if she had wanted to.

Suddenly, she stepped forward and put her arms around Jarrak. He was her closest friend, and she couldn't lose him now. 'I'm free, aren't I?' she asked.

Jarrak's arms went to her shoulders and pushed her back so that he could look at her. 'Of course you're free!' he said.

'No,' said Hestean, pulling away and pointing to her head. 'I mean free in *here*. I know what freedom is, but now I feel it, too!'

Jarrak smiled in sudden recognition of what the argument had really been about. He reached out to hold her once more. 'I hope so, Hat,' he said. 'I hope that from now on, you will always know that feeling.'

13

Jarrak knew the day was going to be long, even before he gathered the men who worked for him into the temple's courtyard. Under the Robes, a man's voice was his own and could not be subjugated. Still, that's exactly what he was hoping to do—or at least, make it appear as though he were.

Almost immediately, as he had hoped, he spotted one of the Black Robes running towards the village. A short time later, the village chairman and his entourage came scrambling towards the dig, a mixture of puzzlement and annoyance on the chairman's face. Jarrak frowned for appearances, but inwardly he smiled.

He turned to greet the elderly man. 'It is good to see you, Chairman. It seems I need your wisdom. I have a dilemma that I hope you can help me solve.'

'I have been told that you're attempting to take the voice of one of these men. You know this cannot be countenanced. What are those devices you have?'

'They are Voice Transference Devices, or simply put, VTDs.'

'And what is a "VTD"? Where did you get them?'

'I brought them with me. I've always had them; I just haven't needed them before. I didn't think they would be the problem they appear to be, as it was one of your own great men who discovered the secret behind their workings.'

'Really?'

'Yes. I believe his name was Heranius Quay, and it was at least twenty years ago when the Museum first became aware of his work on energy membrane stimulation.'

'And what is that?'

'He found a way to make a thin membrane vibrate in order to reproduce sound.'

'So, these VTD's are stolen, then?'

'Not at all. Such devices have been used on your seacrafts for some time. The Museum has had many occasions to observe their use, and once they understood their workings, they simply copied them. I doubt that it was difficult, given the vast resources that the Museum has at its disposal. I believe such devices are now also used on the sky-ships flown by Deserteers, too.'

'I see! But still, what you propose here cannot be allowed.'

Sighing, Jarrak flopped to the ground and crossed his legs. He then motioned with his hand for the chairman to join him. 'I'm tired,' he said, as the chairman seated himself opposite. 'I have reached a point in my excavations where I need to be in more than one place at a time, and as you know, this is not possible. I am spending my days here at the temple and in the new trenches on the mound, and in the evenings I work on analysis late into the night. I cannot ask for help from the Museum, as this is just a minor excursion to them—something on the very periphery of their vision. Aid would simply not be granted, and the men here don't know enough to work on their own.'

'How is this my problem?'

'It's not!'

'I see. Well, you do seem to have yourself a predicament, Maskee, I'll grant you that. But what you ask is beyond my authority. These men will not tolerate it. They are not women, Maskee!'

'Then maybe I should employ a woman,' said Jarrak.

'No, no, no, Maskee. You really must be tired. That you cannot do either.'

'Why not?'

'You know *why not*. Men are above women, my young friend. That's why not.'

'Exactly!'

The Chairman's forehead wrinkled. 'What do you mean by this?'

'Well, I'm not sure. The thought has just occurred to me. I concede that a man cannot hold another's voice, but a woman has no voice, does she? I already have a girl, and she would not be telling the men what to do; I would be telling them *through* her. Women do impart messages, both verbally and through written notes from their husbands and fathers to other men, don't they? Hestean is neither my wife nor daughter, but she is my servant, bound to my will. Being only a woman, could I not take her eyes and voice as my own?'

For a moment, the chairman sat in silence, as if trying to read Jarrak's thoughts. Then he looked towards Gaywin, the most recent of the Black Robes to have arrived in Sharacan. After another moment, he looked back to Jarrak and said, 'You are certain it was the College that first developed these VTDs, as you call them?'

'The VTDs used by the College and the Deserteers are tethered together by a wire, which allows one device to operate the other. These don't need that wire, but are essentially the same, I've been told. The Museum has been using these ones for some time now, but they are limited in their usefulness and will not operate over any more than a short distance. I doubt they can work over a distance further than that between my tent and the well-pond.'

Again, the chairman was silent. Then he said, 'I have been here a long time, Maskee. I know I will never see the citadel of Learnian again, but I cannot relinquish law for anyone. What you say may well be true, but I will have to enquire further into this. I will consult with my fellow counsellors.' The chairman sat for a moment longer. Then, seeing the particularly uncomfortable sneer on Gaywin's face, he abruptly rose, obviously irritated. 'I will study the law and ask my questions. I will let you know what the Council decides.'

Beckoning his confederates to follow, the chairman walked off hastily, as if in charge of the entire world. Jarrak sighed with relief. All he could do now was wait.

* * *

Several days passed before Gaywin appeared at the entrance to Jarrak's tent. In his hand was the chairman's reply of approval, but within it came provisions.

'I presume it was you the chairman had questions for? To see if you could confirm what I claimed,' asked Jarrak.

'It would have been unwise for me to deny your assertions, but you should read on.'

When Jarrak reached a particular section of the document, the Robe's face bloomed into a menacing glow, and his head turned towards Hestean. She was to be constantly scrutinised; a Robe was to shadow her every move in the field. The Council would not have a woman step beyond her place, and if she were to, Gaywin had personally persuaded the chairman to revoke her enslavement to

Jarrak. A fresh punishment would be enforced upon her under strict College law.

* * *

'Petty will find me if he has to, won't he?' said Hestean that evening, as she stared into the cooking fire.

'We knew Gaywin would probably do something like this,' said Jarrak. 'He will make sure one of his young followers is assigned, and like Gaywin, they too will think such a task as traipsing after a woman all day beneath them.'

'And you know this how?'

'You know it too, Hat. We've talked about it. And Petty will find you if things get worse; you just need to find sanctuary.'

Hestean smiled at the thought of their deception. She did know that Petty would find her, but it wasn't this that worried her. Playing more on her mind was the possible humiliation of being stripped naked in front of Gaywin and driven out to blister under the desert sun, before she could reach the safety of Jarrak's organised refuge and its water stash. She knew, as did Jarrak, that from this moment on, they would have to trust each other more than ever.

It was the dig that was important, though. It had become so just as much for her as it already was for Jarrak. She knew he could not continue as he had done, and neither could she. She had learned so much more than she had ever expected to, and if she was to die tomorrow then maybe her brief existence in this world would have been worth it.

* * *

The setting sun was shimmering on the horizon as Hestean sat in the sand, one leg resting over the other, her hands pushed back into the sand. By this time of day, as had become normal for her now, she was mentally as well as physically fatigued. For almost a year, she had been both exhilarated and drained by each and every day.

Beside her, Jarrak looked out at the site of the original temple dig and the newer trenches on the great mound trying to finish his day's summations before the light disappeared completely.

The temple, long since completely freed from its tomb of sand, was still proving hesitant in giving up its secrets. Jarrak had still not discovered any sign of the quarry he'd come for, and the oddities were still a concern, but the beautiful carvings on the stone courtyard floor and alcove walls were a decent compensation for his disappointments.

Hestean looked at him, recalling the many times he had said, *The truth of Sharacan's history is here, all I have to do is find it.*

She recalled too, how everything she now uttered in the trenches mimicked a new vocabulary—one she and Jarrak had skilfully created to give the impression that she was just dumbly relaying her master's instructions. Every day, the thought that she was telling her overlords what to do tickled her mind, although she also wondered what would happen if the Robes found out. Yet she had maintained her composure. She had to remember that the real revenge was not in the deception itself, but in the confidence she had gained.

She was on her fourth guard now. The first three had been young, as Jarrak had predicted, and were obviously aligned with Gaywin. She had kept her composure around them all, and most had eventually asked to be reassigned. This current one, though, was an older Robe, and had apparently requested the posting.

Hestean revelled in the risky game of speaking her thoughts before the guard, convincing him and the other men that she was speaking to Jarrak. She also went out of her way to be courteous to him, playing the woman he expected her to be. One day, when he had stumbled, she had even run to help him, and only later realised that she had done so not because she had needed to, but because she had wanted to. This interaction afforded them a rare moment of intimacy, and she learned that Winnz, the guard, had for a long time had a genuine interest in the dig, and had simply taken his chance to be a part of it.

One afternoon, she had noticed him sitting on a large rock, looking at her with just the hint of a smile on his face. 'What?' she asked.

He got up and walked across to her. He reached out and flicked a switch on the device at her waist. 'You forgot to switch it on this morning,' he said, then went back to his rock.

Hestean had frozen, then turned as pale as a person with her dark colouring could get. They were, luckily, alone.

'Don't worry,' he said. 'If I wanted to tell, I would have done so earlier.'

'You know?'

'You're quite good at this little archaeological game, aren't you? Almost as good as Jarrak himself.'

'But how long have you known?'

'I am not the Robe I once was, Hestean. I may call you that, I hope? "Daughter of Sharn" no longer seems appropriate. I doubt that I was ever a very good Robe; Gaywin and his friends have confirmed that for me. I never wanted to be like them. I have been a clerk for more years than I can remember, and I have seen how often the College rewrites its own history. I doubt that even Learnian knows the truth anymore. You could say that I have become a cynic. What you are doing here is finding the truth, and I find that, at my age, I want to know it, too.'

'But you don't know what we will find?'

'Do you?'

'No!'

'Then we're on the same journey, aren't we! You treat me well, not because you have to, but because you want to, despite the way the Robes have treated you. It's unique, and I respect it. Maybe it is just my age, but I am finding that I must offer you the same.'

'You like archaeology?'

'I have discovered that I do!'

'Then we are alike,' she said, and so they had given birth to one more secret in Sharacan. She looked again towards Jarrak, before continuing her recollections.

Despite their pact, she was wary for some time. But as the moons spiralled and she and Winnz grew closer, so did her knowledge of what went on in Jarrak's tent. Her cataloguing abilities developed, and she was able to do more autonomous detailed work, allowing Jarrak to get out into the trenches more often.

Now, seated on the sand, her thoughts were again drawn back to Jarrak beside her. Winnz had already returned to his sleeping quarters for the night to fill out his reports, which she knew he filled surreptitiously every evening with false observations. As the sun finally vanished, she recalled the very beginning of her involvement with Jarrak, watching him from her rooftop as he entered her village.

'Do you know that you've been here almost twenty-six moon cycles?' she asked. Jarrak lifted his eyes from his script-hold to look out across the sand. He could no longer write in the failing light, and from the corner of her eye she watched him put away his char-stick. 'I don't like the cooler part of the year, I never have,' she continued. 'Although the days are warm, the nights are too cold. I prefer the hot season, no matter how stifling. You arrived just after the coldest season, and the cold has returned twice since then.'

Jarrak stared at her, musing, and then said, 'I wonder whether even the oldest people here have ever seen rain. It hasn't rained once since I arrived, and because of that I've barely noticed the change in seasons. It's been an endless succession of sun-bleached days. There is one subtle change I have noticed though.' He lifted his hand towards the place where the sun had set. 'The sun moves sideways across the sky, as you know. First it moves north, and then retraces its steps increasingly towards the south, and then it starts through its cycle once more. With this, I have noticed that from the top of the giant mound, the tip of the obelisk touches the horizon at the exact midpoint of the sun's north-south trajectory.'

She knew what he said was important, but so was the message she'd been trying to share. She turned to him, looked him straight in the eyes, and said, 'I have been telling these men what to do for nearly one complete cycle now. Gaywin almost caught me again today. I fear that soon he will push me into making a visible mistake! He is just getting too close. He has it in for me. I think he has despised me since the very first day he arrived here. The longer this game goes on, the more certain a fallout becomes.'

'Gaywin hasn't found you out yet. Winnz is the only Robe who knows you. He alone knows what you're doing, and he has no intention of telling. He has a good mind, Winnz, and he's the one who writes everything down now so that I don't have to. He is helping to hide you.'

'But one day someone else will discover me! It's inevitable, and I would prefer not to die now after having learned so much.'

Jarrak sighed. 'To tell you the truth, I've been thinking the same thing. Luck can only hold for a certain length of time. The workload has eased since I've narrowed the search area to the mound, and honestly, I'm thinking of closing it down completely. We've found nothing for a while now, but I don't want to ask you to return to tidying and fetching water. As you said, you have learned so much, and such menial tasks would now feel demeaning to you. And if you or I do slip up, it will not just be you who is banished to the desert, but myself, and possibly Winnz, also. The College has never liked to be made a fool of!'

Jarrak stretched himself out, laying his script-hold under his head to stop his hair from touching the sand. 'You know more about what needs to be done in the tent now. Maybe you can take over full-time in there while I sort out what we should do. Winnz can do the writing. At least in there, prying eyes won't be as prevalent. It will give Winnz a chance to see how the data is collated. It may interest him, since he was a clerk before he was assigned to you.'

'You're not worried about him finding out the truth, then?'

'I'll keep my journals locked in our living quarters. But why shouldn't he help? You'll just have to seem more interested in some things than others, that's all.'

'Who am I?' asked Hestean abruptly.

'What do you mean? You know who you are!'

'No, I mean … Well, that's what we're doing, isn't it? Looking back into my past? Finding out who I am; who the people of my village are and were? I know you're looking for something besides the history of this place. You're finding out about us, too, aren't you?'

They had long ago begun to share nearly everything, yet he still hadn't told her the real reason why he'd come to this place. In the past, whenever she'd asked, he'd simply said it would be better for her not to know. She shouldn't have to hide and protect a secret she didn't understand. Now she saw a familiar glimmer of guilt pass over his face and pressed on.

'It makes no sense—not now. Not with everything else that's a secret between us.' He smiled, and she continued. 'Is this something you keep to yourself just to show me that you're still in charge?'

His smile faded at this. After a long silence, he began to speak slowly. 'I'm not looking for something … I came here looking for someone. But you're right, there is more to this place than just her. Even though I haven't found her, there is something else here. The more I uncover, the more I realise that I really don't know this place. You're a puzzle, Hat. That's what you are, a puzzle! Remember that small book I gave you? The one written in Fem? I'm looking for the person who was possibly the first in over three thousand years to read those words. When she came across the original book, she is believed to have been about your age. She died here. She was from here, and we think she came back here. Before she died, she changed this world. It was because of Andreena and her companions that most of the world survived the cataclysm.'

'Someone as grand as that came from my village?' said Hestean, staring at him with wide green eyes.

'Not exactly,' said Jarrak, breaking eye contact as his head turned towards the small College outpost of the village. 'She was from the greater Sharacan. Andreena lived over two hundred years ago. She was not from your village, but the once magnificent city that existed here. She had a sister who was a priestess, we think. That's why we're digging out here.'

'She brought you here, but that's not why you've stayed. It's those pieces of—whatever they are, which you separate and put into that box in our tent. Isn't it? They're out of place, aren't they?'

It had been Hestean herself who had found the first few fragments around the base of the giant mound. One of them had depicted part of the six-sided houses symbol that Jarrak had shown her, and it was that which had drawn her eye. He'd told her that *Ze Hub* was the word given to the central part of the six-sided symbol. None of the pieces had ever fitted together, though, and like those from the temple site, they all remained just fragments.

'They're out of place, Hat, yes. But more to the point, they're out of time. If they were from the present, I would think they were pieces of some sort of energy router! Some sort of key, perhaps … The Museum uses something like that to open doors, which the general public are not allowed into, but that can't be what these are. They are a technology even beyond my people. I think these shards are something only the gods know of and have chosen for some reason to leave behind.'

'I know now that the sun reenergises your night lamp and the devices we speak through, but there are still things even beyond your people, aren't there?'

'Yes,' said Jarrak. 'It's almost as if someone placed those shards on purpose, knowing that someday, someone like me would come along and realise they meant something. I have no idea why, Hat. No idea at all. I just think that we will understand when we find it.' Jarrak looked up to the stars and said, obliquely, 'Pick a star.'

Hestean studied him for a moment, contemplating the revelations, then lay back to study the stars again. 'When I was young, I used to dream of the day when I would be whole,' she said. 'I will be eighteen soon. I will go from an adult-in-learning to an adult.'

'Why eighteen?' said Jarrak.

'Because of the moons—that's why.'

'The moons? Why the moons?'

'Because, as you know, every eighteen years the sun and the moons realign.'

'Yes, but is that the only reason? I would have thought there'd be more to it than that.'

'You were the one who said my people were once sun worshippers!'

'Yes, but I said that to the Robes, didn't I? Not to you!'

'You're slow today, Maskee Jarrak! The gods, silly! They are the real reason.'

'Oh. And how do the gods come into it, exactly?'

'How do you think they come into it? You really don't know?'

'Why don't you tell me something for a change?'

'Well, six goes into eighteen three times, right?'

'Yes …'

And half of eighteen is nine, which is the age at which a child becomes an adult-in-learning.

'Yes?'

'Well, two times three is six, isn't it? And you need both male and female to make a God, just as you do people.'

'So, you are saying that the gods are people?'

'No. I'm saying that the Comcree are people. Three male and three female, and together they are the gods.'

'They're what?' said Jarrak rising on to one elbow to look at her.

'It's just something I've been pondering lately! You do know that my tree is already cut and there is no one to pledge my stone …'

'What are you talking about now?'

'My stone! I'll be eighteen soon, as I said.'

'You can't just say something about the gods and the Comcree like that, and then just walk away from it!'

'Yes, I can!'

'No, you can't.'

'Well, I have and I am. Think of it as payback.' From the corner of her eye, she saw Jarrak still staring at her. She knew she had given him something to think about.

Finally, he rolled back to look up at the stars once more. 'If you're dead to your parents, then perhaps they are dead to you.'

'Are we talking about me, or the gods?'

'You! The gods are too complicated to think about right now. If your parents are dead, then your rings can be counted, can't they?' His head turned from the sky to look at her. 'You don't need their permission! I don't know about the stone, but I'm sure you'll find someone to pledge your stone when the time comes.'

She propped her head up with her hand. 'But my parents are not dead,' she whispered.

'True, but by law they have declared themselves to be.'

'So, what you are saying is that if they're theoretically dead to me, I can make my own decisions?'

'Your guardian can.'

'And who might that be?'

'Me. I can't perform the ceremony, though, because I'm of the wrong house, but I can give my permission.'

'How do you know this?'

'Give me some credit, Hat! I don't only look at the past; I listen, too. After your banishment, I asked about the small tree left with your things.'

'You never asked me …'

'You were hurting.'

Hestean thought for a moment, then rolled back to look into the sky. 'I will find someone then,' she said, and after a moment's silence she lifted her arm to point towards a star. 'You see that line of three stars, just below the cluster of seven? Tell me about the one at the bottom.'

14

A few nights later, Jarrak tossed a thin cross-section of Hestean's birth tree onto her bedding. 'You'll need that,' he said. 'I was going to give it to you when the time came, but I think you should have it now. You're lucky I scavenged it before it was burnt as firewood!'

For some time, she'd been thinking about the stump near her parents' house. It would still be there, dead and unchanging. She looked up at Jarrak. 'How do you do that? You seem to know what I'm thinking all the time.'

'Not all the time, Hat. I told you, I watch people, and I've seen you looking towards the village lately. You're almost an adult; it's about time you started to look a little closer at people yourself.' He already knew she did, but even now he still pushed her. He smiled and turned from her, walking back to his own sleeping area.

Hestean watched him for a while, then smiled and put down the piece of wood. She picked up the woke horn she had dug from the ground almost two years ago, which Jarrak had finally relented to letting her keep beside her bed.

As he settled himself into his bedding, she began to blow. 'Hestean, please!'

'Oh, just a little! I've almost got it, I think.'

'Sometimes, Hat, I think I should throw you back to them and let them do with you as they please!' She giggled at his annoyance, then started to blow again, teasing him a little more. '*Hat!*' he said, rolling over and pulling his pillow up over his ears.

She smiled again and put down the horn, settling herself more comfortably. She let her mind wander and found herself awake longer than she had intended to be. Late into the night, long after Jarrak had fallen asleep, her mind wove through the story of her past, trying to find a future. She was freer than she had ever been before, but in reality she was still a prisoner of the desert. Banished from her village, she remained separated from the outer world. As she watched the first man she had ever called a friend, a strange new feeling overwhelmed her and she wiped tears of gratitude from her eyes. She knew, as he did, that she would have to leave this place in order to survive.

* * *

Thirteen days later, a woman at the dig noticed a series of dots enter the access gap into the valley. She watched them slowly grow in size. The woman pointed them out to another woman, Aswonnea, when she came to refill the woman's waterskin. On her way back to the water point, Aswonnea entered the display tent and whispered into Hestean's ear. Winnz was watching, and abruptly Hestean turned to him. 'Are the Robes expecting a wagon?'

'Not that I'm aware of.'

'Come on, one of the women has spotted something large entering the valley.' They walked up onto the woman's mound and looked out towards the still distant shimmer. 'Jarrak, are you expecting anyone?' she said into her transceiver.

'A wagon?' his voice asked. She switched off the ear attachment so that Winnz could hear, too, from the box at her side.

'I think so, yes.'

'There was a wagon ordered for about this time. The Museum will be wanting a report. I'll be there in a moment.'

Through the desert haze, the dots slowly formed into a recognisable six-wheeled desert wagon pulled by silver shrows. Their frills fanned rhythmically beneath their necks, cooling their blood, and the large ball of fat behind their four back legs wobbled as they walked. Looking after Jarrak's shrows had become one of the best parts of her day, and she found herself thinking how proud this approaching team looked. There was a joyousness to them that was infectious.

Reaching her, Jarrak put a hand on her shoulder. 'See anyone you know, Hat?'

At his mention, the figure on board the wagon seemed suddenly familiar, but not quite distinguishable. She looked to Jarrak for a moment and knew he was testing her. She looked back, and a night-cloaked figure came into her mind. 'Is it Petty?'

'You have a good eye, even at this distance.'

'I'm Sharacanese. We're renowned for it; I've heard Robes remark on it.'

'That's true,' said Winnz. 'You should see their children play that stone game of theirs. You knew this wagon was coming, Maskee?'

'I knew the Museum would eventually want to know what I was up to out here!'

'And this Petty, who is he?'

'A friend of mine. He's a teamster who works for the Museum. I thought it might be him they'd send, as Deserteers aren't permitted into your territory.'

'And how does Hestean know him?'

'I have another friend who is a fine sketch artist. One night he drew Petty and me. The drawing is in my script-hold; I showed Hestean once.' Jarrak pushed Hestean forward. 'Go show him where we are, Hat.'

Hestean looked to Jarrak for a moment, then noticed that the water-woman had turned her ear towards them, listening. Abruptly, Hestean turned away, leaving the water-woman to wonder what was really going on. Concealing a smile, she strode towards the only other man she had ever truly felt able to speak with as an equal.

She couldn't go through the village, so she skirted it, running to the north of the well-pond. She was out of breath when she reached the slow-moving wagon and pulled herself up. Sitting down beside Petty, she said, 'You're not wearing your cloak or uniform!'

A wry smile sprang from the corner of Petty's mouth, and a grin also grew on hers. To the people of Sharacan he could not seem to be a Deserteer. She knew this even before she spoke. So did Petty. And he said, 'You finished stating the obvious? Got it out of your system?'

'Maybe!'

'It's a strange thing, isn't it? Trusting someone when everything in your life has told you to be on your guard.'

'Are all men like you and Jarrak in the outer world?'

'By the gods, I hope not! The outer world, as you put it, would be empty if it were. Jarrak and I are too into ourselves; too much alone!'

'Jarrak's not like that!'

'No?'

'No! And neither are you.'

'When did you get so smart?'

'It's been almost a year since you saw me, but I've always been smart; it's my curse.'

'Here it is, yes,' said Petty. 'But I think Jarrak is right—it's also your salvation.'

'What do you mean?'

'I'm to be your escort.'

'My *what*?'

'Jarrak is sending some of the findings to Bornn and has decided that you will go, too.'

'The Robes will never let me!'

'Jarrak's working on that, I believe. I'm to take you to the Museum with the shipment. He's found you a position there.'

'He's mentioned none of this to me. What sort of position?'

'I don't think he wanted to disappoint you before he was sure, but I made it my business to find out. I like you, Hestean, and I've always wanted a daughter!' Petty leaned forward to draw his dagger from the inside of his boot. He scratched a mark onto the wagon's footboard and then returned the weapon to its hiding place.

'That's my house symbol!' said Hestean, and then noticed the very small blue-and-red clan markings around the top of Petty's boots.

'It's mine, too,' he said. 'We are kin, you and I.' Incredulous, Hestean looked down and placed her dark fingers next to the tanned white of his. To her, their contrast confirmed the absurdity of his statement. 'Distant kin!' he said, defining his statement more exactly. 'But kin we are, and kin we will always be.'

She recalled Jarrak telling her that the word of a Deserteer was never given lightly, and she looked at him again now. 'Maybe I will have need of another father one day, such as my betrothal day!'

'You are to be married, are you?'

It had been close to two years since she had almost died, and now she had a life. She had freed herself from men, so why would she now think of tying herself to one for the rest of her life. 'No,' she said. 'I'll just have many consorts. I'll need you to get rid of them for me.'

He laughed. 'You can do that for yourself! Do you even know what *consort* means?'

'To keep company—to partner,' said Hestean vaguely, as her thoughts moved on to something new. One day soon, she would indeed need someone to stand in for her father; someone truly capable of throwing her stone. She looked at Petty once more, wondering.

* * *

Jarrak's plan terrified Hestean, he knew this. But she also knew that it was the only way of ensuring the Robes wouldn't come after her. She had subdued her anxiety, but even so, the desert was rarely forgiving. In the following days, she questioned him more than she ever had, making him extend his descriptions of the world. He explained how important she would be as a translator to the Museum, and as someone who had first-hand knowledge of Sharacan and the excavations. Sensing her hesitation, he tried to explain that the time had truly come for her to see the bigger world and finally live her life.

The trenches on the mound had been shut down while he homed in deeper on the temple. For a while, at least, he felt he could manage on his own, and for now, he was focused on treasuring these last few days with Hestean as they packed up the collection. He had become accustomed to sharing his thoughts and life with her, as she had with him, and he knew there would be a hole when she left, but leave she must. She was destined to become an adult, and he meant for her to become one in the outer world.

She knew as well as he did that the Museum and Bornn were just excuses to get her away from the Black Robes. But she, too, seemed to be treasuring this time; he could tell. As Petty and Winnz loaded the last of the crates onto the broad-wheeled desert-wagon, he and Hestean sat to watch the sun set one last time together.

* * *

When Hestean awoke before dawn the next morning, intent on seeing her mother once more, she noticed a parcel on Jarrak's writing table that had not been there the previous evening. The leather binding was old and lightly inlaid with a crusting of sand. From this, she suspected that it had been recently unearthed. Attached to it, written in Fem in a hand she'd never seen before, was a note that read:

Eow Beon To Beon Hestean,
Beon To Beon Opened On Eowr Beran Dag Of Negon Und Negon,
Und Naught Beforan,
Maeg Thes Lf Beran Eow Ure Wyscans.

Knowing that the Black Robes would not approve of her exodus, she had told no one of her leaving. She was puzzled. The only clue was an old blue seal stamped over the package's exterior join. It was an insignia like the one carved into her shoulder.

'It would seem that someone wants you to remember them. Someone besides me, that is,' said Jarrak when she woke him.

'You, I will never forget,' she said.

'I hope not.'

She hugged him to hide her watering eyes, knowing that the package—with its explicit codicil—must have come from within her village. Its late arrival left no time to investigate. Their plan was already set, and she had to be in place before the sun rose.

Jarrak turned to his desk and picked up Hestean's banishment scroll, which he had retrieved the night before from his papers. 'Don't forget this,' he said, rolling it open for one last look. In that moment, he froze. 'By the gods!'

'What?' He handed the scroll to Hestean, and she saw it, too. Freshly written into the bottom margin, in the same hand as the note, were more Fem words. Gasping, she said, 'Why would someone do this?'

'It has been done,' said Jarrak. 'And it cannot now be undone.'

'But why?'

'Well, it does makes sure the scroll adds the missing two years to your tree rings!'

'You must not fear this place,' said Hestean, as a rare vulnerability crossed his face.

'That's not it, Hat. I've always known there was something unseen here. The College don't teach their women to read. They just don't.'

'But all the women here can read!'

'Yes, they can! They can read and write Fem!'

Understanding him now, she said, 'Because of my age, I have not been told of things here. Maybe this is someone's way of telling me that I am just about old enough to know.'

'There would seem to be others who have an interest in your longevity besides me. I hope I haven't prevented you from learning something you were supposed to.'

'I probably wouldn't have lived even this long if it weren't for you.' She looked at him for a moment longer before examining the scroll again. With unexpected reverence, she packed it, alongside the newly delivered parcel and the cross-section from her tree, into her bag. She lifted it, handing it to Jarrak. 'I must be going,' she said. She put her arms around him, holding him briefly, before stepping outside. She looked to her village, towards the small building that housed the matrefem and some of the older women.

'I really don't think you've prevented anything,' she said, turning back to Jarrak. 'You have shown me much more than I would have ever learned here otherwise. For now, this is meant to be kept a secret. But you were meant to see it. Someone, long ago, wanted you to know that this is the way of things here. I will be the first of my sisterhood to leave this village in a long time, and I think they have given me all that I will need.'

'You've never actually pointed out your mother and father's house to me. Is the parcel from them?'

'I think my mother knows that I am leaving, but no, it's not from them.'

* * *

It was still early morning when Winnz hurriedly entered Jarrak's tent and said, 'Hestean has been taken to our House of Authority, Maskee,'

'What?'

'She was found in the village.'

'Take me there now.'

'There is nothing you can do, Maskee. The chairman has already passed his judgment. Gaywin invoked his clause. She is to be evicted into the desert. I was prevented from coming sooner. The chairman now wants to see you and the wagon driver.'

'Why?'

'I don't know, Maskee. Why was she in the village? It was reckless; she knew better.'

'For some reason, she's been missing her mother lately.'

'I know. She told me this, also.'

'Petty!' Jarrak called.

'There seems to be quite a ruckus in the village this morning,' Petty said as he entered the tent. He'd been busy tightening the restraining straps on the wagon.

'We have been summoned by the chairman. Hestean has been foolish.'

The walk to the village seemed long, and all the villagers stared at Jarrak. The women looked at him with accusation and betrayal in their eyes.

The main doors to the hall burst open as if a violent wind had shattered their latches, and Jarrak stormed in. 'Where is she?' he said, marching down the centre of the room. The Black Robes parted in stunned silence to reveal Hestean. When he reached the front, he went straight up to her. 'You little fool! After all I have done for you, this is how you respond.' He slapped her, and the crack of it made even Gaywin wince.

'Maskee,' said the chairman. 'This is none of your concern. This is village business. She was found in the village, and she has long known the consequences of such an act. I just need to ask you a question.'

'And what is that?'

'The wagon. It was to leave today, was it not?'

'Yes.'

'Well, your driver will now be with you for a further few days. No one is to leave here for ten days, is that clear?'

'Why?'

'We want no interference with this judgment, that's why.'

'I see,' said Jarrak, looking at Hestean. 'When is it to be done?'

'Now, Maskee. It is to be done now. Gaywin, you suggested the clause, so you are also to be its instigator. All actions have their consequences, and you are to know that today.'

The chairman said this blankly, and Jarrak knew there was no malice behind his decision, just the law, which had to be followed even if he himself felt uncomfortable with it. The chairman's next words confirmed this.

'Child,' he said, turning to Hestean. 'I say "child" because under Sharacan beliefs, a person is not an adult until they are eighteen years old. Under our law, there is only "child" and "adult", there is no "adult-in-learning" as there is in Sharacanese society. Yet even under ordinary College law, you would not normally be given this punishment. You knew the rulings that have preceded this day, and still you flouted them. I am sorry, child. A life is no easy thing to extinguish, but you brought this upon yourself. From here, you are to be taken to the village square, where you will be stripped bare. You came into this world with nothing, and you are to leave it with nothing. From there, you will be expelled into the desert, which will lay its verdict upon you. Take her, Gaywin.'

If Gaywin thought she would cower when he touched her, he was mistaken. She pulled from him and looked him straight in the eyes. 'You will remember this day.'

Enraged, he grabbed her again. 'Maybe, but you will most definitely not.' He proceeded to wrench her from the building.

Outside, the square was filled with people. As Gaywin emerged, they pulled back to line its outer edge. Jarrak saw Hestean's mother standing beside a man he took to be Hestean's father,, his hand laid protectively on Sathea's shoulder. Except for his age and more masculine features, he looked like Hestean. On Sathea's other side was an elderly woman, and Jarrak noticed her too.

Sathea was not looking at Hestean, though. She was looking at Jarrak, and if looks could kill, he knew he would be dead now. He looked around carefully, then glanced back at Sathea and winked quite deliberately. Sathea's expression changed to one of puzzlement, and she leaned towards the elderly woman to whisper something in her ear. The older woman peered at Jarrak as well, then Hestean. Her head turned towards Sathea and then she turned completely, facing away from the centre of the square. Sathea now also glanced to Hestean and their eyes locked. A moment later, Sathea too turned her back on her daughter. Slowly, one by one, all the women began to turn away.

A voice said, 'She is not an adult.' Another voice said, 'She is not yet whole.' All this time, the man stared at Hestean with a look of sorrow, regret, and love in his eyes. He now turned also. A younger man said, 'She is not an adult,' and even the men in the village began to turn from the spectacle. Gaywin, already fuming, seemed about to explode.

Hestean said, 'You don't know who I am, do you?'

'You are no one!'

'You are right in that. But I am Hestean Descee, and today I have become an idea.'

Gaywin grabbed a small skin of water. 'Drink,' he said.

'Why?'

'Because I want you to feel your death for as long as possible. That's why.'

A hushed murmur spread through the Robes in the square. Then some of them began to turn away also. Hestean watched. A slight smile came to her face, then vanished. She turned back to Gaywin and took the waterskin. 'You will remember this day, Robe Gaywin. But I think now that you will also regret it.' She drank deeply, emptying the waterskin, then handed it back and wiped her chin dry of the drops that had spilled from her mouth.

Jarrak noticed that Petty had already turned his back, so he turned as well. He heard the clothes being cut, then ripped, from her body, leaving her completely vulnerable to the elements. Then he heard her stagger forward as she was pushed violently away. He heard her stumble and fall to the ground. In those moments, Jarrak's hatred for Gaywin grew. Then he heard Hestean stand, and he found himself listening to her footsteps on the dry sand as they faded away. It was a sound that would echo through his mind endlessly over the coming days.

* * *

Ten days later, Petty was preparing to leave when Gaywin approached him. 'I see you have loaded only a small amount of water and provisions for your animals,' he said.

'I left caches along the way so that the shrows would not have to pull a larger load.'

'I see. I thought you may have learnt some of the Deserteers' secrets.'

'Alas, no. The Deserteers still don't give up the secrets of this desert. They may no longer cross the Kalcool by land, but its essence will always be in their hearts. You may rule here, but to them you will never own Sharacan.'

'I think it is a good thing that you are leaving, Maskee.'

'And the girl?'

'As you are aware, no one was permitted to leave this place while her sentence was in play. But I did go to the hills; there was a watch kept to make sure she didn't try to come back. She stopped for a while before entering the desert proper.'

'And then?'

'Then I watched her get up and walk on into the desert.'

'She didn't turn around once, did she?'

'No, Maskee. She did not.'

'I thought as much. After what you did to that girl, I think it is a good thing I'm leaving here, too. So, if you don't mind, I have some goodbyes to say to those who actually care about life.' Turning, Petty walked back to Jarrak's tent. He stopped and turned back to face the Robe. 'I hope you realise, Robe Gaywin, that this will bring an end to you.'

'You think that the College cannot withstand one girl?'

'I wasn't talking about the College. I was talking about you.'

Gaywin's scowl returned, and he said, 'It is indeed a good thing you are leaving, Maskee! If it weren't for your clear passage warrant signed by the College, you wouldn't have dared to say that.'

'Perhaps you're right, but you shamed a lot of Robes by making the girl drink. To punish someone is tragic enough, but to gloat about it is beyond necessity. It's not something I would have done if I had the ambition that you have.'

Gaywin's eyes filled with repugnance. He spun on the spot and strode back towards the village.

Once he was gone, Jarrak approached. 'I think it is a dangerous game you play, Maskee Jarrak,' said Petty, pulling himself up onto the wagon's bench. 'I hope I see you again.'

'Take care of my treasure, won't you?'

'As if she were my own, Maskee,' said Petty, flicking the steer-straps.

The shrows took the strain and the wagon lurched into motion, leaving Jarrak standing alone in front of the tent that had become his and Hestean's home. He felt an empty space in his heart, much bigger than what he had expected. Hestean, seven years younger than him, had become more than just an adopted sister. In this moment, he knew she had become much more, and the tears in his eyes were proof of it.

15

As Petty circled the village, he noticed a group of women ahead of him. As he came closer, he saw that all but two had different clan markings along the bases of their skirts. He pulled the shrows to a halt when the most elderly among them stepped forward and nodded. 'I have her things,' he said, and with an out-stretched finger, he pointed to his own clan markings around the top of his boots.

This time, all the women nodded. One of them said softly, 'I think the gods have been watching over her, so thank them, will you?'

'I shall,' said Petty. 'It will be as if she were my own daughter.' Then he lurched the wagon into motion, and the women watched him go.

It was almost midday when Petty came to a hard patch of ground and pulled the wagon to a stop. Alighting from the left-hand side of the driver's seat, he untied two heavy mats, one from each side of the wagon. He unrolled them onto the ground before fastening them to the wagon's backboard.

He stretched, pulling out all the aches and knots in his arms and legs. Then, getting back onto the wagon, he said to the person now also sitting on its seat, 'You made it, then!'

The dress Hestean now wore was sand in colour, fitting her tightly down to the waist before flaring, allowing for maximum freedom of her legs. 'They didn't follow you?' she asked, as he sat down beside her.

'What side of the wagon did I get down from?'

'The left.'

'And what was the signal?'

'If you got down from the right side, I was to stay hidden.'

'Then why the silly question, daughter?'

'*Daughter*?'

'Yes, daughter. You are to be my daughter, remember?'

'It is a long way to Elora-Bearer, yes?'

'A long way.'

'How long will it take?'

'You will have to wait and see, daughter. There are things you will learn now that are to be seen and not told.'

'Are you going to call me that all the time from now on?'

'Only when it pleases me,' said Petty, as he flicked the steer-straps and set the shrows in motion. 'Are you alright? How's your face?'

'I made a few mistakes that first night, but did he really have to hit me so hard?'

'He did that because he didn't want to hit you at all.'

* * *

A short time later, Petty changed direction. Behind them, the two mats dragged along the ground, one after the other, almost completely obscuring their tracks. A day of the desert's breeze and there would be nothing to reveal where they'd gone.

'Whose dress is this?' asked Hestean.

'It belongs to our loadmaster. She looked about your size.'

'It's easy to move in. I've never worn anything like this before.'

'It's the dress of a fighter. Even off duty, she still likes to be ready.'

'She is a warrior, then?'

'She's a loadmaster and a Deserteer.'

'So, not a warrior?'

'I didn't say that.'

'No, you didn't, did you?' said Hestean with a smile. For the rest of the day, the wagon and shrows bumped and plodded their way round rocks and over sand, between large dunes that ran in broken lines across the desert. It was truly a landscape no one could survive in for long, and Hestean wondered how she'd managed it for ten days. She'd found the cache of food and water, and the dress, but all the stories she'd ever been told of this desert were real. She thought about her parents and the village she would never see again. She thought about the parcel and the scroll. Jarrak was on her mind, too, along with the unknown world she was travelling towards.

When she'd left Sharacan, she had thought the heat of the day would be the worst, but it was the night that had almost killed her. She'd headed east for most of the morning, then turned north. In the afternoon, she'd turned west. After a hard and blistering walk through the hottest part of the day, and the climbing of endless dunes, she had finally seen the hills around Sharacan off to the south again, and turned south-west.

But it was the night that had truly scared her. Naked, alone in the dark, with only the moons and the stars to navigate by, the night had brought monsters into her mind she had never before imagined. Long after she should have found what she was looking for, she'd walked up onto a dune at dawn and seen a trail of her own circling footprints. She knew in that moment she'd let her fears control her way instead of the stars.

She'd almost died that next day. She had stumbled past the tower of stones, not realising she was in the right place until she fell exhausted and dragged herself upright for what seemed like the millionth time. She had truly felt like giving up in that moment, until a gust of wind had saved her. A rare tuft of flutter-weed had quivered at the base of the stone, drawing her eye. She counted the stone and the others on top of it. *One the gods, two the Comcree, three the houses which are us all.* How the largest rock kept its balance on top of the other two, she didn't know. How it got there, she didn't know either, but a little while later she had found the hidden doorway to her salvation.

* * *

'This will do us, I think,' said Petty late in the day, bringing the wagon to a stop on a patch of flat ground. At the sound of Petty's voice, Hestean looked up and noticed they were in a shallow valley of pure sand, with not a stone or boulder in site. This was not a good place to spend the night, for if the wind came up, as it sometimes did unexpectedly, there would be no refuge against the sand's rampage. There was nothing here except …

'What's that?' she asked, pointing to a large metal shaft protruding from the desert sand.

'It's one of those,' replied Petty, pointing out two more of the loop-topped objects, which marked out a large triangle upon the desert surface.

Suddenly, Hestean knew what she was looking at. Back at the dig, she'd looked through Jarrak's books and had read about the shafts. Jolted from her melancholy, she asked, 'When will it be here?'

'I'm sorry, but I thought it better not to tell you in case the Robes came after you. The *Merysands* will be here in the morning. If the chairman had made me stay just one more day, we would have been late. I'll need you to help me when she arrives. I'll go through things when we've made camp.'

Hestean grinned. 'And now you want me to help you catch it? It will cost you.'

'And what will the cost be?'

'You will have to cook tonight.'

Petty laughed. 'Is that all?'

'I'm not sure, yet!' she said, then saw him studying her. 'What?'

'It's nothing. I just think I made a good choice when I decided to like you!'

'You should wait until you know me better before coming to such an opinion.'

'No, my opinion is correct! The only sky-ships you've ever seen are in Jarrak's books, and you have no real concept of how big a sky-ship really is. Yet you have already decided to help me catch it, haven't you?'

'I can do it. Or at least, I guess tomorrow we'll find out if I can.'

'Of that I have no doubt.'

* * *

As the sun broke the horizon the following morning, Petty changed into what Hestean now knew to be the cloak and uniform of a ranking Deserteer. He had retrieved his uniform from the hidden depository where they had spent the night. Once more, his red jewelled dagger hung at his waist beneath his cloak, no longer hidden in his boot.

Hestean and Petty settled by the fire to eat breakfast biscuits and drink the tea Petty had brewed. The shrows had been hitched to the wagon and stood waiting, as if they knew what was coming.

Hestean heard the sound of the sky-ship first. It's quiet whir drifted against the wind to combine with the other desert sounds. She turned to look downwind. 'Is that it?'

From the front, the *Merysands* looked like an irregular oval with its top edge squashed almost flat. The top of the craft was dark, and it seemed to soak in the light that fell upon it as Jarrak's night-light had. Its underside was pale pink, which made its outline hard to see against the blue of the sky. As it drew closer, Hestean got to her feet, realising now that the huge craft was much larger than she had imagined. As it closed on them, the ship's true shape became evident. It now resembled a long, flattened seed pod, with four side-fins and two short rudders, which extended out and down from its tail end. The sun hit the great ship on one side, leaving the other in shadow, so that only the blades attached to the fins' tips on one side could be seen twirling in a blur. Near the nose, protruding from its underside, was the control deck with its large windows. Hestean thought the windows made it look almost like a mouth, and through the still-distant glass she could see the torsos and heads of people within.

'It's bigger than I thought it would be,' she said.

'The *Merysands* was the first of her class, and she's twice the size of most sky-ships,' said Petty, getting up from their small fire. He squashed out the flames with his boot, then poured the last of the tea from the darkened billy over the coals and ash. After stowing the utensils in the wagon's footlocker, he turned to lean lightly against the sideboard. He watched Hestean beam with excitement as she continued to study the ship. It wasn't until the mooring ropes uncoiled from the ship's belly that he moved. 'Come on, this one first.'

She sprang to follow him as the rope passed the closest mooring ring. They slipped the hook through it and fired its spur lock.

'This one next.'

This time, Hestean grabbed the rope first and helped pull it towards its ring. The motor's sound changed as the blades reversed in a roar before neutralising. The two ropes tightened, taking up the inertia of the huge ship, but Petty and Hestean hadn't finished their task.

'Come on, the front rope now.'

The *Merysands* was already starting to recoil, drifting back with the wind. Hestean had the hang of it now, and her young legs sped her ahead of Petty. As the rope drifted back past the ring, she pushed the bar through on her own, then pushed the lever to release its spur. She turned to find Petty standing some distance back with a big smile on his face.

He nodded approvingly. 'You did that as if you were born to.'

'Maybe I was,' said Hestean, catching her breath. This day had barely started, and already she had done things never dreamt of by other women in her village. She strolled towards Petty in a sort of daydream, wondering what she truly would become.

'Quicken yourself, or you'll get squashed,' he said sternly. She looked up to see the *Merysands* winching itself down, then accelerated towards the patiently waiting shrows.

A section of the ship's belly was opening, too, swinging down to form a gently sloping ramp. Petty waited patiently, and when the ship was settled and secure, he drove the wagon up into the cargo deck, guiding the shrows round to their allocated position. Almost at once, he jumped down to the deck and began talking to one of the Deserteers who had started lashing the wagon to the floor. Another group unharnessed the animals and walked them away to their holding pens.

The Deserteer speaking with Petty had an "LM" embroidered on her sleeve. Hestean couldn't stop staring at the woman; she'd noticed the Deserteer's gender immediately. She proved that Petty had been telling the truth about women within the Guild of Deserteers.

The ship jolted as the winch lines started to run out, letting the ship rise again. Petty turned to Hestean. 'Come on, you're not sitting there all day. The captain will want to meet you.' He raised a hand to help her, but she jumped, landing perfectly just as he had.

The hole in the loading deck was closing, and she caught a glimpse of the ground as the sky-ship started to rise. 'That didn't take long.'

'We're professionals! That's what we do here,' said Petty.

They headed towards the front of the ship, with Hestean looking into every crevice and opening. Then, as they turned to ascend a spiral staircase, she turned back, and her eyes met those of the young loadmaster.

Petty's pace was relentless. Just a few digits later, they were descending another spiralling of stairs and clattering onto the control deck. The captain turned in his chair towards them. 'Welcome back, Mister Petty.'

'Thank you, Captain.'

'And who do we have here? I was expecting a passenger, but not one quite so young.'

'I am Hestean Descee of Sharacan, Captain,' said Hestean, forcing her unforeseen nervousness away. She lifted her hand first to her forehead, then to her lips, and then to her heart.

To her surprise, the captain stood up and returned the greeting. 'We are not all barbarians, Maskea,' he said with a smile. 'I hope Mister Petty has been treating you well?'

Instantly, she was drawn to this captain. She sensed a man of great wisdom. She began to wonder if all men of the outer world were like Petty and Jarrak, and now this captain.

'She is indeed the special part of our cargo,' said Petty.

'Then we will have to look after her.'

'Yes, Captain.'

'Is this your first time on a sky-ship, Maskea?'

'My first time anywhere, Captain!'

The captain noticed how Hestean's feet had already spread slightly apart, to better manage the shifting balance of the ship. 'I see you are a quick learner!' he said. 'Come, stand by me and you can see how we do things on a ship such as this. You will enjoy your time with us, I think. Are you sure you have never been on a sky-ship before?'

'Quite sure, Captain!'

While they talked, Petty resumed his duties as first officer, clipping on his sound receiver as the captain began to observe the terrain around his ship.

'Are we ready, Mister Petty?'

'Ready, Captain. We have the light.'

'Wind one finger to the south at three marces,' said the second officer.

Hestean listened to the voices around the room as they formed a pattern; a kind of dance in her head. Then there was nothing but silence as the *Merysands* started to rise, released from her moorings.

'Quota reached, Captain.'

'Thank you, Mister Petty. Do you remember our course?'

'Yes, Captain.'

'Then you have command, Mister Petty. I've had little sleep while you've been gone, and I think it's time I caught up on some.' The captain looked at Hestean for a moment. He nodded his head respectfully before turning to Petty again. 'After I have rested and returned to relieve you, Mister Petty, I think you should show our young friend here around the ship!'

'I will, Captain.'

Until now, Hestean had stood quietly, observing the crew around her as they carried out their tasks. She had taken particular notice of the main helmsman, with his two large wheels which appeared to control the ship's pitch and yaw. She watched the captain leave the command deck, then walked across to Petty. 'You're all very rhythmical, aren't you?' she said as she came up beside him.

'We have to be,' said Petty. 'Everyone on a sky-ship has to know what they're doing. Everyone has to do their job. If they don't, we die.'

For the first time, Hestean saw another side of Petty. Air trade had been his whole life; and he seemed more alive and at ease in the sky. Yet while he made his job look easy, she now realised, it was far from such, for things weren't always as simple as they looked.

* * *

Determined to learn as much about sky-ships as she could, Hestean exhausted Petty as he showed her the *Merysands*. It was a new world to her, and she found herself revelling in its intricacy. Tentatively at first, but then more freely over the following days, she started to talk with other members of the crew. Like Jarrak and Petty, she found they treated her as an equal—not as one would treat a woman in her village.

Increasingly, Hestean found herself returning to the huge cargo deck and chatting to the first woman she'd come across on the *Merysands*. She'd wanted to thank the loadmaster for the dress she'd worn while waiting for Petty in the desert, but soon discovered a sisterly bond with the young woman unlike anything she'd shared with anyone before.

'Do you know that you have Sharacanese eyes?' said Hestean.

'What do you mean?' asked Karree, the loadmaster.

'Everyone else I've met on the *Merysands* has different coloured eyes to me, but yours are the same. Petty's are almost the same, but not quite. Most of the people in my village have the same-coloured eyes as me. So, I thought, well, they're Sharacanese eyes, aren't they?'

'How strange! They're what I first noticed about you, too. Where I come from, the colour of my eyes is a rarity, but I've been told they hold prevalence in my bloodline! It's funny how one thing can be strong in one region, and not in another, isn't it?'

'I wouldn't know! I've only ever lived in one place.'

'Maybe that's it,' said Karree, moving to check the next crate on her list. 'From what I understand, the people of your village haven't been given the opportunity to travel and mingle, so the trait may have come out more strongly in your people due to its isolation.'

'Maybe,' said Hestean. Karree moved on again to identify the next crate bound for Elora-Bearer. Hestean hesitated a moment, then said, 'Tell me. What do you know about Mister Petty? I only ask because since I first met him … I've noticed there are at least two sides to his persona.'

Karree smiled and sat down on a crate. 'Yes, well, it seems everyone comes to ask me about Mister Petty eventually. How did you know I knew him from before the *Merysands*?'

'I didn't. You've known him for a while, then?'

'He was on the first sky-ship I was ever formally attached to as an apprentice loadmaster. He was first officer there, too, but he has known my father for a long time. You are right—there are many sides to Mister Petty. Firstly, he is one of the best navigators I have ever seen, and he is very much a true Deserteer. He takes his profession seriously; he not so much demands but *draws* that diligence from others, also. When he is responsible for someone, he takes that responsibility earnestly, and I think he could tell you the name and duties of every person on this ship if you asked him to. I would hate to stand against him, though, for he possesses a tribal sort of protection. He is from the Sereye, you know, and you only survive there through banding together. It is bred into them, and because of that his Deserteer's dagger is not just a symbol, but a true weapon. If you get up early enough, and know where to look, you will see that time has not slowed Petty nor our captain. They still maintain their skills as powerful sand shadows.'

'I thought there were no sand shadows anymore?'

'There aren't officially, but there are a few of us aboard the *Merysands* who still maintain our training. It was once a part of us, and not something we wish to forget.'

'How do you mean?'

'I mean that I would follow Mister Petty or the captain without question. When he came aboard, I remembered his routine and sought him out. We need to maintain who we are, you see, and others have joined us, too.'

'And who are you, Karree Ladener?'

'I am the loadmaster of the *Merysands*, but I am also a Deserteer. The two are the same! That's what my name, "Ladener", means! There have always been loadmasters in my family, yet I am better than any of my brothers because it's what I've always wanted to be.'

'I envy you that.'

'You will find who you are, Hestean! Of that, I have no doubt,' said Karree. 'You know, I've never had a younger sister. Can you use a dagger?'

'I don't know. I played the stone game when I was younger, though.'

'I've heard of your Sharacanese stone game. I've heard it said that it's not really a game at all.' A knowing smile swept across Hestean's face, which Karree noticed. 'I think I'll come and get you in the morning, Hestean Descee. We'll see then just how good you are in hand-to-hand combat with a dagger. I'll loan you that dress again. You'll need something you can fight in.'

* * *

The next morning found Hestean in the very nose of the *Merysands*. A space had been left clear in the middle of the forward storage bay. In front of her, practising their craft, were Petty, the captain, and several other Deserteer men and women.

Beside her sat Karree. 'See,' she was saying. 'See how they move? It's a kind of dance. You have to anticipate your opponent. Are you ready to have a go?'

'But they're real knives!'

'They're not knives, they're daggers, and that's the only way to learn if you're ever to get good at this. But for a start, we'll use wooden ones, alright?'

'I suppose so. I've never used a knife before in this way …'

'Don't worry,' said Karree, jumping down off the crate. She untucked two wooden daggers from her belt and drew Hestean's attention to her again. 'Firstly, there are two ways to hold a dagger. The first is with the point sticking out like this, and the second is with the blade pointing back towards you, like this. The purpose of a dagger is not to kill your opponent, but to immobilise them so that they can no longer be a threat to you. To kill someone takes a lot of energy, and spare energy is something you may not always have in a fight. So, take one and let's begin.'

'Like this?' asked Hestean, trying to replicate Karree's grip on the dagger.

'That looks good, yes. Now, come at me … No, see your mistake, like this … Now try again.'

By the end of the session, Karree was finding Hestean much harder to defend against. She was having to weave and strike and dance as if she were facing someone who had grown up with a dagger in their hand. 'I thought you said you'd never used a dagger before?'

'I haven't!'

'Then how did you get so good so fast?'

'It's like the stone game, that's how! You have reawakened my instincts for it.'

'How do you mean?'

'The stone game teaches you to see what your opponent is going to do before they do it. I was one of the best when I was a child.'

'A child,' said Karree, coming to a stop.

'Yes. I haven't played the stone game for nearly nine years now. Women are no longer permitted by the Robes once they become adults-in-learning.'

'I can see why,' said Petty from the sidelines. It was only then that Hestean noticed how everyone had stopped to watch herself and Karree practise.

'So, all the women of Sharacan learn this stone game, and then are not allowed to continue once they are old enough to use its skills? What about the men?' asked the captain.

'They're still permitted to become whole.'

'How so?'

'On their eighteenth birthday, they are still permitted to use the game in their coming-of-age ceremony, whereas women are not. They have to show that they can catch the stone before it hits their forehead.'

'And I suppose this stone is thrown at great speed?' asked the captain, shocked.

'Yes.'

Petty began to chuckle, his deep voice resonating around the room.

'What?' said Hestean.

'Gatts,' said Petty, addressing a man standing on the opposite side of the space. A moment later, a dagger flew through the air towards him, and Petty caught it a split second before it hit his head. 'You mean like that, daughter?'

'Yes!' said Hestean, now glued to the floor in total amazement.

'It is a skill taught to all sand shadows, and it would appear also to all Sharacanese.'

'You mean that my people are part of the Shadow Shire?'

'The Shadow Shire is part of antiquity, and so is Sharacan. Even though your people may not know it, it would appear so, yes.' said the captain.

'Then that means I am, too,' said Hestean.

'So, we will see you again tomorrow morning, yes?' asked Karree.

Hestean looked at her, a million thoughts flooding through her head. She handed back the dagger she'd been using, then looked at every person around her, one after the other, before running from the room.

Karree went to follow her, but Petty grabbed her arm. 'Leave her,' he said. 'This is something she must process for herself.'

* * *

Coming to a halt in the hallway near her cabin, through a window, Hestean spied a large scattering of dry bones on the desert sand below. They brought back a recollection of an evening's conversation she'd had with Jarrak.

It had been just three hundred years ago when a sparse blanket of green still stretched almost halfway across the modern Kalcool to Sharacan. It was then that the climate had changed and the College had inflicted their outrage upon the world. The greenery had retreated to the edges of the continent, replaced by the dry emptiness of an expanded desert. To many, it seemed that the gods knew what was coming. They had sent forth their guardians to show the surviving population how to sustain themselves in a changing world, showing them where to migrate to. Then, a hundred years later, the Comcree had come back to vanquish the College, stopping just short of total obliteration.

As Hestean looked at the bones, she fantasised about how the greenery of the past had covered this vast, and now sparse plateau. Unwilling to return her thoughts to the present, she imagined the bones as they once had been. She saw the vast herds of carrowa and nosbi that had once roamed the plateau. They had been the bases for a whole way of life that no longer existed.

From Jarrak's books she'd learned about the people who'd once lived here in settlements and towns that also no longer existed. It was a way of life that had all but disappeared from the plateau, sustained now only in small pockets around its edges. Like her, the majority had been forced to leave, migrating to other parts of Meglia.

These days, shrows were the only animals still seen freely wandering the inner plateau. They were also the beasts of burden that desert communities had become most reliant upon. It seemed that they alone had the genetics to survive in the aridity. Yet here were these other bones.

'Is this why I love shrows?' she asked herself quietly. 'Because they too can survive where I've been raised? Am I bones, and history? Or am I still also part of its flesh and future, moving as others have before me?'

'What are you thinking?' asked Karree, coming to stand beside her at the window.

'I asked Jarrak once who I was, and I've just been thinking about that again is all.'

'From what I've seen, you have the potential to become whoever you decide you want to be, Hestean. You are like me in that!'

'I think I still have a lot to learn about this world.'

* * *

Over the last days of their journey, as the landscape beneath the sky-ship changed, Hestean found herself again drawn to the ship's observation windows, fascinated by what she saw. She knew she had truly left the desert of her youth behind when the sand and stone of her homeland finally gave way to an increasingly green terrain.

Each night, she lifted the parcel, scroll, and cross-section from her tree and wondered at their collective meaning. Then she put them back again, knowing that only on her eighteenth birthday would she find out the truth of it all. She couldn't help wondering about the why of it, though. What did it mean? What if the parcel wasn't for her? How would she find the person it was meant for?

As they crossed the escarpment, on the last day of their flight, she caught sight of the thick coastal forest and stared down in wonderment. She had never seen so many trees.

Ahead, nestled at the foot of the giant cliffs, she saw the tendrils of a small metropolis, which had carved itself out of the forest. The living greenery was a revelation. To the south along the edges of a large river, and to the east towards the coast, she saw a patchwork of farms. The lush crops looked as though they could have supported her entire village for years with just one season of produce. Even with the stories she'd been told and the books she'd read, she still hadn't expected this. This was the outer world—the unknown world; Jarrak's world. It was a world that would now become part of her, and she part of it.

PART II
UNSHEATHING OF A DAGGER

16

Bornn sat at the outer edge of the Museum's courtyard, his eyes taking in its grand facade. He had always been drawn to this building, as many were once they'd seen it. He counted the pillars decorating the facade, then looked again at the surrounding grounds, already filling with people. He noted the scattered benches and sunken seats, the patches of green foliage and flowers, and the playful meanderings of small streams, which no doubt added to the Museum's attraction. But there was something more. Every day, many different people were drawn to the extravagance of the Hassis Museum Historical, and he wondered, for a moment, whether any of them had ever asked themselves why. There was something almost spiritual about this building, which seemed to fill it with the essence of life itself.

Beside the Museum was a great maze. It, too, had a reputation for keeping people entertained for days, but at least its appeal was understandable. Bornn returned his gaze to the sun-yellow pillars, trimmed in blood-red and rich sky-blue. He counted them again; twenty-seven to the right of the main entrance and twenty-seven to the left.

'As always,' he said to himself, 'twenty-seven and twenty-seven is fifty-four.'

His eyes drifted to the top of the escarpment, just over nine hundred paces above him. Visible as mere specks were the six wind-cranks responsible for lifting the giant counterweights back up the escarpment. There, they would be released—descending slowly, driving the cogs and great pendulums. These in turn drove the shafts, which spun the dynamos that produced the electrical energy this magnificent city required. Elora-Bearer had been the first city to ever rely solely on electrical energy, which was established from its conception. As a result, it had not destroyed its surrounding forests. The technology was old by today's standards, but it still worked. Bornn found himself wondering what this world must really have been like before new fragments of knowledge had spewed forth to create this city. It must have been so different before the cataclysm and sky-ships. He wondered, also, about the expanse of time that his work suggested, and of the changes in climate that seemed to have consumed and hidden so much of this world's history. He probably knew more about the early settlement of this world than anyone else alive, but even he didn't know it all. There was still so much that was undiscovered. So much that the myths and legends hinted at but had not yet divulged.

As the giant pendulums continued their unceasing movement at the top of the escarpment, he stood and glanced towards the pillars once more. Then, with the use of his walking stick, he started to hobble towards the Museum's entrance. 'This morning will tell, I know it will,' he said to no one but himself.

This morning he would finally get to meet the girl he had, until now, only read about in Jarrak's correspondence. He had put aside everything to dedicate this day solely to Jarrak's Sharacan hoard. Although Jarrak had not found Andreena, he had at least found something—albeit something he had not sought. Uncertain of what this meant, Bornn, just like Jarrak, was beginning to question all his ideas about this world, Sharacan, and Elora-Bearer itself.

* * *

By mid-morning, Bornn's uncertainties had been replaced by total dismay. They'd begun the process of un-crating the shipment that had arrived from the sky-port. 'Those fools. Those stupid fools,' he mumbled. 'Two years. Two years I have waited just to be sent a mess. Where's that girl?' His shoulders drooped as he sat back on a low crate to look at the mishmash of the shipment's contents in front of him. Wrongly tagged items lay scattered without apparent order. 'Jarrak isn't this inept! What is this? What is it I'm not seeing?'

His assistants continued to open crates and pull free the wrapped and bound items within, but his confusion only grew. He knew he should understand, so why couldn't he? As the sun continued to cross the unseen sky outside, he went over the pages of explanations in the research notes, seeking a clue. 'By the gods, where is that girl?' he said, loud enough for anyone to hear.

* * *

At the far end of the room were the shipping access doors that Hestean had passed through before dawn. Beside them was a gently sloping ramp, which ran up and around the walls of the great space, ending at the top near a set of steps. For quite some time, Hestean had been watching silently from this high balcony as the museum's workers unloaded crates from the carriers and pulled free their contents. Now, as she started down the stairs, she wondered about just what sort of man this professor of Jarrak's would turn out to be.

She resolved not to let herself be diminished by this new world. So when she reached the professor, she raised her voice slightly. 'You know Jarrak is not stupid, and neither am I. What you are seeing is what everyone is supposed to see. But you're not everyone, are you?'

Bornn spun shakily on his weakened leg, steadying himself with his stick. 'Are you her? Where have you been, and what do you mean by your statement? This is a *shambles*.'

She felt him studying her. Her dark complexion and direct words should already have made it clear who she was, but she answered him anyway. 'I am Hestean, yes; Hestean Descee. Jarrak sent me with the shipment. I've been watching you, waiting to see when I'd be needed. We didn't mix the shipment up—it looks that way, but we didn't. We just created an illusion, and I think by now you should know why. It needed to be disguised—because of the Robes. We didn't want to give away what Jarrak is really doing in Sharacan, which could implicate you, too. You *are* Professor Sageling, yes?' She grasped at the security pass hanging around her neck. 'This place is like a jail! I was stuck with your administration until they had this tag made for me, and these corridors are like the tunnels of a skawl's nest. How does anyone find their way around here?'

Silent, Bornn continued to look at her. 'I see,' he said eventually. 'I *was* starting to wonder! Someone I trained could never have been so stupid … Was it your idea? The phonetics, I mean?' The phonetic symbols of the ancient language were in a slightly different order to the modern form—just different enough to make gibberish of any sentence. 'The letters of our modern tongue have been transposed, haven't they?' pursued Bornn. 'And there's something else. A puzzle …' He returned his attention to the boxes. 'Was it you or Jarrak who put together this extra puzzle, Hestean Descee?'

'Puzzles are interesting things,' said Hestean. 'Sometimes, when you find the answer to puzzles, you fail to see what is really hidden.

You can be fooled into thinking that the puzzle itself was the disguise. But if you look beyond what is being presented to you, then sometimes the answer is simple. The story is meant for you, so only you can know what is not being said. Sometimes another key is also needed.'

'So,' Bornn said slowly, 'once these notes are transcribed, only I will notice the mistakes. I am the key to this. Is that what you are saying?'

'You are the one who taught Jarrak, and by proxy, you are also the one who taught me.'

'So, it is not the description that is wrong, but what is being said that is wrong. And only I will know what it is?'

'Exactly! And the rest will be simple. All you have to do is use your life's work as a reference. The numbers are dates, and Jarrak knows your work very well.'

For the first time that day, Bornn began to smile. 'I remember my first day here,' he said. 'It is indeed like a warren. Do you eat lunch, Hestean?'

'Yes,' she replied, wondering what the question had to do with the half-unwrapped collection in front of them.

'In the main entrance hall, Sessam's Eatery is the best. Tell him you're with me, and he'll put it on my tote until we can organise one of your own.'

'And you?'

'He'll give you a dinner box for me as you leave,' said Bornn, turning to watch the work crew unpack.

'Just like Jarrak,' muttered Hestean. 'But at least, with Jarrak, I was more than just a messenger.' Suppressing her annoyance at being dismissed, she followed his gaze and bent down to rearrange the two pieces he was now looking at. 'Like this. I know because I was there.'

'Indeed you were,' said Bornn, watching her rise. He once more gazed out across the collection spread before him.

As she watched his mind drift once more, Hestean turned to walk away. *I've been told to eat and bring his lunch. I am beginning not to like this man,* she thought.

'Follow the green line,' Bornn called as she walked towards the stairs.

She stopped, turning to him. 'Why green?'

'Because green is for the outside!' She started to walk again, but he kept speaking. 'I don't eat lunch till later, as a rule. I would appreciate you collecting it for me, though, while you're there. I like this puzzle,

Hestean Descee. I like it very much. You must tell me later how much of it is yours. I can see why Jarrak likes you.'

Again, she twisted back to watch him study the shipment. *Maybe he isn't so bad after all*, she mused. *Maybe I do look as hungry as I feel.*

* * *

The green line ran along the centre of the hallway, which twisted and turned like a serpent. Hestean rounded corners, passed doors and alcoves, and followed until the line disappeared under a heavy metal door. As the administrator had instructed, she lifted her clearance pass to the little red square on the wall beside the door. The square turned blue and the door slid open.

The smell of humid air instantly confronted her, and she breathed deeply, letting its aroma flood through her. Until yesterday, she hadn't realised how water could smell, or how it could change how the air felt. Its heaviness caressed her skin.

There were other differences to the desert here, too. Fountains filled out the Museum's large foyer, along with garden boxes filled with flowers brighter than she'd ever dreamed they could be. Long green vines twined along the walls towards the ceiling, which was dominated by a huge skylight built from glass in hues of pinkish red, sky blue, and pale yellow. It shone like the sun itself. Groups of people gathered at large information boards, which described the many galleries and reading halls. One board close to Hestean displayed instructions for finding the "Flight Gallery Wing" and "Ancient History Wings".

Hestean was searching for instructions to find the eatery when she overheard someone asking about the "subterranean excavations". She wondered, not for the first time, if there truly were glimpses into all parts of the world here. Jarrak had told her that the Museum held nearly all known information about their homeland. But here and now, she felt utterly amazed. From the books Jarrak had taken to Sharacan, she'd learned a little about all the houses, as well as the clans and tribes of which they consisted. Now, she saw many of these groupings in front of her. There were people working—as she would be soon—for the Museum. She imagined, too, that other people she saw before her might also be on their first big adventure, as she was. There were people visiting with their families, and others who were just, perhaps, enjoying a day away from their everyday lives.

Hestean walked further into the lobby. Next to her, a group of girls chatted to each other like a flock of baby swizzels learning to fly, animated and noisy. Still more people were sitting in patches of coloured sunlight at tables, taking refreshments in tall glasses, metal goblets, painted mugs, and even delicate teacups on dainty saucers. Hestean sought out this place called "Sessam's" amongst the many stalls and eateries filling the hall. She finally spied a sign above a single door, just inside the great glass wall that formed the front of the great, enclosed square.

SESSAM SEBOOM'S. Come Eat in This Room.

She turned to memorise the doorway she'd just come through, knowing she would have to distinguish it from all the others. On her right, she noticed a small booth advertising maps and booklets about the museum's history and exhibitions. Maybe, when she had gotten hold of some coinage, she could buy herself one of these maps.

Turning back to the melee, she baulked for a moment. Her village was made up of perhaps just six hundred people, yet it seemed there were at least half that number crammed into the space in front of her. Stepping forward, she thought longingly of her village as she made her way through the throng of people, wondering if here, amongst all this colour and variety, she would go unnoticed and be allowed the opportunity to grow, as she hoped, into herself.

As she walked into the eatery, a rather short man beamed at her from behind the counter. 'You're new here,' he said. 'I can always tell. Can I help you choose something, perhaps? It is all good, if I do say so myself. Where are you from?'

'East,' replied Hestean, deliberately vague.

'Ah. East. East is a big place. Nearly everything is east of here. I have not seen clothing like yours before, so you must be from *very far* east.'

'Professor Sageling sent me to collect his lunch and get something for myself.'

'Yours to take back, also? Or to have here?'

'He said not to hurry back.'

'Good, good. I like to talk to new people. Sit, perhaps at that table there, and I will bring you something. If you don't like it, I will bring you something else, but you will like it, I assure you. The professor likes you; otherwise, he would not have sent you. He knows I will like you too, but then, I like everyone. Almost everyone, anyway. So, sit. Please.'

Hestean sat and watched as Sessam lifted the lid on a large pot. Steam wafted out as he dropped a few small, whitish balls—dotted with red and green—into the boiling water. He replaced the lid and moved on to a round-bottomed pan, into which he dribbled some oil-of-oleeny. Its distinct greeny yellow colour showed that, even here, the leaves and seeds of the desert shrub were crushed for oil. The pan sizzled. He picked up a set of tongs to place some bean-flour noodles into the pan, then swished them around. He took pinches of several different spices and sprinkled them over the dish as he continued to stir and lift the noodles. Next came slices of towtowee and small pieces of diced green matoze. With professional skill, Sessam then slipped the contents of the pan onto a plate, where they were topped with the white-coloured balls, now boiled and soft. A few broken pieces of fettory were added and a drizzle of something Hestean had never seen before. Sessam placed the plate before her, along with some flatbreads, 'Try this,' he said. 'I think a glass of whinnom tea would also go well. Shall I get you some?'

All Hestean could do was nod as she stared at the plate in front of her, enraptured by the aromas. She tore off a piece of flatbread and picked up one of the balls. She took a bite, and the fettory melted in her mouth, combining perfectly with the texture of the ball and the flavour of the dressing. Hestean felt as though she had bitten into something fit for the gods.

'What are these?' she asked, gesturing to the balls.

'Mashed harrart, a protein plant from the sea, seasoned with tiny pieces of dried asany and sayoosh. They all come from the sea, and have the flavour of the sea, do they not?'

'I wouldn't know. What is the dressing?'

'Ah, some things should remain a secret, do you not think?' said Sessam with a smile. Hestean's throat began to burn slightly. Recognising the signs, Sessam said, 'I should get the tea.' He hurried away and returned with a glass, and as Hestean took a sip, he said, 'It is too hot—I will get you something else.'

'No, no,' said Hestean. 'Don't you dare. This is magnificent.'

'It was my mother's favourite,' said Sessam, beaming again. Another customer came through the door, and he turned to ply his salesman's charm once again.

* * *

When Hestean returned to the unloading bay of the Museum to give Bornn his lunch, she retrieved the part of the collection she'd carried separately in her bag. She opened the pouch and dumped the items onto the bench in front of him, saying, 'These are the "something else". These are the real treasures from Jarrak's excavations.'

'I see,' said Bornn, pushing aside the box containing another of Sessam's masterpiece meals.

'Jarrak said that the workmanship of these pieces would be hard to reproduce, even today,' said Hestean.

Already, Bornn was holding a magnifying glass in one hand and lifting a fragment with the other. 'I think he is right in that,' he said. 'You see here; it has multiple layers.'

As with Jarrak, Bornn's comments stalled after that, as he continued to investigate. An intact tile should have six sides and fit easily into the palm of a hand, but none of these fragments seemed to match up into a full tile. Each fragment had fantastically thin threads of gold wire running through them, and the patterning on each was so different that nothing lined up.

'I recall Jarrak musing about how the wires might indicate an energy router of some kind—whatever that is,' Hestean said.

'Well, if they were made today, I might agree with him, but our ability to manipulate energy is something quite new. We've only understood the production of electrical energy for about two hundred years, so I think this is something else. A map or overlay, maybe. There is mention of that sort of thing being used by the ancients in the library. They are translucent, so light would pass through them. Maybe they were made to fit into something, as tells the tale of the sun's eye—a story that speaks of an image projected onto a wall to reveal the positioning of a door. If some reference exists in the library, it will be hidden in the older sections. Tomorrow, I will introduce you to Bookere Gothen. She runs the literary archives. You should start on the writings before books; the old scrolls and loose manuscripts. I think that's where we will find what we seek. But for today, you can help me here. There is still a lot of unpacking to do.'

* * *

Later, nearing sunset, Hestean rode in a trolley-tram for the first time. She felt fascinated as the trolley-tram was pulled along by a constantly circulating wire rope, housed in a thin trench between the tracks. These tram tracks, she was told, radiated throughout the green foliage of the forest city. This whole day, she had felt as though she had been teleported into one of the many places Jarrak had fabricated in his fanciful tales of stars and other worlds. Lining the boulevards and streets were a myriad of tall, thin batter-palms and fronded trees, which provided a shaded screen between the ground and sky, tinting the light to shades of fluttering green. Away from the Museum and city-centre, the buildings filling the streets were all three- or four-storeyed pyramids complete with stepped terraces and gardens perfumed with flowers.

From Jarrak's books, she knew that these dwellings were called *domicilia*. After exiting the tram, Bornn opened the front door to his dom on the second storey of a pyramid.

'Your room is straight ahead and around to your right, the middle door,' he said.

The polished fibre-reed floor and white stone walls were the first things Hestean saw. Then she noticed the living area to her left. Books and scrolls were shelved along one side, while small sculptures and vases were placed amongst the other furnishings. There were long, cloud-puffed seats, which a person could fall into and not want to get out of for days, and a low table centred on a large floor rug. Beyond this, there was the cookery with its many pots, pans, food stores, and spices. At its centre was a very old-looking table and chairs, decoratively carved on their sides and legs. Further on, on the far side of the living space, was a garden, which still radiated colour in the dull evening light.

Bornn guided her into an alcove and opened a door that gave access to the guestroom. 'It's not very big, I'm afraid,' he said, 'but put your things inside and we'll find K.' While Hestean complied, he called out in a slightly louder voice, 'I have our guest, K!'

Despite Bornn's words, the room was bigger than Hestean had imagined. It was dominated by a soft, raised bed, a closet, a chest of drawers, and a small table and chair in one corner, lit by a night-glow. She set down her bag and turned slowly, taking it all in. Apart from her bunk on the *Merysands*, she had never slept on a proper bed before.

When she left the room, she saw a dark-haired woman—exactly the same height as Bornn—lean in and kiss him on the lips. 'My love,' she said, 'you're late.'

'Yes. Jarrak's shipment involved some unforeseen complications. I have brought the girl home with me, Kuzzea. I hope it's still alright?'

'Was she one of the "unforeseen complications"?' Kuzzea asked. But before Bornn could answer, Hestean stepped through the doorway. Kuzzea's chest heaved in surprise, and she gasped. 'Oh, my dear, Jarrak never mentioned that his assistant was so beautiful. I do hope this is who you are?'

In spite of her initial annoyance at the woman's previous comment, Hestean blushed at the unexpected compliment. 'I am Hestean Descee of Sharacan, yes. And this room—this place—is all much more generous than I had expected.'

'My dear child, we would have you nowhere else; Jarrak would not forgive us. How is my son? His correspondence has been too infrequent.'

In the two years that Jarrak and Hestean had known each other, Jarrak had never mentioned that his mother and Bornn shared a life together. Hestean was stunned into silence. She stared at Kuzzea as she took in her words, then tilted her head towards Bornn, puzzled.

'It would appear, my love, that we are not the only ones your son has been keeping secrets from,' said Bornn, noticing Hestean's expression. He put his arm around Kuzzea's waist, pulling her closer. 'He is not my son, Hestean. I have known K for only six years. Jarrak was one of my students, as you know, and he stayed back often to help me after classes. One evening, this lovely woman walked in, looking for him, and she found me instead!' Tenderly, Bornn tugged Kuzzea closer still. 'He tends not to mention his connections above what is necessary. So, I take it he never mentioned any of this to you?'

'No! I did not know you were now family.' Hestean recalled how Jarrak had always seemed to be trying to prove himself as someone without privilege, and now, at least partly, she thought she knew why. 'I never made the connection between you and Kuzzea.'

'I'm sorry. If I'd realised, I would have made it clearer before we got here.'

Hestean looked again at Kuzzea, curious now. All day, she had seen how women within the Museum were considered equal to men, but even so, the idea of Kuzzea being the one to pursue Bornn felt confronting to her. 'You encouraged the professor?' she asked.

'Of course! What other way would it be, my dear? We are the ones who mostly raise the children, so why would we not also choose who to raise them with? If you choose well, then your children will also thrive. But when you get to my age, that's of little importance. Your children have either survived or they have not. So I chose Bornn just because I liked him. It's much freer, not needing to consider the fate of your children.' She smiled now. 'You and Jarrak have become close, too, I understand?'

Despite her dark colouring, Hestean's face became tinged with a deep shade of red. Kuzzea, a woman who was proud to be a woman, seemed completely unafraid of expressing herself. She reminded Hestean strangely of the women from her own village, who held their pride in quiet reserve. For them, there could never be a consideration for passion—the Black Robes ensured that partnerships were contractual, financial arrangements. Yet things were obviously different here. How could they be the same when men and women were equal?

The village would always be her home. Her upbringing and taught values would be hard to ignore. But now, after Kuzzea's allusion, she recalled the joking conversation she'd had with Petty about consorts. Back then, it had seemed just a frivolous impossibility; one she would never have really considered. In her village, she had never heard any woman talk openly of such things. 'In my village, only the men do the choosing,' said Hestean. 'Women have no say in such matters; it is forbidden by the Robes.'

It was now Kuzzea who stared at Hestean. After a moment, she said, 'Are you wise, Hestean Descee? I think you are wise. There will be a lot of new concepts that will challenge you here, so if there is ever anything you need to ask me, please do. My son would want it.' Bornn coughed, and Kuzzea looked at him pointedly. 'I'm still a mother, and he is my only son, B. But you're right. I'm not being a very good hostess, am I? Such conversations can wait. Come, Hestean.' She took Hestean's arm and guided her towards the open terrace doors. 'Let us go out and enjoy the first of the evening stars. I know my son, but I do not know you. I think you will interest me, though, Hestean Descee. You are Sharacanese, and I know little of the Sharacanese, apart from what I've read in books.'

* * *

Kuzzea smiled at Bornn as she ushered Hestean outside. She knew he thought she was just a little too much at times, but she also knew that she was a woman who longed to be a grandmother, and sometimes it got the better of her. 'Some ferment would be nice,' she said, turning towards a small table holding a decanter and nine glasses. The two women settled onto a bench on the terrace and shortly Bornn came to sit opposite them. He handed each of them a glass from a small silver tray. After taking a sip, Hestean lifted her face to survey the sky.

'So, which star do you think we are from?' Bornn prompted.

Kuzzea knew that this was one of his favourite questions for getting to know someone. He thought it showed a person's openness, and their willingness to explore beyond this world's physical boundaries—something that was not necessarily possible but showed a person's ability to think. Others, like Kuzzea, scoffed at this belief, but Bornn liked that extreme, too. He liked the idea of shaking out people's thoughts.

'Oh, I don't know,' said Hestean dreamily. 'This has been a new day—a long and different day. The stars are different here, too. Maybe that one—I like that one.' She pointed towards a little cluster of stars just to the right of the sky's centre.

'I was rather hoping you would not be one of my husband's fools, dear,' said Kuzzea. 'I live with this silliness all the time. My husband and son are bad enough, but not you, too!'

Hestean's eyes moved to Kuzzea. 'It's just a game, isn't it? I mean, well … Jarrak and I played it all the time in Sharacan. At night, we would lie back on the sand, and he would ask me which one, and I would point, and he would start to tell me about the worlds there … He would conjure up all sorts of mythical beings and wonderful places. I think he did it first to take my mind off my isolation. Later, it became something we just did for fun.'

'Oh, my dear,' said Kuzzea, now thinking herself the fool. 'I'm so sorry. I thought for a moment that you were one of Bornn's thinkers. They think too much, these idle men, and you know that this husband of mine could never travel to the stars, because he can't even travel through a single sentence without deviating.'

Hestean giggled.

'You think this funny, do you?'

'No,' said Hestean, stifling her light laugh, which turned into a yawn. 'It's just that, well, I think you must know the professor very well, like my mother knows my father.'

'Oh, my love, this one I like,' said Kuzzea, turning to Bornn. 'She sees, which I think is better than thinking sometimes. But you have worn her out today, haven't you?' She faced Hestean again. 'Don't let him push you! If he does, you let me know, and I'll do something about it.' She rose from her seat and motioned towards the doorway. 'We must feed you before you rest. B, you can help. Come, Hestean, I want to hear more about you and your family.'

For the rest of the evening, Kuzzea didn't mention her son again. But Hestean spoke of Jarrak often, and Kuzzea began to feel a warmth towards this young woman from the sand.

17

The trolley-tram was almost full when Bornn and Hestean went to board the next morning. So, Hestean stood against its sideboard, hanging from the tram while the breeze blew through her hair. Beside her, Bornn settled into the last remaining seat, his walking stick resting beneath his hands. As they passed the forest buildings, Hestean remembered how upon wakening, she had found Jarrak's name scratched into her bedpost. It had once been his bed, and the realisation had made a strange quiver tingle through her. It was almost as if, through the night, he had been watching over her, keeping her safe. Right now, as she watched this diverse city flow past, she no longer felt alone.

She offered her hand to Bornn for support when they disembarked in front of the Musean. 'Thank you, no,' he said, then stepped to the ground unaided. 'I don't want to get into bad habits that I may come to rely on. It is a nuisance, yes, but my leg is not disabling.'

'How did it happen?'

'A few years ago, I fell down a small cliff on one of my excursions. I was lucky,' he said. Then he pulled something from his pocket. 'Here. Before we go any further, I had this made for you yesterday. You should put it on.'

Hestean took the badge and looked at it, reading its statement.

Hestean Descee. Sharacan Excavation Field Technician, Hassis Museum Historical, Divisions of Anthropology and Literary Research.

'You decided this yesterday?' she asked.

'I saw by mid-afternoon that this place held potential for you, as Jarrak had hoped. You have the enquiring mind and genuine curiosity needed for this work.'

'Do you always make such quick decisions?'

'My decision was not quickly made—just quickly confirmed. Jarrak has been telling me about you for some time.'

'He never mentioned that to me!'

'Well, as we discussed last night, there are some things he likes to keep to himself.'

As they started walking towards the Museum's large square, Hestean's face took on an amused expression of understanding. She pinned the tag to her blouse just above her left breast, and despite having not really done anything yet, she found herself walking with a new sense of confidence and pride. Unlike yesterday's key card, the badge indicated permanency. She renewed her vigilance, watching and listening to everything around her. She knew now that she was experiencing the things that Jarrak had experienced two years before; everything here was as new to her as her village had been to him.

'What are you smiling at?'

'Those pillars. I didn't notice them properly when we left yesterday.'

'Yes, the colours! They're the same as those on your dress, aren't they! Here, they mean belief, knowledge, and truth.'

'It's not the colours, I've lived with those all my life, and am familiar with their meaning. It's the pillars themselves! There are fifty-four, aren't there?'

'Yes, there are,' said Bornn, studying the pillars more closely himself. Then, with a start, he glanced back at Hestean. 'What do you mean?'

'It's nice, that's all.'

He narrowed his eyes. 'How so?'

'I just think it's perhaps a good thing that I'll be working in a place that celebrates the history of the world, and which is also guarded by the gods.'

Bornn came to an abrupt stop, his eyes again springing to the pillars. 'How do you mean, *exactly*?'

Hestean stopped as well, and turned to face him, noticing how his eyes scanned the line of monolithic columns. 'Six times nine—that equals the gods, doesn't it?'

'What do you mean, "six times nine equals the gods"?'

Hestean looked at him more fully, realising that he truly didn't understand. To her, the meaning was plain, despite her being a stranger here. Was she wrong, or did this confirm the conclusion she had slowly been coming to ever since she'd first spoken about it with Jarrak? She smiled, enjoying the fact that she knew something the professor did not.

She pointed with her finger at every ninth pillar. 'They represent the Comcree and the gods. They also symbolise the six great houses of our world, and the people, too. Displayed like this, among the other pillars, they also stand for this world. Do you see how these six pillars are divided into four parts, whereas the others are only in two parts? The bottom part represents the gods, the next is the Comcree, and the two sections on top stand for firstly the great houses and then secondly the people. Starting from the outside edge of the building, do you see that there are sixteen pillars, then two that form the god pillar? This is repeated three times, then the same on the other side.'

'I see only eight pillars before the ninth,' said Bornn.

'Back in my village,' said Hestean, 'they are represented by a ring of batter-palms around our well-pond. It is a similar illusion here. Look again, and you will see that every pillar is made from two separate pieces of stone. Although the god pillars seem to be in four parts, they, too, are made up from only two pieces of stone—one on top of the other. You need both sexes to make a god, the same as you do people. Haven't the Comcree always been comprised of three males and three females, whenever they have appeared in this world? See how the bottom parts form a stylised figure eight? It looks like the bottom half of a batter-palm. They represent the nine cycles of childhood. Now, look at their tops; the top of a batter-palm trunk is a mirror image of its bottom. Nine again, which represent the nine cycles of adults-in-learning. Eighteen cycles in all. I will be eighteen myself, soon,' said Hestean.

Bornn stood stunned. Every day, he had walked from the tram stop and never noticed, yet this girl had walked up these steps once and seen it all. He tilted his head sideways and mentally placed the outline of the eighth pillar over that of the ninth. He could see it now, the symbol of the gods—two figure eights, one on top of the other, each within their own rectangular box. Why had he not seen it before? Although the building was no older than two hundred years, its creation had been drawn from the ancient past. Throughout his tenure, he'd discussed this building's construction with his colleagues, but the only thing he truly knew about the grand facade was its colours—the sun yellow for belief, the red for truth, and the blue for knowledge. He noticed Hestean's yellow dress again, and the word "belief" flashed through his mind.

'Of course, to be a true symbol of the gods,' Hestean went on, 'they should be lying down, but the trees back home are standing also. Because they are trees, their true meaning has been somewhat concealed from the Robes, although they knew enough to cut down every ninth. Yet the gods' trees live on in our minds. Lying down or standing up, infinity plus infinity is still the equivalent to a single infinity, isn't it?'

'It is,' said Bornn. 'You truly are amazing. Jarrak warned me that you see things others don't, and it's true. Perhaps it is a useful thing that you have come here with fresh eyes. When is your birthday?'

Hestean smiled. Despite everything else, he had remembered her birthday. 'In a little over one cycle of the moons,' she said.

'Then we must celebrate this eighteenth birthday of yours. I understand that to the Sharacanese, an eighteenth birthday is important?'

'Do you work there?' said a small voice. Hestean looked down, surprised. 'Was that true, what you said about the gods and everything?'

Until now, the young boy had gone unnoticed by both Bornn and Hestean. Hestean saw that he wore a similar style of dress to the gaggle of girls she had seen in the Museum's entrance hall the day before.

'School group,' said Bornn. 'They're through here all the time.'

'I heard you mention the gods,' the boy said. 'So I came across to better hear what you were saying. Today we are supposed to find out something we didn't know before and write a story about it. Is what you said true?'

Kneeling down, Hestean presented her badge to the little boy, and said, 'Yes, I work here, see! My name tag says I am from Sharacan, but I work here now. It is all true.' The little boy looked at her a moment longer, as if assessing her sincerity. Then his face blossomed and he ran suddenly off, just like the girls had the day before. He joined a small group of children gathered around a tallish, red-haired woman.

'Their teacher,' said Bornn, looking over at the youngsters. 'I think you have just made that little chap very happy. I know you have me.'

Hestean watched the children as they gathered around the boy, then saw the teacher turn to look at her. The woman then took in the building, studied it for a while, then stared back at Hestean with a smile of wonderment spreading across her face. She nodded to Hestean, and without even thinking about it, Hestean brought her hand up to her forehead, then to her mouth, and then to her heart. The teacher responded by repeating the gesture, then bowed in acknowledgement of Hestean's gift.

'What do the hand gestures mean?' asked Bornn.

'For a smart man, you really don't know much, do you!'

'I know what it used to mean, back in the times of the ancients. But you don't see it much these days. I was just wondering if it still meant the same, that's all.'

The teacher had now re-engaged the children. Hestean turned back to face Bornn. 'It means "we think, we speak, we feel". Is that what it used to mean?'

'Yes, pretty much!'

'Then it still means the same thing today.'

'All this knowing,' said Bornn. 'I have heard batter-palms referred to as sustenance trees because of the water contained in their four bulges. I also recall hearing them called god trees, and now you have just given me the answer as to why.' He started towards the Museum once more. 'How do you know about the past Hestean?' he mused.

'I learned a lot when I was young by listening and watching the women in my village. A lot of it I didn't know I knew, until Jarrak taught me how to see it. It's not the past for us—it's our everyday lives. Didn't you learn about the past when you were young?'

'I must confess not,' he said. Bornn seemed a little jealous, but also grateful for the opportunity to learn from history itself. 'Not in the way you seem to have learned, anyway.'

'Back home, the Black Robes resent us knowing about the gods, and that's why we make sure we *do* know of them,' said Hestean.

Bornn smiled. 'You don't know everything, then! The College has good reason to fear the gods.'

'Jarrak has told me a little about that, but is there still something unseen?'

'I think, at lunch, we will have to discuss this further.'

'You don't eat lunch! You pick at your food, like during last night's dinner.'

'I may eat lunch today, I think,' said Bornn.

The doors in front of them opened, and they walked straight into the hallways marked "employees only".

* * *

In the days that followed, Hestean fell into a routine formed by the Museum's anthropology and literary research divisions. At lunchtime, she ate at Sessam's eatery with Bornn, as they had from that second day. Apparently, before Jarrak had left for Sharacan, this had been Bornn and Jarrak's tradition. To Hestean's surprise, Sessam often joined them. She found the little man remarkably capable of holding his own in conversations with the great professor.

One day, Hestean entered Sessam's alone. 'On your own today, I see,' he said.

'Yes. Bornn had a meeting with the chancellor.'

'Ah, the big boss. Bornn may not be in a good mood this afternoon, then.'

'Why's that?'

'Oh, they do not get on so well. It is the Guild, you see. When Bornn first started his investigations, his ideas were way outside current thinking, but the Guild backed him.'

'The Guild of Deserteers?'

'Oh, the Guild is much more than the Deserteers. The Guild is the Museum, and Elora-Bearer itself. The Guild is history, too, you see. Do you know what "Elora-Bearer" means?'

'Not really, no.'

'Elora Sara-Hassis was the last of a dynasty; a family that was once just traders, but then grew to one of guidance. They were an authority, almost, but never dictators. She died where the Museum stands today—it is both her monument and her legacy. She had influence throughout much of Meglia and ran the Hassis estate at the top of the escarpment. It was from the Hassis Valley, you see, that the Comcree and Deserteers began to push back against the College during the Outrage. She died not long before the fight for Sharacan, where the alliance stalled and the Treaty of Truce was signed.'

'Do you know what Jarrak is looking for at Sharacan?'

'You mean Andreena? Yes, I was in the tavern with them the evening they first heard the story. It was a group of Deserteers who told the tale. Elora and Andreena were close friends according to the Deserteers, who also said they were Comcree. I remember how the professor really started to take notice of the Deserteers when they mentioned this.'

'There would be more about Elora in the library, wouldn't there?'

'Oh, lots, I would think! About her and her family, a great and long-lived dynasty.'

'You're not from around here either, are you, Sessam?'

'Me? No. I am from the Western Isles!'

'Where are they?'

'A long way out in the Great Western Ocean. I think that is why people like my cooking so much. It is different, you see. But it could also be because I make people feel at home. That is the real secret to running a business, I think.'

'I must get back to work,' said Hestean. 'I'll see you tomorrow, yes?'

'No, you will see me tonight. Bring Bornn to the tavern. He'll know which one I mean. He will need cheering up after his meeting with Eloro. I will send word to Kuzzea to join us there. She always likes a sing-along, and I am very good on the fluen.'

'Can I bring an instrument, too?'

'You play? What do you play?'

'A horn.'

'Sounds interesting. I would like to hear some of your Sharacanese tunes.'

'I'm still learning, so I'm not very good.'

'The only way to get better is to practise. Is that not so?'

'Jarrak might disagree with you on that, Sessam.'

'At the moment, he is a long way from here, Hestean Descee. So bring your horn and play.'

18

Even with Hestean's unique familiarity with, and knowledge of, the ancient language—and now also with the vast resources of the Museum's library at her fingertips—Jarrak's puzzle still eluded her. Bornn, too. It seemed that nothing in the archives referenced anything like the fragments they'd found. Whatever they were, it seemed as though they had never existed anywhere other than in Sharacan.

Late one afternoon, Bornn came looking for Hestean and found her sitting on the floor, leaning against the wall of a long, broad hallway. She had positioned a portable nightglow above her head. Around her lay a scattering of aged scrolls. In her hand she held a loose page, and more were cradled in her lap. She was reading disjointedly to herself when he rounded the corner. Both sides of the hall were shelved with many thousands of books and scrolls, making it one of the hundreds that comprised the great library.

'It looks like you've been busy,' he said, drawing closer.

Hestean looked up and smiled darkly. 'Bookere Gothen found me this morning. She brought me a stack of cataloguing forms and said that if I was going to be digging around back here, I may as well notarise anything that hasn't previously been done. Then she showed me how, and as a lot of these have never been catalogued, there's been plenty to do …'

'I see. So, have you found anything of interest? You didn't come to lunch today and Sessam was asking after you. He has become quite fond of your daily chats, I think.'

Hestean picked up a another scroll with her spare hand. 'Do you know what this is? It's a copy of the Kalcool Transportation Charter.'

'The what?'

'You know. Jarrak told me about it, so you must know about it, too. It's the charter that was drawn up between the merchants and the desert tribes, for transporting goods across the Kalcool. And that one there—' she pointed with the scroll she'd just picked up, '—describes the proposed route. None of these scrolls are actually that old, though. Most only a few hundred years, perhaps, and Elora-Bearer isn't mentioned in any of them.'

'That's not surprising,' said Bornn. 'Elora-Bearer is only a young city, and it hadn't even come into existence when a new trade link was first being considered. I didn't know we had a copy of the original charter, though.'

She put down the scroll and turned her attention back to the pages in her lap. 'I found these a little while ago. They're really old,' she said. 'They're copies, also, from a section of something called *The Beran Tima*. They're at least a thousand years old, I think. The original *Beran Tima* documents, if they still exist, would be much, much, older again. I have found Sharacan mentioned in these.'

'Where did you find them?'

'In there,' she said, pointing to a small, dimly lit alcove buried in the side of the hallway, with an open door set against its back wall.

'*Beran Tima* means "beginning time", doesn't it?' said Bornn, shuffling some of the scrolls with his stick so that he could sit down beside her.

'Yes. As I said, it mentions Sharacan, but not a Sharacan I recognise. They're hard to read. They're all written with a kind of veiled intent—and Fem, as you know, is also word-placement specific. The same word can mean different things if used before or after another word. It is place sensitive, too—such as when you use it to describe something inside or out.'

'I didn't know that,' admitted Bornn.

'Take this, for instance,' said Hestean. 'It says—or I think it says, anyway—"Beneath the ground, beneath the sky, which is beneath the stars, is Sharacan, which is within Meglan, which holds within itself the six Blues, which are all of us, and which make us whole with the Danannee". "Danannee" is an ancient word for gods, as you know.'

'I did know that, yes,' said Bornn.

'And this bit here, it uses colour again,' continued Hestean. '"Hidden within time is their quarry safe, our salvation, our guide to reclamation, bluest of green, the stars are justly our sovereignty". They are talking about ideas, but don't come out and say anything directly.' She shuffled a few of the pages on her lap and pulled one out from near the bottom. 'Listen to this, though. In all these pages, this is the only bit I think I understand, and I only know this because I am Sharacanese, and because of a discussion I had once on the *Merysands* with a few Deserteers. It says: "The daggers that choose women and men hold within them our blood as testament, as if a stone hurled against the mind to release the soul". This is talking about the Sharacanese stone game, I think. Everything on these pages is written like that. They are descriptions without meaning unless you have the key to understanding them. But there is no discernible key anywhere. Or at least, I can't find one. I've been through them again and again, but there's nothing.'

'You know, you sound like Jarrak.'

'Do I?'

'Yes. And my advice to him at this moment would be to start again in the morning, once you have had time to think. So come on; you haven't eaten since breakfast. First, I'll help you tidy this mess up, so that Bookere Gothen doesn't get too annoyed. We're to meet Sessam and K at the tavern. Sessam said you are to bring the horn; he thinks he has worked out an accompaniment to that tune you played the other night. Often, clarity comes when you're not entwined in what you're seeking.'

* * *

The deep, resonating sound of the woke horn wafted through the tavern, unnoticed at first by the other patrons. Sessam's fluen began its dance along the top of the notes like a flutter-wing weaving between blossoms. It was only once they had finished playing that Sessam and Hestean noticed that the whole tavern had stilled to listen.

'If you keep that up, you might just bring the gods back into existence,' said a female voice directly behind Hestean.

Hestean turned to see a young woman in a sand-coloured dress standing very close behind her. 'Karree,' she said, jumping up. 'What are you doing here?'

Karree pointed to some of the other members of the *Merysands* crew, and said, 'We flew in this morning and finished reloading this afternoon. We will be off again at sunrise, but we have been given the night off.'

'Petty, too?' asked Hestean, looking around.

'Someone had to stay on board. The captain wanted to see his wife and family this time, even if only for the night.'

'Oh,' said Hestean, a little disappointed.

'Don't worry, Petty said to say hi if I saw you.'

'You're a long way from the landing field.'

'It really wasn't a *casual* request from Mister Petty, so we asked at the Museum. We were thinking of coming to find you anyway. We thought you might like another dancing lesson. Can we steal her away for a while?' asked Karree, looking at Hestean's table.

'I've been rude,' said Hestean, turning to the table herself. 'Karree Ladener, meet Professor Bornn Sageling and his wife, Kuzzea. And this is Sessam Seboom. I'm staying with the professor and Kuzzea, and Sessam runs one of the eateries at the Museum.'

'Greetings to you all,' said Karree. 'You play the fluen very well, Maskee. The instrument is from the Western Isle, is it not?'

'You have been there?' asked Sessam.

'I have a brother who is loadmaster aboard a tri-hull.'

'I see. A family business, then.'

'You are very perceptive, Maskee.'

'The last tram runs at midnight,' said Bornn.

Karee smiled in acknowlegement, and assured the professor that they would escort Hestean home.

'I'm afraid I haven't been practising,' said Hestean.

'Then it's a good thing we showed up to give you another lesson, isn't it?'

'Is it alright if I go, professor?' asked Hestean, turning to Bornn.

'Oh, my dear, go have some fun,' said Kuzzea. 'You should live life while you can. It catches up with all of us more quickly than we like to think, so go.'

'Leave the horn,' said the professor, as Hestean went to join the other Deserteers. 'You won't need it if you're going dancing.'

'I suppose not,' smiled Hestean, handing the horn to him. 'Take care of it, for the gods have given it to me to look after. I'll see you both at breakfast.'

'I should hope so. You have research to do tomorrow, remember?'

* * *

Hestean yawned across the table while Kuzzea busied herself making breakfast. 'Kuzzea, where do I get cloth from around here?'

'What sort of cloth?'

'I want to make a dress.'

'Oh, my dear, I have a friend who is a dressmaker. No need for you to make it. What kind of dress are we talking about?'

'Something to dance in.'

'You liked the dancing you did last night, then?'

'A long time ago, my people once danced quite a lot, I think.'

'How wonderful. How do you imagine the dress to look?'

'Well, tight-fitting down to my waist, then loose from there so I can move freely. It must be Sharacanese yellow, with a red sash around the middle. It will also need my clan markings just above the hem.'

Kuzzea slid the pan from the stove, turning slowly. 'You mean a shadow dress?'

'A what?'

'A shadow dress, like the one your friend was wearing last night.'

'Yes, exactly.'

'Hestean! Exactly what sort of *dancing* were you practising last night?'

'Dagger dancing.'

'I see. You're thinking of becoming a warrior, are you?'

'No, I'm thinking of becoming whole.'

'How do you mean?'

'Well, since the College took control of Sharacan, no woman has been allowed to catch their stone, and I have decided that I will catch mine. I found something yesterday at the Museum that says it is my right, and I intend to claim that right. It will be for all the women of Sharacan.'

'I see.'

'Why are they called shadow dresses?'

'I don't really know, but there's one in the Museum's hall of fashion and it's labelled as such. It's blueish green, though, not sand like your friend's, nor the yellow you would like. You should have a look today if you get a chance.'

'I will. So how do we go about getting this dress made?'

'You are sure about this?'

'Yes, I am.'

'Well, if you are still sure tomorrow morning, I will tell B that you're having the day off, and we will go and see my friend.'

* * *

The fashion hall was larger than expected, but still Hestean found what she was looking for. After studying the dress for a while, she noticed its catalogue number. When she reached the library, she looked it up and found that the catalogue card held a short but useful notation: *SHADOW DRESS. One of several that belonged to Elora Sara-Hassis. Donated to the Museum in her memory at the time of the Museum's completion.*

Agitated with excitement, Hestean later burst into Bornn's office. 'The *Beran Tima*,' she panted. 'It's about the Comcree. It doesn't say "bluest of green", it says "bluish green", like a shadow dress. The Comcree were once just the high priestesses and priests of the temple at Sharacan, but as the world grew, so did their role in it. The text mentions *cwen,* too, but it doesn't mean "queen" as most people think. It means something more like "guide".'

'Slow down and sit, girl. Where is all this coming from?'

'From Kuzzea this morning. We were talking before you got up. I have decided that on my eighteenth birthday, I want to perform the full Sharacanese ceremony of adulthood. I first thought about it on the day when Petty came to collect me in the desert. I don't think I've ever really forgotten the thought, so it must be something I truly desire. The ritual is my right; the scrolls say so. While still a child, I listened to the whisperings of the older women, and I know now that I have never really forgotten them. They told of long ago when my sex also caught the stone. Here in the Museum, I have come across the same stories.'

'What are you saying? Are you talking about the Comcree, or yourself?

'Ah … Both, I think. Hestean started to laugh. The sound was tinged with nervousness. She was realising that her complex Sharacanese values were difficult to express.

* * *

After several visits to the shop for fittings, the dress Hestean had commissioned arrived. The tailor, Gwenneetha Dummzy, was a very particular woman when it came to her work.

Hestean formed the habit of rising early, as she had done on the *Merysands*, as if Karree had once again started calling her to practice. Every morning now, she went out onto Bornn and Kuzzea's terrace and followed through the movements of the shadow dance and the "dance of the dagger", which Karree had taught her. The dance of the dagger was the Deserteers version of the Sharacanese stone game, although she also practised the Sharacanese original, as it was what she would use in her ritual of adulthood.

After one of their lunchtime chats, Sessam ordered a device made to throw stones at her. One morning, she had walked up and down a small stream not far from Bornn's apartment to gather stones of just the right size. The device really did help to quicken her reflexes, but it was painful, too. It wasn't a real person, and therefore gave no emotive clues as to when it would throw a stone. She knew she was getting better, and her hand faster, because each morning there were fewer fresh bruises on her body when she left for work.

In conversations with Bornn and Sessam, she learned the square in front of the Museum was used for all sorts of things. With this in mind, she concluded it would be the perfect place to hold her ascension rights. She would be in sight of the pillars, the Museum's symbol for gods, whom she had believed in all her life.

On her behalf, Bornn went to seek permission from the Museum's administration, and afterwards, as a result, Hestean and Bornn spent another evening in the tavern so he could emotionally recover from the experience.

'It's the best tavern in which to get good ferment,' he said.

At the top of her attendance list, Hestean wrote Bornn and Kuzzea's names. After all, they had in a way become her surrogate parents. This thought made her feel closer to Jarrak, also. Some of the staff she had come to know during her time at the Museum were also listed, and of course Sessam. One person was essential to her needs, though, and there were the other Deserteers she had befriended during her short time aboard the *Merysands*. To that end, she sent a special invitation, care of the landing field at Elora-Bearer.

The reply to that said simply: *As a father to a daughter, there is no hesitation at all. We will be there.* It gave the date the *Merysands* was to be at Elora-Bearer, and was signed by Petty.

So, Hestean settled upon a date—one day after her actual birthday. She also found herself hoping that somehow, through sheer will, the giant airship might bring Jarrak to witness the ritual as well. But she knew this was just a dream.

* * *

At work, in the Museum's vast library, she found more references to Sharacan itself. She took every opportunity to read more about the grand history that belonged to her place of birth. Time and again, Bookere Gothen found her cocooned within a pile of books or scrolls. The head of Literary Research would just shake her head and say, 'You will clear this up, won't you?'

Hestean had no idea that many of the obscure books she found had never been read by Bornn, or even by Jarrak, who had himself worked in the archives for a while. She found most of them at the backs of vaults or on high shelves, covered in thick coats of dust. There was something else, too. It was becoming clear that even here, amongst all this knowledge, there was still something hidden about Sharacan; something often hinted at but never actually acknowledged. She decided that, after her ceremony into adulthood, she would concentrate on unlocking these clues.

When the day she had been thinking about for most of her life arrived, Hestean was in a state of numbed apprehension. It was not as she had thought she'd feel at all.

'It's unusual to see so many people here this early in the day,' said Bornn, stepping off the trolley-tram. 'I haven't forgotten a holiday, have I?'

'None that I can think of, my love,' said Kuzzea, stepping down beside him. 'Maybe there is something you weren't told about when you asked Eloro for permission?'

As Hestean herself stepped down, her mind was elsewhere. She was thinking about Sharacan, the College, her real parents, the great temple she had helped to uncover, and what it might mean for the world. Of course, Jarrak was in her head, too. Preoccupied with these thoughts, she trailed behind Bornn and Kuzzea without fully taking in the many people already standing or seated within the square. Strapped over her shoulder was a small bag. Under her other arm she carried the old leather-bound parcel she'd been given in the desert.

'I just hope someone hasn't taken our table already,' said Kuzzea. 'It will be a nuisance if we have to find somewhere else.'

When they arrived at the table, they finally realised that most of the people weren't moving. Instead, they were chatting quietly amongst themselves, as if waiting for something. Even more people were walking towards the square.

'You don't suppose they're all waiting for us?' asked Kuzzea, looking around.

'I think maybe they are,' said Sessam, arriving beside them. Several bystanders turned, and an excited whisper rippled through the crowd. A reserved sign had been placed on the stone table beside them, and Hestean recognised it as one from Sessam's eatery. Sessam held out his hand and presented a small box to her. His face glowed, reflecting the excitement she was now hearing in the crowd around them. 'This is for your birthday,' he said. 'While I've been waiting, I have been listening. All these people have heard about this Sharacan ritual, but none of them have witnessed it. They've all come to watch you become an adult.'

Hestean took the box and looked about, realising the true significance of the crowd. She shrank back onto the stone seat behind her. 'All these people ... Have they all come to see me like I'm an amusement of some kind?'

'Oh, no,' said Sessam. 'You must not think that. For them, it is an honour. In a way, it connects them with their past just as it connects you. Elora-Bearer is a young city, and people have settled here from all over the world. There is a commonality for all of them, and that is Sharacan. Sharacan has lived long in people's minds. It is still considered a special place.'

She shrank even further on to the seat as she fully realised that all these people had come to see her. 'All these people! How did they learn about today?' she said.

'A whisper is always something an ear craves to hear,' said Sessam.

Slowly, Hestean's head twisted from side to side in a negative acknowledgement of what she saw. 'This was supposed to be for me, not for them!'

'But this *is* for you!' said Sessam.

Bornn knelt down beside her and took both her hands in his. 'They *are* here for you! Don't you see that? They are here to see you become a true Sharacanese adult. Look at them. Look at their clothes. To them, this is not some everyday event. This is a special day. You will be the first Sharacan woman in two hundred years to become whole, but these people do not know this. They just see something that connects them with their past. They see someone they wish to connect with themselves. What they don't realise is that, by being here, they ensure that the College can never take this day away from you. Not ever!'

'I had a list,' said Hestean. 'This was to be small and private. That way, if I fail, it wouldn't matter so much, because at least my friends would know I died trying. But with this crowd … If I fail, the whole world will know, and the College will be strengthened by it. I can't have that.'

'Then don't fail,' said Bornn.

Hestean looked around, then murmured quietly to herself, 'They are witnesses, aren't they?' She banished her intrusive thoughts and said, louder, 'Petty's late.'

'Just a little,' said Bornn. 'You know these Deserteers; they love to make an entrance.'

Hestean smiled weakly. 'We will wait, we have to. We can't begin without him!'

She got up and strolled determinedly towards some of the people she'd invited, then chatted to some of the ones she hadn't. Many she had never met before, and as Bornn had said, she found they'd come to look upon a piece of their world's history. Like Sessam, others had considered it an honour, and soon the table behind her started to fill with many gifts, mostly small, gifted by those from all walks of life and from all over the world.

'You have a good morning for it, Professor,' said a voice, making Bornn and Hestean turn.

'Eloro,' said Bornn, seeing the tall and rather plump Museum director with his white hair and overly large moustache. 'I didn't expect to see you here!'

'Oh, I think you did,' said Eloro. 'There are many things we do not agree on, Professor, but there is one thing we do; that knowledge should be free and not hoarded. It is useless when kept hidden. This young woman shows today that she has regained knowledge taken from her. This, I can respect quite sincerely. It is not often I give permission for the Museum's square to be used in such a way. It will irritate the College, so I had no real hesitation. Having said that, though, if I had known that you were to draw this much of a crowd, my permission may have been harder to obtain.'

'If we had known of this crowd, then we may not have asked for permission.'

Eloro Dowging Fife coughed out a muffled laugh at Bornn's sharp inference. The director then set his eyes on Hestean and, with a big toothy grin, said, 'I believe you must be the young lady in question! Am I correct? I am Eloro Fife.'

'I am Hestean Descee of Sharacan,' said Hestean, with all the polite dignity she could muster.

'You seem to have created quite a disturbance this morning!'

'It would seem so!' said Hestean, looking around at the growing crowd.

'They worry you, I see!' said the Director. 'So let me point out a few that may make you stand with strength, the way you should on this day. Over my left shoulder towards the back, a row of men in dark grey and black robes … Do you see them?' Hestean raised her eyes and, seeing her stiffen slightly, the Director said, 'You do not worry them, you scare them. Your simple act of fulfilment here today scares them very much. They are of the College, as you can see. A diplomatic delegation permanently appointed here.'

Hestean's eyes danced towards the director, then back to the group of men. 'Robes! There are Robes here … I didn't know that.'

'You cannot stop information, young lady. Information will go where it wants to go, although those men would stop it if they could. Yet you would like to keep that power from them, yes? I most humbly apologise if I have caused you any distress by pointing them out, but would you not prefer to know they are here?'

After a long moment, Hestean's tense eyes moved back to the director. Her expression changed. 'I think you have earned your directorship, Eloro Fife. You need wisdom to hold such a position, and you are right. It is better to know.'

The director coughed slightly with embarrassment and said, 'I believe it is customary to offer a gift on this day. It is a small gift, but it has brought me luck, so I hope it does you.' He bent closer and added quietly, 'I do apologise, my dear, but I have never liked those men, either.' He placed a small brooch in her hand and said, 'Wear it well. I despise them being in my city and approve of anything that can diminish them.' His gaze then moved to Bornn and Kuzzea. 'I must find a seat. I will see you both later, yes?'

'Director, what is your house?' asked Hestean.

Eloro noticed her finger rubbing across the tiny symbol engraved into the brooch he had given her. 'Counter to what my name suggests, I am of the fourth house, my child, as I believe you are.'

Hestean recalled the director's name, and for a moment she stared at the brooch. Then she looked up and found the College contingent again. 'I was wondering,' she said, 'if you would honour me? As you know, Bornn was going to officiate, but it worries him, as he is not of our house. I think that it would also annoy those men a little more, if officiating were to fall to you.'

The director followed Hestean's wandering gaze, and now he too considered the men of the College. 'It is a dangerous game you play, my child! Bravery is no match for knowledge.'

'Knowledge can be taught, Director. But as a friend once said to me, you need to be brave enough to use it, too!'

Eloro smiled. 'Are you truly trying to challenge me, child?' Then he said, 'It would be an honour. That is, if you really don't mind?' He then turned to Bornn, seeking his approval.

The sound of synchronised footsteps approached, interrupting Bornn's reply. They all turned to see the crowd parting as an arrowhead of Deserteers sprinted towards them. The fifteen pairs of boots came to a halt directly in front of Hestean. Out of breath, Petty said, 'Sorry we're late! We lost something and had to find it. It took a while.'

'What could be more important than being on time?' asked Hestean, glaring at him.

'You'll just have to wait and see, won't you? I must be getting old, though, because that was an exhausting run.'

'Not too old I hope?' said Hestean.

'Never too old, daughter, never too old. Just give me a moment and I'll be fine.'

'It was you that set the pace, Mister Petty!' said Karree, also breathing heavily.

19

The director and Hestean stood facing each other. Eloro's back was to the stone bench, which now held a mound of gifts as well as the objects of ceremony. In his left hand, he held the slice of Hestean's tree, and in his right, her scroll of banishment.

He looked into her eyes and said, 'I hold here this day the rings of age. I hold here this day an affirmation. Adding the affirmation to these rings, we have a circle of time—this time being nine of child and nine of adult-in-learning. This combination we hold to be true and without flaw. To become whole, we ask you now, Hestean Descee of Sharacan, to submit your life to its beginning. Is this your wish?'

Her scroll of banishment had been signed by Jarrak, the village chairman of Sharacan, and two witnesses on the evening that Hestean had been banished. Jarrak had had the chairman date the document, too, stating that she was considered dead, and that she was to be placed under Jarrak's rule from that date onwards. It also stated that, at that time, she was two cycles of the sun short of her eighteenth birthday. He had worded it well, for now that document affirmed she was still alive.

The additional words at the bottom of the scroll gave it its true strength, though. They invoked the Gods and held a wax impression of the symbol for the fourth great house, reading simply: '*Scoran Enn Sehth of Ure Godhood.*' Below these words was an unknown signature beside the blue-stamped impression of Hestean's house mark.

Hestean lifted her hands to hold the tree rings and scroll, and said, 'I, Hestean Descee of Sharacan, in sight of my rings, submit myself to the wholeness of my life. May I also survive its trials.' She paused for a moment, breathing in her strength, and then added, 'To ascend, I anoint my ascender.'

The director handed the scroll and the slice of birth-tree to Hestean, then turned to pick up a shiny red stone from the bench behind him.

As Hestean tucked the scroll and slice of tree into the waistbelt of her shadow dress, the director turned back to her, placing the glittering stone into her right palm.

Petty stepped forward from the group of Deserteers, and with great deliberateness, Hestean placed the polished stone into his hand. 'Trust in me, as I trust in you,' she said, before taking from her pocket a length of red ribbon. Together, Hestean and Petty wrapped the ribbon tightly around the stone, softening its hardness, forming it into a small, firm ball with the weight to fly through the air. When they'd finished, the ribbon fastened firmly, Petty stepped back to a mark that had been made on the grass. Hestean walked to another position where she awaited his onslaught.

Petty stood staring at her, unsure of what he was now about to do. It had been eight days over a full phasing of the moon since Hestean had first arrived at the Museum. Here, in this moment, she stood facing her adulthood in a way Petty could never have foreseen when he'd first met her. He knew she expected this of him, demanded it as her right. Her request had gone round and round in his head, and even now, her voice still lingered in his mind.

He no longer saw the girl he had first met in the desert. He knew Hestean still thirsted for the things she didn't know, but instead of a girl, he now saw a young woman who had taken control of her life. She was a woman who had emerged from under the thumb of the Black Robes, who had ruled over her youth. She was now about to show the world that she had replaced College law with something much older.

As he waited for her eyes to open, he studied her face, watching for the moment when she found the place of seeing. In this moment he faced the daughter who was not his, but who had claimed him as her father. By claiming him, she had given him a deep responsibility. The weight of the stone in his fingers dragged his hand to the ground.

* * *

Nine years had spun by since Hestean had last caught a stone thrown by an actual person. She wondered now if her hand would be quick enough. She stood with her eyes closed, her mind seeking. Would she be from this day forever dead, or could her hand still catch the wind?

In front of Petty, she stood at her mark. Her hands were by her sides, her eyes still closed. All around her the crowd of people stood silent. Time itself seemed to stand aside as she emptied her mind. To see before seeing was possible, she knew this. She had done it before. She cleared her mind to open the eye within.

For a long moment she stood silent and still as a pillar. When her eyes opened, Petty twirled his arm and threw. The stone blurred and Hestean fell suddenly backwards, hitting the ground hard.

With shocked horror, the crowd gasped. Bornn and Kuzzea rushed to her side as she stirred. The fog in her head began to clear as blood crept from her forehead. Slowly, she got to her knees and pushed Bornn and Kuzzea away.

Picking up the stone, she rose to her feet and threw it back to Petty. 'Again!'

Once more, she closed her eyes to let the stillness form in her mind, and once more, she opened her eyes. Again, the stone left Petty's hand, and again, Hestean hit the ground. Again, the crowd gasped. Bornn cried out too, this time, as if feeling the thud of her pain.

Once more, Hestean lay still and silent. *I will do this, I can do this, and I am going to do this*, she said to herself. The thought was stubborn in her head as she climbed to her feet.

Several more times, Petty threw the stone, which hit its mark faithfully, and by now blood was beginning to trickle down Hestean's face.

'I will do this!' she said, pushing Bornn and Kuzzea away again. 'I have to!'

* * *

Across the distance, Petty took in Hestean. Her closed eyes and the redness of her forehead haunted him. He could not do this again. He would end it this time. He knew that Hestean would never yield, and so he clasped his hand around his dagger and pulled it from its scabbard.

* * *

A moment later, Hestean's eyes opened, but instead of the stone she saw the glinting of the sun twirling towards her. With an instinct suddenly remembered, her hand rose to stop the dagger a finger's width from her head. Her body shook. The memory of her blood had defended her. This time, she stood upright, the dagger firmly held. She couldn't believe what she had just done. The red stone adorning the handle of

Petty's dagger glinted as she peered defiantly at the object that had almost killed her.

'By the gods! You could have killed me!' she said with a trembling voice. 'Why did you do this?'

'To bring you to life, daughter. You were too slow. You needed a reason to live. In ancient times, it would have been a dagger, anyway, as it is now with the sand-shadows.' said Petty. 'When confronted with death, some people are made stronger, and that's what this ritual is all about, is it not? No matter what the obstacle, it shows you can survive.'

'You are not of Sharacan, Petty!'

'No, daughter, I am not. But I am a Deserteer of the Kalcool's Sereye, and therefore it is my lore, too. I said to you once that we were family. The Deserteers of the Kalcool and the Sharacanese share a common beginning, as do all these people. You still have things to learn, daughter. So I took a chance and hoped it would be the correct one.'

* * *

Bornn, Kuzzea, Eloro, Sessam, and the whole of the crowd itself were in shock. No one could believe what they had just witnessed, and what Petty had just said. Instead of a stone, they had seen Hestean stop a Deserteer's blade. This was not what they had come to see. The power of the moment surged through them, seizing their bodies into stone.

At the back of the crowd, though, the robed men of the College were huddled. They saw history in what they had just watched, and maybe, too, the future.

Another pair of eyes also watched from amongst the crowd. The red-haired schoolteacher stood quietly in thought. She had come to see the ascension of a Sharacanese girl, who she now realised knew more than most. It was Hestean's dress the woman noticed, and in particular its clan markings. She had never come across someone from Sharacan before, but she knew their history.

* * *

Hestean's voice exploded into rage. 'You took a *chance*?' Her body was still shaking as she glared at Petty. Her fingers twirled the dagger, and suddenly it was in flight. She had learned aboard the *Merysands* the art of throwing as well as catching. But instead of simply catching the weapon, Petty twisted it through his fingers and sent it straight into its scabbard, a drop of blood dripping from his finger. 'Ah! You're not as good as you think, old man,' said Hestean.

'When a Deserteer's dagger is released from its scabbard, it must always draw blood, daughter! Consider this your first lesson.'

Hestean noticed the new stance of Petty's body. 'What do you mean, my first lesson?'

No longer steeled, she saw warmth returning to Petty's face. He almost smiled. 'You are not only whole now, daughter. You're now also as you were meant to be. A Deserteer!'

* * *

The crowd had started to whisper amongst themselves, although they hushed once more at Petty's words. They'd come to see a young Sharacanese woman ascend to adulthood, and were thrilled at a rite so dramatically and unexpectedly concluded. To a greater degree, though, most within the crowd had never seen a person from Sharacan nor even a Deserteer inducted, and they stood with new expectations.

Bornn looked on, too. But unlike the others, he saw a great, unstoppable wind gathering speed. He knew he was witnessing something that went beyond the beginnings of this morning, and wondered what was still to come. At his side, he clutched the parcel Hestean had given him to guard.

* * *

'I am no Deserteer,' said Hestean.

'This is true,' said Petty. 'Not quite, anyway.'

A slight movement of Petty's hand brought the other Deserteers filing past him to surround Hestean, obliterating her from everyone's vision. Before she knew what was happening, the woman she had been was gone. At first there was resistance and cries of indignation, but then silence fell within the knot of Deserteers. One of the Deserteers broke from the huddle for a moment to deposit Hestean's clothes at Kuzzea's feet, then re-joined the contingent. Kuzzea looked down at the clothes and grabbed Bornn's hand, stealing some of his strength for herself. She looked on, as did the rest of the crowd, wondering what was happening within the brewing cauldron of sand-yellow, tinged with a dash of red, and a little blue. Moments passed and the knotted tangle started to unravel, leaving one Deserteer alone at its centre.

* * *

The lone Deserteer stood, looking down at the clothes she now found herself wearing. First was the loose, airy, sand-coloured blouse that dropped to her thighs, bound at her waist by a long length of pale reddish cloth. Trousers, also sand-coloured, billowed out from under the blouse, ending just below her knees and tucked into cross-laced red boots. A cloak—the same colour as the trousers, with a red lining—draped over her shoulders. The hood of the cloak covered her head, held in place by a red and blue bandana. Only her face and hands were left uncovered.

What captivated the young Deserteer the most, though, was the dagger strapped to her side. She found herself caressing it, making sure it was real. She felt the incompleteness of its handle, and looked across to Petty for an explanation.

'That is where your stone goes,' he said, answering Hestean's unspoken question. He walked through the ring of Deserteers and placed the red stone, still stained with her blood, wrapped in the ribbon, into her hand.

'It was not my idea,' he said, acknowledging the circle of women and men surrounding them. 'It was theirs. Especially when they came to understand fully the society you had been living under. You impressed them with your beliefs, understanding, and skill. When you invited them to your ascension, they petitioned for your indoctrination into the Guild. Most Deserteers are born into it; very few are petitioned. You have them to thank. If you had not become whole, you would not have been offered this. It was not a gift, Hestean. You earned this today.'

Wiping away tears, Hestean lifted her arms to embrace Petty, then kissed his cheek. 'Thank you, Father,' she said into his ear. 'But if I had not become whole, I would be dead.'

'This is true. And I would be burying a daughter instead of embracing one.'

Hestean pulled back, smiling tearfully, and turned to the Deserteers around her. She rolled her hand from her forehead to her mouth to her heart and bowed to each, one after the other, acknowledging their gift. They in turn gestured with their hands and bowed.

When Hestean had thanked them all, Professor Bornn Sageling stepped through the circle, carrying the parcel Hestean had given him earlier. 'If this ritual is over, may we now continue with the first?' he asked, offering the package to Hestean.

'That is not part of my wholeness.'

'Normally no, but for you it was clearly meant to be,' said Bornn, and he read aloud the words written on the parcel: *'Eow Beon To Beon Hestean, Onpennian Einga On Eowr Beran Dag Of Negan Und Negan Und Naught Beforan, Maeg Thes Lf Beran Eow Ure Wyscans.* Is that not what it says?'

In the crowd, the schoolteacher caught his words in a gust of wind and strained her ears to hear more.

'You do not understand what that means,' said Hestean.

Bornn looked at her for a moment, then said, 'This is to be opened on your eighteenth birthday and not before; with it, may this life bring you our dreams.' He paused to let his words be understood, then added, 'Is that a good enough translation?'

'Close enough!' said Hestean, looking at the parcel whose origin still bothered her. 'Why does it scare me?' she asked both Petty and Bornn.

'It doesn't scare you,' said Petty. 'It is old, quite old. It is from a past that has become known to you. It is a past, the truth of which you have not been told. It is knowledge, and knowledge is not to be feared. It can hurt at times, but knowledge also makes you free. This is what scares you. Your actual birthday was yesterday, so it is already yours.'

Hestean was quiet as she considered the parcel anew, along with his words. Then, raising her head toward Petty and Bornn, she said, 'I am a water-girl! A water-girl who became a field technician. A field technician who has found herself at the grandest centre of knowledge ever. I have just become whole, and am the first woman of my tribe in two hundred years to do so. I have become part of the Guild. I have a family again. Just when I think I know who I am, I become someone else. Who will I be if I open this parcel?'

'You will be who you were meant to be, daughter,' said Petty. 'You are that person already. Someone out there believes this to be so, or they would not have given you their trust. You have told me that since the day you were born, you have wanted always to know, and that is what sets you apart. Now that you have found you can learn, you cannot stand not knowing, can you?'

'He is right,' said Bornn. 'It is what drives you. You have jumped through life as if catching up with yourself. Maybe this will show you who you are. Or maybe it will show you the path you are already on. Either way, this was meant for you. Don't disappoint their trust, for I have seen you to be better than that!'

'I hate the both of you, you know that, don't you?' said Hestean, a freeing buoyancy building within her. 'You know me too well.'

'Not that well,' said Bornn, a small smile enlivening his face. 'What I know about you I knew long before you came to me. Jarrak is the one who knows you. In his letters, he painted a picture with incredible insight. He wanted me to send him a field technician, did you know that? After reading his letters, I told him to stop being silly and to use the one he already had. He is the one who knows you. He knows you better than he thinks.'

'So why is he not here? Of all the people I asked, it was him I wanted here. I owe him my life. He set me free.'

'It is a long way to Sharacan, my child, both in time and distance. Maybe he first needs to know himself as well as he knows you. Maybe he knows this is your day. A day in which you need to find yourself without him.'

Hestean looked at Bornn, studying him for a moment. 'Jarrak told me about you, too, Professor. You have a way of seeing the truth of things.' She reached for the parcel in his hands and undid the binding securing its outer covering. She then unfolded the hard leather wrapping and found, still covering the treasure, an aged cloth that disintegrated under her touch. She gasped in surprise, having broken apart the cocoon. The larger of the two objects gleamed back at her. For the first time since its entombment, the object's coating of blue and white jewels glittered freely. Nervously, not knowing what else to do, Hestean began to giggle. 'Petty,' she said. 'How many daggers does a girl need when she becomes a Deserteer?'

* * *

Petty's throat dried at the sight of the dagger, and he recalled a particular moment in every Deserteer's life; a moment when every Deserteer ascended, and the red bandana of youth was replaced by one striped both red and blue. Every Deserteer learned, too, to recite a rhyme, an oath, that would never hold meaning for most. Here and now, it suddenly did. 'Daughter,' he said. 'This is not a Deserteer's dagger.'

'No,' agreed Bornn, as he gazed at the weapon, and the blue stone that adorned the end of the dagger's handle. It held the engraved symbol of the Fourth House, Hestean's house. He now realised the connection between the parcel, and this moment.

'It's not?' said Hestean. 'It looks the same, except for the colour and the extra decoration.'

'It is one of a set of six,' said Bornn, somewhat reluctantly. 'In the tellings, there have only ever been six. The stories also hint that there is one that has been missing. It seems it has been entrusted to you.'

'You have been inducted as a guardian to the gods, daughter,' said Petty. 'For this is no gift. This is an inheritance. It is yours alone to hold. It is Comcree.'

* * *

A ripple of sound swept through the crowd. At the back, the line of Black Robes huddled closer together. The schoolteacher saw that beneath their diplomatic robes, they were all wearing battle dress. She watched as they hurried from sight. All but one, that is, who stayed to watch and observe. The crowd's whisper had caught her unawares, and as she wondered what to do, she found her thoughts fraying.

The Deserteers from the *Merysands*, knowing now what Hestean held in her hand, took the lead from their first officer. Petty knelt and placed his hand to his dagger. With one voice, they spoke the oath they all knew but had thought never to proclaim. It was fate that had chosen them this day. Without hesitation, their outspoken words heralded their own transformation from mere Deserteers into a protectorate of sand-shadows.

'Hlaford, I protect.

'As thou protect.

'As thine dagger unsheathed.

'We do thy bidding.'

And without faltering, they filled in the blankness of the last line. *'Hestean Descee of Sharacan and the Comcree.'*

It was the dagger which gave authority, and it was the person they now pledged themselves to. Not all the Deserteers were of Hestean's house, but with this pledge, they transcended their own house loyalties. In this one moment, they became part of the Guild's very centre, where all the houses melded together as one entity. They would not only wear their own house insignia, but that of Hestean's. There would be one more insignia, too; the infinity insignia of the gods. Their red and blue bandanas would be replaced with ones of pure blue, indicating that they were now part of a Deserteer protectorate.

Petty got to his feet, as did the other Deserteers. Unlike Petty, they turned from Hestean, thrusting their cloaks back over their shoulders to reveal their daggers. As if rehearsed to precision, they backed in towards Hestean, their circle diminishing until they stood firm, shoulder to shoulder.

'You are not just one of the Guild any more daughter,' said Petty. 'You are now part of its very construct. These Deserteers, from this day forward, are not only your friends, but also your guardians. They will protect you with their lives. Having found you, we will not lose you again.'

Confusion reigned within Hestean. The Guild, daggers, Comcree, the gods … 'Having found me? Who do you think I am?'

'He means Andreena,' said Bornn. 'You are her successor. One of the stories I have been chasing tells us that for two hundred years, the Comcree hexagon has been incomplete. With you, it may just have become whole again. Most thought the Comcree a myth, but it is a myth I have been researching most of my life. It seems today has just proved a lifetime of thought to be true.' He looked up to where only one Black Robe still stood, and said, 'If it has, there will be consequences. You should go with Petty! You have much to learn, as do we, child, so go. Go and be safe while we find your home, or more likely, until your home finds you. Where there is one, there will be the rest of the Comcree, also.'

'I am no child,' said Hestean, in the most grown-up voice she could muster.

'For the moment, you are as much a child as we are!' said Bornn. 'So go!'

Fear was building in him, and he knew it showed. A moment later, Hestean leaned forward to kiss his cheek and whispered, 'I will not be a child again for very long, Professor.' Bornn smiled at her gathering strength.

She stepped back and brought her hand to her forehead, then her mouth, then her heart, nodding to her most recent mentor. She looked again at the dagger, bridled by its intricately patterned scabbard and belting, feeling its power, contained but not diminished. It knew who she was. She could feel it. So, she turned to Petty and said, 'Where do we go?'

'We need time, while the truth finds us,' said Petty. 'The *Merysands*—you'll be safe there. The landing field is under the preserve of the Guild, and controlled by Deserteers. It is a refuge with a point of withdrawal if need be.'

'The last of the Robes has just gone, child,' said Bornn.

Her eyes rose up to where the Robes had been, as her protectorate formed a wedge around her and began to drive a path through the crowd. As she started to move, instinct encouraged her to grab the second object from the parcel. Falling to the ground, the wrapping was now empty.

* * *

Emerging from behind the protectorate, Bornn stood watching. In an instant, Hestean was gone.

'What does this mean, my love?' asked Kuzzea, coming to Bornn's side.

He reached out and pulled her closer to him, feeling her solidity. With uncertainty and wonder, he said, 'It would appear, my dear, that we have been hosting an apparition.'

'A ghost, you mean?'

'Yes, my dear, a ghost! Jarrak has spent the last two years looking for Andreena, and now it seems she was closer than we thought. It would seem that Hestean is the Comcree Andreena's direct descendant, anointed from the grave by the ancestor herself in front of us all. Can you believe it? It seems that what I have been striving to uncover has just made itself very visible.'

Bornn pulled Kuzzea closer still. From the depths of the desert, this had been planned as a warning to the College, to show everyone that the Comcree had returned. The Comcree were now once more amongst them, again a force in this world.

'It is a day I will tell my grandchildren of,' said Kuzzea, and Bornn's eyes rolled towards her. Kuzzea raised her hand to grasp his. Turning to face him, she said, 'I will always have hopes. If it is not to be her, then Jarrak will find someone else, I am sure.'

* * *

The schoolteacher, having watched the last of the Black Robes hurry off, did what she should have done moments earlier. She, too, began to move. But unlike the Deserteers, for whom the crowd parted without any resistance, she had to push her way through. By the time she reached the edge of the crowd, the Deserteers were already gone. This time, without any hesitation, she began to run quickly towards the Great Maze.

20

At the steady pace of the Deserteers, Hestean and her protectorate had covered quite a distance in the short time they had been running.

Cautious when running into the unknown, Petty took them first south along the old streets that hugged the base of the escarpment. Even here, though, instead of a more obvious route, he took them along the pioneer road that twisted and turned between small, aged buildings. These had once housed the workers who'd constructed the beginnings of Elora-Bearer. If the Black Robes of the College were attempting to follow, he told Hestean that it might look as if the protectorate were setting out for Sheer-Top, instead of the relative closeness of the sky-ship landing field.

Around them, this oldest part of Elora-Bearer was built from the same grey stone as the Grand Museum and the rest of the city. However, this stone was roughly cut and lacked the fine workmanship for which the city was renowned. There had been no planning here. This part of the city had grown organically, as men and women had poured into the area to help build the memorial. Hestean could feel these buildings telling their story; the same story Sessam had told her. From the outset, the main part of this city was designed to reflect the enlightenment that the Comcree brought to this world. Here, within these streets, for the people who made this enlightenment possible, it had been much more personal. Elora Sara-Hassis had been someone who needed to be remembered. It was in the stronghold of her valley, the Hassis Valley, that the Alliance had eventually found a way to surge forth and contain the stifling College.

When Hestean felt her body urging to stop, her mind would not allow it. She fought against the pain in her lungs and thighs by sheer will alone, forcing her body into a state of endurance. Even though she had become more than just a Deserteer, she was beginning to think of herself as truly one of them.

Keeping her in their centre, her protectorate rounded one bend after another, never letting up their pace. She had no true knowledge of who they were running from; until today, she hadn't even known the College had a presence in the city. But if the Deserteers thought there was danger, then she would trust them. She was concentrating now just on moving.

Then, as they rounded a sharp bend to the left, she almost ran into the Deserteer in front of her as the entire protectorate abruptly came to a halt.

From within the shadow of a batter-palm, a single, shimmering figure blocked their path. The apparition wore a bluish-green dress that clung to her upper body, then draped seamlessly and loosely to the ground, its silken fabric fluttered in an unseen breeze. The woman's stance demanded attention. She had been beautiful once and still was, thought Hestean, although now her face held the lines of age and wisdom. The woman's red hair flared around her, further defining her tall form. Through her glowing aura, the woman's eyes glistened the same colour as her dress, and Hestean wondered if they might be the same unusual green as her own.

She knew this woman. She had met her before. But if she had, surely she should remember where. A woman who demanded this much attention could never be forgotten.

* * *

The woman knew these Deserteers had never seen such an image before, and she transfixed them with her penetrating gaze. She needed to. There could be no mistakes in this moment. 'Do you still have her?' she asked.

The Deserteers braced themselves, firming up their stance. Petty flung back his cloak, revealing his dagger. Immediately, the other Deserteers mimicked his movement. Inwardly, the ghostly figure smiled, recognising the determination she had hoped to find. Slowly, she removed an orange scarf from her waist. The Deserteers of Hestean's protectorate saw a blue-and-white jewelled dagger bridled as the signature of a true Comcree warrior.

The woman heard the word "Elora" whispered from within the Protectorate of Deserteers, and a smile spread fleetingly across her face. She now demanded more forcefully, 'Do you have our sister, or do you not?'

Petty stepped forward with his hand around his dagger. Without mentioning a name, he said, 'We have within us our charge. Is this who you mean?'

Upon hearing his careful words, the woman allowed her satisfaction to show. She smiled again, more fully this time, then said, 'Does she have the earpiece?'

Petty looked to Hestean. 'Do you know what she means, daughter?'

Hestean was still breathing heavily from the run, but she stepped forward from the group. She presented her matching jewelled dagger, still in its scabbard, to the woman. She then lifted her other arm, opening her clenched fist to display a small hexagon-shaped brooch.

'Open the brooch,' instructed the woman. After pushing the scabbarded dagger carefully into her waist-belt, Hestean examined the brooch. Finding a small latch, she used her thumb to click it open before again presenting it to the woman. 'You must put them on,' said the woman. 'The brooch just above your left breast, the dagger to the left of your waist, and the earpiece in your left ear with the red tip outwards. You must do it now.'

With that said, her apparition vanished, leaving the way ahead clear once more.

Petty walked forward to where the woman had been. Finding nothing, he walked back to Hestean, then lifted her hand to look at the brooch and the object it contained.

'It was in the parcel with the dagger,' said Hestean. 'Until she spoke of it, I had no idea what it was. It's important, isn't it? It has to be. It was with the dagger.'

'It's tiny,' said Petty looking at the thimble-like object. 'Looks almost new.'

'The brooch and the dagger both looked old when I took them from the parcel, but they seem to have rejuvenated in my hands,' said Hestean.

Petty looked back to where the woman had been, and said, 'Do as she said, daughter. You should put them on, I think.'

'Do you think it's a communicator? It's much smaller than the one I used at the dig.'

'I don't think the Comcree would be playing games right now, so you should do as she wants. As you said, it's important.'

'Is that truly who you think she was?'

'Don't you?'

Hestean looked at him. Then, looking at the small object within the brooch, she removed it to study it further. With her breathing now calmer, she used her right hand to push the object into the cavity of her left ear. As she did, she unknowingly depressed the minute red button on its outer edge, and the tiny thimble bit into her skin.

'*Ahhhhhhhh,*' she cried, as she fell to her knees in extreme pain. Then, almost as quickly as it began, the pain dissipated, diminishing to such a degree that she had no sense of the earpiece at all. Seeing the concern on the faces of her protectorate, still cupping her ear, she rose and straightened. She pinned the brooch on, but before attempting to strap the dagger to her waist, she stilled herself to listen for a moment. 'I don't hear anything!' she said.

'That's because no one is saying anything, sister! But you do hear me now, don't you?' said a voice from within her mind.

'Yes ... Yes, I do!'

'Not quite what you expected,' said the amused female voice.

'It stung me!'

'They always do! It is now a part of you. It will never leave your body until the day you die.'

Hestean could almost see an image of the woman in her mind now. She asked, 'Why did you disappear?'

'To vision someone takes a lot of energy.' said the woman.

'The earpiece is tiny …'

'Did you know it was a communicator?'

'I have used something similar before, but not so small.'

'Similar it may be, but it is not the same,' said the woman. 'You move fast, which is good, but another two marces and we would have lost you. With the earpiece in place, we will never lose you again. You are one of us now!'

The woman let the statement sink in before giving Hestean her first lesson. 'Everyone is the maker of their own destiny, sister,' she said, 'but we suggest that you now come back.'

'Come back to where?'

'To the Museum. Its southern garden.'

'We were just there.'

'I know, you ran straight past me before I could get out of the crowd. It took me until now to find you. Your Mister Petty has good instincts.'

'You know him?'

'No, I was in the crowd, but you surprised us.'

'I surprised myself.'

'I am Gorean Dowee of the Hub-Comcree,' said the woman, 'and you are our missing sister, it would seem—Hestean Descee, formerly of Sharacan.'

'Formerly? What do you mean "formerly"?'

'Formerly, yes. You have a larger family now; you are Comcree. There is no turning back from this, Hestean, for the earpiece has chosen you, and so has the dagger and the brooch. They are all a part of you now.'

The woman's words whirled in Hestean's mind as she began to realise just who she had become. Finally, she said, 'Why me? I am no one.'

'You are indeed very much someone, or the earpiece would not have chosen you. They do not make mistakes, Hestean Descee. You are of the old blood, with a direct line that travels back through your house to the time of beginning. That is who the Comcree are. We are the beginning, and we are the end.'

'What does that mean?'

'It means that it is up to you, to be who you are! Now, you should meet the rest of your new family, don't you think?'

'Perhaps one should know one's family, as you seem to already know me?'

'You and I have introduced ourselves once before, Hestean Descee. I didn't know who you were, though, and my young students took precedence.'

The image of a tall, red-haired schoolteacher came flooding back into Hestean's mind, and she said, 'That's who you are! I knew that I'd met you somewhere.'

'I should have guessed, then, when I saw you,' said Gorean. 'I should have seen it when you showed courtesy, but I didn't. It's my fault you are now running from the College, for it should not have been this way.'

'That's not the truth of things,' said Hestean. 'This was meant to happen just the way it has. I am beginning to think that if you were meant to know, then you would have. Sharacan did this to me, not you!'

'You may be right,' said Gorean. 'Even we are not fully aware of what is in the mind of the Danannee.'

'Then they really do exist?'

'Oh, yes,' said Gorean with a laugh. 'And they are quite annoying at times, too.'

'Are you allowed to mock the Gods?'

'Understanding is not mockery, Hestean Descee!'

'I see.'

'Do you?'

'I don't know!'

'Good answer, Hestean Descee. But you will. You will learn to see this world very clearly.'

'Then I suppose we should head back. But what of the Robes?'

'I see no sign of the College,' Gorean said. 'If they are looking, then they are looking in the wrong place. It will likely take them a while to fully understand this day. Their hierarchical dogma stifles their agility at times. You have surprised them, as you have us. While you were still just a Sharacanese woman who dared to stand against them, they would have had no hesitation in taking your life. When you became a Deserteer, all that changed. To harm a Deserteer for anything other than a breach of treaty would defy the Treaty of Truce. And now, as one of the Comcree, the ramifications of who you are will be profound.'

'I see,' said Hestean. 'You said before that you were looking in the wrong place for me?'

'Your Mister Petty has good instincts, sister. You have chosen well.'

Hestean turned to look at Petty, who stood listening to her half-audible conversation. In a whispered voice, she said, 'I think we chose each other.' Today, Petty's and Hestean's placements had switched. The one who had lead was now to follow. Turning, Hestean began to walk back through the protectorate, back towards the Museum and another future. 'Come,' she said to the Deserteers. 'We go this way now.'

'Hestean?' said Petty. He rarely called her that anymore. She had become his responsibility, his charge, and in that moment, she knew he had sensed a change.

No longer the woman she had been, she said, 'This is the way for all of us, so come. Together we will find our future.' Hestean picked up into a slow run, and Karree immediately fell into pace beside her. In doing so, the loadmaster cemented herself in a position she would hold for the rest of her life.

* * *

The others turned, too, leaving Petty stranded and alone with his thoughts.

At forty-nine, he had lived a good life, an exciting life, and he had been looking forward to spending the last of his working days as the first officer aboard a sky-ship. It seemed now that the gods had other plans for him. He watched the others for a moment longer, resigning himself to what lay ahead, then pulled his feet forward into a run.

Karree was running to Hestean's right, shadowing her every move. When Petty caught up, she switched to Hestean's left, to allow Petty the favoured position beside the newly risen Comcree, who still wore the clothes of a Deserteer.

'Here, hold this,' said Hestean, handing the Comcree dagger to Petty as she ran. She undid the Deserteer's dagger from her waist and re-buckled it, this time on her right side. She held out her hand to Petty, and he handed back the Comcree dagger. She looked quickly at its scabbard and belting, then brought it to her left, where she buckled it firmly into place. Bridled, just as Gorean's had been. 'That's better, don't you think?' she said.

From the corner of his eye, Petty looked across at her and said, 'Only this road will tell us that, Hlaford. Only this road will tell us that.'

Hestean looked to him, acknowledging his honouring word, then reached across to grasp his hand. They ran on, Petty to her right and Karree to her left, the rest of the protectorate also shadowing her.

21

Just inside the entrance to the southern garden, they slowed to a walk, allowing their vigour to quieten. Hestean released Petty's hand, then walked ahead into the middle of the garden. She turned towards the maze and said, 'Now what?'

'Within the maze, starting with your dagger, you must follow your steps—left-right, left-right, left-right, then enter into the house of us all,' said Gorean's voice in her mind.

The walls of the maze were tall and stony, their greyness long decorated by a rich mosaic of red-and-yellow lichen and thick green creepers. Hestean knew that, guarded within these walls, hidden retreats were spaced out where scholars and students could study quietly, or lovers could meet for secluded passions. She knew now that she had just been told the way to its greatest secret. 'Come,' she said, addressing her protectorate.

Once inside the entrance, she turned first to her left, then took the next opening to her right. She followed the zigzag until it branched, and she turned left once more. As she walked, Gorean gave her more instruction about what she would find, and what she must do when they reached their destination. At the next junction, she turned right, then once again turned left. As she turned right for the last time, she came into a small courtyard against the wall of the Museum itself. A long stone bench sat in the middle of the square. Along each side of the bench were six stone stools. She studied the enclosure. Along the back wall, she found what she was looking for; seven free-standing monoliths, each inscribed with a house mark, except for the middle stone, which instead held the six-sided polygon to bind them all.

'This way,' she said, 'and do exactly as I do.'

She walked around the bench to the far wall, and paused in front of the central monolith. Then she stepped behind it. Her protectorate followed, and one by one they vanished from the everyday world.

In the hidden room behind the stone, Hestean turned to watch the others materialise. Not knowing what to expect, each Deserteer came through with their hand upon their dagger. Petty was the last, having made sure no one had followed or been left behind.

It was only then that Hestean allowed herself to marvel at what she had just done. She recalled watching her hand rise to the set of house marks on the wall behind the monolith, where she touched the mark of her own house. She remembered Gorean's voice in her ear, saying "gently now", as she lowered her arm and slowly pushed it into the stone itself. She had walked forward in amazed silence as the wall swallowed her.

After pushing his hand slowly into the wall, Petty had backed through the veil, and now stood looking at the wall from the inside. He poked his finger into the illusion and watched it disappear.

Standing beside him, Hestean also poked the wall. 'What do you make of this, Father?'

'It is indeed of the gods, I hope,' said Petty. His other hand grasped more firmly the handle of his dagger.

* * *

Karree and one of the other Deserteers were the only two who saw Gorean quietly come into view at the other end of the room. The Comcree warrior put her finger to her mouth as a sign to be silent, before nodding to them both in turn, acknowledging their alertness. Karree then watched closely, her hand still on her dagger, as the warrior turned her attention towards Hestean and Petty, who were still examining the wall. 'The curtain was a gift from our ancestors,' explained the warrior, causing Hestean and the rest of the Protectorate to turn as one towards her. Even as they recognised the familiar figure standing in her corporeal form, none of them lessened the grip on their daggers. Gorean noted this, and grinned slightly.

'The first Comcree,' she said, 'who dwelt in Sharacan before their descendants moved to the Sereye, were our direct ancestors.' She walked towards Petty and Hestean. Her dress no longer wafted in an unfelt breeze, but seemed almost a part of her body. Karree had the distinct impression that if the warrior wanted to, she could immobilise the whole protectorate without being harmed. She was the Guild at its most potent. 'Hit the curtain hard with your fist, Mister Petty,' suggested the warrior.

Still grasping his dagger, Petty's eyes captured the warrior's. His gaze didn't leave hers as he flung his free hand back against the wall. His fist hit hard, stopped by an unexpected and painful solidity. He turned back to the wall, questioning.

'It reacts with equal force to that imposed upon it. But if you are gentle, it will offer up its reward. I am Gorean,' she said, putting out her hand to gently touch the same spot Petty's fist had hit. It passed through as if it had touched nothing at all. Even to her, it was still a wonder. She'd lost count of how many times she'd stepped through this veil. She then reached up to where another set of house marks had been carved into the wall. The blue stone at the end of her Comcree dagger flashed, as Hestean's had, unnoticed by anyone. She turned to Hestean and said, 'You must always switch the gateway off again.'

'Who were the Sereye Comcree?' asked Petty.

'The Comcree sought shelter in the Sereye after leaving Sharacan centuries ago, but the catastrophe there brought the Comcree here to the Hassis.'

'The great upheaval,' said Petty.

'Exactly,' said Gorean. 'As a sanctuary, this world is not ideal, but then maybe that is why we survive here.'

'But the Hassis is no more, either?' stated Petty.

'The Hassis is more than a cascade, Mister Petty! It is more than just a mere waterfall. The once overflowing river of the Hassis may no longer hold water, the valley's fertile fields may no longer blossom, but the Hassis still exists as it truly was, I can assure you.' said Gorean. She glanced again towards Hestean, studying her more closely. 'You look like her,' she said.

'Like who?'

'Like the woman who last wore that dagger!' Gorean noticed the other dagger hanging at Hestean's waist, and added, 'Are you expecting a war?'

'I have become a Deserteer and Comcree on the same day, so I will honour them both,' said Hestean.

'Silly girl! Have you not worked it out yet? The Comcree *are* Deserteers, just as the Deserteers are Comcree. We all come from the same place, have the same heritage. We are two fingers on the same hand, and we all come from you. You are our genesis!'

'I don't understand.'

'No, but I think you will one day.'

Most of the Deserteers had gathered closer, paying attention to Gorean's words about the Comcree and the Deserteers. Astounding them even more, though, were Gorean's comments about Hestean as their inception.

'How can I be your beginning? I don't know what you mean,' said Hestean, studying Gorean. 'Aren't there four fingers on a hand, not just two?'

The older woman smiled, wondering how much this young woman really did know. 'There is also an opposing thumb,' said Gorean. 'Come, Dan wants to see you. You are one of us now, even if you are too young. But we cannot change that now!'

'I'm not young. I'm eighteen. I am an adult,' stated Hestean.

'I mean in your mind, Hestean. Most of us have spent years becoming who we are, you've had it thrust upon you. You still have a lot to learn.'

Gorean turned and began walking towards the open passageway leading from the room. Unseen, her smile became thoughtful. 'Keep the two daggers—they suit you,' she said.

The passageway was long and tunnel-like. Catching up with Gorean, Hestean said, 'Who's Dan? Is he one of the Comcree, also?'

'No. Dan is … Dan is just Dan. For a very long time now, he has been just Dan. You will know what I mean when you meet him. If he likes you, you will know that too.'

* * *

The two women continued side-by-side down the passageway, followed by Petty and Karree and the other Deserteers. Hestean's head filled with more questions, but before she had gathered her thoughts sufficiently enough to ask any, their small procession reached a closed door to their left. The passageway continued on, but Gorean stopped here and held out her hand. 'Your Comcree dagger. Use it there.'

Hestean looked to the slot beside the door, then glanced at Gorean.

'Slide its blade into the slot,' prompted Gorean.

Hestean did as she was told, drawing out her dagger and inserting it into the wall. The end of the handle flashed brightly, and the door slid open to reveal a small room. Hestean glanced up at a restricted entry sign, which she had only just noticed above the door's frame, and then looked towards Gorean.

The older woman grinned at her knowingly, and said, 'I still remember the first time my dagger opened a door for me. Yours, too, will take you to places few others are allowed to go. Use it with care, though. Everything must be done with care here. Unless accompanied by an authorising dagger, no one can enter this elevator. It will take you up to see Dan.'

The door revealed a space lavishly decorated with two upholstered bench-seats. On the far wall, below a painting, were three actuator buttons, which Gorean pointed to.

'They tell their own story,' she said.

The painting above them was of the deep desert, and in a way, it seemed like a window into the very essence of Hestean's homeland. She found herself staring at the image.

'The ride will take a while,' said Gorean, drawing Hestean back. 'You may like to sit. When you get to the top, just follow the yellow line. You will find Dan at the end of it.'

'You're not coming?'

'No. Dan wants to see you alone. He has some questions for you. You have intrigued him, I think! Besides, I have to outfit your protectorate. Red is no longer their colour.'

'Did you know anything of this?' said Hestean, looking at Petty.

'Not until now! Until this morning, the Comcree were but a myth. This is as new to me as it is to you.'

Hestean, unsure about this separation, turned to enter the elevator. She pushed the upward button and took one last look at her companions. Not since the first day she'd arrived in Elora-Bearer had she felt so alone.

As the elevator door closed, Gorean said, 'The rules have been broken before. You are not the first. It must be a trait within your family's line, so smile.'

The lift jolted as it started to slowly ascend, and Hestean reached out a hand, touching the wall to steady herself. Sitting down, she studied the little room again. What had Gorean's last words meant exactly? The dagger was at her side, and the brooch and earpiece were fastened to her body and clothes. For the first time since that morning, she had time to wonder who in her village had given them to her, and who had thought her worthy enough to hold them. Had they actually known what was in the parcel? Just when she thought she was beginning to know who she was, she became someone else with a completely different history. 'Is this who I really am, or is there still more?' she asked herself.

Gorean had said she was the beginning. The elevator shuddered slightly, and she again put out her hand, touching the wall not only to steady her body, but to steady her nerve.

22

The elevator door opened. Hestean found herself looking out into a long and almost empty room, carved from solid stone. Along the wall to her right, small windows let in the brilliance of early afternoon. To her left, through a broad archway, stairs could be seen descending from above. At the far end of the room, two huge doors—each at least five paces wide—reached up to the ceiling. What really captured her attention, though, was the thing hovering in the middle of the room, between six kneeling metal figures atop a hexagon-shaped box. It was a small ball of light, illuminating the entire space with a brightness greater than the light outside.

After a long moment of wonder, Hestean broke her gaze free and stepped from the elevator. She saw the yellow line Gorean had told her to follow. She scanned the room, listening, but the only thing she heard was the sound of her own footsteps. 'Is anyone here?' she asked, her words echoing around the room. 'Gorean sent me.'

There was no reply. She turned to follow the yellow line.

In front of the stairs, she stopped, tracing their spiral up and round to the left. She continued past as she followed the yellow line. She studied the illuminated statues in more detail. The kneeling figures, arms outstretched, seemed to be holding the glowing ball aloft. She could see that three of the statues were female, the other three male. From the elevator, it had looked as though the statues were paying homage to the light, although now she saw that the palms of their hands were actually supporting it, even though they never touched the ball.

Just past the statues and glowing ball, the yellow line turned and ducked under a door she hadn't seen from the elevator. She stood in front of it for a moment before knocking. When no one answered, she knocked again, then waited some more. Above the door, too high for her to see through, was a window. The room on the other side was lit with the same soft glow as this one. She knocked again, although this time, when no one answered, she opened the door just enough to peer inside. 'Is anyone there? Gorean sent me.' She let the door open further.

The room was spotlessly clean. At the far end stood some sort of machine. There was another hexagonal object in the middle of the room, although this one stood as a table, attached to the floor by a thick central column. Surrounding the table were six lavishly upholstered chairs, also fixed to the floor by central columns. Through the long narrow window connecting the rooms, diffused light was reflected by the ceiling, sending it into every corner.

She entered, hoping she wasn't breaking some unknown taboo, and said, 'Is anyone here? I am Hestean Descee. Dan wanted to see me, and I was told to follow the yellow line.'

There was still no response, so she closed the door behind her to walk slowly around the room. She stopped in front of another feature, attached to one of the walls. It was a framed rectangle about a pace and a half in length, which reflected the room and herself. But unlike a mirror, the image didn't change as her point-of-view changed. It was more like a painting that displayed movement. This intrigued her for a while, but then she walked on to observe everything else. She pondered the why of it all.

Finally, she took a step closer to the table. As she did, a small light came on in the middle of its upper surface. She took a step back and the light went out.

Stepping forward, the light came on again. She seated herself on one of the chairs and spun around to face the table. The middle of the tabletop sloped up to form a six-sided pyramid. On the side facing her sat the illuminated light, below which a small, narrow, diamond-shaped slit was visible. The other faces of the pyramid had lights, too, but none were glowing. She shifted in the chair and looked across to the door, wondering how long she would have to wait for this Dan. She touched her earpiece, and an image of her inserting her dagger into the wall when she had entered the elevator flashed through her head. She looked again to the centre of the table.

Reaching to her waist, she pulled her Comcree dagger from its scabbard and lifted it towards the pyramid. Gently, she slipped it down into the slot, and as the dagger's handle touched the surface, the light went out and the blue crystal at the dagger's end began to glow.

'By the gods,' she exclaimed quietly to herself. She lifted the dagger out, then pushed it in once more. She watched the glowing end of its hilt first extinguish and then light up. She did it for a second time, and then sat back down, leaving the dagger in place as she surveyed the room.

'It was you that did it, not the gods!' said a voice.

Hestean jumped to her feet and spun around but saw no one. She froze. Searching the room more thoroughly with her eyes, and listening for the slightest of sounds, her attention finally landed on the machine at the back of the room.

Not quite believing the thought, she asked, 'Are you Dan?'

'I am, yes!'

'But you're some sort of machine!'

'I am that, too, yes! But to be more precise, I am the DANANNEE.'

'You're the gods!' said Hestean, stepping back a pace.

'No,' replied the machine. '*You* are the gods. You are the people, and you have your own destiny. Destiny must be free to make its own decisions. All I can ever hope to do is guide those decisions. I just help out from time to time, you could say, as you yourself will also do from now on.'

'If not the gods, what are you, then?'

'It was Andree who first called me Dan,' said the machine. 'I prefer it! After all, that is what I am. I'm the Data Assisting Nucleus. I am knowledge. The rest of my designation stands for what I was created for, but have never had the chance to do. Your enemies tried to destroy me at the same time as they tried to destroy you, so now I am just Dan. One should always know who one is, don't you think?'

'At this moment, knowing who I am is still a work in progress,' said Hestean, dryly.

'Yes! You talk like her,' said the machine. 'You have her complexion, too, and you have her dagger. But you are not her, are you?'

Continuing after only a momentary pause, the machine said, 'You all only live for such a short time! Only I get to see you come, to see you go, to see you grow old, and to see you become the person you were meant to be.' The machine paused again before saying, 'I'm the one that sees if the person you become is the person your parents and grandparents would have wanted you to be. Her, I did not get to see grow old, and I would like to know why.'

'You mean Andreena?'

'Yes. You have the dagger and earpiece that were last hers. She was a scoundrel, but I have always liked scoundrels. In fact, they were both scoundrels in their own way.'

'Both? Who are you talking about now?'

'Andree and Elora, of course,' said the machine. 'You could never have one without the other! Are you a scoundrel, too, Hestean?'

'There are some who would have a tendency to think so!'

'Good ... Then I shall like you, too.'

'You really liked this Andreena, by the sound of it.'

'She was one of my mothers. I had four mothers and two fathers who brought me back to life here at the Hassis. Normally, as you know, the Comcree should consist of three females and three males. At the time of her existence, they were in a state of complete rebirth. It's rare, but it does happen. She was one of the youngest, but one of the best, too. I know what became of the others, but I do not know what became of Andreena. Do you know?'

'Me! How would I know?'

'You have her dagger.'

'It was a gifting,' said Hestean. 'On the day I became whole, which was today! I turned eighteen yesterday. It was given to me, but I don't exactly know by whom.'

'I see!'

The conversation meandered for a little, before circling to arrive back at the same place. Hestean found herself warming to the machine. She rested herself against the edge of the table, then folded her arms loosely in front of her.

Once again the machine asked, 'Do you think you should find out who gave the dagger to you? The dagger has a story to tell. A story you were meant to know, that Andreena wanted you to know. Know this, and you will know what you are and who you are. You will also discover what happened to her.'

'Do you always talk in circles?'

'It is a good way to have a conversation,' said the machine. 'One discovers things that way. It is hard to repeat a lie twice in the same way.'

'I think you're the scoundrel,' said Hestean.

'One learns from one's parents,' said the machine.

Hestean's mind drifted for a moment, seeing her own mother in a way she had never seen her before. She remembered things that were done and said that had held no significance until now. She smiled with newly found gratitude. 'I guess we do,' she laughed.

'You understand, don't you, that the dagger gives you the right to sit at that table? You are the true succession.'

'I know nothing of this,' said Hestean, pushing herself up.

'This is true. You have had no apprenticeship, but nor had Andree when she first came to this place. She learned, and so shall you. She knew only the tellings, as do you. You have her mind—I see that! I see also that you were chosen with thought.'

'*Can* you see?'

A ridiculously distorted image replaced the reflected image in the framed rectangle, and Hestean laughed. 'That's not me,' she said.

'No, but this is,' said the machine. The image slowly morphed into a better likeness of a young woman. Unlike Hestean, though, the image showed a Comcree warrior wearing a blue-green shadow-dress and two daggers. Hestean took in the image. The machine spoke again and brought a second image onto the screen. 'You are from her. Andreena was very much like you, as you can see.'

Hestean walked closer to the screen, and slowly ran her hand across the image of the woman placed beside the image of herself. Her finger stopped when she realised that both women wore two daggers.

'I said you were alike,' said the machine. 'She also wore two daggers. You are both unique in that.'

'Was she also a Deserteer?'

'No. Her second dagger had a different beginning from yours.'

'I am of her, aren't I?' mused Hestean, studying the woman's features anew.

'I knew Andreena, but I do not know you!' said the machine.

'I don't know you, either,' said Hestean.

'Then perhaps we should get to know each other.'

'Yes … I think perhaps we should.' Hestean returned to the table and faced the machine. She lifted herself up to sit on the tabletop as she said, 'We should start at the beginning.'

'Always a good place to start, but my beginning is much further past than yours.'

'It does appear that way,' said Hestean. Then, hoping he understood humour, she added teasingly, 'So I shall talk slowly, and you can talk quickly.'

'Yes, indeed!' said the machine. 'You are a scoundrel.'

Hestean smiled widely at the machine, which she was beginning to think of as Dan. She found his eye and, looking straight at him, let him know of her discovery.

As the unseen stars outside began to fill the sky, Hestean listened to Dan's latest recitation. Her chin resting on top of her arms, she asked, 'Don't you ever get lonely?'

'The earpiece. I see what you see.'

'I don't think I like that!'

'You can turn it off if you feel the need! Just press its outer red tip.'

'If you can see what I see, why don't you know what happened to Andreena? Surely you would have seen what she was seeing?'

'While you are in this room, I cannot see through your eyes, only my own. It is a cloak. Your ancestors built this cloak so that I could not be seen. It is within me, so none of the earpieces work in my presence. I believe there are other cloaks; cloaks that hide other parts of this world. There are other things and places that are also not to be seen. Sharacan is one of those places. As for being lonely, let's take a walk, shall we?'

'A walk? You can't move, can you?'

'No, but you can! Come, go out the door to the stairs. The earpiece will work there. We'll climb to the top floor.'

'Is there a kitchen?'

'Eventually, yes!'

'Good! I'm starting to feel a little hungry.'

'Yes, I forget that about your kind at times,' said Dan.

Standing, Hestean realised she had been still for too long. Her legs felt sleepy and slow to move. She retrieved her dagger, and then walked to the door.

* * *

Gorean giggled to herself.

'What?' said Petty, sitting beside her at an outdoor dining table.

'I think Dan has decided to like your friend! He is giving her the grand tour.'

'Tour of what?'

'Our home, of course!'

'Your home? I thought *this* was your home.'

Gorean smiled at the idea. 'This is work! I have a life too, you know, just like you.' From the Museum's highest roof, Gorean stared at the stars. She pointed into the darkness, guiding Petty's eyes towards the cliffs towering over the great Hassis Museum Historical. 'We live up there, Maskee,' she said, getting up and walking to the edge of the small rooftop courtyard. 'The Hassis Estate, in the upper Hassis Valley. That is where I'm free! I work here, that's all. I'm a teacher; I teach children. I first saw Hestean because one of my children overheard her talking with Professor Sageling. I should have known then who she was.'

'Hestean is up there, on top of the escarpment, and you're a schoolteacher?' said Petty, putting aside his napkin, having now finished his meal.

'You don't believe me?' said Gorean.

He picked up their two glasses of ferment and, getting up himself, walked across to her. 'After today, I'll believe anything. Thank you for the supper. It was much appreciated.' As the ferment set free its delicious fragrance, Gorean took her glass from him, and turned to walk further along the castellated edge of the courtyard. Petty followed.

'With Dan,' she said, 'things can take an age. Your Deserteers needed feeding!'

Behind them, at the far end of the long table, the rest of Hestean's protectorate sat talking amongst themselves. Gorean and Petty could still hear them discussing their new blue-trimmed uniforms, which now set them apart as the rare elite. It was a life they had not chosen, but no one had refused it.

'Why don't you have protectors?' asked Petty.

Gorean smiled and said, 'I have them. However, no one knows I exist, so I'm better without them close. That may be about to change, though. Hestean made a statement today, which the College will heed. They will know she is of Andreena's line, too, whom they have reason to fear. I think something has been set in motion that will touch us all.'

'But I thought the College had submitted?'

'It is a truce we live by, Petty, not victory. It is only our skill over the past centuries that has kept the vast majority of people safe from the College. They have never given up, but hide merely within our sight, constantly looking for weakness. We know this because, secretly, we have always ventured amongst them, even within Learnian. We have to if we are to keep them at bay.' Gorean's voice cooled as she said, 'It is probably time for the secrecy to end. Hestean may have been right when she said things happen for a reason.'

Gorean and Petty were now hidden from the other Deserteers. Gorean stopped her slow walk and turned to look out over the city, reaching up to press the red tip of her earpiece.

'You call Hestean "daughter". Is she?'

'Not biologically, no!'

'But you have known women?'

'A few, but not for a long time.'

'Good. I don't like to lust after a man who is already taken.'

Leaning against the top of the parapet, Petty stood silently beside Gorean. Without flinching at her words, he said, 'It has been a long time since I was lusted after.'

'Maybe it should happen more often,' said Gorean. 'You're still a handsome man.'

Petty glanced towards her, 'Gallantry is not dead, then?'

'Not where I'm looking.'

* * *

Hestean ascended from the below-ground rooms to find herself on the main floor of a grand house. Opening the almost hidden iron-gated doorway, she entered through a narrow alcove to stand at the crossing of two long, wide hallways. One of the hallways exited onto an expansive patio, past which she could see nothing more than the growing shadows of dusk. The second hallway ran the length of the building, from one end to the other, quartering the floor into four distinct parts. Tightly joined blocks of stone formed the walls, and a colourful mosaic floored the halls. Every offshoot or doorway was topped by a carved arch. Between these, the walls were covered with paintings and tapestries that told of this place's status and purpose. Everything was lit by a soft glow, similar to that of the downstairs rooms. Hestean turned slowly to take it all in.

'There are people here, yes?' she asked.

'You and Gorean are the only two Comcree presently located within sight of the Hassis,' Dan said, directly into her mind through her earpiece. 'There are others, though. Most have finished for the day, but there are some here still.'

Slowly, she began to walk down one of the hallways towards what she thought must be the west. Off to her right, she discovered a reception and entertaining area fitted out with finely carved chairs, plush couches, and low tables. Along the outer walls, curtains covered the floor-to-ceiling windows. A huge fireplace—big enough to stand in—dominated the room. It's exposed copper hood topped by a flue, rose to the ceiling before splitting into many smaller pipes running off in all directions.

'This part of the house hasn't been used in a long time,' said Dan.

'It looks like it,' said Hestean. 'Why not?'

'This is the main house of the Hassis Estate. There have been no grand parties here for more than two hundred years.'

'Shame,' said Hestean.

'Maybe you will change that,' said Dan.

Hestean moved on down the hall. She poked her head into a magnificent dining room. Two chandeliers lit up when she entered, sparkling with a subtlety that spoke of true wealth.

'There are one hundred and fourteen chairs!' counted Hestean.

'This room was also the war room during the fight against the College. All six houses from all the regions, plus the Comcree, once sat in this room.'

'You mean the Alliance operated from here?'

'It still does. The Guild is the Alliance by another name. Come, there is more for you to see.'

Back the way she had come, Hestean discovered a small waiting room, a larger study, and then an even larger book room. Within this library, every wall and alcove was filled with books, manuscripts, and scrolls.

'Does the Museum know of these?' she asked.

'Some of these are the oldest documents known to us. The Museum Hassis Historical must never know of them. Within this room is the entire history of the Comcree. It is their knowledge and stories. In time, Hestean, these books will tell you who you are, and who you must become.'

She felt the weight of centuries overpower her and walked across to finger some of the bindings. She knew that in here she would at last find her true and complete story. 'Could you not simply tell me what is written here?' she asked.

'I could, but you must find your own destiny. Some Comcree read just enough to become very good at what they do, but there are others who strive always to know more. Every Comcree must find this out for themselves.'

'You mean the freedom to choose?'

'Yes.'

'But I did not choose to become Comcree!'

'No. That was a gifting, and it cannot be given back.'

'So, there are some choices we may not make?'

'Do you not always choose to be the best that you can, for others as well as for yourself? Someone must have thought so, or you would not have been given this gift.'

She studied the walls again, realising she did want to know what was shelved here. It was a responsibility. She wondered if those who had done this to her really knew what they were asking. She knew, however, that they had been right about her. If she had been given the chance to choose this place, she would have. Was she worthy of such an offering? Would she be able to justify such belief?

'Come,' said Dan, 'there is still more to show you.'

What more could there be than this? thought Hestean.

Dan guided her up a set of circling stairs. She stood on a landing overlooking the floor below. Here, she could see more clearly the patterns in the tiles. Most of the shapes and symbols were abstract, but the six house marks and their seventh link were clearly visible. There was also another symbol made up of two daggers placed side by side. She had seen it somewhere before but couldn't remember where.

The hallways stretched out, lit by the same soft glow. She was beginning to wonder if this whole building was alive in some way, for it seemed to follow her with its light. On this level, walkways gave access through large glass doors to a front terrace that overhung the carriageway in front of the building. She would love to see outside.

'This floor holds the living quarters,' said Dan. 'We will go to your left.'

'Will one of these rooms be mine, then?' she asked, a little disappointed.

'Gorean seems to like your Mister Petty very much,' said Dan.

Noticing Dan's avoidance of her question, she said sharply, 'What do you mean?'

'She has switched off her earpiece. She only does that when she is being … intimate. All else she allows me to hear.'

'Should you be telling me that?'

'Probably not,' said Dan. 'I usually do keep such things to myself, but it's because you remind me of Andreena, I think! Andree and I talked, you see. We had few secrets.'

'I thought I was getting something to eat?'

'First things first,' said Dan. 'We must get you properly dressed. You must look Comcree, as well as be Comcree. It is the image people look to, as much as the act. Open this door just ahead.'

Hestean opened the door, which revealed a suite of rooms. The first was a drawing room and study, while the next was a bedroom with its own ablutions alcove. In the first room along the outer wall, positioned near the window for light, sat a soft and comfortable reading chair. Beside it, a large desk was covered with a few old books, a ruler, a box of paper pins, and some char-sticks standing upright in a small glass container. In front of the container was a small stack of writing paper, yellowed with age. Again, this room looked as though it hadn't been used in a long time. It smelled old, as if it had been locked away.

Hestean walked across and pulled back the curtain, then saw that the window over-looked the entire front of the house. She opened the window and stared out into what must have once been the most beautiful view of a lush green valley. Now, the distant scenery was brown and dry. The air carried the same dryness as her homeland. Here, too, as in her village, the only greenery was in the close fields and gardens surrounding the house. She realised that even here, the desert's influence encroached.

She closed the window and walked back into the bedroom. Along the far wall, she saw a wardrobe, then a large bed with short, round posts rising from the corners of its footboard. Beside the wardrobe was the entrance to the large ablutions alcove, where she could see part of a sunken bathing pool, now empty. Against the dividing wall was a mirror and a dressing table cluttered with combs, brushes, jars, a few small bottles, and a small red varnished box made from fibre-reed. She lifted its lid and saw it filled with sand. Although the whole room was clean, like the desk and drawing-room, Hestean sensed its disuse.

A sudden flicker in her mind made her put down the box and step back. Turning, she walked out into the hallway. Above the door frame, she confirmed the symbol that had jumped into her head. 'Andreena,' she said. 'The red box belonged to Andreena, and the sand is from Sharacan.'

'This is to be your room,' said Dan. 'Andreena was the last to use it, yes. She worked here, but rarely slept here. Especially towards the end.'

'The end?'

'When she was here, after Elora died, Andreena slept every night alone in Elora's room. They were close, you see.'

'You mean they switched off their earpieces?' said Hestean.

'You are quick for your years' said Dan. 'But don't be too quick to judge. You have much still to learn.'

Much still to learn! The words were loud in her mind. 'Must everyone say that? I do know some things, you know. I don't judge people for caring! Love is hard enough to find at the best of times. It is rare! Very rare. So, I know you should hold onto it when it comes. Seldom have I known its meaning, and for me, its understanding comes too late to be held.'

The thought had been festering inside her all day. She wished Jarrak were here. She needed to see his face; to talk to him; to smell him next to her. For the first time, she started to realise what she was feeling. She missed him. She really missed him.

'Can you see thoughts?' she suddenly asked.

'No,' said Dan. 'But I am a good listener. Andree and I knew each other very well. It is time that gives you true wisdom, and that you will gain more of. I see this within you.'

'Do you really?'

'We all miss someone. Even me, it seems!'

'I thought you said you couldn't see thoughts?'

'And I also said that I am a good listener.'

'Did Andreena ever say you were annoying?'

'Many times.'

'Good, then you won't mind if I do?'

'You need to be properly dressed,' said Dan. 'In the wardrobe, Andreena's things should fit you.'

'Clothes that old will be frail!'

'These are the clothes of a Comcree warrior! There is nothing frail about them, and there never will be. Look for yourself and see.'

Hestean walked back to the wardrobe, her emotions slowly subsiding. Behind the folding doors, she found a row of blue-green dresses, similar to the one Gorean had been wearing. She drew out one of the dresses, felt its fabric, and examined its form. Holding it up to herself, she looked at her reflection in the large mirror. She pulled open one of the drawers and found an old, fragile skirt and blouse carefully folded within. They were similar to the desert clothes she herself had once worn. She gasped at the sight of them, reading a similar history here to her own.

After a long stillness, she pushed the drawer in and pulled out the one below. Here she found a collection of orange scarves, one of which she lay on the bed beside the dress. She then opened the next drawer and found a single folded cloak. The cloak was like a

Deserteer's cloak, but longer, and lined with blue instead of red. She drew it out and watched it unfurl, imagining it hanging over Andreena's shoulders.

'This, I think, is me,' she said. She turned and put it on the bed beside the dress, then started to undo her own cloak. 'Can you see me?' she asked, pausing.

'Only if you look in the mirror! I see what you see.'

'Ah, right,' she said. 'Good to know!'

She began to undo her cloak once more, and a little while later stood fully clothed in the shadow-dress that now wrapped round her body. She turned to the mirror. 'What do you think?'

'You truly are of Andree,' said Dan. 'Her temper never lasted long, either, but there are differences.'

Hestean smiled wryly into the mirror, then bent down to pick up the cloak. She buttoned it around her neck and flung it back over her shoulders, the way a Deserteer would.

She looked again into the mirror and Dan said, 'Better.' The brooch was next, then the daggers, the Comcree's to the left and the Deserteer's to the right. The orange scarf was last, which she used to cover the Comcree dagger, leaving the Deserteer's exposed for all to see. In her ear, Dan said, 'Now you can eat.'

Hestean smiled, pleased. As she walked towards the door, she said, 'You call Andreena "Andree" sometimes. Why is that?'

'She only allowed her friends to call her Andree.'

'Will we be friends one day?'

'Maybe we already are,' said Dan.

'Maybe. But not just yet, I think. When we are, though, I will allow you to call me "Hat".'

On Dan's instruction, she descended the stairs, and turned towards the back of the building when she reached the ground floor. As she entered the kitchen, she saw two people engrossed in their task of washing and drying dishes. Their backs were turned to her.

'Oh, I'm sorry!' she said.

The two figures turned abruptly and instantly the old woman's hand faltered, letting a plate fall to break on the floor. The young man's hand, however, went straight to his dagger as he stepped in front of his older companion. 'And who might you be?' he asked.

Before Hestean could answer, the old woman said softly, 'She is a ghost!'

The young man looked at the elderly woman, seeing recognition on her face. 'You know her?' he asked.

'She is Andreena, from the painting. Don't you recognise her?'

Hestean began to grin at the colourful assumption, then corrected the woman. 'Maybe I should be, but no, my name is Hestean.'

The old woman brushed the young man aside and walked forward. 'But you look so much like her. You have to be at least of her, yes?'

'I think so. Or some people seem to think so, anyway. I do know that I'm hungry,' said Hestean. 'I forgot that Dan told me there were still some people in the house.'

'My poor girl, yes,' said the old woman. 'That wizard! I'll cover him with dust the next time I do his room. Tell him that. He should have told me. Shenn, find Gorean and see why I was not told! I am Whittn, by the way, and the boy here is Shenn, Gorean's apprentice. We have been wondering where she is. She told us she would be back before dark.'

Shenn slowly removed his hand from his dagger and looked to Whittn.

'Be off with you, lad' she repeated. 'I may be old, but you know I'm as good as you anyday. Besides, this girl and I have things to discuss.'

'But, Whittn …'

'Don't "but, Whittn," me, Shenn! Find her now!' There was no dagger at Whittn's side, but even so, Hestean sensed an air of authority about the woman.

'Gorean didn't say she had an apprentice.'

'You have seen her, then?' asked Whittn, starting to wander around the kitchen, opening cupboards and setting things upon the table. 'Where was she?'

'I'm not sure. We entered through the maze.'

'Did you get that, Shenn?'

'Yes?'

'Then go.'

Shenn looked towards Hestean once more, then hurried off.

'Everything has been such a blur today,' said Hestean.

'Why? What is this day to you?'

A sigh drained from Hestean. 'Today started simply as my day of ascension. My eighteenth birthday was yesterday, and it has brought me here. Today has been a journey, that's what it's been!' Feeling the length of the long morning and afternoon, Hestean realised the truth of this, and she pulled out a chair to drop into it. 'Can I help?' she asked, watching Whittn move around the room.

'No, no, no. A story! I like stories,' said Whittn. 'You sit and talk, and I'll get you something to eat. Did Gorean say if she would be up soon?'

'I don't think so. She is seeing to some friends of mine. Her earpiece is off.'

Whittn chuckled and said, 'Good-looking, is he?'

Hestean smiled at the old woman. 'You know, then?'

'Everyone knows, child. She doesn't hide it. It is simply the way she is!' Whittn stopped her fussing to look at Hestean directly. 'You will need to be as true to yourself as Gorean is to herself. It is what will sustain you. You must be true to yourself first, if you are to be a good Comcree, for there is no turning back.'

23

Through the windows behind her, only the very top of Hestean's head could be seen above the tall-backed chair she'd curled into. Just before dawn, she had risen from Andreena's bed and ventured downstairs to the room where she now sat. All around her, the paintings and tapestries told their stories, but it was one particular painting she had come in search of. It hung above the main entrance to the dining room, and her eyes had scanned it again and again, seeking out every nuance within its frame.

'You can see why Whittn thought you were a ghost, can't you?' said Shenn. His voice made her eyes rotate quickly towards him, and in that moment take in his physical form. He was leaning against the frame of the smaller side door. She sat up straighter in the chair, her eyes focusing on the partly shaved twig he twirled steadily between his fingers.

'I don't think you like me very much,' she said quietly.

'I don't know yet. You're not much older than I am, and you know nothing, yet you have come amongst us as one of the six. I am still deciding!'

Shenn had risen early, too, and sitting on the back patio, he'd noticed the top few strands of Hestean's dark hair through the window. Now, without warning, most likely hoping to prove his own preconceptions, he flung the piece of palmwood towards her. Before it had time to reach her, Hestean unleashed her own weapon and rose from the chair. She caught the wooden stake in her hand, and a fraction of a moment later Shenn felt her Deserteer's dagger find its target.

'By the gods! H—How did you do that?' he said, looking to his sleeve, which was now pinned to the door frame.

Sensing his action more than seeing it, Hestean had reacted on instinct, surprising even herself. Realising that her dagger had landed exactly where she'd intended, she tried to behave with only authority and control as she walked towards him.

'I am Sharacanese, so don't play with me, boy. I know I have much to learn. You can either help, or you can stay clear of me. You cannot do both. This is no game, Shenn! I am here for a reason, and I have no time for childish indulgences.'

* * *

Her green eyes seemed to fill with fire as she lectured him, pushing aside the girl he had seen the night before. In front of him now, Shenn saw a young woman who knew who she was.

'The others in this painting. Who are they?' Hestean demanded, recovering her dagger and pointing it towards the image above the doorway.

Shenn pulled at his sleeve and noticed a small red stain. 'You cut me!'

'I nicked you! Of course, I did. A Deserteer's dagger must always draw blood if it is unleashed. I am Sharacanese. If I wasn't, the hole in your sleeve might also be in your arm.'

'What do I know of Sharacan? No one has come from the desert in a long time. Sharacan is almost a myth!'

'Ah, so now I am an imagined phantom?'

'I am no child, girl.'

'Good. Then we'll have no more of this, will we? I have been summoned, Shenn. My presence here was planned, and I mean to know why. Who are the others in the painting?'

Beginning to think that maybe she was truly one of the six, Shenn wondered if he ever would be, too. Although it was something he wanted, he also knew he had been chosen by default. Now wary of her, he moved around her to better see the painting.

* * *

In the hallway, Gorean listened to the youngsters as they sorted out their ranks. Now, as Hestean and Shenn moved away from the side door, she entered silently behind them. She touched her finger to the fresh knife mark in the door frame and noticed the small piece of wood that Hestean now twirled through her fingers. She watched the two as they examined the painting, the young woman venturing to be more than she was, and the young man already starting to see her as the person she might one day be.

She looked again at the mark left by the knife, and remembered the very beginning of her own apprenticeship. Even she had not fully understood her future, then. Hestean had not been given the charity of an apprenticeship, and she wondered what that might mean. She had read the histories about the last time this had happened. Then, Elora had been the only one of the Comcree warriors to have received any sort of formal apprenticeship. There had been both the good and the not-so-good to come to the guardians in that period of rejuvenation. What would Hestean bring to them now? She turned to observe the young woman for a moment, knowing that there was something inherent about this untrained girl. Hestean already moved like a warrior, cautious or quick when needing to be, always vigilant.

'You know Andreena, of course!' said Gorean, stepping forward to make her presence known. 'The woman to her left—the one with her arm on Andreena's shoulder—is the Lady Elora Sarah-Hassis. To Elora's left is Zukara. Zukara was the only name she was ever known by. To Andreena's right there is Sjeda and Benjam Sym, and in front of them is Florenz. It is believed that Florenz was more closely related to the Sereye Comcree than the others, but this isn't known for sure. You remember the painting in the elevator? It was painted by his great uncle. Together, these six were the original Hassis Hub-Comcree. This valley belonged to Elora's family, but she was the last. She left this estate and all her family's wealth to us.'

'The little plump woman with Elora and Andreena—who is she?' asked Hestean.

'Ah, now, there is a question. That is Mearda, the housekeeper. She raised Elora from childhood. We know little of her, but it is believed she taught Elora the ways of the Comcree. She became the first Matrefem to the Hassis Comcree—their guide, you could say; their Ze Hub. Some say she was related to Elora, but there is no proof of this. She belonged to the Shadow Shire, though, and must have been what we call "Shirey". She was only a few generations removed from the Comcree. If she was kin, it would make Elora closely related to the Sereye Comcree, also, explaining many things.'

'Are you related to any of them?'

'No, not that I know of. Not closely, anyway; only in the way that we are all related in some form. My relationship starts with Andreena's and Elora's apprentices, Deckon Thames and Lillia Dowee. After Elora was killed and Andreena vanished, they—along with the other four Comcree—were the ones who eventually drove the College into submission and created the Treaty of Truce.'

'Elora was killed? Dan said only that she died! Do you know how she was killed?'

'The Museum marks the place of her death. That is why it is the Hassis Museum Historical. As all Comcree must, you will read the records yourself and make your own judgments,' said Gorean. She knew there had never been any real proof of College guilt, only speculation, as there was with Andreena. Still, it was what she believed, although she could not influence the decision Hestean would soon have to make.

* * *

'I know that Andreena vanished,' said Hestean as if sensing something about Gorean's answer. 'Dan did tell me that. I thought he would have known why because of the earpiece, but he doesn't, does he? No one knows what happened to her.'

'Dan blames himself!' said Gorean. 'You remember the glowing ball of light downstairs? Back then, that was the only energy machine in existence. When they took on the College, they needed energy to recharge the armour and weapons they had rediscovered and built. Dan suggested taking the machine on the campaign. He could have survived without it if he'd shut down his systems. But it meant he was no longer in contact with the earpieces, so he failed to hear what happened to Andreena. It is said that she changed, too, when Elora died. She was in charge on her own, then, and driven by Elora's death. In those days, Sharacan was still the centre of trade. Its water kept the desert in check, making it possible to cross the mighty Kalcool by foot or by wagon. Andreena was winning, then, and keeping the College from Sharacan. One morning, she was simply not there anymore. She and her entire Protectorate had vanished. In the confusion that followed, the College took the city, and you know what became of it then. The Alliance regrouped, but were never able to retake Sharacan, and so the Treaty of Truce was devised to allow the world to continue.'

An image of Sharacan's ruins came into Hestean's mind, then another thought grabbed her. 'The energy machine … Couldn't they have made more?'

Gorean looked at Hestean, wondering when the young woman would realise there had once been another world beyond even this hidden one of the Comcree. That was a world Gorean had only glimpsed through her reading in the estate library. 'Today we capture light, wind, and even heat instead of using machines such as that one,' she said. 'And even today, we don't understand it. The heart of the energy machine was a gift from our ancestors, you see, formed from something still unknown to this world. It was partly because we didn't have the means to make more machines that we lost Sharacan. After Andreena's disappearance, the Guild didn't want the College to discover the machine, so they brought it back to the Hassis. To this day, the College knows nothing of its existence, and they must never know. With Dan restored, they eventually found other ways to power the boxes, but by then the College had destroyed Sharacan and the Deserteers had taken to the sky.'

'Dan said that there was a "cloak" over Sharacan.'

'There is a cloak, yes. Even when Dan returned to full power, he still could not find Andreena. Even today, Sharacan is a hidden place to him, and it silences us, too.'

'But I've used a transceiver there!'

'Our new toys worked for you, then? Even we can communicate with one another whilst there, but we can't breach the cloak.'

'So, Andreena's mystery is Sharacan's mystery!' said Hestean, starting to understand.

'The two are the same,' said Gorean.

Hestean was beginning to realise that if she were to find Andreena, she would need to return to Sharacan. Had Jarrak and Bornn been right? Was Andreena's fate indeed linked to that ancient city? As she considered this, she started to understand that if Andreena and Sharacan were truly linked, it might be in Sharacan, too, that she would also find herself. From the edge of her consciousness came an unexpected query. 'Who amongst them were musicians?' she asked. 'There are instruments in this painting.'

* * *

Intrigued by Hestean's question, Gorean replied, 'All of them, except Zukara and Andreena. Zukara was their songstress and Andreena was their technician. Come, come and see.'

The two women walked down the hall, with Shenn trailing them. They entered another room containing the instruments Hestean had just seen in the painting.

'I was expecting to see Petty with you this morning,' said Hestean casually, as she surveyed the room's interior.

'Why is that?'

'This world works differently compared to my village, so I notice the differences. But actually, it was something Dan mentioned. Don't play with him, Gorean. I have seen Robes play with women, and I have seen it destroy those women. I will not stand by and see the reverse happen here!'

'Your Mister Petty doesn't allow himself to be played with, sister, and I don't play either. I like him! But there is no permanency between Petty and me. I am not the one who will take his heart.'

'I see. Then perhaps you have my permission.'

'Your permission?' smiled Gorean. 'He doesn't need your permission.'

'I know that. But he has become a friend. He has given up his navigation career to protect me. Right now, I need him. He needs something else, though, and from what I've heard, you can distract in ways I don't know much about yet. If you can help to realign his life, then you have my permission!'

'Ah, I see what you mean,' said Gorean. 'We are indeed at the beginning of a journey, aren't we?' She saw now why Hestean had been given Andreena's heritage. Good warriors cared about this world, but more importantly, they cared about its people, too.

Hestean turned back to the room. 'Dan didn't show me this last night!'

Gorean almost smiled as she said, 'Yes, but Dan *did* show you the library, didn't he!'

'He made a point of it. Especially with the older books!'

'Then let's just say that books are more his style.'

'Music I like, too!' said a voice in their minds.

'Ah, he's awake and eavesdropping, as always.' said Gorean.

'Gorean,' said Dan. 'You learned a long time ago that I am always awake, and I do not eavesdrop, I listen!'

'It's been a long time since I was eighteen,' said Gorean. 'Do you still have to throw that at me?'

Although Hestean didn't know to what they were referring, she realised that Dan had learnt to use his words with just the right inference to punctuate a moment to his advantage. She held back a grin, then rescued the woman by saying, 'If Petty isn't with you, then where is he?'

Gorean glared at her, then softened to say, 'He was still asleep when I left him. You know how men are when they've been with a woman most of the night.'

'No, actually,' said Hestean, surprising even herself with her honesty. Her thoughts leapt from Gorean to Kuzzea and then, by progressive association, to Jarrak, and her face flushed. 'I am from Sharacan, remember,' she said. 'The rules are different there.'

'But might there not have been someone if the rules had been the same?' asked Gorean, with a smile.

'I doubt it. I was banished,' said Hestean, now strangely unsure of herself. The time between getting banned from her village and arriving at Elora-Bearer was a part of her life she had never thought of as intimate, but now her mind flickered again to thoughts of Jarrak. Had she thought of such things back then? Had Jarrak thought of such things? *No*, she thought to herself, face flushing so red she thought it would burst into flames.

'Banishment,' said Gorean. 'So, you do have something of a past, then?'

'What?' said Hestean, her mind still on Jarrak. Even though she knew the principles of intimacy between women and men because of the animals in the village, she had never actually gotten round to asking her mother about it before her banishment. It just hadn't seemed important back then, but now who was there to ask?

'You said you were banished?' prompted Gorean.

'I forgot my place,' said Hestean, only half hearing. 'In Sharacan, I was but a lowly female to the Robes. I stopped a stupid man from harming a relic, and for that I was banished. I would be dead now, if it weren't for Jarrak.'

'Jarrak! Ah!'

'He is the one in charge of the Sharacan dig.'

'I know! We sent him. I've never actually met him, though.'

'You sent him? I thought Bornn sent him.'

'Yes, and Professor Sageling thinks so, too.'

'But why?'

'We plant ideas,' said Gorean. 'We needed a way to uncover Sharacan—to find the source of the cloak there.

'But Jarrak is looking for Andreena!'

'Yes, but he's found something else, hasn't he? The fragments that are unique to Sharacan. Pieces that were once part of six-sided keys.'

'Bornn said they're not keys, but maps.'

'A key can be a map, and a map can be a key,' said Gorean. And perhaps you are the door.'

'Door! Door to where?'

'The door to that part of our past that we are now supposed to find. Dan thinks that neither you nor the fragments are a coincidence. You are both part of Sharacan's story.'

'Jarrak bluffed the Black Robes,' said Hestean. 'After that, we played a game with them. He is the only one I miss from back there.'

'What about your family?'

'My family … I am unsure of my family,' said Hestean, as an image of her mother and father flashed through her mind.

'Then you have a few reasons to go back.'

'Go back!' exclaimed Hestean. She glanced around for something to shift the conversation away from herself, and her gaze landed on the instruments. 'Do you play any of these, Gorean?'

'Oh, no, not me. I'm all thumbs when it comes to things like this. But Batteen, Thace, and Heggon do! When his hands start tapping, Thace is a wizard on the drums, and Batteen plays that instrument over there.' Gorean pointed to the far wall, which was covered in pipes. At its centre were two shelves, just a little more than an arm's length long. One shelf was recessed above the other, and each was made up of thin wooden finger slats.

'What is it? I've never seen anything like it before.'

'No, you wouldn't have. There are only three like it; this one, the one in Chime Town, and that smaller one over there.'

Hestean turned to see a rectangular box. She crossed the floor to run her hand over the top of the strange instrument. 'No, I do not think so, this is not the same as that,' she said, taking in the similarities between the two.

'Yes and no! The one along the wall and the one in Chime Town were made by Elora's grandfather, but that one is as old as time. It was made by the ancients.' Gorean pointed to a few more instruments. 'Those are ancient, also. They were thought to be toys until Andreena got to them. She discovered their secret.'

'What secret?'

'They need energy! The energy amplifies their sound and allows them to be heard. Without energy, they are mute.' Gorean twisted to the large box sitting on a table beside her. 'This controls them! Andreena was no musician, but she could play this very well.' Gorean's hand felt its way slowly across levers, dials, and switches. 'She could mix the sounds so that it seemed the gods themselves were playing. My great-grandmother first told me that, and when I came here and mentioned it to Dan, he allowed me to hear for myself.'

'Your great-grandmother?'

'Yes. Her great-great-great-grandmother was Elora's apprentice, remember?'

'You mean Lillia! The one who helped defeat the College?'

'No, little sister,' said Gorean. 'They did not defeat the College. They stopped them, yes, but defeating the College is your job. I think we all agree that it is time this stalemate was ended. We should hear from the others soon, and we will see what they say.'

Gorean turned to Shenn and said, 'Tell Whittn there will be five for breakfast, then go to the Museum's upper level and find a Deserteer named Petty. Make sure his companions are given something to eat, then bring him up here to join us. You understand?'

'Yes, Gorean.'

'Oh, and Shenn,' said Gorean, grasping his arm. 'You may have to grow up quicker than we had planned! Today is not the world it was yesterday! From today, you will have to use what you have learned. As Hestean stated earlier, there will be no more time for childish indulgences.'

He nodded his agreement, then turned to take in Hestean's youth once more.

Hestean knew that Shenn had just been reprimanded for doubting her rank. As he turned to walk from the room, he bowed slightly to her. She returned the gesture, handing back the twig he had thrown at her. Her eyes followed him as he withdrew, feeling sorry for him in a way. She understood completely what he had tried to say to her. She knew that, in a way, he had been right. She did have a lot still to learn.

'Whittn is not merely a housekeeper, is she?' asked Hestean.

Gorean looked at Hestean out of the corner of her eye, then smiled. 'No,' she said. 'She is not! Housekeepers in this house are never what they seem. She was once as you and I; one of the Comcree. I didn't quite tell you the truth yesterday. The earpieces will relinquish their hold before death, but you have to want it. When you decide you are too old to be a good Comcree, or when you become the Ze Hub, they will surrender their grasp. In this latter case, another earpiece is given to you. Whittn is now our centre, our guide, our Matrefem—the Ze Hub. She now wears that earpiece. If you ever have a question, ask her.'

'So, I was right,' said Hestean. 'There is someone like that in Sharacan. Last night, I had the same feeling about Whittn as I had about Reglean. Jarrak told me once that "Ze Hub" is the name given to the centre of the symbol used to depict the six houses. It is more than just that isn't it? What does it really mean?'

'In a way, your Jarrak was right. "Ze Hub" does mean the centre, but it also means "the Keeper". The Ze Hub has no power. She cannot make decisions. But what she does do is help *us* make the right decisions.'

'I thought that would be Dan?'

'No. Dan is the seer. He is the one who has seen the past and future. If you ask him the right questions, you will get the right answers, but he guards his knowledge closely. The keeper and the seer hold two different forms of knowledge. If you use them both properly, you will always get the right answer.'

'So, they're a bit like parents, then, aren't they?'

Gorean exploded into laughter. 'Yes, you could say they are.'

Hestean caught sight of something shadowed in the far corner of the room. She walked across the floor and stopped in front of the s-shaped instrument standing as tall as her waist. 'A woke horn!'

'You know it, then?'

'One of these is my nemesis. It is the reason I am here—the cause of my banishment.'

Picking up the horn, Hestean placed it carefully to her lips and started to blow. She circled air in through her nose, then to her cheeks and out through her mouth. She created a full, throaty tone that never stopped as her right hand started to manipulate the body of the horn, bringing it to song.

The accompanying words of the song she had taught herself flowed through her mind. *There is a place where I come from, and I know this place is with you. My heart, my mind, knowing all time, I, my love, am always with you.*

'You can play that thing! No one has ever been able to play it.'

'Just a few tunes. I taught myself on the horn I dug from the ground at Sharacan. It's down in the Museum, now. You have to keep the air moving through it to make it vibrate inside. That's the trick.' Hestean put the horn back onto its stand. 'There is more to the tune. That was just the first verse.'

'What's it called?'

'It has two names,' said Hestean. 'My mother told me that its real name was *In Lament of Sharacan*, but no one ever called it that. It's normally just known as *My Heart*. The words never quite made sense before, but knowing what I know now, they do. I think my mother was speaking of the ancient Sharacan, and so is the song.' Hestean smiled knowingly, realising something for the first time. Her mother must know at least something about the old Sharacan, or she would never have been able to tell her that the song had another name.

Her eyes twinkled as this glimmer of recognition flushed up her spine. As the words of the song echoed in her mind, she knew she *was* meant to return to Sharacan.

24

Whittn was busy warming breakfast biscuits and putting water on to boil for tea when Gorean and Hestean entered the kitchen.

'Hestean, you take that seat, and Gorean, you're to sit opposite,' she said. 'I'm at the end, and when they come, Mister Petty and Shenn can take the next two seats.'

'Are you sure about this?' asked Gorean.

'Dan has said she is truly of blood, Gorean! You would already know that, if you had left your earpiece switched on last night. Batteen is not here, so until I know different, I will treat each of you equally. Would you have me do different?'

'No.'

'Then Hestean will sit there, where her strength will be strongest. She has a decision to make.'

'What do you mean, *of blood?*' asked Hestean.

Whittn turned to her, as did Gorean. 'I thought you had talked long with Dan yesterday?' said the Matrefem.

'Yes, but he never mentioned any blood!'

'What did you talk about, then?'

'Many things. About Sharacan, and about how I grew up. About Andreena and Elora. About Elora's family and the Hassis. About his reincarnation—'

'His reincarnation?' asked Gorean.

'Yes. He said he has had many lives. He said that he had once been destined to be something other than what he is now, and that the ANNEE was that part of him. That's why he likes being just DAN, because that is what he is now.'

'Well, that's more than he's ever told anyone else! Did he say why he told you?'

'No, but he said that I reminded him of Andreena, and that they discussed everything. He kept twisting the conversation round, and coming back to things a lot, too,' said Hestean, remembering how tongue-sore she was by the time she'd walked from his room. 'Everything we talked about, we talked about many times.'

'He does that, yes. Did he tell you why? Nothing about blood?'

'No!'

'Dan! Why didn't you tell her?'

'It was not my place,' said Dan's voice in their heads.

'It is as much your place as mine.'

'I wanted to leave something for you!'

'Did you, now!'

Hestean found herself smiling at Gorean. Whittn looked at them with suspicion. 'Sit down, child,' said the elderly woman. 'It seems I have a history lesson to give. I think, though, that our expert wants to know if I remember it all as he once told it to me.'

'Exactly like parents!' said Gorean, with a smile towards Hestean.

Whittn pursed her lips, showing her annoyance, then began to explain. 'The light in the middle of the table downstairs—it came on before you inserted the dagger, didn't it?'

'Yes.'

'It only did that because the dagger had already accepted you. You have the blood of the Comcree in your veins. The daggers always know if you have a true relationship with the first six guardians. All Comcree since then have within them this blood, no matter how distant the connection.

'But I thought only Florenz, and maybe Elora, were related to the Sereye Comcree!'

'That is a known and suspected link, yes, but we are all related to the six great houses! If Gorean was to take your dagger into that room instead of her own, no light would illuminate. Her lineage would not match that of the dagger. Each of us is from a different house. We are the hidden centre of each house. You complete us, Hestean. With you, we no longer have to just wait. We can once again guide this world the way we were meant to.'

'Anlice abrocen cwens ond cyings,' said Hestean.

'What was that?' said Gorean.

'I was just remembering something my mother occasionally said when she was exasperated or unable to do what she needed. It translates as: *Like broken queens and kings*. And I've heard other women in Sharacan say it, too.'

'Really?' said Whittn. 'Well, they were right. We are the guardians! But we can only guide when we are complete. All six daggers are needed to guide. It is time you met the rest of your brothers and sisters, then there is some lore you must be told before you make your decisions.'

'Which decisions?'

'We will come to that, but first you should meet the rest of the centre.'

Whittn guided Hestean to her seat, with Gorean opposite. When Whittn had seated herself, a dark-haired man about the same age as Gorean appeared in Hestean's mind. His words came as Gorean's had the day before. His reflected image, from a wall mirror, began to form in her head. 'I am Thace,' he said, 'and the young woman standing beside me is my apprentice, Layatty. The room you see around us is on the second floor of a tavern, far away in the south-west corner of the Kalcool plateau, at the headwaters of the South Whay River.'

An image of a woman, younger than Gorean, with auburn hair and dark brown eyes, was next to form. With it, Hestean noticed a feeling of cold. She realised she could sense even the environment around her fellow Comcree. 'I am Batteen,' said the woman. 'This is my parents' home below the Barrier Ranges. It's even further south than Thace is, near the very bottom of the Meglia landmass.'

The last for this morning was Heggon. This time, though, Hestean's mind brought forth only an image of the man's surroundings, and none of himself. 'At the moment, I am quite unkempt and bearded,' Heggon joked. 'But, as you no doubt have become aware, the earpieces only see what the wearer is seeing. I have no reflector available to me here.'

Hestean remembered Dan telling her the same thing the night before, and she took in the image of a small, flickering campfire. She also observed two men looking back at her from the other side of the flames.

'I am traveling for an annual survey of the College's home region,' said Heggon. 'It is their stronghold, where their city of Learnian is situated. It was from Learnian that the College first started to control and tax-trade along the southern trade line. It was this that forced the traders to cross the Kalcool and employ Deserteers as their guides. In turn, Sharacan grew from a small, isolated religious community into the great city it eventually became. I understand that you are Sharacanese.

Seeing you through Gorean's eyes has confirmed this to me. It has been some years since I looked in on Sharacan.'

'You have been to Sharacan?' said Hestean.

'Of course! I have always liked the desert. Were you already aware of what I just mentioned about Learnian, Sharacan, and trade?'

Heggon was studying her. He looked into her mind and felt the way she reacted to his questions.

'A lot of it, yes, but much only recently learned from the Museum,' said Hestean.

'Upon hearing of your existence, one of my companions here has brought forth a bladder of ferment to celebrate the end of the time of waiting,' said Heggon. 'I feel sure that by tomorrow, you will have caused many more sore heads to manifest themselves. Do you know that the Comcree had stalled without your dagger, Hestean?'

'Dan told me last night.'

'Two hundred years is a long time to be silent, but this world has progressed in that time, too. It has discovered things. Perhaps it's again ready to take another step forward.'

'You mean forward into the past?'

Heggon's big frame heaved with laughter. 'Yes. You already speak like a true Comcree. Perhaps you *do* know enough to be where you are, but there is always more to learn. Never stop learning, Hestean Descee.' After a moment, he said, 'There is one more of us you have to meet; Deleev. But Deleev likes to be alone with his thoughts, and often turns off his earpiece. As yet, he does not know of your existence. When he feels ready to re-join the world, he will be in touch. He'll be annoyed that he has missed this moment, as he, more than any of us, has hated this waiting. We all know he will affirm your decisions, if they take us forward, so that we can extinguish the blight on this world. To make your decision, we felt it best that you have someone you already know and trust with you. Gorean thinks your Mister Petty would be a good choice. Do you think so, too?'

'Yes, but why do I have to decide?'

'Andreena was your ancestor.'

'I already know that I need to return to Sharacan!'

'Yes, but you have to decide whether or not to finish what Andreena started. You have to decide whether or not the College is answerable for Andreena's disappearance.'

* * *

When the introductory meeting had concluded, Hestean knew it had been a more intimate experience than she had ever thought possible. These people had been inside her head; in such a short time, she already felt as though she knew them. She had discovered her clan lore, the lore of the Sharacanese, at the Museum, and now, as Whittn and Shenn dispensed breakfast, Dan told her of Comcree lore, which the College had tried unsuccessfully to purge from Sharacan. It gave depth to the local lore, and expanded it to encompass the whole world.

After they had eaten, and after much discussion with Petty and Whittn, Hestean concluded that Andreena had indeed sent a message from the grave. She was to finish what Andreena had started; to vanquish the College and bring forth enlightenment. But she was also to find out what had happened to Andreena. Under the combined lore, only one's own house could determine the wrath of the slain, and as young as she was, Hestean had become the most senior authority of her entire house. By late afternoon, she knew she intended to fulfil what Andreena had requested of her, and thus made her first decision as a Comcree.

First, she'd take back Sharacan.

* * *

'Although the demise of Andreena cannot be assigned as yet,' she said to the other Comcree through her earpiece, 'a starting point for investigation has been uncovered. At Sharacan, and elsewhere, the College have pushed aside part of Meglia lore. Dan has confirmed to me that no person can hold dominion over another. Most prominent in my thoughts are the women of Sharacan, but this also includes the men. In Sharacan, even the men, to a degree, have been forced into submission by the Black Robes. As I am Sharacanese, I am responding to this injustice by determining to expel the Robes and their influence from Sharacan. I will leave further judgement of the College until Andreena's fate is truly known. If it is then deemed fitting, I will revisit their transgressions as we force them towards Learnian. Is that enough?'

'Is it enough reason to go to war,' said Batteen. 'For that is what we will be doing. Sharacan may only be on the edge of their territory, but it was Sharacan that stopped their advance. For that reason alone, it still lives in their memory. They will not take this lightly.'

'It's enough reason to go to war if they have stifled other places and peoples in the way they have stifled the Sharacanese,' said Hestean.

'I don't think the Comcree exist to allow that to stand. I may have the authority to take back Sharacan and start this, but it is the Comcree hexagon as a whole that will take us further. Is this not why we are here? Why you have continued your surveillance, even though without me, you could go no further? We take Sharacan, then we push on to their citadel of Learnian. Once there, we determine its fate.'

'I think I see what she means,' said Thace. 'It will tip the College off balance. If we can make them think Learnian is our destination and take Sharacan silently, then the rest of Meglia will stand with us. If I have learned nothing else, it is that deep within the tribes and clans, there is still a longing for the Comcree to exist. All we need to do is show them that we do, and that it is time for our return.'

'What about the Robes from yesterday?' asked Hestean.

'You have shaken them, as Thace said,' said Gorean. 'I think they are bound for Learnian, shaken by your ascension. Most of their number were seen heading for the coast this morning. They have no sky-ships. From Sequria, they will take a tri-hull south and around to the closest port to Learnian. Tri-hulls are not as fast as sky-ships, but are still much faster than taking an overland route.'

'Then we still have some time before the College can react fully.'

'They will call into ports wherever they have a contingent, but yes, nothing will happen until Learnian is notified.'

'Then all that is left to find out is whether Deleev agrees,' said Hestean.

By the time this second meeting drew to a close, it was fully dark. With Hestean's decision made, it was now truly a time for conflict.

* * *

The next morning, Hestean was in her bedroom—having just finished a long soak in her small bathing pool—when Dan confirmed to all of them that Deleev had affirmed Hestean's decision, as everyone knew he would.

'Can I speak to Deleev?' she asked.

'Of course you can,' said a voice that was not Dan's.

Her first impressions were of wisdom and pain. It was something she instantly recognised, and she knew it came from harsh lessons in life. She had been told Deleev's childhood had been tainted, like her own, by the College, and she felt an instant kinship with him. 'I will never get used to this! I forgot you would probably be listening,' she said.

'You will get used to it,' said Deleev. 'It will become part of your normal thinking after a while. Eventually, you will feel lost without it. That's why I switch off my earpiece from time to time. It reaffirms my commitment. It helps me to remember that I have become part of a group of people who can also feel and understand my hurts and desires and joys.'

'Where are you, Deleev?'

'I am halfway around the globe from you, sitting on top of a cliff and watching sea qwols fly. They only come out just before the sun sets.'

'Half a world away,' said Hestean, and she heard Deleev laugh. 'Is that what they are?' she mused. 'I've never seen them before.' She watched them through his vision.

'Did you know that Elora built a machine that could fly like them? She was in it when she died. I have always wished I could have seen it, or even flown in it, but there was nothing left after she fell. It was completely destroyed. It's in the Comcree stories if you read back far enough. The College crept into range, you see, and sent flaming arrows at her on one of her reconnaissance flights.'

'So that's what happened to her …'

'Yes,' said Deleev.

'Your sea qwols are magnificent.'

'And so are you! You're the first Sharacanese woman I have ever seen.'

'Oh, by the gods,' said Hestean, turning away from the mirror that reflected her naked body. 'I didn't think! Why didn't you say something?'

'I just did! The earpieces can be both a privilege and a curse. You will also get used to knowing when to turn your eyes,' said Deleev, laughing. 'But one day, you will have your revenge upon me. It is inevitable, sister. We all forget occasionally. Eventually, we all get to know each other better than we know anyone else. It is what gives us the insight to do what we do. Like the others, in time, you will not have to talk to me in order to know what I think. You will be able to tell with your own thoughts. In truth, courtesy will be the only true reason for talking to us. That and friendship, I hope.' Deleev paused for a moment, then said, 'I should perhaps also tell you one more thing that

I don't think you know yet. Dan can isolate us from one another if he wants to, but always he hears. We believe he is the system that binds the earpieces together, but he is of the opinion that there is something beyond him as well. There is never any true secret, but this however has been a private conversation between you and me. At least as private as it will ever be, for guardians such as us.' He paused for a moment. 'I was not present yesterday, so wanted to get an impression of you for myself.'

'And what is your impression?'

'From what Dan has said and from what you yourself have told me, I am looking forward to meeting you in person.'

'I haven't told you much.'

'You have told me more than you think, and that is enough for now. Dan has informed me that I have a long ride ahead of me. I will travel as fast as I can.'

25

The Deserteer on night watch took his time verifying the warrant, the likes of which he had never seen before. The three unknown Deserteers, with their blue-lined cloaks, had simply presented the boarding warrant at the loading hatch of the *Merysands*, and requested to see the captain immediately. They also stated that because it was a blue certificate, there would be no need for them to sign the embarkation log. It was only a short time later, after having spoken to the captain, that the three Deserteers left the *Merysands* without signing the register of disembarkation, either.

'Watchman,' said one of the three Deserteers, before jumping from the side of the loading ramp. 'It is our understanding that the captain wishes to see you again, immediately.'

The watchman waited until the three had disappeared into the darkness, then went to present himself at the door of the command cabin.

'Ah, yes!' said the captain, opening the door and ushering the watchman in. 'You need to strike any references you may have made about our three visitors from the boarding log, and tell no one else of this—at least for the time being. There is to be no record of these Deserteers having ever been aboard the *Merysands*. You would do well to grasp that this is not a request, but a Guild order. Do you understand?'

'I think so. Yes, Captain.'

'Then make sure it is so.'

After the door had closed, the captain's forehead wrinkled. He was puzzled. Sky- ships had been Petty's life since he'd met him, and so his sudden resignation had come as a complete surprise. His written resignation had cited family reasons, although Petty had never mentioned a daughter before. Coupling that with the blue certificate, the captain knew his world had changed again, as it had two years before when the man named Jarrak had boarded his ship. Now, for the second time, he had been given orders bound and sealed in blue.

The three strange Deserteers had only suggested to him that maybe the maintenance crew should find a reason for the *Merysands* to stay tethered for at least another sixteen days, and perhaps a little longer. Sixteen was a critical number, meaning that the *Merysands* would have to give up all its cargo to other sky-ships. The Guild had a reputation to uphold, and punctuality had always been the mantra of the Air Deserteers. Ten days or even eleven and he could have held onto his trade, but sixteen was just too long. He knew this was why sixteen had been suggested. Orders of leave had also been suggested for most of the remaining crew, while a search began to replace the members of his crew who would also now not be returning along with Petty—crew members who had suddenly been transferred in bulk. He knew there were always periodic losses of crew, illness, and Deserteers just wanting advancement or a change. But to have so many leave at once, as well as his first officer and loadmaster, meant he would need time to rebuild.

He knew from within the reported history of his own family that there had once been a connection between the Deserteers and the Comcree. He knew, too, that the Comcree were historically known for making suggestions. And the colour assigned to them had always been blue …

He found himself thinking of the young Sharacanese girl they'd brought back to Elora-Bearer. He'd wondered, then, why she had been important to the Museum. Now he wondered if it had had little to do with the Museum at all … He had not seen the missing members of his crew for three days—not since they'd gone to witness her adult induction ceremony.

The Deserteers had also been wearing blue-lined cloaks, which stated that they were part of a Deserteer protectorate. A protectorate meant one thing—that one of the Comcree was nearby. Although he had never been told officially, he knew now that the Comcree were also part of the Guild.

* * *

Thace couldn't remember much from the night before, or the day before, or the night before that. He lay in bed, trying to gather his thoughts and hoping that his head hurt too much for him to be truly dead. If he were dead, it surely meant that his head would throb like this for eternity. *By the gods,* he thought to himself. *Why and why now?* Slowly, he lifted his legs over the side and shifted up into a sitting position.

'That's done,' he said to himself. Then his right eye opened to let in the light before quickly closing again. His hands rose to massage his temples. *By the gods,* he thought again. Had it been real? Yesterday? Had Dan really said the words he was remembering? Had he really spoken to Andreena's chosen successor? All his life, he had been one of the hidden—a Comcree ghost guiding from the side, making sure this world headed in the right direction. But he'd never made himself known; walked out into the light. How could he know if this was something he could do?

'Layatty. She believes in me,' he said softly. 'She knows the reality of my world and she follows me! So maybe others will, too.'

Just then, the door to his room opened and a short, white-haired girl backed into the room, carrying a tray. 'I heard your feet touch the floor,' she said. 'So come on, old man, time we were gone!' She wore a blue-green dress with a red sash around her waist; the sign of an apprentice. A Comcree apprentice.

'By the gods, girl, have you gone mad?'

'No,' said Layatty, looking at him with assured brightness. 'Last night, you said that we have an army to find!'

'Who has seen you in that?'

'Only the lady downstairs—who, by the way, is still in the kitchen and seems slightly annoyed with you!'

'And what has she said?'

'She only asked me if the dress was real.'

'To which you said?'

'Yes!'

'Of course, you did,' said Thace, shaking his aching head.

'She still thought you should have this, though,' said Layatty, holding out the breakfast tray.

'What else did you tell her?'

'I'm not that silly,' said Layatty sitting down beside him. 'Eat. Your clothes are over there on the chair. Now that you're awake, I'm going to the barn to get the shrows ready. You come when you're dressed, and make sure you apologise. I don't know why she allows you back here time after time.'

Thace sat and stared at his blue-green tunic. He thought of Batteen, thousands of marces to the south, and Deleev and Heggon to the east. He knew that none of them had ever worn their Comcree uniform in public either.

Layatty stood and walked to the door. 'Eat, old man, or I'll force it down your throat.'

In his life, Thace had travelled through this region many times without anyone knowing what he did or who he was. Everyone had always presumed Layatty to be his daughter. From the day she had first started to travel with him, she had never told, either. "Look, learn, and listen" had been the first instructions he'd given her, and she'd taken them to heart. From this moment on, though, he would no longer be anonymous. He would be who he really was—one of the Comcree. And that scared him. The thought of fronting the woman downstairs scared him more, though. Lovers didn't like deception. Even occasional lovers.

On and off over half a lifetime, Thace and the independently minded owner of the tavern and chandlery had known each other. It wasn't the fact that he was Comcree that seemed to annoy her; she said she could understand him having his secrets. What affected her more was the fact that, the night before, the last night she might ever see him, he had drunk so much he had been useless to her.

'You were a waste of manhood last night,' she said when he entered the barn, before slapping him and promptly bursting into tears. Then she threw her arms around him.

When Thace and Layatty rode back from the barn, past the tavern's porch, the tavern keeper cried out after them. 'Take care of him, lass! If at all possible, I would like him to come back in one piece someday.' She turned and walked inside, pulling her shawl up over her shoulders.

'I told you to apologise to her,' said Layatty, hitting him now on the shoulder.

'I did!' said Thace.

* * *

Far to the east of the Kalcool, near the most eastern edge of the Meglia land mass, Deleev stood in the twin mooned shadows of a hangar building, looking out across the sky port of Fiskay. It was nearly midnight. Only moments before he had, for the first time outside of the Hassis, changed into his Comcree tunic.

He looked towards a smallish sky-ship—a type used in the windy regions of Meglia where landing space was minimal. The *Aquasands*' reputation for being quick had also aided in his decision. It was definitely the ship he needed for the purpose he had in mind.

A storm had prevented him from catching a boat across Fiskay Bay to the north-eastern port city, so for the last two days he had ridden around its lengthy perimeter without stopping. He was tired. He knew sleep would only come once he was in the air, but now his mind wandered to how he would be received in his garb.

"Bad luck" were the words his father had uttered the day his family had been discovered near the walled city of Learnian. The College had always thought of themselves as superior. Their arrogance had grown until they'd eventually stifled their region into accepting this belief. For generations, Deleev's family had put up with these black-robed thugs by submitting to their laws. But his father had decided enough was enough; he'd had enough of seeing his son and wife being treated like bound servants on their own land. It was his father's determination to rebuff the College that had led to their discovery. That had been the day Deleev had lost not only his father, but also his mother.

The Black Robes had thought Deleev young enough to be swayed, but he never was. The images of his father and mother being slain remained vivid in his memory.

It was a Comcree warrior, disguised as one of the Black Robes, who retrieved him from his nightmare five years later. The warrior had been undertaking a clandestine survey of the College stronghold when she'd allowed Deleev to notice her. Later, after realising she was a woman, he'd thought her the bravest person in the world. He'd known that if the Black Robes discovered her disguise, her life would have ended immediately and violently.

She had observed his conviction against the Robes and the inner strength that had held him calm. As she was leaving Learnian, she had sought him out again, and allowed him to see the blue dagger hidden beneath the folds of her disguise. It was only after they'd escaped together that she'd made a further decision, and petitioned for him to become her apprentice.

Right now, as he looked out at the sky-ship, he remembered her words throughout his apprenticeship. They'd told him that one day, he might have to walk out into the light of this world, whereas she had only ever walked in the shadows. 'If you must show the world your true identity,' she had said, 'then that will be the day of true bravery. To guide a world from the open, instead of from the shadows, will take great strength.'

The *Aquasands*' young captain awoke to the knocking on his door, at first confused by the unexpected presence of the stranger dressed in a blue-green tunic. 'I have a suggestion for you, Captain,' said Deleev, as he held out his warrant for the young captain to inspect. 'You are to provision your ship for a trip south. An excursion of at least sixteen days.'

The captain rubbed sleep from his eyes and looked again to see if the Comcree warrior was still there. He took the warrant, noting its seals and statements, and looked again at Deleev. Like all Deserteer captains, he'd been taught that one day this might happen. He had never really expected it, though. No one ever did. His father and grandfather had both been sky-ship captains, and nothing like this had ever happened to either of them.

'May I see your dagger?' asked the *Aquasands*' captain. Deleev looked at him for a moment, then drew out his weapon and handed it over. He watched the captain pace back to his bunk and pick up his own Deserteer dagger, then examine the two weapons side by side. 'Have you ever used this?'

'I use it all the time,' said Deleev. 'But not to draw blood, no.'

'Do you think you ever will?'

'It has become a possibility.'

'And you intend to involve my ship in this?'

'No, Captain. That is up to you.'

The captain stood in thought for a moment, then handed back the Comcree dagger. 'Mister Henny,' he said turning towards the door. It opened, and the man on night watch appeared within its frame. 'Wake my first and second officers if you wouldn't mind, Mister Henny.'

'Yes, Captain,' said the night watchman.

When Mister Henny went to close the door, the young captain said, 'Just a moment, Mister Henny. The door to my cabin is rather thin, so I am wondering if you have any personal qualms about taking this … *irregular* excursion we've been asked to involve ourselves in.'

The man looked at the captain for a moment, then at Deleev, then back at the captain. His eyes shone with awe. 'Not if you don't, Captain!'

* * *

From her bedroom window in her parents' house, Batteen looked past the trees, out over the misty waters of the southern sea. She wondered what her mother and father would think of her in just a few moments' time. She had delayed enough, but couldn't stop thinking about her life up until now, and imagining what it might be like from now on. Since her late teens, she had been one of the guardians of this world.

Her mother was still agile for her age and continued to work hard. Batteen smiled at the thought of the tough, rotund woman who had helped guide her. She thought of her father, how he had aged since his illness, even though his mind remained brilliant. He'd always been much more to her than just the fisherman he thought himself to be. She wondered how he would fill his days now that his illness had permanently taken the sea from him.

It seemed fitting that she'd been here when Dan's voice crackled in her ear, telling her of Hestean and the ramifications that came with her new sister's arrival. The news had made her more scared than she'd expected to be. Not scared of the College, but of her own deceit. She had kept her secret hidden from everyone, including her parents. She turned to look in the mirror again, at her blue-green dress, and thought to herself, *They are about to see a daughter neither of them knew they had.* She retrieved the blue dagger that lay on her quilted bed and belted it to her waist. Then she turned once more, back to the mirror. She lifted her head to make herself look stronger than she felt, then moved off towards the door, stepping from her room into her father's house. She walked through the rooms to where her parents sat together, still wondering what they would make of her. She took a deep breath before presenting herself.

There was a long pause. Then, from his pillowed reading chair, Batteen's father looked up and said, 'You look good in that. It's about time you wore it!'

'You knew?'

'We might be old, but we aren't blind,' said her mother. 'By helping to keep your true nature hidden, we helped keep you safe.'

'How long have you known?'

'Years,' said her father, having already returned to his book.

'I've been awake before the sun, wondering how to tell you both!'

'And now you have,' said her mother. 'I gather, too, that you must be telling us because this world is about to change.'

'Yes,' said Batteen. She dropped into a chair. 'Two days ago, we found the last of the Comcree, who has been missing for a very long time. We are once again whole, and once again we have the strength to push back against the College. I have to leave today.'

'I suppose you'll want a full breakfast, then, will you?' asked her mother, putting aside her darning and getting up to walk to the cookery.

'Is that all you have to say? Don't you understand? I don't know when I'll be back!'

'We understand, Batteen,' said her father, putting aside his book. 'But we have always known this day might come. We knew something was bothering you yesterday; I happened to hear you talking to yourself in the morning. Afterwards, we noticed the weight that descended upon you. For many years, we wondered why you chose to wander the world instead of settling down. Then one day, your mother saw a piece of blue-green cloth poking out from one of your traveling bags. We have known since then who you are. Your mother is Shirey, don't forget. From that day, all we have ever been is proud of you. It takes strength to be who you are, Batteen, and strength you have always had.'

'But Father,' she said, approaching to tuck the blanket further around his legs. 'I came to spend time with you.'

'And you have, and will again. I'm not ready to leave this world quite yet, you know.'

* * *

Later, as she rode through her village in her Comcree garb, she knew that the two people she loved most accepted her for who she was. One cycle of the moons had passed since she had first arrived back in the village of her birth. She had spent most of that time with her recuperating father. Now she knew that this sleepy south-western fishing village would finally understand why she had never given her parents a grandchild. She also realised why her father, many years before, had stopped pressing her to cease her endless travels and settle down. *Happenstance is a wondrous thing*, she thought, smiling to herself.

She headed east along the beaches and outcrops of the southern coast, skirting the Ice-Palm Forest with its tangle of lichen and moss. It wasn't till well after dark that she finally stopped, settling down to a restless sleep. She had read stories of the famed, ancient warriors of Sharacan, and she wondered now how she would compare to her newfound sister.

The morning after, while she sat finishing the last of her tea, she heard two riders enter the clearing behind her. *They're good*, she thought. *I should have heard them before now*. In one flowing movement, she rose, spun, and drew her dagger.

Still seated on their shrows were two startled young Deserteers. Or at least they looked like Deserteers; their uniforms fitted them badly and showed creases from generations of storage. Their daggers, however, looked polished and well-loved.

'Our grandfather sent us, Hlaford,' said one of the Deserteers, riding forward a few paces. 'He told us that a Comcree should never ride alone. He said that they should always be surrounded by a protectorate. He told us that for a Comcree to be seen riding alone at speed, there has to be something very wrong.'

Until yesterday, she had been but a myth, yet these two youngsters had still come to protect her. She looked at the youths, recognising both of them now. Riding down the wet sandy beach the previous morning, past the first village, she'd spoken to a familiar old man near his boat, mending his fishing nets. She now recognised his grandchildren; twins—one boy and one girl.

'And how does a fisherman know so much about the Comcree?'

'He didn't send us, exactly,' said the young woman. 'We volunteered. As you can see, the members of our family haven't always been fisherfolk. The uniforms belonged to our great-grandparents, but the daggers are ours. They were handed down to us some years ago, and we know how to use them.'

Batteen looked to their worn-out animals. These two make-believers had ridden through the night, and tracked her even in the dark. Impressed, she replaced her dagger in its scabbard. 'I will need a full protectorate, and more,' she said, 'by the time I get to where I am going. But on those animals, you won't be following me much further.'

'We don't intend to ride these,' said the young man. 'Our uncle lives in the next village. If we hadn't caught up with you by the time we reached it, we were going to swap our mounts for a couple of his. We still can.'

At least they are thinking. But how far ahead had they truly thought? She glanced at the red-and-blue bandanas around their heads. 'Red is not the colour of a protectorate,' she said. She turned to break camp. 'If those are real Deserteer bandanas, then the red can be uncurled from them. Blue outranks red; in times of conflict, entire protectorates can be killed before they have a chance to receive or wear the blue-trimmed tunics they deserve. It is now a time of conflict we find ourselves in.' She didn't look around, keeping her eyes off the twins while she collected her things. She hoped they would see she was doing it on purpose.

Her bedroll was the last to be stowed. As she climbed up onto her shrow, she wondered if they had understood her. She wondered if their bandanas would be blue or still interwoven with red. She even wondered if they would be still there, or if they'd melted back into the trees.

'There will be others, soon,' said the young man, and Batteen turned towards them. Their bandanas now consisted of only blue. 'In your wake, we saw other uniforms being donned throughout the villages, and shrows being outfitted for long journeys.'

'Where are we heading?' asked the young woman.

'East, then north,' replied Batteen, riding past them. 'Then we're going further north still. You are to see where your ancestors came from. Blue suits you both, by the way.'

'I am Onee and this is my sister, Onea,' said the boy.

'I know who you are,' said Batteen. 'Your mother died just after giving birth to you. You get your names from the words she spoke before she died—one boy and one girl.'

The twins looked to each other, then moved to follow this woman of the gods.

The twins flanked Batteen where they could as they continued to ride eastward along the coast. They ate and drank on the move, and only in the latter part of the afternoon did they stop.

After coming to the bank of a large river, Batteen—unaccustomed to explaining herself—halted within the shadows of the adjacent forest. The exhausted twins drew up beside her without questioning her stillness. They were tired after their travel and took advantage of the unexpected rest.

In silence, Betteen looked at the small coastal town on the other side of the Cleofan River, which flowed down through a broad valley to their north. Eventually, she saw what she had been waiting for. 'It's time we were going.' She shifted her shrow abruptly forward, exposing her presence to the village, and headed north along the western bank of the river.

That evening, by the time the night had closed around them and they were setting up camp, their small group had increased by four. By the following night, their number had increased again, and over the days that followed, Batteen's protectorate expanded to its maximum of fifteen. Then, as more novices joined her, the beginnings of her squadron took shape. Not in two hundred years had the blue-green dress, flowing cloak, and blue-jewelled dagger of a Comcree warrior been seen in this southwest province, but even here, the Alliance had left its legacy. The sight of a Comcree warrior riding alone, at speed, without protection, had brought the first of the volunteers. Just as Onee had predicted, it had then brought forth many more.

* * *

Far to the east, Deleev wondered how Batteen's march north was going. Yet he had his own task to worry about. The Toughs was a foul place. Most of it was frozen, except for hot mud pools that bubbled up from the bowels of the earth, smelling of sulphur. It was into this unwholesome region, below the Escales Ranges of the southeast, that the *Aquasands* had flown. Deleev had suggested to the captain that they search for a small island, just off the coast of the Toughs, within the Frozen Sea itself.

Now, five days after leaving Fiskay, the *Aquasands* hovered above a rocky outcrop, having found no suitable place to land. On the captain's command, the crew fired the grapples, hauling the *Aquasands* still closer to the rocks. Within moments, three men appeared, carrying a box between them. They scrambled hastily aboard the still floating sky-ship. Immediately, the ship's loadmaster signalled for the winches to run out, letting the *Aquasands* rise to a safe height above the hazardous terrain.

'You found it, then,' said Deleev, greeting the first man to hoist himself up.

'Of course, brother. It was right where it was supposed to be,' said Heggon. His great size now towered above Deleev. He turned to the loadmaster, and with calm authority, said, 'We are done here. You can uncouple your ship from this cold piece of hell, if you wish.'

'I wish to very much,' said the loadmaster, turning to Deleev. Deleev nodded his agreement, and the loadmaster spoke into his voice receiver. The grapplers released their hold and the *Aquasands* lifted into the sky.

'You saw and spoke to our new sister,' asked Heggon, turning to Deleev.

'Yes,' said Deleev, grinning. 'She is definitely Sharacanese.'

The big man smiled. 'I told her I like the desert. How far do you think she'll take us?'

'I don't know, brother, but it was her decision to make, even if I do wish it had been mine. How far she goes will depend on what we find at Sharacan. I do hope she will take us all the way to Learnian. As you know, I have a personal score to settle with that city.'

'You mean if she finds Andreena?'

'Yes!' said Deleev. 'But it is already a certainty that when she's finished, the College will no longer control her desert village. Generational remnants of the Alliance are, even now, flocking to Batteen in the southwest, as you no doubt know.'

'I have seen that, yes,' said Heggon.

'I am sure our Sharacanese sister seeks more than just Sharacan,' said Deleev.

'You think so?'

'It is something Dan said. He said that cwens are formed from history, and so are great cwens. I think Hestean Descee is meant to go a long way.'

'The future is never known, brother.'

Deleev's grin grew a little stronger. 'Gorean has told me she wears two daggers. Just like Andreena. I think that if she sets her mind to it, she will free this world of the College completely.'

'Maybe, then, she is already a warrior, like the rest of us!' said Heggon. As the cargo door started to close, he said, 'I should get changed. The captain knows where we are headed?'

'First to Dell and then to Sinkar, where Batteen will be waiting. Then we rendezvous with Thace. The captain estimates about five, maybe six days to Sinkar. Do you think it was luck that you were here, and Batteen was with her parents?'

'Stranger things have happened.'

'That's exactly what I mean. Don't you ever wonder why we are just where we are supposed to be, sometimes?'

'We work for the gods, Deleev, even if the gods say we don't!'

The ship started due west, flying into the wind as they crossed the lacework of green slime separating the ice and the boiling mud of the Toughs. If the College had become aware of Deleev's or Heggon's journey, they hadn't shown it. There were no settlements to the west of the Toughs—the sheer spires of stone that formed the southern peaks of the Escales had always been a barrier to settlement.

The mountains began as steady undulations, but soon became sharp spires of rock that, for nearly six thousand marces, rose towards the inland plateau, then kept rising. Amongst these mountains were vast, uncharted canyons and valleys, blocked from daylight, and filled with deep, icy coldness. The *Aquasands* passed through these valleys, using them as shelter against the constant westerly blow, twisting through each valley's dangerous bends and turns. The Escales formed a long peninsula that divided the Frozen Sea in the east from the slightly warmer currents of the Southern Sea to the west.

On the morning of their fourth day westward, the *Aquasands* lifted from its nightly tethers and broke from its shelter into the turbulence that assaulted it without restraint. With the blades of the sky-ship roaring at their maximum, it pushed slowly forward. Deleev saw just how good his choice had been. Any ordinary captain would have allowed his ship to flounder here. But his was no ordinary captain. Giant, jagged spires appeared as if from nowhere as they were dangerously tugged by the wind, but the captain and crew were masters of this ship, and when all seemed lost, the *Aquasands* would swing free from disaster.

Finally, the *Aquasands* descended back into the more sheltered valleys on the other side, where the mountains were now rounded and polished by the constant onslaught of the wind. Here, the *Aquasands* once again hid in valleys, then headed, unseen, out over the Southern Sea towards the island of Dell.

26

When entering the remains of Sinkar, a settlement that had slipped from living memory a thousand years before, Batteen had pulled aside the twins to watch nearly a full squadron—almost two hundred men and women—trail past her. Behind her, spreading out in a line, sat the fifteen Deserteers of her protectorate.

The ancient tribes of the inland plateau had dispersed and scattered, but they'd taken with them their beliefs. It was from within these myths and legends, clothed now in antique Deserteer uniforms, that she had gathered the force she required. Fisher-folk, farmers, and tradespeople of all sorts had flocked to her as if from legend. She now hoped, as her fellow guardians did, that this time that force might actually banish the College.

'Hlaford,' said Onee. Batteen looking up at him from where she now sat beside one of the many campfires, which sent shadows flickering on the ancient stone walls like ghosts. 'This is Sett. He only caught up with us this morning, and he has told us something we think you should hear.'

She looked at the newcomer, putting aside her thoughts of tomorrow. She got to her feet and placed her hands behind her back, close to the flames. 'I was born to the cold, but I have never come to terms with it,' she explained. Sett stood in front of her, silent, mouth slightly open. 'You can talk to me, you know!' smiled Batteen. 'I'm not a god. I only work for them.'

Her remark caused the twins to smile, too, and Sett said, still wonder-struck, 'Yes, Hlaford … I mean … I am from the small town at the mouth of the Cleofan.'

'Spitford,' said Batteen. 'I know your town well.'

Again, Sett was startled. 'Then you probably also know that the College maintains a presence there,' he said. 'We are at the very edge of their territory, so they don't interfere overly much. But at about the time I was told you passed Spitford, they became very agitated, and began to tighten restrictions. Then, a few days later, two College tri-hulls arrived. One of them carried a College delegation. After they'd talked to the town's chairman, one of the ships continued east that very afternoon, under full sail. The other ship left the next morning. It, too, continued east, and took with it most of the town's Robe garrison. From what the twins here have told me, I think you were seen, Hlaford!'

'Does this bring your plans undone, Hlaford?' asked Onea.

Batteen turned back to the fire, her face taking on a look of concerned satisfaction. She rubbed her hands together over the flames, knowing that the College ships had arrived earlier in the south than expected. The tri-hulls must have had good winds. She realised now just how big a disturbance Hestean's ascension had caused amongst the Robes of Elora-Bearer. *They aren't just scared*, she thought. *They're terrified.* 'If nothing else,' she said aloud, still looking into the flames, 'the College is predictable. It's this predictability that will bring them undone.'

She turned to look back at the newcomer. 'Does your uncle still run his tavern, Sett?'

'Ah, yes,' he said, and again Batteen knew she had surprised him.

'Good. He is a good man, your uncle, I've always liked him.'

'Do you know everyone?' asked Onee.

'Within my own region, yes. Those that are important, anyway.'

'I thought everyone was important!' said Onea.

'Everyone is,' replied Batteen, turning to look straight into the young woman's eyes. She was almost identical to her twin, despite their genders.

'Not only do you know everyone,' said Onee, 'but I think you know *about* them as well, don't you, Hlaford?'

She considered his observation but said nothing for a moment. Her demeanour shifted, becoming colder and more pointed. 'You know that neither of you volunteered, don't you? It was your grandfather who volunteered you. He thought you ready and worthy, just as everyone else here is. You should think about that. Even though I've made you my lieutenants, never forget that you are no different from anyone else here.' She watched the twins for another moment, then moved to look at Sett. 'Where is your brother?'

Sett's eyes opened wider, filling once more with awe, then moved shamefully away from her. She saw his throat gulp with his fear. He swallowed before saying softly, 'On one of the ships!'

'I thought he would be,' said Batteen. A misty vision of the past floated through her head. 'It's a shame. But trees in a forest never fall in the same direction, do they? Some people take the shorter road to knowledge, but the true road to knowledge is never short and never easy. Still, you are here, aren't you, Sett? And you would not be if your uncle had not thought you worthy. It is his dagger you carry, isn't it? That's what matters most.'

'Why does that matter?'

'Because, Sett, your colour is now blue. The twins will explain what I mean by this later. You were right when you said I was seen across the Cleofan at Spitford. They were meant to see me, and I hoped, too, that your uncle would hear of it. In the morning, I want you and the twins to divide the others into three groups. Each of you will lead one of these groups from now on, is that clear? And each group will take a turn at the task required.'

'What exactly will we be doing?' asked Onea, stepping between the two young men.

'Tomorrow, you will be digging,' said Batteen. 'You should get some rest. You will need it. That goes for all of you!' She turned to address the many other recruits who had crept within the glow of the firelight. She scanned her eyes across the many faces and said, 'There is much to be done in the next few days, and much you will learn and see, too.'

* * *

Further to the north-west, most of the settlements along the Southern Whay River were ruins now. Their inhabitants had long ago moved further south and east as the Kalcool had expanded, although the river itself was still used for trade. It transported goods to and from the small, productive pockets of lush green flutter-weed that still remained in the corner of the plateau. A day after leaving Tavern Springs, Thace and Layatty had taken passage on a barge heading downriver towards the Junction. There, the Southern Whay and the once-mighty Whay River joined. River travel had given Thace time to think and form his plans without inebriation, as there was no drinking allowed on river barges.

'Did you know she cared for you that much?' asked Layatty, who sat watching him fork out hay for their two shrows, which stood in the open hull beside them.

'It was safe,' he said. 'Neither of us wanted commitment, but sometimes things have a habit of creeping up on you. Sometimes you only find there is a chance when it is taken.'

Layatty changed the subject. 'How long before we get to the Junction?'

'Both moons fully light the sky at the moment, so we should keep travelling after sunset. The captain thinks we will have an escort north.'

'Why is that?'

'The Shadow Shire is everywhere, it seems. The captain's sister is Shirey.'

'That's good, isn't it?'

'I think everyone is about to find out how much this world truly remembers,' he said.

* * *

As the sun reached its zenith, Batteen's three new groups started pulling chests—sealed long ago—from their hiding places. Enclosed within, the Deserteers found strange treasure, which made them recall some of the darker tellings. 'Thunder staffs,' said Sett, recalling the story his uncle had once told him. 'Do you intend to start a new war?'

'No,' said Batteen. 'We are destined to end one.'

In the late afternoon, when they had finished uncovering all the boxes, the blue stone at the end of Batteen's dagger flashed. She turned to look towards the southeast. Thunder staffs were weapons that could not work without the power of the Comcree, and as if on cue, her group of new Deserteers became aware of a droning in the darkening sky. The *Aquasands* had finally reached Sinkar.

Later, as a light breeze moved in the darkening twilight, the campfires began to flicker. Batteen and her two Comcree brothers sat sipping tea. 'The only thing wrong with desert tea is the grit it contains,' said Heggon.

'I thought you liked the desert,' said Batteen.

'I do, but not always its sand.'

She paused. 'You said they saw you. Are you really sure?'

'I certainly hope so,' said Deleev. 'Do you know how hard it is to look as if you don't want to be seen? Unless they were all blind, at least someone at Healfweg must have seen us coming from the south.'

Batteen glanced towards Heggon. 'Don't look at me like that,' he said quickly. 'I had my head mixed in with a bunch of wires at the time. Whoever dreamed up those boxes didn't want it to be easy.'

'Isn't that what our ancestors wanted?' said Deleev. 'Without the diagram I brought from Fiskay, even you would have found it completely impossible to install.'

'As opposed to being just slightly impossible, I suppose?'

'Yes, brother, that is exactly correct.'

'Igniter boxes are machines designed for conflict, and now we are once more about to use them,' said Batteen. 'Do you know if it works yet, Heggon?'

'It works!'

'You sound sure of yourself.'

'I tried one of your staffs earlier, when Deleev was showing you the installation within the *Aquasands*.'

'That was you?' exclaimed Deleev. 'We heard the discharge but thought it was just static grounding from the sky-ship.'

'You could have been killed!' said Batteen. 'What if your work had been flawed?'

'Exactly,' said Heggon. 'I wasn't going to let one of your young Deserteers pay for a mistake I may have made. Besides, I had the captain and one of your Deserteers with me. The captain was wondering what we had done to his ship, so I thought a demonstration would be the best way to explain it to him. As for the Deserteer, I asked your lieutenants if there was one among them with medical knowledge. You have a fully qualified physician, you know!'

'I have three, actually,' snapped Batteen.

'I do also have Layatty, remember,' said Heggan. 'As I recall, neither of you two have replacements yet!'

'I still wish you would have waited,' said Deleev, sounding just as annoyed as Batteen. 'I must admit though, I am curious. What was it like?'

'You will find out for yourself tomorrow,' said Heggon. 'I can assure you, though, they are well named as thunder staffs when at their full strength.'

'You tried it at full strength?' exclaimed Batteen.

'Well, we would have had to sooner or later.'

'Boys and their toys,' grumbled Batteen. She'd always had trouble hiding her feelings from Heggon, and she pulled her mind away from thoughts of him lying dead. 'How long can we afford to stay here?'

'If I've added it up properly,' said Deleev. 'We need to be gone from here in six days if we are to make our next rendezvous.'

'Then let's hope these young recruits are quick learners.'

'No one is quick to kill, Batteen,' said Heggon.

'I, too, feel your reservations,' said Batteen. 'But in conflict there are necessities.'

'What about the shrows?' asked Deleev.

Batteen looked towards the corralled animals that had brought her squadron to Sinkar. 'I've been wondering about them myself. I think we should assign a couple of Deserteers to herd them south again. It will add to the illusion of encirclement and will keep the College off balance. I have been told of their reaction after seeing me at Spitford. I think they are assuming, as we'd hoped, that we are circling, skirting the southern edge of the Kalcool to come at Learnian from the desert. It was only by chance that I was at my parents' village when the sixth dagger came back to us. I think it shook the College to see me on their western boundary so soon. If they saw you to the south, they might be wondering if we are intentionally surrounding them. The sheer cliffs of Dell make it reachable only from the air, and that's a resource the College does not possess. They may be thinking that Dell is where we've been hiding since we vanished. So, if a number of shrows were also amassed by Deserteers near the coast, it could help with our deception.'

'Sounds good to me,' said Heggon.

'Me too,' agreed Deleev. 'Those Robes are just arrogant enough to think that what they have, we want. Personally, though, I do hope Hestean will include my justice with hers.'

Batteen looked at Deleev, sensing that his long-held pain had been uncaged. 'We are in agreement about the shrows, then,' she said, still studying the other Comcree.

* * *

From the Junction, Thace and Layatty headed north towards the once thriving settlement of Chime Town. They were accompanied by ten young men and women, who had simply appeared, dressed in ill-fitting

Deserteer uniforms. 'I guess we are not the only hidden part of this world,' said Layatty, as her shrow trotted beside Thace's.

'And hopefully there are more still to come,' said Thace in return, doing his best to visibly project the authority he had never needed to show before.

Once in Chime Town, he led them down a deserted side street, then down another street towards some derelict barns and former liveries. The doors to one of the larger liveries opened and they rode in. They were immediately surrounded by cavaliers, who had been sent directly from the Hassis to meet them.

'I see you have made a start without us,' said a man, coming forward to hold the head of Thace's shrow.

'It's good to see a familiar face, Steph! Have you been here long?' Thace dismounted and grabbed hold of his friend's forearm as Steph grabbed hold of his.

'Six days. Gorean wanted us gone from the Hassis before the College thought to alert their spies. It would not have done for them to see us materialise as a force from a valley they thought had been deserted for centuries.'

'I suppose not! Have you seen my new sister?'

'No, it was Gorean who dispatched us. I believe the gods are keeping your new sister mostly engaged in the library.'

'Sounds about right. She will have a lot to learn, and quickly, now that her presence has turned this world upside down.'

'She has certainly done that,' said Steph. 'I've never seen the Hassis so alive.'

'How many do you have?'

'I've got one hundred; exactly half a squadron!'

'Then at least some of us will look as if we're professional,' said Thace.

'None of us are professional in this, Hlaford. We may look the part, but we are like those you have brought with you. We are all still just barge hands, stone masons, and gardeners, with the odd bookkeeper like myself thrown in for good measure.'

'But you are a bookkeeper who can ride, Steph, and you are a trained Deserteer. That's what we must impress with now.' Thace looked about him, at all the faces staring back at him. He decided that he would need to be honest with these Deserteers if he expected them to follow him. 'The rest of what we need to know, we will learn together! We'll press on in the morning, and there will be little time for sleeping until we reach Tear Salt. I suggest you get what rest you can.'

'And where to then, Hlaford?' asked Steph.

'We are going home, Steph,' said Thace. 'We are going to where the Comcree and the Deserteers first came into being.'

'History tells us that the Comcree are from the Sereye.'

'That it does, Steph, but I'm afraid you will have to wait to see if history is correct. Do you trust me, my friend?'

'I always have!'

'Good! That's why Gorean put you in charge of this contingent. And I trust you.'

After everyone had eaten and the sun had left the sky, Thace extracted himself from his protectorate and walked alone through the abandoned streets of Chime Town. For a while, he stood in its main square, contemplating. Then he took a small flask of ferment from his pocket. He swigged down the last of its contents and flung it away. He walked across the street and pushed open the decoratively carved doors of the grand hall. Even in this decrepit state, it was still a place to behold. It had been meant to last for millennia, and even without any maintenance, its polished stone was still intact. He walked through to the rows of seats, where he sat down just beyond the upper balcony. In silence, he sat looking down upon the far wall. The huge pipes, which no longer brought forth the music that had once filled this place, made his mind drift. The instrument was three times the size of the one at the Hassis.

He closed his eyes and heard himself say, 'If only this one still worked …'

'That would take a miracle,' said the old, withered man, who suddenly appeared beside him.

'Yes, but what a miracle it would be!' said Thace, to the ghost from his past.

'It is the first time I've seen you dressed as you should be, my apprentice.'

'I'm afraid we have another miracle to perform. One that is potentially much harder and will possibly change this world a great deal more. We are now six once again.'

'Then I wish you luck, warrior.'

'I'm getting tired, my teacher. Conflict is a young person's game.'

'Is he ready?'

'No! Gorean thinks Shenn still has some learning to do.'

'Will this bring him out, do you think?'

'It may, but why did I wait so long? Until now, it has all been a game to him. This may show him it is more than that, but I'm not sure.'

'Before Shenn, there was no one,' said the ghostly image. 'It had to be him! Gorean has not found any one yet to replace her, and as I recall, she is of a similar age to you.'

'Yes, but at least she has more to choose from than I did.'

'There is Layatty.'

'She has become better than I first thought she would, but as you know, she belongs to another house.'

'And what of this newly found warrior?'

'She is but an apprentice herself! Within her, though, I do feel the ability to wage conflict and win. Despite her youth she is strong, I believe.'

'Andreena was like that. As for Shenn, I wouldn't worry about him. He will be ready when his time comes. My dagger, which is now yours, will choose him; this I already know.'

* * *

Before the sun had started to light the sky, Thace awoke from his uncomfortable sleep. He stood, wondering how long he had been in the hall. He turned to see Layatty sleeping just three seats behind him. At his touch, she woke with a start.

'I got worried about you,' she said.

'I had some things to sort out.'

'You were sleeping—that's what you were doing.'

'Yes, that also,' said Thace with a smile.

From Chime Town, the cavaliers followed Thace northeast towards Tear Salt. Over the following days, even in this now desolate part of Meglia, their numbers started to grow.

By the time they arrived at what was now not much more than a watering hole, surrounded by neglect and abandonment, one-hundred-and-ninety men and women accompanied Thace. At Tear Salt, he set up camp and began to hone the skills of the newer recruits. The time for conflict was nearly upon them.

27

Looking out at the Hassis Valley through the expansive windows of the reading room, it finally became clear to Hestean why Dan had shown her the library. Since coming to the estate, she had spent most of her time in the reading room. Day after day, she had waded through its vast array of books, which had been added to by each generation of Comcree, going back thousands of years. Somehow she knew that each book she picked up had either been read or written by Andreena.

She lowered her eyes from the view outside and returned to reading. She imagined Andreena sitting in perhaps this very same chair, writing the words she was now reading. She read again the line that had sparked her imagination, and saw Andreena with a different book in her hand, sitting on a wagon as it trundled toward the Hassis.

Andreena, reading one of the oldest books, had found that in order to kickstart and maintain a new civilisation, the original Comcree had written what Hestean now thought of as a survival manual. It fascinated her. Now, from the notebook in front of her, she also knew that Andreena had made many more discoveries. All of the old books were written in an archaic form of the ancient language, but even most of the newer ones were deliberately written in Fem, too. Very few of the books were written in the modern tongue, and those that were held no real secrets. Was this the true reason why the dead and worthless language had been taught to her as a child?

Just as she had many times over the last few days, she put down the book and descended the stairs to talk with Dan for a while. Then, after listening to everything he told her, she returned to her books.

'You don't have to follow me everywhere, Karree,' she said to the woman who had become her shadow.

'You didn't see Petty's face the last time I let you slip away without me.'

'He worries too much.'

'It's his job!'

'Now that Gorean and Shenn have headed north, it's his job to oversee the *Merysands*' refit! That's what his job is.'

'Yes, and since that contingent of blue-clad cavaliers left, he has also been put in charge of provisioning the ship with enough supplies to sustain eight hundred Deserteers. He told me himself, he would have me torn to shreds if I left you alone again. Poor man doesn't know whether he's up or down!'

'They wouldn't have assigned him if they didn't think he could do it!'

'But it still doesn't stop him from worrying about you, does it?'

Hestean looked at the sleeves of her friend's blue-trimmed uniform and noticed the newly added letters stitched to them. 'You're not a loadmaster anymore, you know!'

'I know! But they mean more than just "loadmaster" to me. They denote my family, too. Where I go, these letters will always accompany me!'

* * *

In the library a while later, Karree looked across at Hestean. She knew she wanted to take on her new role as one of the young Comcree's protectorate with the same thoroughness she had given to her job as loadmaster. 'Can I read some of these books?' she asked, running her hand along one of the shelves.

Hestean lifted her eyes from her reading and watched Karree's fingers drag from one book to the next. 'If you can find one you understand, I don't see why not,' she replied. 'I've noticed Whittn doesn't seem to mind you hearing about what I read.'

Karree turned and frowned knowingly. She had already discovered that most of the books were unfathomable to her. 'How did you come to learn this language, Hestean?'

'I was taught it as a child. It's the language of the women in my village, but I realise now that it's also much more than that.'

'Can I learn it?'

'It's no secret, Karree, I'll teach you myself, if you like. When I have time, that is.'

'I'll hold you to that.'

'Make sure you do.'

'Do you have an exam or something at the end of this?' asked Karree. 'My father gave me lots of tests when I was learning to become a loadmaster.'

'By the gods, I hope not,' said Hestean, returning to her studies.

Karree smiled at the dark young woman, who had truly become her friend. She walked back out into the hallway to study the wall hangings and paintings she'd become fascinated by. As part of her training to become a loadmaster, she had learned to seek out and understand patterns within designs. Here, she was finding patterns again—all sorts of patterns with hidden meanings. They were telling her about a past she'd never dreamed of, nor even been told about. She was becoming as much a student of them as Hestean was of her books. In one of the older tapestries, she had even found a depiction of something that resembled the *Merysands*. In the tapestry, it was upside down, and appeared to have no rotors at the end of its winglets. It was only one of the many puzzles that kept her engaged.

* * *

Every evening, Hestean sat wearily at the kitchen table while Whittn made her something to eat. Usually Karree was with her, and Whittn found herself observing the two women together. She noticed their similarities. There was the pale white of Karree's skin and the deep blue-black of Hestean's, but that was where their differences ended. She had noticed that the two young women were physically the same athletic build, and they both had the same green eyes. The intensity of those eyes fascinated her.

One evening, Hestean came into the kitchen and pulled back a chair before collapsing into it. She brought her arms round onto the table and lowered her head to them.

'I am being pushed too hard, Mother!'

Whittn turned to the exhausted youngster and huffed. 'It is you who pushes yourself, child! You have had no apprenticeship and you are young for a Comcree, yet you have already absorbed much. Maybe it is your lack of schooling that allows you to ask questions of Dan that no other has ever dared to ask, but I think he likes you, my young one. He answers your questions, doesn't he?'

Hestean lifted her eyes to Whittn as the housekeeper put two bowls on the table. 'You should eat, and while you do, tell me a story. Your mind is like a dry sea that has found water. I want to hear what it has sucked up today.'

Karree reached for one of the bowls, and as she did, Hestean asked Whittn, 'Why do you allow Karree to hear my stories?'

'Because she needs to know them. There is a connection between the two of you. If she could read these books, I would allow that, but she can't. You both are to travel this road, and so you both need to know why. And besides …' Whittn looked to the Deserteer, whose blood ran closer to that of the warrior than even she realised. 'What I allow to be said in my presence, Karree will never mention elsewhere. Is that not so, Karree?'

'Always!' said Karree. 'But why should I know?'

'I didn't get to my position in life by accident, young woman, and I don't say things until they need to be said. Occasionally, though, two heads are better than one, and I see that in both of you.' Whittn now looked to Hestean. 'A story, if you please. I need a story.'

'Do you mean that I've been telling you about what I've read because you wanted Karree to know as well?'

'No, child. You tell me so that I know you know. But I think Karree is to hear them, too. I felt it the first time I saw you both. You may be one of the guardians, but she is *your* guardian, and to be a good guardian she must know you. What you learn here will determine who you are. So, she must know that also.'

'I see.'

'I don't think you do. Not yet, anyway, but you will. So, a story please.'

'Yes!' said Karree, reaching towards the centre of the table to ladle out some stew. The stovepot was still steaming, and she filled both their bowls.

'So now I have a bossy sister as well as a bossy mother?' asked Hestean.

'Yes!' said Whittn and Karree together.

* * *

By the morning of the fifteenth day, Hestean hadn't read all the books, nor had she fully understood some of the ones she had read. She knew by now that to understand them all would take years. She had, however, read enough to understand these warriors of the past. The Comcree had once been part of a great people and had enabled the Sharacanese to survive in this world. She'd read their history and some of their science and technology. She also knew, now, what the College would do if they ever again possessed more power.

She had grown up knowing of the College, but now she really *knew* them. She knew what beliefs like theirs could do to a world if there was no constraining them. They believed that only those at the top should hold the power of knowledge. It would stifle the world. She had learnt that at their centre was a craving for power. A craving that had, as of yet, not been fulfilled because Andreena had stopped them. They also thought that what they were seeking dwelt in the Sereye, but Andreena had also stopped them from finding that destination.

But the College were wrong. Hestean had a deeper interest in Sharacan, and it was because of this that she'd come across how the wells of Sharacan truly came into existence. She had confirmed her realisation about the wells with Dan, and it was then that she'd heard something that he told her to keep to herself. Not even Whittn or Karree were to know. Not yet, anyway. The secret startled her, and she began to wonder if he really was just the benevolent benefactor he was pretending to be.

* * *

The next morning, Hestean walked downstairs, having been summoned by Dan once more. In her usual way, just one step behind, Karree trailed her. They entered the below-ground chamber, where Karree then opened a door to a second room she had never been allowed into. She closed the door after Hestean had passed through and stood guard outside.

Hestean had been cocooned in her world of books up until now, but now Dan said, 'It is time for you to re-join the larger world. There, Karree will do for you what I am not able to do! But first, I have one last thing to show you. After that, you must be like twins.'

'What do you mean?'

'As you have been told, there is a shield over Sharacan, and so I cannot help you there. Rarely have I seen one as diligent in her protectiveness as your companion outside; I think she is someone you should keep close to you!'

'She has become a good friend, yes.'

'She is indeed that,' said Dan, studying Hestean through his eye. 'Keep her close. You will have need of her.' He paused for a moment, wondering, then decided and said, 'I did not, however, ask you here to discuss one of your protectorate! Like a dagger, the Comcree have unsheathed themselves once more, and you have unsheathed your history. So, stand in front of the screen, if you would, and touch just inside its top left corner.'

'Why?'

'You always have to know *why*, don't you? Well, if you do it, you will find out why.'

She walked across and touched the screen. It lit up to display a contents list. Facing away from the bottom corner, on the right-hand side, was an arrow, then an X, then an arrow facing towards the corner. In the bottom left-hand corner, there was a small box, displayed with its lid open.

'Normally' said Dan, 'I can display anything you ask me to, but there may come a time when I am unable to do so. So, this is how the screen works if I am unable to talk to you, or you me. Choose any one of the items on the list—for now, it doesn't matter which—and touch it with your finger.'

Hestean selected an item and instantly the screen opened out into another display.

'If you stroke your finger across the screen—either up, down, or sideways—the image on the screen will follow, allowing you to see more.'

Hestean moved her finger up and down. She smiled. Then she stroked her finger across the screen a few times until the display refused to move any more.

'If you touch the screen with a finger from each hand, and pull them apart, the screen will magnify. If you bring them together, it will do the reverse. Touch the left facing arrow at the bottom right.'

'I am back to where I started!' said Hestean, as the contents list reappeared.

'Yes, and if you touch the right facing arrow, it will jump you to the next section—if there is one. The X in the middle will switch off the screen. If you touch your finger to the edge of the screen and pull it around the edge, the image displayed on the screen will rotate.'

'What about the box here in the bottom left corner?'

'If you touch your finger to the screen and then circle a piece of information, you can drag it to the box. It will save whatever you've circled into a special heading of your own description, so you can find it quickly later. Within that heading, you can create sub-headings, too. You write the identifier with your finger on the screen in the space provided. There is more, but you will be able to work out the rest on your own now.'

'Why have you really shown me this, Dan? You think there are more screens out there somewhere, don't you?'

'I don't know what you will find, Hestean. As you know, I cannot see into every place, but at Sharacan there may be screens like this one, yes. This screen is as old as I am, and the journey you are about to make will lead you further into the past than any who have ever travelled this road before. You must be as prepared as you can be, for it is you who will lead your people back to their beginning. We have waited three thousand years, and now it is time. This is what Andreena was supposed to do, but because we needed her dagger, she has handed the task to you. There are new rumblings from within the ranks of the younger Robes. They seem to be setting aside their adherence to the old beliefs, including the rule that the obelisk at Sharacan must always stand. To that end, we set in play a plan that we hoped would draw Andreena's dagger out, if it was at Sharacan.'

'Did Gorean and the others know of all this?'

'Not all, no! They know what they needed to know. I told you, Andreena was the one I talked to. Now that you have taken her place and are so much like her, I talk to you. Only you have been told it all. You are the inheritor of her bloodline, Hestean, and as such, you must now go forth and complete what she was unable to finish. Your bloodline is unique on this world, Hestean, and one day I may confirm to you why. But you will first have to find out why yourself.'

'Did Andreena know?'

'She did! And the same rule applied to her, as it does you and those who inherit after you. You will know only what you deem to know.'

PART III
THE UNVEILED KEY

28

The day Hestean turned eighteen was also the day the elderly chairman of Sharacan died. Winnz came into Jarrak's tent, mumbling unhappily to himself. Preoccupied, he pulled two books from under his robe and sat down without saying a word. There had been no "good morning"; no explanation for his late arrival, nor for why he'd silently begun copying the words from one book into the other.

Puzzled, Jarrak had watched the scribe make a mistake and tear the page from his book. He did this three times, crumpling each into a ball before flinging it to the ground.

'By the gods, Winnz, what is the matter? And what are you doing, anyway?'

'Copying! He'll kill us all! He wants to change everything and seems blind to the consequences that will flow from such changes.'

'Who will? And what changes?'

'Gaywin has become the new chairman.'

'What? How did that happen?'

'Robe Elless, the under-chairman, relinquished his claim to the position, so it was left open for anyone to claim. Once relinquished, he could not take it back. He wanted to, but it was too late, and Gaywin was the only challenger.'

'But surely there would have been someone else?'

'Elless thought there would be other challengers better suited to the role than himself. But they backed down after a short adjournment. I didn't see what happened, but something went on during the recess. When we resumed, the two expected challengers seemed pale, and announced they wouldn't go ahead with their claims.'

'And you?'

'Me, no. I'm too old to be chairman. It's not something I would be suited to, anyway. I'm just a scribe—that's what I am.'

'You're more than just a scribe, Winnz. You would have been a good choice for chairman.'

'Maybe once. Once, years ago, I tried to challenge, but I was much too young then. Now I'm too old, and time has passed me by. As you can see, they think I'm now only good for keeping an eye on you, and as a keeper of books.'

'Is that what's worrying you? Reporting things you don't want to report, to someone you don't like?'

'Like I said, I am old, but from me, Gaywin will hear only what I want him to hear. What troubles me is that he is going to stop the women here from using the ancient language and bring Sharacan into line with other College enclaves.'

'But he can't. It's written into the Treaty of Truce.'

'Exactly! He will kill us all.'

'But hasn't anyone told him that?'

'He is of the younger thinking, which is making itself heard within Learnian these days. Little by little, our history has been altered over generations to justify new interpretations. It has resulted in a lessening of the truth.'

'That is what happens when knowledge is kept by only a few at the top. There is nothing to back up alternative thoughts.'

'Yes, Maskee, that is exactly so. It happens here, too, with each new chairman. Because of my position as a scribe, I know this, and Gaywin is probably already looking through the old chairman's books to see what he will remove. However, he cannot actually do anything until his appointment has been ratified by Learnian.'

'And how long will that take?'

'A courier will take ten days to get there and ten to get back, but if the High Council has other priorities, then the courier will have to wait there for a hearing.'

'So, twenty days!'

'Yes. And he also intends to stop the Sharacanese from working for you. He cannot stop your work until his position is confirmed due to your contracts, but he can stop the Sharacanese now.'

'But I don't employ all the men who are working here now. Not at the temple, anyway. They may work to my directions, but I don't employ them.'

'And that is why he can stop it! Hestean may be dead, but she stood up to him the way the rest of the villagers are now starting to. The way he treated her has emboldened them.'

'Like her father and Qworeel, you mean?'

'Her death sparked a rejuvenation in the Sharacanese. More and more of them are flocking to restore the temple. She died helping you, and that is why they are starting to do the same in their free moments. She threatens Gaywin more than she did when she was alive.'

'I can't stop them from rebuilding the temple if that's what they want to do.'

'No, and neither will he if he doesn't stop it soon. There will be too many. We are only a small contingent here, Maskee, and we rule because the Sharacanese allow us to rule. And only because they fear Learnian—not because they fear us. Something bad is coming, Maskee. I am sure of that!'

'So, what are you intending to do with these books?'

'I have twenty days to copy the old chairman's journals before they can be altered. If you don't mind, I would like to hide the originals here with you.'

'You can do that?'

'I might be old, but I am a very good scribe. It might be the only protection you have.'

'Do you think I should tell Sharn and Qworeel? They came to the temple first, and the others look to them for guidance.'

'I have no real idea of what is about to happen, Maskee, but Sharn was her father, and if a child's nature blossoms, it must have been nurtured. Gaywin will think of this, too. Now that Hestean is gone, he will take his frustrations out on her closest kin. He's a vengeful man, and for some reason he has always hated Sharacan.'

'Yes, I've seen that, too. How long will it take you to copy the books?'

'More time than I have. I will copy what I think are the most important volumes first.'

'Then you would do better to slow down and not make any more mistakes. I'll find a place to hide them, but first I will find Sharn.'

* * *

As Jarrak looked around at the temple, he recalled the day he'd first seen Sharn and Qworeel standing in its courtyard. It was shortly after Hestean had walked out into the desert, and only a few days after he'd made the decision that had—in part—led to this day. The actual decision had not been his; until that day it had just been an idea, something he'd talked about with Winnz while walking amongst the excavations. Sharn and Qworeel had been standing at a distance from those who were actually employed on the excavations. As one of them turned towards Jarrak, he immediately recognised him. 'I don't believe I have employed you,' Jarrak had said, flipping back through his script-hold.

'We have come because I believe I have a debt to repay,' said Hestean's father, stepping forward. 'And to start repaying that debt, I have asked Qworeel here to assist in your reconstruction. He is our village stoneworker.'

'Reconstruction? What reconstruction? And what debt are you talking about?'

'The day after my daughter walked out into the desert, I was more ashamed of myself than I have ever been, crosslander. Her actions have also made many of the men in this village feel ashamed, too. She was not yet an adult, and we should have stood up for her. But we have become cowards. We were the reason she died that day, not the Robes. Until yesterday, I wished for death, too. She was my light, you see. My reason for living. According to the Robes, she was not supposed to be, but she was. She was the one who made my existence here worthwhile. I never told her that, and I should have. I thought I was protecting her by restraining her. I may have shunned her for nearly two years, but I always knew where she was. She has been the only one to continually defy these Robes, and although I showed my disapproval, in a way I admired her, too. Her mother was the same when she was younger; I have known for a long time that this is what I most admired about both of them. When I asked Sathea's father if we could be tied, I hoped back then that her strength would allow me to survive here. Like most here, I chose to simply survive, not to find my strength. When the time came for me to stand, I failed to protect the one person I should have. When Hestean walked out into the desert, I spiralled so low that I couldn't get up in the morning. Yesterday, though, Sathea said something that woke me up. She said that our daughter will be eighteen in a few days' time. She didn't say "she would be, if she had lived"—she said "she *will* be". Sathea has always been right. She then proceeded to tell me that we had not actually lost a daughter at all. Instead, she explained how you had planned Hestean's escape.' Pausing for emphasis, Sharn then continued. 'So you see, crosslander, it is as I said—I owe you a debt for giving me a reason to find the strength I should have found many years ago. Qworeel, here, is one of those who also felt the shame. I have only told Hestean's secret to him. He needs to know so that he can do what is to be done now.'

'And what is that?'

'I understand,' said Qworeel, 'that you would like for the inside stones to be placed back where they came from in these walls. Is that correct, Maskee?'

'It is something I've been thinking about, yes, but as yet I've not decided. I want to see if there is any patterning on the inner surface of the wall, and to find out what they may be covering on the courtyard.'

'These patterns are important to you, then?'

'I came in search of a story, and these patterns tell a story. Not the story I was looking for, but another one about Sharacan's beginning. It is this story that has increasingly taken my attention since I arrived. Hestean was helping me to understand it.'

'My daughter was helping you to understand this temple?' said Sharn.

'Yes.'

'But how could she? She knows very little about it, like the rest of us, and because of the Robes she wasn't even schooled.'

'Your daughter had a brain, Sharn, and she is more schooled than she let on. She was helping me to understand the Sharacanese, and in doing so, to understand this temple, too.'

'Truly?'

'Yes, Sharn. And like you, I have also come to realise that she holds more than just my gratitude in the time since she left. I would like to tell her that one day.'

'I see! Does that mean that one day you may also ask what her bind-price will be?'

Jarrak smiled at the thought, but said, 'She has never shown any interest towards me in that respect. But if she had, then maybe it might have been something I would consider. Her interest in the history of this place is what drives your daughter, not an interest in me.'

'I said before, crosslander, that Hestean reminded me of her mother when she was younger. Perhaps, like her mother, she has become a woman without knowing it. I know Sathea didn't care for me the way I cared for her when we were younger. She accepted me because she knew I cared very much for her and would do my best to protect her in this world of the Robes. Since then, we have become close, and now neither of us would untangle ourselves. We have truly become bound, as I had hoped to all those years ago. This is not something I would normally talk about with someone I barely know, but I am telling you this for a reason. You should not give up quite so easily. I am told my daughter laughs because of you, and you should ask yourself why she laughs. I warn you, though, her price will be significant. Don't you think her price should be high?'

A smile again spread across Jarrak's face. 'Yes. I do indeed think her price should be significant.'

'See, I told you! Don't give up, crosslander.'

'That is not for you or me to decide, though, is it?'

'Maybe not. The Robes would like us to believe that we men do the choosing, as I thought all those years ago when I chose Sathea. But the more time passes, the more I think the reverse is more likely true.'

'Then perhaps we should talk about something else.'

'Perhaps we should. Qworeel, do you think the rebuilding of this wall is possible?' asked Sharn, turning towards his companion.

'Anything is possible, Sharn! I will have to think about it, though. I will survey what is here and tell you tomorrow if I think there is enough stone to do what is being asked. I do think it is possible, though, yes. It looks as if most of the stone is still here. The Robes used some temple stone to build their meeting hall, but my father said it came from the temple's living quarters, not the walls. I would not have used this stone if I'd been stonemason then; it belongs to the temple, and is sacred because of that.'

* * *

Now, as Jarrak looked around, he wished he'd never had that first conversation with Sharn and Qworeel. He recalled entering the temple's courtyard only a few days ago and looking towards the section of wall that Qworeel had started on. He'd found himself marvelling at the stoneworker's expertise. In Qworeel's workmanship, he saw the original builders of the temple and knew that their skills had been handed down through each generation. This was what Qworeel had been born to do, and Jarrak hated that he now had to tell him to stop.

It was Sharn who saw him first, as he turned to pick up one of the smaller stones before handing it to Qworeel. 'Ah, crosslander. It is coming along well, don't you think? It is as if it never fell.'

'It is that,' said Jarrak, not really listening as he viewed the wall. The reconstructed section was directly opposite where the main entrance would have been. A crudely carved inscription had been forming on the wall over the past several days. Now it was complete. He had thought the inscription done in haste, as if it was not really meant to be part of the temple's decoration. It was only his trained eye that had seen this new development. It was written in Fem, too, which had helped to disguise it. And now he knew why. He mouthed the last word silently to himself, to make sure he was seeing what he thought he was seeing. He stood back to look at the whole inscription again.

Binnan Eower Beran Licgan Ure Dohtor Andree.

'Andreena,' he said quietly to himself. Was he really looking at the first real evidence that she had existed? Was this about her? He saw something else. The rest of the words were the same as on the plaque, which Hestean had deciphered the day he found out she could read the ancient language. It was just along from here that the plaque had been found. He knew now, though, that it originally came from above the altar, in the vault next to the obelisk. Is this why it had been found near here? Did the similarity of the words also mean something?

Binnan Eowr Beran Licgan Ure Beran.

'Qworeel,' said Jarrak. 'Why did you decide to rebuild this section of the wall first?'

'Because of the way the stone had fallen. I realised that this was the last section to be knocked down, Maskee. Its stone lay at the top, so it was the place to start. Also, there was this section still standing, which I could use as a gantry. Wood is scarce, and I need to use ropes to lift some of these stones. Why do you ask?'

'No real reason. I was just wondering,' said Jarrak, breaking his thoughts free from the past. 'But I'm afraid I have some bad news for you. I think you should stop work on the wall. Robe Gaywin has become chairman this morning.'

'I thought Robe Elless was to become chairman,' said Sharn. 'The under-chairman always becomes chairman.'

'Apparently not. He stepped aside. Winnz thinks the more appropriate candidates were threatened in some way. If that is the case, then you working on the temple may no longer be a good idea.'

* * *

Just as Winnz had guessed, Gaywin revoked permission for the Sharacanese to work at the excavations. Now Jarrak saw two years of his life in the form of the empty temple that his workers had dug from the sand. It was an excavation that had started with the discovery of a woke horn by Hestean. Who knew, then, that it would result in this?

In his mind's eye, he saw it as it once had been, grand and imposing, its wall intact. The living quarters were in the south-west precinct, administration was to the north, and the obelisk and temple alcove were to the east. Joining these segments—and surrounding the massive and magnificently engraved courtyard paving—were the walls, intricately covered in engraved decorations. The western wall had been tall, with several windows high up in its structure, but all the other walls had been short and solid. The whole temple complex had been painted in the traditional colours—blue, red, and golden yellow.

'So close,' he said quietly to himself. 'I am so close now. I can feel her here, somewhere.'

He looked again at the inscription, and in particular at the symbol above the words; two downward-facing daggers, side by side. On the Great Mound, only days earlier, his workers had finally found something—a single column, which had been toppled and buried. It, too, had had a symbol like this, although unlike this one it carried remnant flakes of red pigment on one dagger and blue on the other. They'd also found another fragment beside the column, and for the first time it had matched with another piece, which Qworeel had found beneath some stone, belonging to the very section of the wall he had started to rebuild.

'What does it mean?' he said again. 'What does it all mean?'

Now, looking at the spot where Qworeel had found that piece, he noticed a few fragments of chipped stone that had fallen between some paving stones. On an impulse, he bent down to pick them free. He placed them in his hand, moving them around and forming them into a line. His mind wandered. Still crouching, he swivelled to look around at the temple once more.

'The Sharacanese will not like being told they can't rebuild this place. They have again found a reason for their existence. Winnz was right. Something is about to happen here, and just when I was getting somewhere, too. She is here, I know she is.'

He stood up and looked back to the inscription, puzzling it over. While his brain whirled, he placed one of the stone fragments into the cavity that formed one of the letters in the inscription. It fitted, and so he selected another piece and found it fitted, too. The next piece fit also, and he now stood staring at what he had just done. The answer to the question he had been asking himself was now staring back at him.

'They fit,' he said, turning again to study the demolished walls of the ancient temple. They were already getting pulled down. The temple was already being destroyed when this inscription had been made, so Andreena herself couldn't have done it. She had already vanished by then. So, who had? And why? He looked at the inscription, then stepped back to take in the reconstructed section of the wall. 'Someone knew! Someone knew that this was where the reconstruction would start. They knew this stone would still be here. Like Qworeel said, it is sacred, and not just to the Sharacanese, either. Maybe to the whole world.'

He took in the inscription once more.

'Andree! It's her familiar. It is Andree, rather than Andreena. Someone knew that only someone close to her, who knew enough to be looking for her here, would make this connection, but why?' His eyes scanned across the stone. 'The plaque! The plaque was found just along from here, but it belongs in the …' His eyes darted towards the alcove, from which he now knew the plaque had been taken. Then he looked at the giant obelisk. 'The obelisk!' he said, with a smile. 'The oldest part of this temple is around the obelisk.'

'What are you smiling about?' said a voice that made his smile vanish instantly.

He turned to see Gaywin walking from the shadows. He said the first thing that came into his head: 'I was just thinking about how magnificent this place must have been once.'

'Once, yes, but it will never be again.'

'Really? Why is that?'

'Because I have decided I am going to knock it all down, that's why. Even the obelisk. The well-pond, too, and the village itself. I intend to obliterate Sharacan from the face of this world.'

'But why would you do that?'

'Because Sharacan has destroyed my family's prospects for long enough—that's why. If there is no more Sharacan, there will be no more dishonour for my family to endure.'

'But even if there is no more Sharacan, people will remember.'

'People will not remember. It will be written out of history. I will see to that.'

'And you think the Sharacanese are going to allow you to do this?'

'They will have no choice. They will be forced from here, and it will cease to exist. I have family in Learnian, and when I send word of what I intend to do, the Sharacanese will be outnumbered tenfold.'

'And what of my research? Learnian will not be pleased when they hear what I have found, nor that it will be lost because of your wish to obliterate your family's dishonour.'

'And what exactly have you found, Maskee? A few vases, some carvings that show men have always been meant to rule this world? We already know that, Maskee. We don't need history to tell us that.'

'And what of the story that says if Sharacan ceases to exist, then so does the world?'

'Those tellings are fairy tales, Maskee. Just stories. In the Learnian library, there is no evidence that such a story ever existed. I do not believe in unsubstantiated tales. When I am fully confirmed, I intend to revoke your contract. I came to find you, to tell you in person. You should start to think about leaving, Maskee. You are no longer wanted here.' Gaywin's ever-present scowl had slowly turned into a slight smile. He went to leave, but then turned back. 'What is that inscription on the wall that was intriguing you as I came over?'

Jarrak was now pale, and he saw that Gaywin was enjoying this moment. 'Andreeneol,' he said, as fury began to overtake his thoughts, 'was a warrior from many centuries ago. Surely you have heard of him? He was one of the founders of Learnian and the College.'

'So why is his name on a wall in Sharacan?'

'Because he came from Sharacan, that's why!'

'Really? And how do you know this?'

'Because that's what the inscription says, and I have heard it before, too.'

'Where would you have heard such a thing?'

'I can't recall exactly, but I have heard or read it somewhere. Maybe in Elora-Bearer. When I went to the College Mission to get my permits to cross the desert, the chairman of the Mission allowed me to look at their books on Sharacan.'

'I see.'

'Yes. I think that maybe you do now. If you really want to obliterate Sharacan, then you go right ahead. But I think Learnian will not be pleased with you at all. That is the problem with rewriting one's history. Sometimes, the truth that needs to be remembered is lost, but other times it is not.'

Huffing to himself now, Gaywin turned abruptly and began to stride away. 'You should leave, Maskee,' he said, without turning back. 'You should leave. And soon.'

Jarrak could almost see steam coming from the Black Robe's ears, and he knew he had gone a little too far. But he knew, too, that his own blending of the truth would be hard to counter without a lot of research in records that had already been corrupted.

29

Water, left by storms, glistened in puddles as the crew from the *Merysands* returned from their leave. It was a certainty that there would be more rain soon. Already, clouds were building, and they found that their ship had moved.

Caze trudged across the soggy ground, following the footprints of others who had arrived before him. When he had entered the sky-port, no one had told him that the *Merysands* wasn't where it had been when he'd left to spend a few days with his brother. In ignorance, he had walked in the wrong direction. He wondered now why the ship had been shifted, recalling how everyone he had met since coming through the entry gates seemed slightly aloof. He wondered if he had been somehow tainted by the shroud of isolation now segregating his ship from the others.

Coming closer to the seldom-used part of the busy sky-port, he heard the echoing of hammers and the roar of forge furnaces emanating from within the long-abandoned workshops surrounding this part of the field. It was believed by many Deserteers that this was where the first sky-ships had been created. Yet no modern sky-ships were ever brought here for repairs these days.

A scud of rain caught him, and he began to run towards the shelter of the *Merysands*' shadow. He stepped quickly onto a fibre-reed walkway, laid between the workshops and the sky-ship. However, slush still sprayed up through the gaps between the planks. By the time he stopped outside the *Merysands*' loading hatch, his boots and the lower part of his trousers were soaked. He took off his cloak and shook it dry, then looked back towards the, antiquated, workshops.

'Welcome back Mister Caze,' said the *Merysands*' new loadmaster.

'Things have been happening while I've been away, it seems?'

'You haven't seen the half of it, Mister Caze! There have been blue boffins crawling all over this ship. They've changed everything, and there are even some places on the *Merysands* that we aren't allowed to go to now.'

'What do you mean?'

'They're Blue Cloaks, Mister Caze! You know, from the tellings! The godly ghosts of legend.'

The loadmaster turned to point at the wall, where the insignia of the Deserteers had once been painted. The emblem was still there, although now it was smaller, and surrounded by one loop of an infinity symbol. Painted within the other loop was the polygon, which represented the six great houses of the world.

'They've done that throughout the ship, Mister Caze, and that was only the start. As soon as the *Merysands* was moved, they came on board and began to pull her apart, then to rebuild her. We're no longer just a cargo ship, Mister Caze! I don't know exactly what we are anymore. If you ask me, we're going to be carrying a lot of people soon. For the first few days, I tried to be sociable, but they wouldn't talk. None of them will. Unless you have a blue bandana around your head, that is. The ordinary Deserteers working for them don't say much, either, but they did tell us that they live where they work. It seems they're stuck here, too, just like we are.'

'Stuck here?'

'Yes, Mister Caze. Once back on board, I can't allow you to leave. Captain's orders.'

'Where is the captain?'

'In his cabin, as far as I know. He said I was to send you straight to him the moment you came through the hatch.'

'Well, then, I suppose I should stow my gear and find him.'

'I'll have to see your personal warrant and get you to sign in first, Mister Caze! Everyone has to sign since these Blue Cloaks came on board. That's the captain's orders, too. You can leave your stuff here, if you like—I'll look after it. I can't leave until I'm relieved, though.'

'Have you chosen a number two yet?'

'Not yet. I was told not to bother for the time being.'

'That's odd!'

'That's what I thought, but everything is odd these days. So, instead, I've been cycling all the top-loading crew through the watches.'

'At least that will give you a better idea of who to choose eventually.'

'I hope so, Mister Caze! After all, it still seems like only a few days ago that I was number two, myself. I thought that the captain would bring in someone new, but he said he wanted a person he understood, this time. Something weird is going on, Mister Caze. Something real weird.'

'Take it as an opportunity, Fenn. Once a Deserteer climbs up a notch, he doesn't often get put down again!'

'That's what I'm hoping, Mister Caze. That's what I'm hoping.'

Later, when Caze left the captain's cabin, he recalled this conversation. *Once one rose in rank, they tended to stay there.* He knew his own navigation skills were fair, but he also knew that he still needed the wisdom that only time could teach. Like Fenn, the captain had offered the position of first officer to him instead of to someone more qualified. Caze had not refused the advancement. For him, it was another step up the ladder. In fact, to become first officer on the *Merysands* took him several steps up the ladder.

It was weird, though, just as Fenn had said. He knew that the captain usually preferred experience over familiarity. Karree may have been young for a loadmaster, but she was also one of the best, and Mister Petty was renowned for being an elite navigator. The *Merysands* was now filled with secrets, and it seemed that these Deserteers in their blue-lined uniforms were the cause. No proper explanation had been offered, and he knew it would be better not to press the matter. Before this morning, he had never even seen one of these blue-clad legends, but now here they were, infesting the ship. His one consolation was that the captain didn't seem overly concerned about their presence.

* * *

On the seventeenth day after its grounding, now extensively reconfigured, the *Merysands* awaited its first test flight. All sky-ships went through evaluations after any alterations, and these ones were more than just superficial.

Standing to the side of the control deck, where Petty had once stood, Caze looked out towards the mooring lines while awaiting the captain's orders. He knew, of course, what the order would be. It was a well-known series of rituals that lifted a sky-ship into flight, and he had already issued the "all clear".

It was a strangely silent man who sat in the command chair this morning. The captain had still not revealed a great deal about what was going on. 'It will all become clear in time, Mister Caze, and when it does, you will not need me to explain it,' he had said.

To take his mind off the captain's unusual behaviour, Caze turned his head and glanced at the man inducted into the newly vacant position of second officer that Caze had once occupied. Mister Lees was of a similar age to himself, and Caze himself had approached the lower ranking officer of the *Hindasands* regarding the advancement. Caze saw that Mister Lees also looked puzzled by the captain's stillness. However, being new to the ship, he was unsure of how to go about resolving his query. One evening was not enough time to get to know a new crew or ship.

Caze knew that their commander would speak when his mind was cleared of whatever thoughts consumed him, but the silence was now causing unease to spread through the control deck. He felt that soon he would have to say something. He turned to look out through the window; the wet weather had still not cleared, and already the clouds were building. If they didn't lift off soon, they might not be able to leave at all.

Unbeknownst to his two officers, it wasn't the view outside that the captain was looking at. It was the faintly reflected image of the control deck's interior. The positioning of his chair not only gave him an excellent view outside his ship, but also of what was happening behind him. 'I think you are wondering why I have not issued the order to launch, Mister Caze,' said the captain, finally, turning his head towards his first officer.

'The thought was on my mind, Captain.'

'You have to be observant, Mister Caze. Always observant. There is a hierarchy, Mister Caze, and even I cannot issue an order on my own ship if I am no longer the highest-ranking officer.' The captain looked back at his reflected image. 'Do I have permission to launch, Commander?'

Caze cocked his head, wondering if he had heard the captain correctly. He swivelled to take in the control deck, expecting to see some high-ranking Deserteer come into view, but instead he saw only the young woman whom they had carried from the desert nearly two moon cycles before. He had a good memory for faces, and Hestean's he remembered well. She stood alone, just out from the back wall, steady and strong-looking, encased in a hooded cloak that covered her from head to toe. Only her face remained uncovered. The cloak, which displayed no insignia of rank nor trade, made her almost blend into the wall.

* * *

Hestean had come onto the control deck quietly, moving as a shadow, almost unseen by any of the people who now ran the *Merysands*. Recognising that the captain had seen her, she decided to continue observing. The captain's little game of suspense had amused her, and she had played along while using the delay to study the men around her.

She nodded to Mister Caze in acknowledgement, then looked back to the captain, who had still not stirred from his seat. 'How did you know, Captain?' she asked.

'As you heard me say to Mister Caze, one must always be observant, Commander.'

'To see the world reflected in everything is not just the realm of the Comcree, then, is it, Captain?'

'Not necessarily, no.'

* * *

Caze looked back at the captain. "Commander" was a military rank, not a civil one. The person the captain had addressed was but a young woman; someone who had not the cycles of time expected to accompany such a title.

'It is no wonder that Petty wanted your ship for this, Captain. You have a good eye,' said Hestean.

'You don't really expect me to think this was Petty's idea, do you?'

'No. But he did think our choice was the best one we could have made.'

'How is my old friend?' asked the captain, now observing more fully the overcast sky.

'He is once again aboard, Captain, busy making final arrangements for our cargo.'

'Good. I have missed his conversation! We have been rather starved of it here.'

'An unavoidable consequence, Captain. One I'm sure Petty would also like to remedy.'

'Then I suppose we should launch, Commander?' Again, Caze noticed the word.

* * *

Mister Lees was also looking at Hestean. As if signalled by the captain's request, she folded back her hood, undid her cloak, and swept it back over her shoulders. She took a moment to pin it in place with her epaulettes, knowing that for the first time aboard the *Merysands*, she was revealing her Comcree dagger and dress. She walked to stand by the captain's side. The next phase of her life had now truly begun.

'Yes,' she said, in the most authoritarian voice she could summon. 'You have my permission to launch. Do you know your orders?'

'I do, Maskea.'

She smiled at his familiarity. He had not, as most others had done recently, called her "Hlaford". She found herself liking him for that. It was an unexpected piece of normality in a world that no longer felt normal.

'Do we have the light, Mister Lees?' asked the captain.

Hestean took in the expressions of the officers and helmsmen, still scrambling to understand the sudden meaning of things. Here and now, in front of them, the myths of time were becoming much more than history.

'We have the light, Captain, captured and locked,' replied Mister Lees, regaining his professionalism.

'Rotate blades then, Mister Lees,' instructed the captain. 'Mister Caze, release aft lines and bring us into the wind.'

'Rotate blades, hold neutral,' said Mister Lees into his voice receiver.

Meanwhile, Caze also spoke. 'Aft lines released, helm to the wind if you would, please. Sixteen points starboard.'

'Sixteen points to starboard, coming around!' the head helmsman echoed.

'I take it then, Captain, that this is not a test flight?' inquired Caze.

'Very insightful of you, Mister Caze. I apologise for the ruse, but I was told it was necessary. You are right. I have been assured that in this configuration, the ship needs no test flight. It would appear that the *Merysands* is once again in its original configuration. I suggest, however, that we still be vigilant.'

'A wise strategy, Captain, but I thought that you had always captained this ship!'

'I was supposed to have, Mister Caze, but at the time of her launch I took ill with forest fever. It was half a year before I was fit to command again. By then, all her testing had been done. I've only ever seen her handling reports, but she has always done what I've asked of her. I see no reason for that to change.'

'We have the wind, Mister Caze,' said one of the helmsmen as he centred his wheel.

'Blades ahead one quarter, Mister Lees,' said the captain.

'Bow line slack, Captain,' added Mister Caze.

'Then you should set us free, Mister Caze.'

This time, Hestean understood the silence that filled the control deck as the *Merysands* rose through its most critical zone. Once clear, the captain spoke again.

'We will continue straight up, Mister Caze. When we reach our height above the plateau, loop us around as if heading south. Once we have crossed the escarpment, bring us down into the Hassis Valley. You will see our landing site!' The captain then turned to Hestean. 'Commander, I think it is time we found Petty.'

'Yes, Captain,' replied Hestean with an enthusiastic smile.

The captain rose from his chair and smiled too. 'I still remember the first time I commanded a sky-ship into flight. It is something you will never forget, Maskea. Mister Caze, you have control!'

'Yes, Captain,' said Caze, noticeably hesitant, wearing the same ghostly expression that had taken control of Mister Lees. Just as the captain reached the exit stairs, Caze said, 'Captain, the Hassis … It's a no flight zone, and dangerous to sky-ships.'

This was exactly what the captain had hoped to hear. The last thing he wanted was unquestioning compliance. The success of what lay ahead depended on the crew he had gathered around him. 'Is it indeed, Mister Caze,' he replied, seeing that he had chosen Caze and Mister Lees wisely. 'The reason for something is not always what's stated. You are one of the best tacticians I have ever come across, Mister Caze. The Hassis is no more dangerous to sky-ships than you are. The very first sky-ships were built within the Hassis, not in the port we've been tethered to for the last seventeen days, as most believe. It was actually in the upper Hassis Valley where the blockade runners came into being, not the lower. We are taking the *Merysands* home, Mister Gaze. Make your run from the inland and call me when you start your descent. We get one chance at this; one chance only. It is the turbulence swirling from the escarpment that is dangerous, not the Hassis itself.'

* * *

Caze was still staring at the now empty staircase when Mister Lees walked across to him. 'Do you think it's true, Mister Caze?'

Caze looked at Lees for a moment, then turned back to the empty space. 'When you get to know the captain better, you will find he never says something he doesn't believe. He makes a hobby of studying Deserteer history. I am wondering, though, whether you have made a wrong choice in joining us. It would seem as though the gods are on the move, and we are to accompany them.'

'Is she really one of the Comcree warriors that the legends speak of?'

'Did you notice her enter the command deck?'

'No!'

'Nor did I, Mister Lees, and we both should have. I get the distinct impression that the captain knows a little more than we do. He seems convinced that she is who she appears to be, and I suspect he's right.'

'What are your thoughts, Helm?' asked Caze, turning to the head helmsman behind the control wheels.

'It's not the Comcree that worry me, Mister Caze, for that is not my place. It is this ship that concerns me! The blockade runners were tiny compared to the *Merysands.* If the Hassis is truly their origin, then it is the Hassis that will be worrying me.'

'Exactly right, Helm. Our minds should be on the task at hand. The rest is but an adjustment to reality. Besides, we have a reputation to uphold. Even if the fleet never get to hear of this, we should endeavour to maintain that reputation.'

'Is that really what you believe, Mister Caze?' asked Lees.

'If you do something just to show others, Mister Lees, you end up not doing your best. We always do our best here, Mister Lees. Isn't that right, Helm?'

'I have always found that to be so, Mister Caze.'

'What's our altitude, Mister Lees?' asked Caze, turning to look at the clouds gathering around them.

'It's just coming up on five hundred, Mister Caze.'

'Then I think we should take the crossing at one and a half instead of two. It will be a little rough, but seeing as we have no cargo to worry about, it will allow us to descend quicker. From what the captain said, I think he would want us to prioritise stealth. So, on my mark, take us to the south, Helm.'

30

Preceding the captain up the spiral metal stairs, Hestean stepped out onto the suspended upper-level walkway that ran the length of the *Merysands*.

'You have not forgotten your way around, Maskea,' the captain noted.

'Little chance of that, Captain. Last time I was aboard, I explored every part of your ship. She was the very first sky-ship I ever saw. Even with these new changes, her design is imprinted on my brain.'

'Yes,' the captain smiled, 'they have a habit of doing that.'

'Petty should be down this way, in the aft storage bay,' Hestean said.

The large gas-filled envelopes that inhabited this upper realm of the *Merysands* were tethered in rows on either side of the expanded metal walkway. They made it look long and narrow, their huge forms creating a shadowy gloom. The only illumination came from the skylights in the ship's upper surface, and as the captain fell in beside Hestean, the top of his bald head gleamed every time they went beneath one. It was the riggers and maintenance crew who used the walkway most, and along its length, several spiral stairways led up from the decks below, allowing quick access from one end of the huge ship to the other.

'Why are sky-ships always thought of as female?' asked Hestean.

'I don't know, Maskea! It has always been that way, right from the very first blockade runners! Perhaps, though, it is because those first small sky-ships were nicknamed the *Shara*.'

'Shara, as in Sharacan?'

'No, I mean "Shara" as in the woman's name.'

'Really! I've never met anyone named Shara!'

'A Comcree that admits to not knowing everything. Now that is a rarity.'

'We never know everything, Captain.'

'You know more than most, Maskea. If it weren't for the Comcree, I doubt that this world would exist as it does.'

'Do you really believe that, Captain?'

'As you no doubt are aware, I am a student of Deserteer history, Maskea. So, yes. Since your friend Jarrak first took passage on the *Merysands* and diverted our route to within sight of Sharacan, I have come to believe very much in the Comcree.'

'Mister Caze seemed concerned when we left the control deck. Are you sure of him?'

'It is true that he has a bit to learn as a navigator, Maskea, but he is one of the best. As a tactician, there are only two that can surpass him. I am one, and your Mister Petty is the other. We are in safe hands, I assure you. Mister Lees will do just fine, also! He grew up in the north. I pick my crew because of their strengths, Maskea. The blending of those strengths will make us all stronger. I have every confidence in them.'

At the very back of the *Merysands*, it was the captain who led the way down another of the spiral stairways to the lower storage bay. He pulled open its access hatch, letting Hestean enter first. 'What exactly have you done to my ship, Mister Petty?' he asked, upon seeing his former first officer.

'It is good to see you also, Captain,' said Petty, getting to his feet. Beside Petty, a blue-cloaked technician was kneeling, working his fingers along a tangle of wires in unbroken concentration. Petty glanced at the man before walking across to embrace the captain. Pulling back, he said, 'I have not liked this concealment, old friend!'

'Nor I,' said the captain, releasing his own grasp from his friend.

There was a moment of silence, and then Petty said, 'Tell me how Mister Caze and the new officers are doing? I felt the lift-off; it seemed well done.'

'Mister Caze is not you, Mister Petty. But they both acquitted themselves well enough!'

The captain's eyes were drawn past Petty to the strange-looking machine behind his friend. He walked across to stand in front of it. 'Your daughter here was kind enough to go along with a little game I played. I wanted to see how Mister Caze and Mister Lees would react in an unforeseen situation. I sensed no rivalry, so they should work well together.' He watched as the expression on Petty's face changed, and smiled. 'It took me a little while, my friend, but I did work it out. I know you have never had any children!'

'Yes, well, my daughter here—as you called her—says I'm old, but to my recollection, there is only a moon cycle between you and me. In all that time, there have been few secrets between us. Until now, the guardians wanted the true nature of my resignation obscured. They seem to like things blurred.'

'I thought as much when I puzzled it out,' said the captain. 'The Comcree have always been a blur.' He gestured back to the machine. 'So, tell me, can you now disclose more about this game you've got me mixed up in?'

'It was not me that offered you to them, it was your own reputation, my friend. That, and the fact that this is what the *Merysands* was created for.'

'Then they have us both, I think,' said the captain, looking at Petty's blue-lined uniform. It reversed the status of their ranking for the first time in their lives.

'In truth, yes, Captain!'

'Then this is big, is it?'

Petty looked to Hestean for a moment. She nodded her agreement. To his lifelong friend and colleague, he said, 'It would seem that our young archaeologist did, in a way, find what he was looking for, Captain. May I present, formally, from Sharacan and of the fourth house, Hub-Comcree Hestean Descee. The blue dagger she carries was once held by the Comcree Andreena, and is hers by inheritance.'

Hestean bowed her head formally, and said, 'There has been no deception on my part, Captain. When last we met, I did not know of this either.'

For a moment, the captain studied her, remembering the young woman he had welcomed onto his ship for the first time, not much more than two moon cycle before. 'Do you bring a smile back to this world, Hestean Descee?'

'Along with some tears, yes, I think so.'

His eyes skimmed over her blue-green dress, taking note of the two daggers hanging at her waist. She was no longer the young woman he had first met; he could see that within the last cycling of the moons, her world had truly grown beyond the confines of her childhood. In her eyes rested the whole world, and not just the world that he also knew. He considered her for a moment longer, before saying, 'Then my blade is with yours, Hestean Descee. You have my ship, and you also have me.'

'Thank you, Captain. We are asking a great deal of you, and of your ship.'

'Your friend Jarrak first did that, Maskea! This is merely an extension of that.' The captain now turned to Petty. His hand fanned towards the machine. 'So, tell me, Mister Petty, am I able to know what it is you have done here?'

'Was it as you thought, Joss?' asked Petty, noticing that the technician had finished his adjustments and was waiting patiently with his tools in hand.

'It seems so, Mister Petty' the technician replied. 'This new calibration seems to be holding, but I'd still like to check that switch board in the engine room again.'

'Then do it. We need to make sure it's right this time.'

'A problem?' asked the captain.

'It is Comcree technology, Captain,' said Hestean. 'It was not designed for these modern sky-ships, and we have had some unforeseen hiccups. When they have it working properly, it will give the *Merysands* protection. It's an energy shield.'

'And what is an energy shield?'

'It resists against the force of movement. The quicker something is moving, the harder it is for that object to penetrate through the shield's protective ring. It absorbs an object's energy and turns it back on itself. It will protect us and the *Aquasands* when she catches up with us. The *Merysands* must always be in front of the *Aquasands*, as the shield lies mostly in our wake, Captain!'

'The *Aquasands*?'

'Yes, Captain!' said Hestean. 'Yours is not the only ship we have asked to help us. You must protect the *Aquasands* and the *Aquasands* will in turn protect you. If she is lost, so are we all. She holds within her another device from the gods. I intend to take back Sharacan from the College, Captain, and depending on what we find, it may only be the beginning of a much larger campaign. My village has lived under the doctrine of the Robes for too long. I intend for it to never do so again. If the Robes surrender Sharacan willingly, I will accept it. If they don't, then we will take it back. Sharacan is our heritage, not theirs.'

'I don't remember her being so bossy, Mister Petty?'

'No,' said Petty, grinning. 'She scares me, too, at times.'

'Are the blockade hangars still in the Hassis?' asked the captain, remembering that he had always wanted to see them.

'Some are. Ruins now, but they're still there. I have seen the drafting room; the place where the first plans were drawn up. You will find that it, too, is filled with our ancestor's ghosts.'

'You must show me! If we get the chance, that is,' said the captain.

* * *

Hestean smiled as she watched the two grown men become little boys rediscovering their favourite toys. She observed them before turning to leave them to uncover their shared history. She walked to an observation window, wondering whether she would still be able to smile in a few days' time. Would she find Andree? Or would she wake up in the morning and find that this had simply been a dream.

She had told the captain only a little of what was intended. She wondered if perhaps, instead of reclaiming her past, she was merely further unleashing the wrath of the College. She found herself missing Jarrak. Over the last few days, he had increasingly entered her thoughts. Knowing that she would soon see him, she had come to think of him as part of her again. She wondered whether he would see her as the woman she had become, or as the girl who had only a short time ago ridden away from him on a six-wheeled wagon built to traverse the mighty Kalcool.

Cloud had almost obscured the coastline in the distance and the forest below them. She turned her attention towards the now familiar Hassis Valley to the east. Later, she watched the valley swing to the north as the sky-ship turned. It buffeted as it crossed through the updrafts at the edge of the escarpment. When they found still air again, the giant ship began to circle widely, and Hestean looked out towards where the distant ocean sat in the west. Out to sea, the clouds were thinner, and the mixture of white clouds and blue-green ocean made her think of the gemstones—blue, green, and white—decorating the pommel and cross-guard of her Comcree dagger.

Finally, they began their descent onto the ancient landing field of the Hassis. Her thoughts felt like a mixture of reality and dream. She saw the landing field as a part of the past, and now, once again, that same landing field was the starting point for an unknown future.

31

After returning to the control deck to oversee the *Merysands* being caught and tethered to the ground, the captain walked to the cargo hold. He saw another Deserteer who, not too long ago, had also been a member of his crew. Karree had again taken charge here, and now she stood beside Hestean, instructing the new loadmaster.

He smiled when he noticed her sleeves. Her new, blue-lined uniform was emblazoned with a unique insignia, the letters "LM", which not only indicated her previous rank, but also her family. He wondered if her father would be as proud of her new status as he had been when she'd first become a loadmaster.

'She was the first aboard when we came to ground,' explained Petty, coming to the captain's side. 'She wanted to see the changes for herself before the cargo started to come on board. She may no longer be a part of your crew, Captain, but she still thinks of this ship as hers. When she learned that I would be overseeing the refit, she was most put out to be staying at the Hassis Estate. As with everything she does, though, she has devoted herself to her new charge. If you observe them for long enough, you might mistake them for sisters.'

'But isn't that what the fifteen of you are supposed to be? The arms of the guardians?'

'One particular guardian, yes. I think that in time, Karree will completely forget the *Merysands*. The bond between them has gone both ways. It's deeper than for the rest of us. Karree wears her uniform just as intently as Hestean wears the garb of a Comcree.'

'It's odd that you should say that. I was just wondering whether her father would like this new honour and prestige she brings to his family. He has been very proud that she's upheld the Ladener family tradition to such a high degree.'

'Perhaps she will start a new tradition!'

'Perhaps! But for the moment, we should leave her to get on with loading my ship. There is no one I would rather perform that task. You said that there are two hundred Deserteers and a mound of stores to come aboard. It will take a while, yes?'

'You are persistent, my friend!'

'I mean to be! I've never been here before, and this may be my only chance. Who knows what lies ahead of us.'

'I have a couple of things to do first, but then we should be able to explore a little!'

'Good. I also have something I need to do first. The *Merysands* took a bit of a shaking on the way down, and I need to see that she's still alright.'

* * *

The sky-ship seemed gigantic when resting on a landing field built to hold ships only an eighth of its size. As the captain walked around her exterior, he satisfied himself that Caze had been right to test the integrity of the ship's reconfiguration while it was without cargo. After his inspection, he found himself walking up the slope towards the large front gates of the estate complex. The whole place looked run down, but then, perhaps, that was the way the Comcree wanted it to look.

From on top of the small ridge that spurred out from the southern edge of the valley, the grand family home of the Sarah-Hassis had an expansive view of where the captain's ancestors had first taken to the skies. To the east, he could see the old access road twisting its way back and forth over the distant wall of this seemingly impenetrable valley. This road had once been the only way into this isolated holding. To the west, beyond the *Merysands*, the valley fell gently away until it ended at the escarpment's edge. There, the now-dry river had once flowed out into nothingness as a magnificent cascade.

Just to the side of the river, he saw an old, narrow building on the very edge of the escarpment, and for a moment, he wondered what it had been for. He saw the wind cranks further to the south, which had once helped power the city of Elora-Bearer far below. The expansion of the Kalcool had changed everything, it seemed. Even here.

Behind the gated estate complex, on the lower side of the ridge, stood the supporting outbuildings, and it was here that Petty found the captain. He pointed out the small side canyon he had told the captain about, and they started towards it. During the conflict of two hundred years ago, it was this canyon that had become the enormous construction hanger for these blockade-breaking sky-ships. It was a small, isolated space within the Hassis, with rock walls that dropped vertically to its flat, level floor. To hide the enterprise, a roof had been constructed and suspended by metal ropes, which spanned the chasm halfway up its walls. The stream that flowed through the canyon had been encased to flow beneath the ground to drive a large water-wheel. Three hundred paces wide and a thousand paces long, what Petty and the captain now saw was the roof of this winning experiment lying in decay, half-collapsed on the canyon's floor.

It was a depressing end to such a success, the captain thought. But at the same time, he was filled with exhilaration from knowing that what had been spawned here had eventually become the *Merysands*.

As they walked through the debris, they noticed a huge metal cylinder along one wall. This they surmised to be the remains of the pressure tubes, used to steam the long lengths of fibre-reed required in the skeletons of these first sky-ships. Beside it were huge, misshapen jigs, which had once been used to bend and create these frames. There were other discarded machines and equipment—old drill presses and lathes which had once been powered from long drive shafts. A few broken hand tools lay in the worn tangle of decay. He picked up the remains of a hand plane and tried to picture the worker who had once held it.

Compared to the present, the primitive nature of this site made him marvel at the greatness his ancestors had achieved. Fibre-reed was no longer used in sky-ship construction; these days, they used a lighter and stronger alloy. Yet in the heat of conflict, with few resources, these people had forged the beginnings of the Sky Fleet that now dominated trade throughout Meglia.

The normally staunch man found his heart swelling with pride, and he wiped a tear from the corner of an eye.

A while later, they walked back towards the main house. Petty slid the door of the drafting room open and walked in, followed by the captain. They stood silently, as if in another godly place. Below a window sat a dusty drafting table, with two chairs still set before it. Pinned around the walls were faded sketches—original preliminary drawings. The captain's eyes moved slowly as he imagined the revolutionary discussions that had paved the road for turning fiction into fact. He saw ghosts in the chairs, their char-sticks solving vast, abstract sums.

Yet when he looked closer at the drawings, he saw that their designs would never have worked. They were close enough to fool someone who wasn't familiar with sky-ships, but just different enough to bring any ship based on them crashing to the ground. He began to smile, then a chuckle of understanding erupted from him. Even here, in their own stronghold, the Comcree had taken no chances. This whole room was a deception.

'Have you really looked at these drawings, Petty?' asked the captain.

'Yes! If taken separately, none of them work, do they? But as a whole, you do have the Shara. They were quite cunning in their deception. You change one thing, and it all falls apart unless you put it right again. If you change one thing on each drawing, it is like a maze that is impossible to get through, unless you know the way.'

A while later, both men sat on the edge of the drafting room's front porch, looking out towards the *Merysands* as it finished taking on its cargo.

'There hasn't always been this many Blue Deserteers here, has there?' asked the captain as he watched the last of the squadron board his ship.

'No,' said Petty. 'But apparently there have always been eyes at every sky-port. A few select Deserteers knew the truth about the Comcree. When the rumours started to percolate through Elora-Bearer, those eyes looked harder. They listened at the taverns and eating halls, where sky-ship crews liked to congregate. Quite a few of the sky-ships that came through Elora-Bearer over the last seventeen days left shorthanded. The sky-port of Elora-Bearer is a busy place, and not much attention was drawn to this. It was quietly suggested to the Deserteers that if they left their ships, they would find a position within a new, specialised squadron. These men and women boarding the *Merysands* are those Deserteers. They were chosen for their skill and the depth of their beliefs. I suspect the same thing has been happening at the sky-ports of Fiskay and Meranzy, also.'

'All this time, the gods have been closer than we ever thought,' said the captain.

'They never left,' said Petty. 'They just wanted the College to think they had. Without all six daggers, there are some things they cannot do, it seems. I'm not exactly sure why, but it is because of Hestean that they have regained their resolve.'

'Then perhaps we should not hold them up any longer,' said the captain, getting to his feet. 'I see that they have just about finished loading.'

* * *

When the captain boarded, Karree was standing ready to close the loading hatch.

'They have given you back to me for a while, I see,' said the captain.

'Just for a while, yes, Captain. I had to check out my replacement, didn't I?'

'And what do you think of him?'

'He will do, Captain. I trained him well enough.'

'Yes. But it will be a while before he is as good as you, I think.'

'I had my father to teach me, Captain.'

'You did, indeed!'

'It sounds as if you knew him, Captain. You never said.'

'Some things don't need to be said. I was based out of Fiskay for a time before I was offered the *Merysands*. It was your personal reputation, Karree Ladener, that brought you to this ship, though. Not your family's. That is why I never mentioned it. You were the one who was suggested to me, but you were also the one I wanted.'

The captain glanced across the valley, sensing a privilege not offered to many. After a nod of respect to his ancestors, he turned and set off towards the command deck. By his side was Hestean. Behind them both was Petty. Karree closed the loading bay doors, and with the new loadmaster by her side, no longer her second but her equal, she set off for a final check of the cargo and all entry and exit points.

32

'Flotation is neutral,' said Mister Caze as the captain entered the control deck.

'Thank you, Mister Caze. You got us here, so let's see if you can get us out again. Stay clear of the escarpment. I'm sure you agree that one shaking a day is enough for any sky-ship.'

'Yes, Captain!' answered Caze, the quickness of his reply bringing a glow of amusement to the captain. 'Do we have a course?'

'We are heading to the far north, Mister Caze! To the Salvation Lands.'

Mister Lees looked towards the captain, but it was Hestean who said, 'When you have time, Mister Lees, hopefully before we get there, you will tell me about your homeland?' A knowing smile appeared on her face, and even though Lees knew it wasn't by magic but simple observation that she had discovered his background, it appeared to be magical.

'Do you have a more accurate destination for us yet, Maskea?' asked the captain.

'Not yet, Captain,' replied Hestean, still looking at Lees. 'For the moment, you are to follow the River Whay north. When I know more accurately, you will know also!'

'You make it hard, Maskea.'

'Not hard, Captain, just challenging. Mister Lees is from the north, is he not?'

'That's not the reason why he was asked to join us, Maskea.'

'That may be true, Captain, but it is not a hindrance, either is it? Nor is his knowledge of the Ingress River and Ingress Way, for they are not normally flown over by sky-ships the size of the *Merysands.*'

'You know me and my crew a little too well, I think.'

'This is your ship,' said Hestean, turning to look at him. 'We do not dictate your choices of crew. We do not rule this world like kings and queens. We never have. We guide and suggest like the *cyings* and *cwens* from the tellings! We show this world a path, but it is up to this world to travel it.'

'What is it you are doing now if not meddling, Maskea?'

'The Comcree do not like restrictions, Captain. What we are doing now is removing an obstacle. This world has a destiny to achieve, and the College would subvert that destiny for their own purposes. They are small, whereas this world has a much bigger fortune to find.'

'Do you know this destiny, Maskea?'

'All things have a destiny, Captain. If it is known, it's only by the gods themselves.'

'The Comcree follow the gods, Maskea! They protect them, but perhaps you are right. The gods do know a great many things that we do not.'

As he listened vaguely, Lees' mind was whirling. North, but not north along the coast, as would have been more usual. The young Comcree warrior had mentioned the River Whay. They were to head north along the interior of the Escarpment Ranges, over-flying the remnants of Chime Town and Tear Salt, where his ancestors had once run their businesses. His three brothers still operated tanneries, but now they did so far to the north in the Salvation Lands.

Only since the Kalcool's expansion had the thawed paradise north of the Fibre Reed swamps come out of its frozen hibernation. There, only five generations of his family had seen the green flutter-weeds thrive, as once they had on the high plateau of the Kalcool. This new region of green had been the saviour of the highland settlements. The settlers had moved north as the land unfroze, softening from its white iciness. The herds of carrowa and nosbi had been the reason for the move; the animals had known where to go. Within just a few years, places like Chime Town and Tear Salt had ceased to exist, except as ghost towns. Only a few people survived there now, and the old settlements had become but a memory to the people who now lived and worked in the far north. For the first time in his life, Lees would get to see where his people had come from.

'Lees! Did you hear me?' said the captain. 'Do we have the light, Mister Lees?'

'Ah, yes, Captain. Sorry!'

'Then rotate blades, Mister Lees. We do, after all, have a schedule to keep.'

'Yes, Captain.'

* * *

Sixteen days earlier, Gorean and Shenn had set off themselves for the Salvation Lands. To get there, they had at first headed south-west to the sea port of Sequria. There would be no sky-ship flight for them; nothing that could alert anyone to their destination until they arrived in Port Reed.

Just before dawn, they rode through the still-sleeping streets of Elora-Bearer and ventured out through the batter-palm forest towards the coast, taking the old road that twisted between trees and around rocky outcrops. After a day, they saw a pebbled beach and began travelling south. It was a back way into the sea-port, and a road on which they hoped they would not be noticed. Although still in her disguise as a schoolteacher, Gorean was now surrounded closely by her protectorate of fifteen Deserteers.

Above them, the blue sky flickered through the canopy of leaves and palm fronds. Rolling waves covered the sound of the shrows' footsteps. When they ventured out onto the beaches, the brightness of the light dazzled their eyes, and when they returned to the forest, the shadows were at first dark and menacing. At one point, the track led them into the sea itself, as they were forced around a large stone bluff that jutted defiantly into the vast ocean. If they had been travelling with wagons, they would have needed to wait for a lower tide, but without such hindrances, their shrows splashed eagerly through the shallow waves.

After a solid day and a half of riding, the batter-palm beaches gave way to low scrub. Here, they entered the coastal merchant town of Sequria and sought out a tri-hull called the *Firsea*. It was only then they were finally heading north, across the waters of the Great Western Ocean towards Port Reed.

Only after they had set sail did the crew of the tri-hull discovered the true value of their cargo. Now, Gorean was surrounded by blue-cloaked Deserteers, her protectorate having discarded their disguise. Even amongst sea folk, the influence and history of the Comcree was still strong. Gorean came up on deck and walked slowly towards the bow of the *Firesea*'s central hull. She swept back her cloak so that it draped behind her shoulders, and only then was her Comcree dress and the blue dagger at her waist revealed.

For a long time, Gorean stood at the front of the ship, thinking and smelling the sea air. The wind whistled around her as the ocean's water curled in ribbons of spray. On a calm sea and under full sail, the *Firesea* could cover almost a thousand marces in a day and night. It was like flying, and Gorean had always loved that feeling. To someone like her, not accustomed to its everyday familiarity, the sea was exhilarating. She had always felt free here, but for the first time in her life, she was exposed and no longer cocooned.

Four days later, when Gorean left the ship at Port Reed, the group set off through the swamp, giant stalks of the valuable fibre-reed swaying majestically and unsympathetically around them and whispering eerily. Tiny, winged crawlies buzzed and bit at Gorean and her contingent, and they took to covering their faces with cloth and placing sand-goggles over their eyes. Each settlement they travelled though was surrounded by a ring of smoky fires to deter the ever-present insects, but even so, the people of the Fibre Reed camps had become hardened towards these tiny creatures. It was a seasonal thing, and unfortunately this was the wrong time of the year to be traveling the Fibre Reed in comfort.

The roads through the swamps were formed from a footing of reeds, which were tied together in bundles and stamped into the ooze, one on top of the other, to create a platform above the acrid waters. The bundles of fibre-reed were impervious to water and resisted rotting. These rafts were then covered in layers of soil and gravel to form roads. Straying from the paths was unwise, as in places the swamps were bottomless.

It was another two days before Gorean and Shenn rode free of the Fibre Reed with their entourage trailing out after them. Gorean knew these green, rolling hills of the Salvation Lands, for she had kin here—family that had moved north with the migration generations before. She'd visited on several occasions with her parents in her youth. It had been a special time in her life, a time of naivety and childish things, before the Shadow Shire.

A lot had happened since then. She had been back to the Salvation Lands since that time, but this was the first in which she had come wearing her robes. She wondered now what these relatives would think of her when she appeared amongst them as one of the Comcree.

Her contingent had increased to forty-seven by the time they left the Fibre Reed, swamp folk having also recalled the tellings. Even here in the Salvation Lands, the stories of the Comcree had never been forgotten. Gorean found that there was no reason to worry that she wouldn't find the numbers she needed. For eight days, Gorean headed north-east across the expanse of green rolling hills, quickly gathering a troupe of one-hundred-and-forty. They consisted of both kin and non-kin, some new to the Guild while others had their own secrets of belonging. As with elsewhere, these northerners felt the pull of allegiance to a common, though distant history.

Now, having reached the destination she was striving for, a voice spoke behind her. 'You have done well, Gorean. Even in the heat of passion, this is one secret you did not disclose.'

Gorean turned her head towards the familiar voice and smiled cautiously. 'Maybe you just weren't as good as you thought you were.'

'Oh, I was good, but obviously you were better,' retorted the man before her. 'What has brought the Comcree to within sight of the Frozen Alps?'

'We're to wait for a sky-ship!'

'A sky-ship. That tells me a lot.' Even now, his voice made her heart thump.

A visible sorrow fell across her face, and she asked, 'Do you understand me better now?'

The man, whose name was Leen, was looking at her as though seeing the young woman he had once known, remembering a time when they had been close. 'We have lived a long time, you and I,' he said. 'It has been many years since we were eighteen. My life has been good, as I trust yours has been, also.'

Gorean smiled now in recognition of his forgiveness. The hurt and sorrow had left them, allowing their long-ago friendship to resurface. 'I have thought of you often, but as you can see, I had something else to do with my life. And yes, it has been good,' she said, holding out her arms so that they could embrace as only good friends could.

A short distance from them, a young female recruit stood talking cheerfully to some of her friends. The recruit's expression changed suddenly to one of astonishment at the sight of her father embracing the warrior she had come to follow. She had no idea that her father walked in such high circles. Breaking from her friends, she walking slowly towards him.

'Ah, Kattea,' said Leen, having noticed Gorean glance towards the approaching girl. 'I would like to introduce an old friend of mine. She will look after you and your friends well, but she is a hard taskmaster, so do not disappoint me. Gorean Dowee, this is my daughter, Kattea Dowee-Soo.'

Gorean's eyes widened too. 'I didn't realise it had been so long. She was just a baby when I saw her last.'

'She is the youngest of my children, Gorean, so take good care of her! This is what she wants, so I must grant her this wish to be amongst the legends of our clan. She is smart and has learned well. It is only because she is my last girl child that I worry. When she told me what she wanted, I said that I would first have to see this Comcree before I assented. I didn't know then that it would be you! She is only sixteen, which means she still needs the consent of her parents.'

'You will not be coming with her, then?'

Leen lifted up his right arm and said, 'No. I hurt my hand a few years back. You Comcree will most likely be wanting able bodies. She will carry my dagger, though, so I will be there in spirit if not in body.'

Gorean looked at his hand, then gazed into his eyes as she remembered conversations from years past. 'One of the guardians was lost, but now the Comcree hexagon is whole again,' she said, sizing the girl up for herself. 'I am your mother's cousin, Kattea. I think I will enjoy your company, as your father and I are old friends. You can catch me up on his misdeeds.'

Kattea looked at her father scoldingly, then back to Gorean. 'I am glad to know you,' she said. 'It is good to know family when you finally learn you have them!'

Gorean smiled at the girl's words. 'Indeed, yes, you and I will find much to say to one another, but right now, I need a word alone with your father. Have you eaten yet?'

'Not since this morning.'

Gorean looked around, seeking out her apprentice. 'Shenn,' she called. 'Take this one to her friends and find food for them.'

Gorean watched Kattea walk off to her friends. Without turning to the man beside her, she said, 'Now that you know I am one of the Comcree, you want to ask me a favour, don't you? And I think it is a big favour, isn't it, Leen?'

'You and I always did know each other's minds before anything was said. Are you and I not worthy of big favours? Although her mother never said she was Shirey, I always had a feeling she was. I always thought that you might be a part of the Shadow Shire also. There was always an air of mystery about the two of you. Maybe that's why I liked you both and found it hard to choose.'

'I cannot train my own replacement, Leen, and that is what she would be. She and I are of the same house, and a house cannot train its own. Also, she is a woman, and under Comcree lore, a woman must be apprenticed to a man, and a man to a woman. Only once—that I know of—was this lore ignored. Its result is partly the reason why I am here today, asking these men and women to forgo their lives. The best I can do, Leen, is ask one of the male Comcree if they would be willing to take her on. It will be up to one of them to decide her destiny.'

'That is all I ask of you, Gorean. She is my last surviving girl-child, as I said, and without her mother, she needs guidance, which I cannot give. Even if her destiny is not to become Comcree, with you she can gain knowledge of the Shadow Shire, and surely that is deserved.'

Gorean looked at the girl, then to Leen. She saw the love he directed towards his daughter, and in that moment, she knew that, years before, she had made the right decision. 'Then that is our business done, Leen. I hope you will join me at the fire for some ferment?'

'I was hoping you would say that!'

'You haven't changed, have you!'

'I have become older and wiser, as have you, Gorean. Now tell me of this sky-ship you're waiting for.'

* * *

Over the next few days, Gorean began to find out exactly what sort of recruits had joined her. She started with rudimentary exercises, and soon discovered that only a few had any kind of real training in the skills they would need. Amongst these few, she was glad to see that before her death, her cousin had at least started to train her daughter. She could see that Kattea was not just a foolish young girl whose head had been filled with wonderful stories of her ancestors. Instead, she had already begun to absorb the subtleties of the ancestry that destined her to be one of the Shirey, if not more.

On the morning of the fourth day at their encampment, frequent laughter burst in waves from a group of young recruits. Kattea was amongst them, listening to and relating recollections of the tellings. As she listened to one young man share his reason for allegiance, she looked up and around, needing to survey her surroundings. She saw that her mother's cousin was once more alone and talking to the air. She had observed the Comcree warrior doing this before. And again, she wondered at her strangeness. She watched Gorean stride purposefully up the small rise surrounding their camp, stop at the crest, and look out towards the east. Intrigued, Kattea followed. Since becoming part of this contingent, she was like a flutter-wing to a flame, always curious. Absorbed in their discussions, her companions never even noticed her leave.

'What are you looking for?' she asked, coming up beside her mother's cousin.

Gorean turned at the sound of the now-familiar voice, which had become a trailing shadow by her side. She observed the girl for a moment before pivoting back to observe the east. 'One of my sisters is coming,' she replied. 'Can you see her? Just above the horizon.'

'The pink, you mean? It's big, isn't it! I've never seen a sky-ship that big before. It looks much closer than it actually is, doesn't it?'

Gorean smiled. Not many people would have noticed the pale pink dot in the sky. Keen observation, it seemed, was one of the skills her cousin had taught her youngest daughter. Gorean pondered this for a moment, wondering why the youngest of Leen's daughters had received the training when it should have been the eldest. Maybe her cousin had started to train all of them. She would never know now.

The end of Gorean's dagger flashed, making the young recruit flinch. 'What was that?'

The stone flashed again, and Gorean said, 'I think if we do not move, we will be squashed. My sister has found us. Go tell Shenn; I need to speak with him. Start telling the others to get ready. It's time to leave this place.'

* * *

'As you see, Mister Lees,' said Hestean, fanning her dagger across the horizon for the second time in just moments. 'Right where they should be. Just as you predicted! You still know the landmarks of this region very well, it would seem! The *Merysands* has indeed done well to have you aboard.'

'I wish all sky-ships harboured one of your daggers,' replied Mister Lees. 'It would make navigation much easier.'

'The dagger only allows me to locate my brothers and sisters, Mister Lees. It would be of little use in day-to-day navigation. Besides, would you have all our magic for yourself? Surely the Comcree are allowed to hold some secrets back.'

Lees smiled at the young Comcree's statement. Despite her youth, he had come to admire the breadth of her knowledge. After leaving the Hassis, she had sought him out and asked many questions about his homeland. He thought her questions strange. As one of the Comcree, she should surely already know this world very well.

Apart from the helmsman and his second, Mister Lees and Hestean were the only ones in the control cabin. The captain and Mister Caze had headed off with Petty in search of Karree, to make some final decisions about the loading of Gorean's contingent. It was time to land the sky-ship, and Lees wondered if his transfer to the *Merysands* had indeed just been happenstance.

* * *

The people in the camp watched as the crew of the giant sky-ship fired its harpoons and began hauling it to the ground. When the access door opened, Gorean saw Hestean standing, deliberately framed within the ship's hatch. To one side of her was Petty, in his blue-trimmed uniform, and on the other side was a female Deserteer in hers.

'Follow us, Kattea,' said Gorean when the loading ramp touched the ground. Shenn and the head of Gorean's protectorate accompanied her up the ramp. Kattea trailed behind.

'I see you have learned how to make an entrance, sister!' said Gorean, making herself heard above the residual whir of the sky-ship's dwindling propellers.

'Hopefully I have learnt how to do more than just that!' replied Hestean.

Gorean, heard in Hestean's voice the authority required by a Comcree. She knew then that the young guardian had indeed grown considerably. She looked towards the female Deserteer beside Hestean, noting the "LM" insignia of her previous calling on her uniform. With one glance, it was clear that the Deserteer was closely bound to Hestean.

Gorean's and Karree's eyes met. 'I have one-hundred-and-forty. Will the ship hold them all?' she asked bluntly.

'This is a big ship,' replied Karree, 'so, unless they are giants, there will be room. We will have them come aboard single file, carrying only what they need and nothing more!'

Gorean replied with a single nod. She turned back to Shenn and the young recruit by his side. 'Kattea, go with Shenn and let the others know what this loadmaster has stated. Then have them present themselves here for boarding.'

'At once, Hlaford,' said the girl, turning. Gorean saw Shenn glance at the girl as she ran down the loading ramp, and then he turned to Hestean for a moment before descending also.

'What was that about?' asked Hestean.

'Don't ask! I think a pet has found me, and Shenn has also seen how good she is with a dagger. Maybe she reminds him of someone.' Gorean didn't know whether to smile or frown.

'I can think of worse things than being worshiped,' said Hestean.

'You just wait till it happens to you! You won't think it so funny then. All my life, I have been invisible. This visibility has challenged me.'

Hestean's eyes lingered before shifting to the girl, now racing from one group of recruits to another. 'I fear that is a risk we may all face now. Who is she? She has your eyes.'

Gorean turned to look at the girl herself, watching the sheer, youthful exuberance that exuded from every pore of Kattea's body. 'Having family is never simple,' she said, and then she felt a pair of eyes on her. She turned to see Petty observing her. 'She's not mine, Mister Petty, if that is what you're thinking. She's my cousin's child.'

'I didn't say anything! Would a mug of ferment help?' said Petty.

'I fear I already had too much of that last night,' said Gorean. 'We gather to ourselves unforeseen responsibilities at times, Mister Petty, and sometimes they turn out to be the best things we have ever done. I do wish, though, that some things were easy to put aside. Some complications we could do without, right now, but you have just helped me decide on something. Thank you.' Gorean looked deeper into the ship, putting aside her personal thoughts as she returned to the task at hand. 'Come, sister. While my contingent is coming aboard, you and I should see the captain. Does he know where we are to go next?'

'Yes, sister. And also, what he is to do after that.'

* * *

The head of Gorean's protectorate and Petty followed the two Comcree warriors as they went in search of the captain. Karree stood watching them, along with the *Merysands*' new loadmaster. 'What did that mean?' he asked.

'I have no idea, but I would like to find out!' said Karree. 'Now, though, I think we should ready ourselves to sort her motley contingent as they come aboard.'

Karree turned to look at the line of women and men. Their addition would bring the number aboard the *Merysands* to nearly three-hundred-and-ninety. With the large number of supplies onboard, it would bring the ship close to its maximum weight. She knew her calculations would be tested if they were to get back into the air, and this was likely why the new loadmaster had quickly deferred to her as the hatchway had opened.

It was with notable relief that she later felt the giant ship's buoyancy restabilised as it lifted gently from the ground. 'The ship is yours, Captain,' she said into the voice receiver hanging around her neck. 'All hatches have been secured.'

33

The *Merysands* had turned east, setting course for the place where Hestean's journey had first brought her aboard the huge sky-ship. It seemed a lifetime ago now. With her head on her pillow, she closed her eyes and found herself thinking of Jarrak.

Of all the people she'd met in her short life, he was the one who'd been able to stabilise her thoughts and give them direction. He understood her, and it seemed that the closer she came to Sharacan, the more the past and history of this world tugged at her. Her brain was becoming crowded, and she longed for his made-up stories about stars and far-off worlds. They'd seemed so fanciful back then.

Now, though, this world could turn in her hand if she wanted it to.

She feared she'd changed into something she didn't want to be, and she found herself needing to know if the man who had begun her journey was still there for her. She needed to look into his eyes and feel his closeness; needed to know what he'd found in her absence. Rolling over in her sleep, her dreaming mind was uneasy.

There was more to Sharacan than anyone had ever imagined, and she needed to know if what she had read was true. The ancient books that Dan had shown her spoke of hiding, and she could see it now—a gigantic ship coming to ground, its people surviving. She saw knowledge, too, far beyond what existed in her world today. It had been written down in a way that hid its true origin, but it had been described nevertheless, so that one day it would be seen for what it was.

Images of vast caverns and tunnels forming came into her mind, their sand walls turning to glass due to heat blasted in ribbons of light. The books had served as manuals that had allowed her people to survive … So much learned and lost. Her head whirled. Before she told her fellow Comcree, Dan had suggested strongly that she expel the College from her place of birth. By doing so, there would be less chance of the

Robes finding out what they held within their grasp. Her newfound knowledge was something she hated concealing from her new sisters and brothers.

The anomalies Jarrak and Bornn had struggled to understand were now clear to her. She knew that they had both been right. In the two hundred years since Andreena's disappearance, no one had asked Dan the questions she had asked. She had discovered that the greatest anomaly was her own kind. Why did no one else see this? Her mind twisted as she wondered how this revelation would be taken. Should it be revealed that they were not truly a part of this world?

Jarrak had been correct when he had said the anomalies were meant to keep someone digging, but it was not for him that the map had been laid down. It was for the Comcree. Her uncluttered mind had allowed her to see what others had not. She had come upon this truth as only Andreena had done generations prior to her. Perhaps the College hadn't even had a part in her disappearance. Maybe, in a way unknown to even Dan, the gods had been the ones to take Andree. She winced at the thought as her restless sleep continued.

If it were true, the College need only be punished for the destruction of Sharacan and for their treatment of the village women. This was still enough, though, to secure her wrath. The College would receive their rightful retribution.

She would need the collective insight of all her sisters and brothers to properly unravel the past of the world. As of yet, though, the whole hexagon had not been together to discuss things. Dan had also advised that she would need to better understand the truth for herself before revealing the world's true origins. But should she disclose that they were from another world? Refugees who had found a place to hide, and also found a way to stay hidden from the stars hunting them? The single blanket fell to the floor as Hestean tossed and turned, and she curled up into a ball, making herself small.

It had been Dan who had suggested she first find her proof and take back Sharacan. Sharacan had been the birthplace of the Comcree, of the Deserteers, of the Guild and of Dan himself. The College had spawned later as a bubbling within the walled city of Learnian, considered a place of great thought by the Robes but a place of corruption to everyone else. It was to Learnian that they would be returned. Sharacan was not theirs.

However, she would never again let a bound person within Learnian's walls, and this meant no women. Without women, there would be no longevity for the Black Robes, meaning that the College would slowly but assuredly die. This decision was what the Comcree were now acting upon.

Yet she still needed to disable the shield so that the Comcree could use their weapons at Sharacan. From the very beginning of their time on this world, these were weapons that were designed to build, to powder stone or forge glass.

An image of Kattea flashed into her mind and she knew she was seeing something of herself, but in the way someone was normally supposed to come to the guardians. Was it just circumstance? Or was there another reason? Something that she was still unaware of?

She felt her shoulders being gently shaken as her body thrashed. She heard a voice; an anxious, worried voice. 'Hestean … Hestean. You are dreaming, sister!' She lurched upright and found herself in bed aboard the *Merysands*. Gorean was by her side. 'You have been dreaming,' said her fellow Comcree. 'Your unease was so loud that it roused me from my own sleep next door.'

Hestean's heart was thumping, but her mind began to settle. She knew she was experiencing no dream. After a moment, she said, 'It was just a jumble of thoughts … I'll be fine in a moment.'

'You have come a long way,' soothed Gorean. They talked for a while, and when Gorean finally left to go back to her own room, Hestean found the lure of sleep to be non-existent. Instead, she lay on her bed, looking up at the darkened ceiling. She recalled Jarrak telling his stories about the stars. Unbeknown to even him, some of those stories were true.

* * *

The next morning, Hestean and Karree watched as Gorean took some of her new recruits through training. Time was beginning to run short. Hestean knew that over the next few days, Gorean intended to teach her new recruits all she could in the time left to her. As a warrior, she needed to know what she could expect from those under her command.

A space had been left clear in the large storage bay. As Gorean positioned small groups of the recruits against her protectorate, Hestean noticed someone watching. Sitting atop a mountain of crated supplies, Kattea mimicked Gorean's every move. Hestean studied the girl with interest, recalling her dream. The night before, Gorean had said that Kattea had no idea what was being planned for her. Hestean found herself wondering how the young girl would react when she learned. She wondered how she herself would have reacted, but then realised it was far too late to wonder about that.

When Gorean called for the next group to come forward, Kattea turned to see Hestean opposing her. Hestean's dagger darted high and to the right before its cold edge came to rest against Kattea's throat. The young Comcree vanished from in front of the girl only to materialise, as if from thin air, behind her. 'I think you already know the dance of the dagger well enough. It's time you learned the shadow dance,' Hestean whispered into her ear. She glanced up and saw Karree smiling. She recalled the Deserteer saying the very same thing once. That time, it had been Karree holding a dagger.

'Kattea doesn't have to know that yet,' said Gorean.

'No, but she already knows her dagger better than the others. I think she has already had some training, and it won't hurt for her to know a little more.'

'Alright, but take these two as well; they're almost as good. Karree can help you.'

The next afternoon, Kattea managed to get her dagger closer to Hestean, but even as she did so she felt another blade at her throat.

'Never forget,' said a voice into her ear, 'that wherever there is a Comcree, there is also a protectorate. When you are fighting a Comcree, you are never just fighting one shadow. Now, let's try it again, shall we?' Kattea turned to see the other two recruits sprawled on the floor. Karree sheathed her dagger and put out her hand to help up the nearest.

'How long did it take you to learn all this?' asked Kattea.

'I've been training all my life,' replied Karree. 'But you are getting better. In another few years, you might even be good. Let's try it again.'

* * *

Two days later, the *Merysands* began disgorging its cargo of people and supplies. The great ship's winches had pulled it to ground just before the sun's zenith, allowing the combined contingents of Elora-Bearer Hassis and northern Deserteers to be finally set free. Immediately, they set to work establishing a temporary camp. They would spend only three days here, waiting for the return of the *Merysands*, for the giant sky-ship was yet to finish its journey. One more excursion to the south-west lay ahead of it.

After the Deserteers had disembarked, the supplies from the ship's cargo bay were also unloaded, forming a mountain of sustenance upon the sand. This was later camouflaged with netting and bound firmly to the ground to protect against desert winds. The *Merysands* was once again free to move, but for the remainder of today's light, it would sit empty and silent as it waited in anticipation of the next morning's sun.

Gorean finally set forth to do what she had been born to do; outlining the camp's structure and setting its perimeter. It was as far from teaching children as she had ever been, but even here, she was a teacher. Here, she was to continue schooling the Deserteers in arts that had been hidden or partially forgotten over generations. In this place, she would teach her new recruits the real power of a Deserteer's dagger, although she had just three days remaining in which to do it … She set the Elora-Bearer Hassis contingent against her own, time and again.

On the evening of the third night, she set forth to surround Sharacan in a thin, continuous line, hidden amongst the waves of sand and hills. She needed to have blended these two groups into one giant double squadron of nearly four hundred strong. There, they were to wait for the return of the *Merysands*, accompanied by its smaller cousin, the *Aquasands*—and within them both, the southern and central west squadrons.

* * *

Hestean, however, hadn't seen the mountain of supplies form. She hadn't seen Gorean at her finest, either. Within moments of the *Merysands* coming to ground, Hestean and her protectorate had emerged from the opening in the *Merysands'* belly. They were heading east, and they, too, had just three days to find what they were looking for.

'She will need a seconder, won't she?' asked Hestean, making a last-minute decision before jumping to the ground.

'Who will?' asked Gorean.

'There is no time for hiding, sister. I know that Kattea will not come to us as I did!'

'You are right in that!' replied Gorean.

'I thought so! I have been observing her over the last few days. That's the real reason why I took her from you. If you think she truly is who you want her to be, she will have my vote. I see talent in her.'

Gorean smiled. Hestean had shown an uncanny ability to see all that was around her. 'Coming from one who was selected by the gods themselves,' she said, 'this means a lot to me. But, sister, you do scare me. I didn't know I would become so accepting of the world's changes. I hope the gods protect you!'

'I hope the gods protect us all,' replied Hestean, her feet hitting the ground. A moment later, she was gone, hidden within her scurrying protectorate.

Towards the end of the following day, just as she had been warned—and just as it had happened to Andreena two hundred years before—on her approach into Sharacan, Hestean's connection with Dan and the other Comcree dissolved.

Abruptly, she knew that she was once more alone, with only her protectorate to watch over her. Now, only her own thoughts guided her. For a while, the shield around Sharacan had puzzled her; the communicators she had used with Jarrak had worked there. Gorean had explained that Comcree within Sharacan could also talk to one another, for they were only communicating to each other from within the ancient city itself. The shield served as a dividing wall. It also worked in a similar way to that of a thunder-staff's shield, and was of a similar technology to the shield that wrapped around the *Merysands*. Maybe Dan was right, and maybe her dreams were right, too. The past was the future, and the future was now.

34

Nearing mid-morning on the day after Thace's cavaliers had ensconced themselves amongst the ruins of Tear Salt, the *Aquasands* came from the south.

Its young captain had never been here before, and the terrain was a mystery. He marvelled at the accuracy of their course. Directly in front of them was the oasis that had once been a thriving settlement. On the other side of a now dry stream, he could make out a collapsed fabric mill, and further back—near a dry salt pan—a tannery. These were the industries that had once made this town. Now, the soak was the only reason why this place remained. Later, he would find that the cemetery, containing some headstones dating back a thousand years, housed Tear Salt's only permanent residents.

The captain felt he had come to know the Comcree warrior who stood beside him, although there was still an air of otherworldliness about the man. The warrior listened to a device in his ear, as did the other Comcree, and his dagger lit up when held before them towards the horizon. This was true magic. In the short time of their acquaintance, he had come to truly believe in these Comcree who served the gods.

These warriors knew the landmarks of this world very well. He had seen, too, the power of the Comcree thunder-staff, which could powder stone to dust at the will of its holder. He had seen them used to form holes in the ground, which were used as places to lie in—a technique called caverning, which when activated, kept its user hidden and safe. He had asked Deleev a few days earlier if the Comcree intended to rule this world, and the warrior's reply had startled him.

'And what makes you think we don't already?' the warrior had asked. After a moment, he'd added, 'But you are right, of course. We don't rule. We never have. It is not our place. We guide this world, like the *cyings* and *cwens* in your tellings. Have you never wondered why the tales of the Comcree persist? It is because we have always been here! We do not force ourselves onto this world, and it has accepted us without really knowing that we were here.'

'Until now,' said the young captain.

'Yes. Until now,' agreed Deleev. 'The College would rule this world if they could, and this we can never allow. For the first time in two hundred years, the Comcree hexagon is complete, and we have again been able to show ourselves. This will make the College fearful, as it is meant to. But they will assuredly still come forth, as they have in the past. Their own arrogance is their one true enemy.'

There had been history in Deleev's words. The young captain had thought about it for a moment while waiting for Deleev to continue, but the warrior had not—his words defiant in their conclusion. Now, approaching Tear Salt, his mind suddenly skipped with a thought. *What if the College are indeed able to capture and unleash upon this world the technology of the Comcree?* He was filled with alarm as he remembered the Comcree's thunder-staffs.

He had already firmly resolved to stand by these Comcree warriors. The guild's heritage was no longer a myth. It was real to him, and he knew he had always been part of it. He had realised, not long after leaving Fiskay, that this was what the Deserteer's oath meant.

The *Aquasands* came to rest, tethered to the ground near the remains of the ancient town. The captain watched on as Deleev, Heggon, and Betteen disembarked to be greeted by a fourth warrior. Beside this person was a young woman, obviously not Comcree, but close to becoming one. Her dagger was red, yet she wore the distinctive garb of a Comcree.

After the squadron of Deserteers had disembarked, some of the boxes brought from Sinkar were unloaded. The young captain watched as Betteen's Deserteers were paired with cavaliers, to instruct them on the use of the thunder-staffs. To the captain, the inevitability of conflict was now clearly on display. He had seen that these weapons were not just offensive, but protective. If held correctly, they were capable of producing a shield to defend their users. This, he saw, was the first line of knowledge shown to these novices of war. The Comcree were assembling a mighty army that would be capable of protecting itself. It wasn't big in number, but large in the force it could wield. He knew there were more Deserteers amassing in other places, too. At first, he'd thought the Comcree were gathering to take on the city of Learnian. Now, he found himself wondering. Why had they come so far north?

Later in the evening, he was told the reason. His ship would not, as he had first thought, be heading south again. Instead, they would be heading east, towards the ancient desert city of Sharacan.

'Why would the taking of Sharacan—just a desert village now, I am told—require such a force?' he asked Deleev.

'The truth of it is that it won't,' replied the warrior, 'but the keeping of it might. We have vowed never again to let Sharacan be taken!'

'But why is a desert village so important?'

'You will just have to wait and see, Captain.'

'But if I am wondering, then so might the College be.'

'And now you see the reason for the force we are building,' said Deleev.

* * *

Just before dusk the following day, the *Merysands* also appeared in the sky above the encampment at Tear Salt. More than twice the length of the *Aquasands*, it dwarfed its smaller cousin as it came to ground. Once landed, Shenn stepped from the huge ship, followed closely by Kattea, who Gorean had—without explanation—assigned to him.

Just as Gorean had stated, Shenn's responsibilities had grown quickly since his first encounter with Hestean. It was he who had represented the Comcree during this last section of the *Merysands'* journey. It was now also he who would give the other four Comcree warriors their first report.

'I need to see your captain,' said Kattea, presenting herself to a young man lounging against the edge of the *Aquasands*' main hatchway.

'Do you? And what exactly do you need to see him about?'

'I was given a note for him, from the captain of the *Merysands*.'

'A note?'

'An invitation. Now, can I speak to him? I have somewhere else to be right now.'

'Then you had best hand it over.'

'You're not the captain!'

'And why shouldn't I be?'

'You're too young to be a captain!'

'Not all captains are old and grey-haired, you know,' said the youthful-looking man as he moved to hang his legs over the edge of the hatchway. 'Now, let's see that note. An invitation, you say? To what?'

She handed over the note and said, 'To sup aboard the *Merysands*!'

'You shouldn't read other people's letters, you know.'

'I didn't. I was there when it was written. Tomorrow, I believe both your ships will again be in the air. Oh, and by the way, our captain is bald, not grey! If you look for a grey-haired man, you will find the wrong person.' With that, Kattea turned and walked away.

* * *

The scent of brewing tea wafted through the air as Kattea arrived at the fire. As she settled herself into the ring of Comcree and apprentices, she wondered where the ritual offering of tea had come from. She also wondered why she had been asked to attend this congress of warriors and apprentices. It had not really occurred to her that she would be an oddity seated amongst them. Slowly, she found herself taking a keen interest in what was being said. As with everyone else, she glanced expectantly towards Shenn as the Comcree Battean said, 'Are you afraid of my new sister, Shenn?' Kattea watched as Shenn breathed in his thoughts to form his answer.

'No,' he said. Kattea was sure he was backing away from some implication.

'Then what did you do to her? Or what did she do to you?' asked Thace. 'There is a disturbance within you lad, as Batteen has seen.'

'She cut my arm!' said Shenn, heatedly. 'She could have stabbed me, the way she threw her dagger at me!'

From the opposite side of the circle, Heggon started to laugh. 'If she had wanted to stab you, lad, then she would have! She is Sharacanese!' said the big man.

'That's what she said,' retorted Shenn. 'You say that as if it is known.'

This time, Heggon was joined in his laughter by the other warriors, and even Thace's apprentice, Layatty, gave into a small giggle. Kattea was the only one who remained silent.

'She is Sharacanese,' repeated Heggon, in his large, cheerful voice. 'No one goes against a Sharacan dagger and expects not to bleed. Not even me, lad. From the day they are born, they learn the stone game.'

Heggon put out his arm and fanned it across the horizon. 'How many people do you see before you here, lad?'

Shenn's eyes surveyed the encampment. 'Maybe four hundred?'

'And how many are with Gorean?'

'Nearly that number again.'

Kattea leaned forward as Heggon, still chuckling, spoke again. 'Sharacan is a small village, Shenn, but even so, if it was the Sharacanese that we were going up against, we would possibly still lose half of our Deserteers in a single day. If what you have told us is true, then the women of Sharacan have not forgotten their skills as the Black Robes believe. It is the women of Sharacan who were always the danger, not the men. But I would not want to come up against a Sharacanese man, either. There is a question here, Shenn. If the women of Sharacan have not forgotten how to fight, then why have they allowed the Robes to think they have?' Heggon's voice had turned cold, but now it lightened a little. 'They are brethren, yes, but it would appear that they are still real Sharacanese. That is why the women have hidden themselves. They have allowed the Robes to become complacent so that Sharacan could slip from the centre of the College's sight. As you know, we have been reinforcing this attitude, so they will think that we're attacking Learnian. But when we take Sharacan, things will change rapidly. The women of Sharacan have known this was coming.'

Kattea looked to Shenn, and saw him gulp in understanding.

'Would you follow her, Shenn?' asked Layatty, bringing the conversation back to Hestean. Kattea realised that this was what they needed to know. The young Comcree warrior was the key to all of this.

Shenn looked to his fellow apprentice, whom Kattea knew had been one for longer than him. The young woman was obviously trying to find her own reasons to believe in this new warrior. Shenn appeared to think for a moment before answering. Calmed since his previous outburst, he said, 'Hestean walks with the gods. One does not walk against her, so neither will I.' Layatty nodded, and Kattea knew that she'd found meaning in his words.

The four warriors had also taken this in. They seemed to make their conclusions. 'You have done well, Shenn,' said Thace. 'In time, you will do your ancestors proud.'

Shenn nodded his gratitude.

'Then does she fly as one of us?' asked Heggon—a question that Kattea would come to realise was the most important of their assembly.

Kattea had observed that all the warriors thought Hestean young, still the age of a mere apprentice. But a blue Comcree dagger had been thrust into her hand, and she had held it with confidence. Hearing from Shenn, the only person who had actually seen Hestean throw that dagger, gave legitimacy to her claim.

'She flies as one of us,' said each in turn.

Heggon now looked at Kattea and asked another question. 'And what of you, young Kattea, what do you think?'

From the outset, Kattea had felt him observing her, as had the others. Every movement of her face, turn of her head, and look of her eye had been noted. 'Me?' she asked. 'What do you mean? I have no say here. Besides, you already know what I think.'

Heggon smiled at this. 'Good Comcree never look in one direction to make up their minds, Kattea. They survey every viewpoint before deciding on a course.'

'It seems to me that you have already made your choices.'

'With your help, yes.'

'But I've said nothing here!'

'You have said things without words. You made decisions on every question posed here, and I would like to hear you share them aloud.'

Kattea looked at the big man, suddenly aware of everyone's eyes upon her. She felt herself to be as exposed as Shenn had been earlier. She braced herself, then said, 'I have noticed one thing that may confirm your thinking. Aboard the *Merysands*, she began to teach the best of us the shadow-dance. Until now, I never even knew she was so recently inducted, but I have seen Gorean's respect for her. I have also seen how passionately her protectorate guard her. And she also guards them in everything she does. It is just a natural way with her. She seems to care very much about this world and its people.'

Layatty let out a little giggle. 'My cousin has been playing with you, Kattea. He might appear big and oaf-like, but he is one of the smartest amongst us. If you are inclined to accept his offer, you could do no better.'

'Offer? Offer of what?' asked Kattea, watching as Layatty drew forth a large red scarf from the pocket of her dress.

'He would not be asking if he thought we did not agree. I, for one, do agree,' said Layatty, flicking out the scarf and then refolding it into a triangle. She drew the newly folded fabric around herself to demonstrate its positioning.

'They both like playing games,' said Shenn, stepping forward to pull the scarf from Layatty's hands. 'It is a family trait they share. They once played a similar game on me!' Layatty poked out her tongue at Shenn. For an instant, Kattea saw the closeness that bonded the two apprentices. Shenn turned to Heggon and handed over the scarf.

'You should lighten, Shenn,' said the big man. 'You are too stern! This world is full of tragedy, and the exactness of our decisions demands our strength. The only ones we can afford to be frivolous with are ourselves, and this may be the last opportunity we have to smile for a while. These are serious days, and you must play while you can. At the same time, Kattea must be serious right now. This will affect the rest of her life. She will have to think about my offer, Shenn, as you once had to with Gorean!'

'Are you offering me an apprenticeship?' asked Kattea suddenly.

'Yes,' said Batteen. 'It must be your choice, though. Everyone's life is their own.'

'Who put me forward?'

'Your mother did, but it was Gorean, your mother's cousin, who applied. Do you know who the Shirey are, Kattea?'

'I am one, I suppose. They are family to the Comcree, aren't they?'

'Yes, descending down though the female line. They are collectively known as the Shadow Shire. More precisely, they are the eldest surviving daughters of their families. Your mother was Shirey, and not even your father knew it.' Batteen stood and took the scarf from Heggon before walking across to the girl. 'Take your time to decide. If you choose to put this scarf on, then Heggon will be your mentor. But if not, return the scarf and no more will be said of this. You will however, always have you birthright and a place within the Shadow Shire.'

'I can say no, then?'

'Your mother did.'

'In favour of Gorean?'

'That is why Gorean is repaying the favour now!'

'But I was not my mother's first-born girl child!'

'No! But you are the oldest still living, are you not?'

'I see. How long do I have?'

'We may be at battle in two days, but there is no hurry. Do not rush your decision.'

* * *

The following morning, the two sky-ships lifted into the air and set their course for Sharacan. Kattea kept out of the way during the embarkation. It was only once they'd departed that she appeared beside Heggon, wearing the red scarf and a blue-green dress she'd borrowed from Layatty. 'You make your decisions quickly,' the Comcree warrior said.

'There was no decision to make. I made it a long time ago. Although, I must say, I didn't know it then. My father would approve because you were wrong in one thing—I think my father did know. I would not have been allowed on this journey if he had not. My mother would not have wanted it if I had not wanted it for myself. I do have a question, though. Hestean … She didn't come to the gods in the same way that I have. That was the reason for yesterday's discussion, wasn't it?'

'You are partly right, yes. We used her to discover you. Hestean's arrival was a gifting through the line of inheritance. It happens rarely, but it has happened before in her line when there is no clear succession, or when the line has been shattered and needs gluing back together again. It happened to all the lines at once over two hundred years ago. The whole hexagon needed to be rebuilt, that time. Back then, it was Hestean's ancestor Andreena who received the honour of her lineage, but then she vanished, breaking the succession completely until now.' Heggon pulled out his dagger, allowing Kattea to look upon it. 'It is not just the person that is the authority; it is the dagger, also, that decides the legitimacy of a claim.' In demonstration, he held up the dagger, scanning it across the horizon. Its handle glowed a brilliant blue as it told the direction to Sharacan.

'I have seen Gorean's dagger do that,' said Kattea. 'Can I try?'

'The only dagger that will affirm you is Gorean's, and only after she's dead. It will not accept another while she still lives as one of the Comcree.'

'I have a long wait ahead of me then, don't I?'

Heggon smiled. 'Daggers don't like things to be rushed, and they have a habit of finding out when things are. Besides, unlike Hestean, you have a lot of learning to do.'

'Why is she different?'

'Take this as your first lesson, Kattea. Hestean is a true Sharacanese. There can be no other explanation for the dagger's acceptance of her. From birth, she would have been shown the way of the Comcree—all that needed to be done was for the dagger to be awakened so that she could find the truth of what she already knew. Sharacan is the centre of this world, Kattea! If we go back far enough, we can all trace our lineage to Sharacan. Even you. All Comcree are equal, but there has always been something special about those who are true Sharacanese. At the Hassis, there is a library. In it, you will find this for yourself. With the help of the gods, you will understand what you find. Don't just take what I say as true. You must find your own way to becoming yourself. I am your guide and your teacher, but to become Comcree, the conviction must come from within you. Do you understand, Kettea!'

'I think I'm beginning to!' she said, looking up at him.

'Good,' said Heggon, smiling.

'With Gorean, you mentioned an exception?' said Kattea.

Heggon's smile expanded. 'See, you are learning already! Never lose track of a thought, Kattea, until it's understood. Gorean may become our next Ze Hub. Or it could be Batteen, who I must say would make for a better cook. Only a woman may hold the title. The Ze Hub is our centre,' Heggon explained. 'Our Matrefem. The one who keeps our existence purposeful.'

A comprehending smile came across Kattea's face. 'Shenn was right about you,' she said. '"Cook" indeed. You're not talking about food, are you! I will have to look out for your little jokes.'

'Always remember how to smile, lass. This world is too small for malady. Unknown to them, it is the College who are ailing, and it is how they want us. Do not allow your heart to become like theirs!'

35

Hestean undid the fastenings attaching her daggers to her waist, then knelt down, placing the weapons just within reach on the rug covered floor of the tent. She discarded her cloak, covered the weapons to hide them, and moved closer to Jarrak's sleeping body. In the dark, the colour of her dress could not be seen. The earpiece in her ear was now the only clue remaining that might tell him who she had become. She leant forward, placing a soft kiss on his lips, then sat back to watch as he licked the kiss from his sleeping mouth.

She couldn't help but smile at his dream. For a while, she sat there, observing him. She was closer than she had ever dared to be before. She took in the pattern of his face, then skimmed a finger lightly across the rise of his hair, watching as his hand brushed the imagined disturbance away. Again, she leant forward and ran the tip of her tongue lightly across his lips. *He looks so tired*, she thought as she played this new, seductive game, which Gorean had recently explained to her.

* * *

Slowly, Jarrak's eyes opened, adjusting sleepily to the gloom. His dream seemed somehow real. His eyes were transfixed by a ghostly figure, which slowly turned into the more solid and real form of Hestean.

He lurched upright, and Hestean only just managed to avoid collision. 'It *is* you!' he said.

'You take a lot of waking up,' replied Hestean with a smile.

Still partly in a dream, his mind took in the unexpected words. 'What do you mean?'

'Do you love me?' she asked, still as an apparition, soft and unfocused in his eyes. He quivered at the question, which had been on his mind for so long. He thought of all the previous times her image had floated before him. He saw again the times she had made him laugh, when there had been no reason to laugh. He remembered the warmth that had lingered whenever she had come close to him. It flushed through his veins once more. He felt, again, the unexpected loss that had begun the day she'd left. This was the first time his mind had actually dared answer the question.

He heard his voice say, 'Yes.'

He reached up to touch her lips, and found form to his ghost. The words he had heard were real, as had been his reply.

* * *

Hestean felt the touch of his finger confirming her existence. 'Well, then,' she said. 'You had better make love to me while I'm still feeling brave.' She closed her eyes and felt sparks tingle across her lips. She heard herself say, 'You do know how, don't you?' And suddenly the spell was broken. Her eyes opened. 'I mean … I haven't. I'm just hoping that at least one of us knows what they're doing, that's all. I've gone and spoilt this, haven't I?'

Jarrak quietly laughed, and said, 'Perhaps just a little, as only you could, Hat.'

All at once, she felt embarrassed and shy and naive. 'Should I be quiet now?'

With his finger, Jarrak combed a few stray hairs from her face. 'I think it's my turn to ask a question, don't you? Do *you* love *me*?'

Assembling her thoughts, she said, 'I've never felt like this before. How do you explain something that you haven't previously experienced? It scares me, to be this close to you, and it scares me not to be. It scares me that I don't know how to make love to you yet. Right now, I know that there is only one person I want to make love with … You make me feel good. Loved. And I just know … I think I do, yes!'

* * *

It was her ramblings that amused him this time. He lent forward and kissed her before falling back onto his bedroll, his hands dragging her down so that she fell with him, too.

'It sounds as if you feel a bit like I do,' he said. 'You are right, of course. About other women, that is. There have been a couple. However, to love you—to make love to you—the thought has scared me ever since you left. I fear you have unexpectedly become part of me, and I don't want to lose you because of desire.'

Hestean moved close to feel his body, and said, 'I'm right in thinking that we're not just friends anymore, though, aren't I?'

Jarrak breathed in a lungful of air, then released it. 'No, we're not just friends. We haven't been "just friends" for a long time, although neither of us knew it. When you were here, I never did. It was only after you left that I realised how much a part of me you had become.' Suddenly he pushed himself up, as if suddenly putting everything together, and said, 'Why are you here? You shouldn't be here! I sent you away to be safe.'

* * *

She didn't want to think about this, and looked up into the blank darkness of the tent. Her mouth opened, and in a whisper, she said, 'I think you know why. You've been expecting it for the past two years, just as I have.'

'And what makes you think this?'

'Your mother! She says hello, by the way.' In the darkness, Hestean grinned.

'I should have told you, shouldn't I?' he said, with a groan of regret. 'But for some reason, I didn't want you to think that I was here because of my family's associations. I needed to do this for myself, not for my family, but Bornn's reputation obscures that.'

'You are quite silly at times, aren't you? Anyway, I don't want to talk about this now. Not tonight. Tonight is for us. Tomorrow, I'll show you the next.' She snuggled closer to him, and he collapsed onto his bedroll once more. 'You do smell a bit,' she said.

'So, you've become soft to your new comforts, have you? You smell a bit too, you know. Are you on your own? You still haven't told me why you're here!'

'That's not for now, either. Tomorrow.'

For a long time, they lay there, endless and unobservant, revelling in each other's closeness. Something new had begun, but now they were both unsure of how to continue.

After a while, Hestean got to her feet and walked to the water jug. She pulled the wash basin close to decant some water, then picked up a small bar of soap, a cloth, and a towel before walking back to him. 'Come on, sit up.' She had become the bossy young girl whom Jarrak had first seen on the day she'd thrown her hat at him. She placed the basin on the ground and grabbed his arm, pulling him up. Then she pulled his tunic over his head.

'What are you doing?'

'Doing what needs to be done! You do smell! How did you become so lazy? I used to be the lazy one, not you!' Kneeling beside him, she splashed water over his back and started to rub soap into his shoulders, neck, and underarms.

'Do you know what you're doing?'

'It's my first time, but I suppose men smell in the same places that women do!'

He felt her hands against his skin and became aware of the movement of her fingers. His muscles started to relax as he felt her towel him dry. She shuffled her way around him to work on his face and arms, then his chest. As she went to undo the knot at the top of his trousers, she froze when he reached up to undo the lacings of her dress.

She hadn't thought about undoing his trousers; she had just begun to without thought. It had crept up on her and she'd realised that for the first time in her life, she was about to shed her clothes in front of a man—and more so, that she wanted to.

Jarrak's fingers lingered for a moment, having loosened the lacing to reveal the very start of her breasts. But then she felt him pull away, as he noticed the look of uncertainty in her eyes. He stood, taking her hand to help her rise with him.

'How about if I go first?' he suggested.

She knew that they had returned to the same awkward moment of before. Instead of letting the awkwardness grab hold of them, this time, she saw that Jarrak had pushed it aside. He let his trousers fall to the ground and Hestean stood looking at his face, wanting to look down, knowing that at this moment she wanted to see him, feel him, touch the man of him. But instead, she pulled the shoulders of her dress down. She pulled each arm from its sleeve and let her dress fall to the ground. Leaning forward, Jarrak kissed her lightly on the lips and said, 'It must have been me! You don't smell very much at all now.'

She smiled, giggled, and said, 'I haven't finished cleaning you yet. Then you can wash me.'

He pulled her close, and she felt her breasts flatten against his chest. Driven by a feeling she had never known before, she quickly fastened her mouth to his.

Then, without warning, the archaic law of the Black Robes jumped into her mind, flashing through her like a thunderbolt. She pulled back. For a moment, those Black Robes haunted her, but then she rejected them. No; never again would they bind her. The Robes would not steal this moment from her. She was free now. This was her moment, full of sensations, excitement, and uncertainties. She was going to surrender her very being to this moment, not to the College.

She pushed her lips to Jarrak's once more, and felt his tongue as it explored her mouth. In that instant, the College was pushed from her mind, and she felt herself respond to his touch fully. That night, she became a woman, no longer just a girl.

36

In the first glow of morning, a middle-aged woman walked towards Jarrak's tent. It had become routine for her now—waking before the sun to walk the distance between her village and the diggings. As always, she carried in one hand a small sack of bean flour, and in the other a basket. The quietness at this time allowed her mind to drift, in sharp contrast to later in the day, when she would need all her wits about her. She had become a target now—the only member of her family left for the new chairman to harass. One wrong action could result in death, as it had for her husband. She was alone now, and Sharacan was no longer the place it had been. Unlike in the case of her husband's brutal death, though, she would just be stripped and cast out into the desert, as her daughter had been.

Now the tent had become a refuge for Sathea, as it had been for her daughter. The young man employing her as a servant gave her a way to survive. Ironically, the job had given her some status and respect, not only amongst the women of Sharacan but also amongst the men. At the tent, she would set to work making the morning meal for herself and Jarrak, before fetching water and generally tidying. She would make the time drag out as much as possible, and even liked it when the elderly Robe visited to perform his clandestine scribing.

Unexpectedly, she found herself liking him a little, despite his title as a Robe. Though he had always been a little different from the others. Slowly, she was finding out why. He hadn't been born a Robe but was one of the stolen. The College indoctrination had never fully taken with him; all he knew was that he had no home to go back to. While still a novice, he had heard whisper that Sharacan was treated differently from other places under College rule, and so he had contrived to be stationed here. He was eventually forgotten and never reassigned. At first, it had surprised her that he had chosen to stay, but she now understood why. What choice did he have?

After the death of Sathea's bind-mate, her house had been taken from her, and so she had been assigned a room in the shared house where widowed women were permitted to live until new bind-mates could be found for them. Each afternoon, she would walk back to the village. Having noticed her unease, Winnz accompanied her whenever he could. It was through his conversations on these strolls that she'd started to see that the College was forgetting the lessons of its past. This was why things had changed in Sharacan. She remembered how Jarrak had kept at work, never allowing his own mind time to wander. This place had become treacherous for him, too, although she knew it wasn't the Robes he feared most. His work didn't stop him from missing Hestean, just as it didn't stop Sathea.

Sathea had seen Hestean blossom in Jarrak's company, but even she knew that her daughter could not have stayed. Sathea was proud that Hestean hadn't allowed the past to consume her future. Sathea was determined that she, too, would have a future somehow.

It had been Reglean who had pulled her back from the edge after her daughter's banishment. Later, it had been Reglean who had established her suspicions about what had really happened on the day of Hestean's expulsion. The old woman's strength had helped her to survive the pantomime.

This morning, she was again wondering how much longer she could contain her increasing disdain for the College. The more she learned from Winnz, the more she knew it was time to do something. The Robes had taken everything from her—her house, her autonomy, her husband. And although Hestean was still alive, they had in a way taken her.

She had known with certainty that her daughter's destiny would have been short if she had stayed within sight of the Robes. Hestean's personality would have allowed no other outcome. She remembered the night she'd spent guarding her. It was something she hadn't been able to do with her older sister, who had also been targeted by the Robes. She and her daughter had been two female forms alone in the dark, saying many things, yet not saying the things that should have been said. Now, gone from here, Sathea hoped that her daughter would flourish. She missed her very much, but to see Sharacan obliterated would be worse.

Rounding a bend in the path, she thought she saw the sand move in her peripheral vision. She stopped, then stood for a moment, staring out across the dunes, seeing nothing. 'A ghost,' she told herself. 'A fragment from my mind, or maybe an ancient spirit this young man's digging has disturbed.' She sighed, expelling her fantasy, and walked on, almost wishing that it *had* been a ghost. To be scared to death would perhaps be preferable to the long starvation she would probably face after Jarrak was gone. But at least she would have repaid her debt to him.

A moment later, she again noticed the sand move. A chill ran down her spine. This time, she did not stop. She walked on with her anxiety hidden. She ignored her desire to run and hid her disquiet from the observant shadows.

She entered the tent feeling that something was amiss. After a moment's pause, she dropped her basket to the floor. The walls of the tent had been tied down for the night, so it was much darker inside. As she parted the curtain to the young man's living quarters, she called out in a low voice, 'Maskee, Maskee Jarrak. Maskee Jarrak, are …'

The curtain dropped as another ghost leaped out of the gloom in front of her.

* * *

Rising from where she lay uncovered and naked beside Jarrak, Hestean had moved quickly to stand and unsheathe one of her daggers. She now held it out towards her mother. The eyes of the two women locked as they took in this unexpected moment.

Behind Hestean, Jarrak moved at the sound of Sathea's voice, and for a moment his eyes blinked open. Then they closed again, and he said, 'It's still dark outside, isn't it? What is it, Sathea?'

'I think she has seen my shadows,' said Hestean.

Once more, Jarrak's eyes blinked open, but this time they stayed open. He scrambled round to see Hestean's outstretched arm and the dagger held firmly. Facing her, with an expression of utter disbelief, was Sathea. 'By the gods, Hat,' he said in a loud whisper, reaching to pull some bedding over himself. 'What are you doing?'

Hestean's arm didn't move. 'My protectorate, Mother! Is that what you saw? Did you see the desert move in the corner of your eye?'

* * *

As still as a rock, Sathea continued to stare. Her daughter, was supposed to be safely away from here. Was this a dream?

Hestean's eyes disconnected from her as a shadow entered the tent. Sathea turned to see the man she knew as Petty standing behind her. Unlike last time, though, he was now wearing a cloaked uniform. Without thinking, she instantly stepped between him and Hestean, and hissed in a loud whisper, 'Avert your eyes! Do you always look upon the gods in their nakedness?' She wondered if this was all an hallucination.

* * *

Amazed at the quickness of her movement, Petty took in the middle-aged woman, seeing her likeness to Hestean. 'Only when my job demands it,' he said, lowering his dagger.

'And what is your job?'

'As mother to one of the Comcree, I thought you would know that!'

'What are you talking about, Petty?' asked Jarrak, taking the opportunity to rise and pull on his tunic.

'Remember last night?' said Hestean. 'When I said that I would show you my world tomorrow? Well, it's now tomorrow, and this is my world!' Hestean, now flushed with embarrassment, began to pull on her own clothes. She strapped the daggers to her waist, then moved sideways towards Petty. 'Some protector you turned out to be!' she hissed. How did my mother get in here?'

'I didn't realise that you wanted protection from your mother!'

'And I suppose you thought we were just talking in here all night, did you?'

'The light,' said Petty. 'It's getting brighter outside, and it was a matter of judgment. I didn't want to make a disturbance that could draw unwanted attention.'

Huffing, Hestean eyed him for a long moment. Then she turned to look at Sathea. 'What are you doing here, Mother? And don't you dare judge me. We could all be dead tomorrow, and I wanted to die as a woman. Do you understand?'

'Things have changed here,' said Sathea, without turning from Petty. 'That was not what was on my mind, daughter! For a moment, I thought you were a ghost.'

'A ghost?'

'Yes. In the gloom, you reminded me of my sister! But then I saw the blue dagger and my mind began to search for a more exact understanding.'

'And what exactly do you think you now understand, Mother?'

Sathea turned to see a fully dressed Comcree warrior. She gasped. 'But how …'

'"How" is not important! "Why" is what I want to know about, Mother. I am Comcree, yes, but it was not the gods who did this to me. This is because of you, and I think you know that, don't you? You have something to tell me, I think.' Hestean undid the lacing at the top of the dress, then pulled down her sleeve to reveal the mark carved into her shoulder as a baby. 'What exactly does this mean, Mother?'

Sathea stared at the mark, then at the two weapons now strapped to her daughter's waist—the red dagger of a sand-shepherd and the more meaningful blue-handled weapon of a Comcree. Her face filled with pride. 'It means the same as the mark on my own arm,' she said, 'and it is also the mark on the end of that blue dagger.'

'You knew of it, then?'

'I have been told the tellings, just as you would have if you'd stayed in Sharacan to come of age.'

'Was it you, Mother, who gave me this destiny?'

'No. I had no idea it had been given to you.'

'Do you know who did?'

'There are many secrets within Sharacan, but yes. There is only one person it could have been. This would not have been done without her knowledge.'

'Reglean?'

'Our Matrefem, yes.'

'Do all the women know what position she held here?'

'Most of the adult women here know that we held the world within our silence, but only a few knew the exact secret. It is what gives us the strength to survive here. For that very reason, Reglean allowed us to believe that the parcel was still here.'

'How widely is the term "Ze Hub" known here?'

Sathea smiled in acknowledgement. 'Only the same few women have ever called Reglean that! Where did you hear it?' she asked.

'I'm not talking about Reglean,' said Hestean. 'Maybe there is not as much known here as I had hoped.'

'What else is there to know?'

The tent filled with silence. 'A lot,' said Hestean after a pause. 'There is a lot to know about Sharacan, Mother.'

As they spoke, Jarrak watched the woman standing beside him, who he now realised was the very being he'd come here for. With every moment, her status as a Comcree warrior was becoming more real to him.

'Do you hate me, daughter?' asked Sathea.

'What! No … Why would I hate you?'

'When you were growing up you asked so many questions. Maybe that's why Reglean chose you.'

'Questions are not answers, and right now I need answers,' replied Hestean. She turned to Jarrak and studied him. 'Has he been looked after, Mother?'

'For as long as you have been gone, yes. I made it my duty.'

'Then no, I don't hate you, Mother. You have done all that I could have asked for.'

The curtain separating the living quarters from the rest of the huge tent moved, and a female Deserteer appeared. 'The sun has breached the horizon, Mister Petty,' said Karree. Sathea gasped again. She turned to see another ghostly reminder of her sister. The woman was a younger and much paler likeness of her sister, but with the same voice.

Noting her mother's reaction but saying nothing, Hestean surreptitiously smiled and said to Petty, 'You had better get the others in here and out of sight. Unfortunately, it seems there will be much to do this day, and little time in which to do it. We cannot afford to be seen while I work out how to find what we came here for.'

'How many of you are there?' asked Jarrak.

'Fifteen' said Petty. 'We'll all fit, don't worry!

'There won't be any workers today, but Winnz usually comes mid-morning.'

'That's all we need,' said Hestean, rolling her eyes. She breathed deeply. 'What's going to happen here when a Black Robe walks in?'

'I don't think Winnz will be a problem,' said Jarrak. 'Things have changed here since you left.'

'How?'

Looking first to Jarrak and then to Hestean, Sathea said dryly, 'You really weren't talking much last night, were you?'

'I said don't judge me, Mother!'

'I wasn't! I happen to approve of your choice, and one day I would like very much to be the grandmother of your children! So, I was not judging you. I was merely saying that you two need to talk.'

'Then why didn't you just say that?' hissed Hestean. For a moment, Jarrak saw the Hestean he knew, whose mind would head in one direction while venturing also in another. The corners of her mouth broke into a smile—of acceptance, sorrow, and also recognition. Her mother still knew her well.

Sathea kissed Hestean's cheek and said, 'I no longer live in fear of not having told you of the things you needed to know. It appears that you have come to know more than I knew, anyway. I should have words with our Matrefem.'

'You think we should talk to Reglean?'

'Don't you? After you talk with Jarrak, you should talk with her. She will have the answers, I think.' Abruptly, Sathea looked at Karree, before turning to Petty at the entrance to the tent's private chamber. 'So, you're a shepherd,' she said. 'You hid that well. Last time you were here, you gave no hint of your association with the gods.'

'Last time I was here, I was just a navigator on a sky-ship, nothing more.'

'I see! Then everything is changing at once. I think you and I have some things to discuss while Hestean and Jarrak have their own little chat. You and the others might also like to eat. My daughter must eat before her world grows beyond this tent again!'

Petty's forehead wrinkled as he glanced towards Hestean. A smile crossed his face. 'I think this day will be longer than expected, so some food would be good, yes. May I call you Sathea? "The Comcree's mother" is a formality that doesn't quite suit you, I think.'

'Mothers are always something more, Mister Petty!' said Sathea, eyeing him flirtatiously. She then said to Jarrak, 'Tell her everything, and I will be out here if needed.' She turned back and preceded Petty into the tent's work area, followed by Karree.

Once the curtain fell behind Petty, Hestean looked puzzled. Without effort, her mother had just turned her back into a little girl. Jarrak watched her listen to the conversation in the outer tent, and started to wonder how to say what now needed to be said. He knew that what he was about to say would truly test her soul.

He heard Sathea set to work preparing a larger than planned morning meal, using extra stores from his food locker. He knew that

Sathea had set this task as a test for him—to prove that he really was the man her daughter needed.

The winds of change were about to descend on Sharacan. Hestean had said that they might all be dead tomorrow. Was the Descee family about to become extinct, or would it live on to bear future generations, as Hestean, Sathea, and now he, hoped?

37

'Do I get a say in children?' asked Jarrak, turning to Hestean as he untied, then retied, the pull-string of his trousers.

'No,' said Hestean, mischief glinting in her eyes. 'No, I don't think you do. Children are my department, and whether or not we have them will be up to me!'

She watched as her words took hold, seeing the incredulity spread across his face. A smile came to her lips as she walked across to him. 'I know my judgment is limited in such things,' she said sternly, reaching to tie the lace at the top of his tunic, 'but I have made this decision. My body is mine, not yours!' Glancing up, she saw that it was time to end her teasing. 'I said last night that you can be witless at times, and you can, can't you? Do you honestly think that if there ever were to be children, we would not both make such decisions? I will never again emulate the values of the College, nor impose the opposite ideology.'

Jarrak gazed at her, his eyes moving over the blue-green of her dress and the veneer of her daggers. 'You're not the girl who left here, are you?'

'Not quite. Not anymore.' Hestean pulled the bow knot tight at his neck. 'Remember the parcel we found the morning of my leaving? The person you see is its consequence!' Hestean drew the blue-handled dagger from its scabbard, then held it out to him. 'This was once Andreena's. Two hundred years ago, she set it in motion to become mine. Bornn knows this to be so, for these were his words. As my mother pointed out, it has her mark, see! And it is my mark, too. This dagger is the reason why the mark is on my arm! Now, tell me, what is going on here? I need to know everything.'

* * *

She was once more a living ghost. Hestean had gone, and in her place was the historic woman Jarrak had been searching for. It occurred to him now that there was no longer such a need for his dig, not that he was really in charge anymore. His fingers brushed Hestean's cheek, and his thumb ran lightly across her lips. He was glad that she had returned how she had. In a moment of decision, he picked her up and carried her across to where two large cushions sat on the floor. He let her plop onto one before seating himself on the other. Feeling that they were heading towards a shared destiny, he asked, 'What is it you are looking for?'

'That's just it—I don't know,' she said, before pointing to her earpiece. 'You see this?' She turned her head, and he wondered how he hadn't seen the small object the night before. But then, he'd been distracted by other things.

'It doesn't work here,' she said, 'and it should. Of all the places in this world, it should work here. Here, it only works like the communicators you and I have used, but it should do much more. There is something here that stops me from joining with the gods. I have two days to find out what that something is.'

'Why two days?'

'Because in just two days, the Comcree are to take back Sharacan.'

'*What*?'

'Sharacan belongs to the Comcree, Jarrak!'

'But what about my work?'

'It was never your work. It was the Comcree who planted the idea in Bornn's mind. It was Andreena who made the decision for us to return here, but also me. Andreena and I made it together, for I am her heir.'

'So, you are telling me that it is because of the Comcree that I have just spent two years of my life here?'

'It is what Andreena wanted.'

'Why is that? Because of what the Robes have done to Sharacan?'

'Not completely, although partly. It is because of what these women have managed to keep hidden.'

'And what is that?'

'Me! I am what they kept hidden. It was the Sharacanese women who kept Andreena alive, refusing to let her die. Sharacan belongs to the Comcree, not the College.'

Jarrak recalled again the artefacts he had unearthed. He knew that what she was saying was true. He had almost forgotten why he had originally come to this village. It wasn't just to dig holes in the sand or to uncover a temple. He had come to find Andreena, and miraculously, in an unexpected form, here she was sitting opposite him. He lent forward to kiss her, saying goodbye to the girl she'd been. Then, pulling back to greet the Comcree she had become, he said, 'You should talk to the woman who has kept this secret!'

'No,' said Hestean. 'Reglean cannot help me right now. I will talk to her, but not yet. I need to talk to you first, as my mother wanted. There is something here that not even these women know about. Have you seen anything? Sharacan is the beginning.'

'The beginning of what?'

'Our beginning! All the peoples of this world have a beginning here! Sharacan is our genesis. There is something hidden in the old city. This is why I need your story.'

'You honestly believe this?'

'I know this! I know this as fact! That's what your anomalies are. They are a map.'

'Can't you just wait till the Comcree take back Sharacan?'

'No. We lost Sharacan last time because we no longer understood Sharacan. We need to understand it again. We have to find the source. The College did not defeat us last time; Sharacan let them push the Comcree away. It needed to protect itself, so it protected itself from us, too. We have to know Sharacan again; it will not allow us to return until we do.'

'You speak of Sharacan as if it is a living thing.'

'It is! It has always been a living thing—as alive as any other of the gods. Sharacan is one of the gods, and the temple is its eye. So, tell me, what have you found? There must be something!'

Jarrak stared at the floor for a moment. Then, getting up, he started pacing as his mind whirled.

'What?' asked Hestean, seeing the reluctance on his face.

'I need to tell you something, but I need to start at the beginning. A lot has happened since you left.'

'Did someone die or something?' asked Hestean with a smile.

'What! No. I mean, yes … Look, I need to tell this my way, so just listen, will you?'

* * *

While Jarrak and Hestean talked in the adjoining room, Sathea watched Petty and Karree slip from the tent and vanish. Their mottled, sand-coloured cloaks blended so well with the sand that they quickly became just a faint suggestion under the morning sun.

'My ghosts,' she said, before turning to put water on to boil. As she worked, the other members of Hestean's protecterate began to appear at the tent's entrance, one by one. She beckoned them in, saying, 'Sit where you like. I'll have some tea ready shortly.'

Karree shimmered back through the opening, followed by Petty. Setting himself down beside Sathea, he pulled a satchel from his back and said, 'I have biscuits!'

'Not this morning,' said Sathea. 'I'll make some fresh breakfast biscuits, and you can top them off with sweet lush-melon. There should be enough.'

'Thank the gods for that!' said Karree.

'What, you don't like my travel biscuits?' shot Petty.

'Does anyone?'

'They keep you alive.'

'Yes, and that's all they do!'

A wry smile came to Sathea's face. She glanced at the female Deserteer. 'The letters on your sleeve—what do they mean?'

'They represent my family—we Ladeners are a family of loadmasters.'

'A tradition, then! Were you good at it?'

'Karree is one of our best,' said Petty.

'Your eyes …' Sathea mused.

'What does my profession have to do with my eyes?'

'You have Sharacanese eyes.'

'That's what Hestean said.'

'Did she? And what else have you learned from her?'

'About what?' asked Karree, with suspicion.

The kettle was starting to steam. Sathea lifted it from the fire to pour the boiling water into a spouted pot, into which she had already put a handful of tea flakes. She slowly stirred the brew with a long ladle. 'I get the feeling, Petty, that you are desert-born. Am I correct?'

'I'm from the Sireye,' said Petty.

'And the others, you have trained them?'

'For the last few years, we have trained together, yes. We crewed together on the sky-ship that plucked Hestean from the desert. It was aboard the *Merysands* that she first began to learn more about her heritage. The stone game, for instance, is much more than just a game.'

'And is she still as good as she was when young?'

'Once I showed her the moves, it was as if she had known them all her life,' said Karree.

Sathea once more observed the female Deserteer. 'So, it was you who trained her?'

'I didn't have to, really. After just the first day, she was almost as good as I am. I would say that now she is easily my equal!'

'And you are good, are you?'

'Karree has always been one of our best dancers,' said Petty.

'Dancers!' said Sathea, smiling a knowing smile. 'A nice word to hide the skills of a shepherd. With those eyes, you would have to be good, I think.'

'The eyes of Sharacan, I know. But I am more than just my eyes,' said Karree.

'Yes, and no,' said Sathea. 'I said "Sharacan eyes", not "eyes of Sharacan". However, you are more right than you realise. Remember the Sharacan women I was talking about earlier? We are the descendants of the temple priestesses. In truth, you have priestess eyes. They only come out in those deemed eligible.'

'So now I'm a priestess?'

'No. It merely means that you would be accepted as one. When Sharacanese women become adults, we are taught the reverences, of which there are one-hundred-and-eight. A godly number. Within one of those reverences are the words, *Only with temple eye within both red and blue will Sharacan be entered.* Also are the words, *With eyes of temple, the protector shall see the past as does the protected, keeping her safe from within all the houses.* The reverences tell us what to watch out for and what to see. I see around me all six houses, do I not? And the red dagger was given to Hestean first, was it not?'

'Yes,' said Karree. 'We inducted her into the Deserteers on the day she caught her stone during her ceremony of adulthood.'

'Ah … Then you are where you were meant to be, Karree Ladener,' said Sathea, as she filled two glasses with tea. 'Help yourselves. I'll be back in a moment. I'll just take this next door.'

* * *

'So has my father gone back to his gardening now that the Robes have put a stop to the work on the temple?' asked Hestean. 'I could never imagine him working with stone, although he did rebuild the mud-brick wall of our house once.'

At that moment, Sathea entered through the curtain.

'No …' Jarrak hesitated.

'They killed him,' said Sathea, putting the two glasses down on a small table.

'What …'

'We believe that some of Gaywin's followers kicked him to death. In defiance, even more of the villagers began to work on the temple. Your father and Qworeel were always the first to start work every morning. They were found barely alive by some of the other villagers, and your father died three days later. Qworeel, although still alive, has been unable to say a word or move from his bed.'

Her mother's words made Hestean feel as if a dagger had been plunged into her heart. She had never liked her father's passive obedience to the Robes, but even he, it seemed, had defied the college. She began to fume. She rocked slightly as she said, 'No, no, never again …'

'It is not just women the Robes control here, daughter,' said Sathea. 'Men here are trapped just as much as we are. The world of the Robes is damaging to everyone. I did not choose your father freely. In another world, I probably would never have chosen him, but within the confines of our marital circumstances, he was a good man. He was found dead, daughter, because you showed him his heart. You have always shown him his heart, and when he learned of your escape, you gave him his freedom, too. It was a disobedience these Robes would not allow, and he did it *for* you, not because of you.'

Jarrak lowered himself to sit beside Hestean, pulling her close to him. He held her and her raging mind. 'You have succeeded in dividing the Robes,' said Jarrak. 'A few of the older Robes don't like what is happening here but have been powerless to stop it. One of them tried to leave for Learnian, but was dragged back. He is now being held in custody. I think Gaywin is spiralling towards something from which Sharacan will not recover. That is why I have not left yet. Winnz needs my help.'

'To do what?' asked Hestean, anger filling every pore of her body.

'Women can no longer move unaccompanied within Sharacan. He and some of the older Robes have taken it upon themselves to be chaperones. They don't trust the Robes who have fallen under Gaywin's influence. He will come later; he always escorts your mother back to the village.'

'But Mother came here on her own!'

'Yes, but Gaywin's Robes don't know that! They don't keep watch on the older women's quarters after dark and before dawn. They feel more threatened by the men.'

'Well, that's a mistake!'

'Yes, it is,' said Sathea with a smile. 'The Robes have never really understood Sharacan.'

'So, what is Winnz doing here if the dig has been closed down?'

'I can still do my work,' said Jarrak. 'I just can't have help doing it, that's all. And I persist because it gives Winnz an excuse to come and do his copying.'

'Copying?'

Yes, he is copying some of the more important records before Gaywin can change them. Gaywin can't, you see, until he has been fully confirmed by Learnian, and the courier has not returned with his confirmation.'

'And I doubt that he will anytime soon,' said Hestean.

'And why is that?'

'It seems that Hestean here has shown the Comcree to the College,' said Sathea.

'Yes,' said Hestean. 'We have further directed their thoughts away from Sharacan, towards the south—to Learnian itself. To make it easier for us to take back Sharacan.'

'Is that why you're here?' asked Sathea.

'Yes, Mother! I have to do something else first though.'

'Then I think it is time you talked to your Matrefem, as your mother suggested,' said Jarrak. 'She knows about the mark on your arm. She is the one who gave you Andreena.'

Having calmed herself somewhat, Hestean turned to her mother and said, 'Can you bring Reglean here?'

'It won't be easy! But if I can enlist Winnz's help, then maybe I can.'

'It would be best if Winnz doesn't know we are here yet.'

'Then I'll meet him back along the path before he gets here.' Quietly, Hestean started to laugh. 'What's so funny?' asked Sathea.

'Oh, I was just wondering if he planned this, too.'

'Who?'

'One of the gods—Dan. He has had a way of making it impossible for me to do anything but what is required of me. It would seem that we have arrived just in time. I would have preferred for it to be as before, but we will manage. We will have to.'

Jarrak leaned across and picked up the two cooled glasses of tea, handing one to Hestean. 'So, shall we see what else your Matrefem has to say?' he said. 'Remember, you are Comcree, so be Comcree. Your father was a man of this village, so do this for him. There are more good men like him, but they are afraid. So, give them a reason not to be. I have worked with these men, and I have listened to them. There are those among them who only follow the College laws because they have no choice. Give them a choice, and you will see that most of the Sharacanese are still Sharacanese.'

Listening to Jarrak, Hestean realised that Gaywin—this aspirant to the chairmanship of Sharacan—had made a big mistake by trying to force Sharacan to obey his will. Instead, he had pushed them to the edge of rebellion.

Putting her hand on Hestean's shoulder, Sathea said, 'He is a good man, this Jarrak of yours. Trust him.'

Sitting straighter, Hestean looked into her mother's eyes, then into Jarrak's. After a moment, she sipped her tea as she gathered her thoughts. When she turned to Jarrak again, it was not the village girl who spoke, nor was it the young woman who had lost her father. In this unfolding moment, it was once again the Comcree who said, 'While my mother finds Reglean, you will tell me again what you know and have found while I've been gone. There must be something you have overlooked. Something I haven't seen yet.'

'Not until you've had something to eat, though,' said Sathea. 'Come and be with your friends while I make some breakfast. We can't do anything until Winnz is due later, anyway.'

38

As Sathea set to work making breakfast, Hestean came up behind her mother and said, 'Can I help?'

Sathea looked up in surprise. 'You learnt to make jokes while away, did you?'

'I do know how to make breakfast biscuits, Mother!'

'You know how to burn them, you mean!' There was a snickering chuckle from somewhere behind them, and Hestean turned towards Karree with a scowl.

Jarrak watched as Hestean seated herself beside the Deserteer, and he recalled the day when Sathea had first come to his tent. He had awoken to the smell of freshly brewed tea drifting through his living quarters. Rising to open the flap separating the back section of the tent from his work area, he had noticed the woman sitting cross-legged beside the cooking fire. He had also seen fluffy breakfast biscuits baking in a pan, and off to one side was the freshly brewed tea that had initiated his curiosity. He'd recognised her as Hestean's mother at once. 'My girl has gone, yes?' Sathea had said, without looking at him.

He had stared at her, wondering why she was in his tent. Then he had said, 'Yes, she's gone!'

'Is she safe?'

'I believe so, yes!'

'So, you're not sure?'

'I received an invitation to attend her ceremony into adulthood.'

'I see,' said Sathea. 'Our Matrefem said that you were to be looked after in repayment for your kindness. You need someone to cook for you now, so I will take Hestean's place.'

'She never cooked for me.'

Sathea smiled and said, 'No! That is something she never has done well!'

'Don't you have other obligations?'

'They buried my husband yesterday, so no. Today, I am homeless.'

'I'm sorry.'

'Don't be sorry,' she had said, but he knew she was experiencing deep feelings. If she had accepted sympathy, she would have fallen apart. That was something he now knew she would never allow herself to do. She had cared about the man she had bound herself to, and Sharn had cared for her. He knew this because Sharn had told him. 'You were the girl's friend, so I will cook for you now,' was all Sathea had said. What she didn't say was that without her bind-mate, she needed a job to survive. She wanted to put off tying herself to another man who might perhaps not be as caring and generous as her first bind-mate had been. At least for the time being, he had decided to let her continue with her perceived obligation.

He had entrenched himself in his work, rising early and only finding his bedding again late into the night. It was the temple that took up his time and interest. This was where most of the anomalies had been found. The mound in the centre of the old city had also showed some promise. Outwardly, the mound showed no sign of ever having been built upon, but within its sand, there were fragmented and interesting glimpses of the past. The mound had not been built upon because the mound itself had been built. But why had such a large hill been built in the middle of a metropolis and left without settlement? Religion was the most likely reason, and he was sure he was right in this thinking.

The more of the temple he unearthed, though, the more questions he had found. Andreena had no longer been the only thing of interest to keep him going. There was a lost civilisation here, which appeared to have once dwelt solely within the walls of this temple.

He had found star maps engraved into the temple's floor, if indeed that's what they were, for they showed no relevance to the night sky above. There were also receding spirals, ellipses, and what looked like bursting stars covering the temple walls, along with many other engravings. The temple's alignment with the mound was also becoming more obvious. A suspicion was beginning to grow in his mind that the mound had a more significant connection with the temple itself. Somehow, they were two parts of the same entity.

The single pillar they'd discovered on the mound seemed to have been deliberately toppled and covered with sand. The column was hollow. At its top was the remains of a polished reflector, which seemed to have been used to send light down through the column's hollow core. The pillar had been inscribed with the six house marks, and above them, on a separately inlaid disk of stone, was another set of hieroglyphs. It had become just one more of the puzzles of this place. Was this what Hestean was looking for? The strange depiction of two downward-pointing daggers on the engraving had puzzled him. He'd told her about the engraving on the temple wall, and how they hinted at Andreena. It seemed that the temple had been in use right up until the arrival of the College Robes, who'd partially demolish it. The Black Robes had then left the temple in its wounded state, almost as a symbol of conquest. The desert sands had then reclaimed it.

'Here,' said Hestean, drawing him back to the present.

'What?'

'Breakfast! Do you want it or not?'

'Oh, sorry! I was trying to remember if there was something I had forgotten to mention.'

'And is there?'

'Not that I can think of! I mentioned the pillar on the mound and the blue and red dagger mark we found there. Like on the plaque and the wall.'

'Blue and red! You didn't mention that before. You mean like these blue and reds?' asked Hestean, pulling her two daggers free of their scabbards.

'Could be, yes!'

'What do you know about dagger marks, Mother?'

'Nothing,' said Sathea. 'I've never seen the mark you're talking about, but blue and red are mentioned in the reverences.'

'Time's running out,' said Hestean, yawning. 'What did you put in this tea, Mother?'

'It is not the tea, it is your lack of sleep from last night.'

'Have you had something to eat yet?' asked Jarrak, awkwardly.

'Not yet, no!' said Hestean, avoiding the eyes around her.

'Then have these. I'll have the next lot.'

'Can you take me to the temple?' asked Hestean, taking the plate.

'When we've eaten. And what of your protectorate?'

'They won't let me go on my own. They're glued to me.'

'Just what we need, an entourage!'

Hestean's patience lasted just long enough for them to eat and see Sathea off to intercept Winnz. Hestean's protectorate were next to leave, to scout ahead. Jarrak then watched as Petty and Hestean vanished, before he, too, set off towards the temple.

When he made it into the temple's vault, Hestean's voice instantly came from the shadows. 'All right, then, where is this engraving you've found?'

Jarrak smiled slightly, and he took hold of her hand in reaffirmation of their new-found bond. With his other arm he pointed, 'Over there—on that reconstructed section of wall.'

Hestean then looked further down the wall. 'And the plaque? It was found there, wasn't it?'

'Yes, but it belongs here. Up on this wall.' Jarrak turned to look above the altar. 'When we cleaned the wall, I found residue. The plaque's clay had still been damp when it was placed in position'. He began to recite the plaque's message. '*Within your birth lies our birth.*'

'What? No!'

'The plaque! You told me that's what it said, remember?'

'Not in here, it doesn't! The written language of Fem can be particular to a place. In here, it would mean, *Inside your beginning sleeps our beginning.* It would translate more appropriately today as, *Who we were, you are destined to become.* It is a prophecy. It is one of the oldest Comcree dictums. It is belief itself,' said Hestean, sighing. 'Back then, when I first read the plaque, I didn't know of this place's true heritage, so how could I make the connection? It is only now that I see its truth.'

'You are correct in this thinking,' said an aged and withered voice from behind them. Twirling as one, Petty, Hestean, and Jarrak looked towards the entrance. Just within the vault's shadow, away from the doorway's light, stood Sathea and an old woman. 'It was something you had to learn on your own, child, and for that I am sorry. We can never find out everything at once, or there would be no reason to life, would there? Even here, within this village ruled over by Robes, I have found life to be full of wonderful discoveries.' She took a step forward and held out her arms to Hestean. In one hand, she presented a long, thin cylinder, and in the other, a mirrored-glass prism. 'Along with what you have already received, these are for you, child. I don't know their meaning; it was not for me to know. This one,' she said, indicating the glass prism, 'is from the top of the temple's altar. The other is from the sun's eye.'

'The sun's eye? What is that?'

'I regret, child, that these words are all that were handed down to me!'

Hestean observed the old woman for a moment, then said, 'It was you who started my journey, wasn't it?'

'Did I choose you well? Was I meant to choose? These are things I have wondered.'

'I think we are about to find out,' said Hestean. She walked across to the Matrefem and took both objects from the old woman. As she did, she lifted one of Reglean's withered limbs to kiss the back of her hand. 'Let's put faith in your belief, shall we, Ze Hub of Sharacan? For you stand not behind me, but by my side.'

'Ah,' said the old woman, her eyes brightening. 'A true Comcree you have become, for belief is the most powerful of things.'

Smiling, Hestean turned and said, 'Let's find that out. The mirrored one is for the altar, you say?' Hestean walked along the inner-most wall of the vault, then came to a halt in front of the most holy part of the ancient ruin. There were three small holes in the altar's upper surface. She leaned forward and blew the remaining sand from one of them, coughing as dust rose around her. She repeated this blowing twice more with each of the other holes, coughing each time.

'Maybe not such a good choice after all,' Sathea grinned. Chuckling, both women continued to observe Hestean as she turned the object in her hands and seated it in its place.

'Is it to catch an image of some kind?' asked Hestean. 'If so, from where? She stepped back and handed the second object to Jarrak. 'Any thoughts?'

'The triangle is a reflector, and this is a pair of lenses!'

'I can see that,' said Hestean, peering into every part of the vault's inner walls. 'It fits into something, but what, I can't see.'

Sathea, along with Reglean and Petty, started to search, too, but found nothing.

'Maybe it's not from here,' said Hestean finally, as she looked out through the entranceway. 'That collapsed wall to the west … Was there anything on it that could have held the cylinder, do you think?'

'No! It was just a solid wall with three windows,' said Jarrak, coming to her side.

'A solid wall does not have three windows,' corrected Hestean. 'Where were these windows?'

As Jarrak's finger pointed towards where the uppermost part of the wall would have been, Hestean noticed the mound's summit in the distance. She began to wonder. Then said, 'You're going for a walk.'

‘A walk! Where?’

‘Up there!’ she said, pointing towards the mound. ‘You said that you found a hollow pillar with a reflector. In its side, it had a hole through to its core, didn’t it?’

‘No!’

‘Yes, it did! The priestesses filled it in, though. You told me there was a double dagger mark on an inlaid piece of stone. Did you try to remove it?’

‘Yes.’

‘But you couldn’t, could you?’

‘No.’

Hestean brushed his cheek and nose with her hand before pulling his hat up over his head. Tightening its chin strap she said, ‘You still burn easily, don’t you?’ Looking at him, she realised again just how much she had missed him.

‘I don’t know if you and I are such a good idea,’ grumbled Jarrak, as he began to walk across the temple’s courtyard.

‘Really? I think we make a good team.’

‘If I can, I’ll catch the sun and point it through the entranceway.’

Hestean watched him walk from her and smiled.

‘Why does he have to go up there?’ asked Sathea, coming to her daughter’s side.

‘It is a lens, Mother, with a fixed focal length. The image that it projects will only become clear when sent from the place from which it was intended to be sent.’

‘So, we wait again,’ said Sathea.

‘Yes. We wait.’ Hestean walked back through the alcove and sat down, leaning against the altar. She looked out through the entrance, her eyes following Jarrak’s every movement.

‘You are winning, child,’ said the elderly Matrefem, coming to sit down beside her.

‘Am I? What if I’m wrong?’

‘If you are, then the answer still lies inside.’ The old woman fanned her arm across the room, and Hestean’s eyes followed, searching the walls of the vault again. Scanning the detailed scrolling, she tried to see whatever she was meant to see. She could almost feel it. As she looked, the ghosts of the past started to fill her mind as they had never done before.

39

Going back generations, only one Sharacanese woman at a time knew that one amongst them was more important than the rest. This woman was the Matrefem, the secret-keeper. With the same dark complexion, jewellery, footwear, and decorative clothing as every other woman in the village, the Matrefem was indistinguishable from other women.

Each day, she sat with the other old women, mending the belongings of her fellow villagers. This was something that had been worked out intentionally by the first of these secret-keepers. By perpetually fulfilling a duty to the village, the older women continued to receive a meagre but adequate ration. They knew that if women were not considered useful under College rule, they would be discarded.

The ancient city of Sharacan had been almost deserted when the College had taken control, most of its inhabitants having already fled. But amongst those that remained had been a young girl from the streets, whom the other women soon realised was different. When she spoke, she had an authority that far exceeded her age, and only to the women did she ever display the mark that had been carved into her upper arm. They found, too, that she knew the ancient language, which showed she had been schooled at the temple. It was only later that the women discovered that the girl, and her younger sibling, had been the only ones to survive the slaughter that had transpired at the temple. The young girl was ignored by the Black Robes—the first mistake they made in conquering the Sharacanese. Their second mistake was in not recognising the false history of Sharacan that the girl had brought into being.

Within days of the city's capture, the girl made it look as though the older women of Sharacan had always played this role in society, allowing the younger women to do the more necessary work of cooking, cleaning, and collecting dung. In doing this simple thing, she had provided the elderly with a necessary purpose. She knew what a future under the College would bring to the lives of these women, and she was determined to lose none of them.

But the real advantage to this unseen fabrication was that the older women were now able to come together unobserved, and could quickly pass information around the community. And there was something else the Robes of the College never noticed. One day, the baby whom the girl had always carried in a pouch was gone. She had finally found a way to get the child out of Sharacan, and to relatives in the east. Now, even if she died, her lineage would live on. By the time the young girl did die, she had children of her own. Two daughters, who were also to carry her lineage forward. By then, the great city had already begun to dissolve back into the Kalcool, to be replaced by the remnant village that was Sharacan today. She left behind a legacy of bravery and hidden dreams, which would carry on for centuries.

* * *

Having been accompanied back to the village by Winnz, who had seated himself next to the other elderly Robe chaperoning them, Sathea sat down beside Reglean and began to whisper in her ear. Reglean returned the whisper and then stood and walked to the doorway of the older women's communal house. A short time later, she returned with a basket of clothes, and Sathea got to her feet. After a short conversation with Winnz, he rose and walked off towards the washing well, with a small group of women who had also gathered with baskets of clothes.

At the washing troughs, the women began to scrub the clothing, spreading each piece over the stones to dry. Amidst the activity, Sathea and Reglean quietly slipped away.

The tunnels carrying Sharacan's precious water were the height of a man, so they could be easily maintained. It had been Hestean who'd told her mother of this secret network, which she'd explored while younger. Jarrak's additional clearing of the tunnels now made it possible to get to the dig without being seen. It was into these tunnels that the two women descended.

A short time later, Sathea looked out from the draw hole near the temple. A moment later, the two women scrambled to the surface. They were once more hidden amongst the outer ruins. It was hard for the

Matrefem, not only because she was old, but because she also held two objects in her hands.

'Let me carry them,' suggested Sathea.

'No,' said Reglean, not wanting to surrender her items to anyone. 'It is for me to do.' Generations of women had waited their entire lifetimes to rid the Black Robes from their village. Reglean had no intention of ceding her task to anyone else. They rested for a moment in the shadows of the temple's fallen walls. Across the expanse, the old woman watched two figures enter the temple's vault. A few moments later, she saw the young man they were seeking enter the same opening. She sat, relieved and happy to have caught a glimpse of the blue-green dress she'd never thought she'd see. She would have to wait no longer.

* * *

At first, Gaywin thought it was just his imagination, but the shapes—huddling low to the sand and scurrying towards the temple—refused to leave his mind. He knew that there were no longer workers at the temple, so who were they?

'When I am chairman, I will fully discipline this place,' he said quietly to himself. He knew he could not entirely remove the stain of history, but he had decided that removing its memory would be the next best thing. From the very place where his ancestral uncle had splattered shame upon his family, he would regain his lost honour.

It was now only a matter of time before the young archaeologist packed up and left. He knew he was no longer welcome, yet he'd shown no sign of leaving. Instead, he'd continued to spend his days alone within the dig site, or staring out over the old city's roofscape. He still had to be watched. Gaywin was beginning to think that he would need to take more decisive action soon. Until Jarrak was gone, the authorisation of the last village chairman held sway.

Even so, there was still time. In a way, Gaywin felt gratitude towards the young man, for it was his arrival that had given him his opportunity. It was only now, since the temple had been fully uncovered, that he could destroy it as it should have been destroyed. He had never understood why it had been left standing at all. To him, it was nothing but a blemish left on the world. He would prove himself to the High Council by doing what needed to be done, and his ancestor's stain would be wiped from him afterwards. The previous chairmen may have come to believe in the stories of this place, but he didn't. A well-pond was a well, with no fanciful power. It was an absurdity.

He knew that what he had seen was not Jarrak, but Gaywin gave up after a few puffs on his pipe. Whatever it was had gone—most likely night animals scurrying from the sun.

A while later, though, he got up again and started to walk through the village. He knew that what he had seen was odd. His dark robes ruffled in the light breeze, and a group of children parted to let him pass unobstructed. The closed doors of the village houses—always closed, now—magnified the separateness of his College status. He passed the washing troughs near the ancient well. On reflex, he counted the baskets, and the women attending them. There had always been something that disturbed him about these older women. He saw one of the older Robes watching over the women and seethed—something was out of place. Steadfastly, he explored his surroundings, seeking to find a reason for the unease in his mind.

Finally, he rounded the corner onto the temple's courtyard and stopped. His eyes scanned its perimeter. There was something here, he knew it. He walked slowly along the courtyard's edge and stopped again. Motionless, his eyes skimmed across the collapsed masonry, glowing in the already harsh morning sun before him. Amused, he imagined this entire place after he destroyed it. Nothing would remain.

A speck of light started to dance upon the courtyard, drawing his eyes up to the summit of the high mound. He saw Jarrak moving something in his hands, deflecting the sun towards the temple. A moment later, a flash of light shot from the entrance of the temple's vault, taking him by surprise. He turned in puzzlement. Jarrak was just standing there.

Stepping out into the light, his black robes rustled as he crossed the temple's courtyard to enter the vault's shaded darkness. He waited for his eyes to adjust, then peered around before walking further in.

He had never been in the temple on his own. He turned, seeing nothing, despising the emptiness. A gust of wind lifted sand from the floor and twirled it towards the walls, where it chattered on collision with the stone. A chill climbed his spine. He feared this place, he realised. He turned to leave, then stopped. He turned to the altar, noticing for the first time the triangular glass instrument sitting atop it. He then stepped out into the brightness to wait as Jarrak descended the mound.

* * *

The moment Jarrak had seen Gaywin enter the vault, his heart had skipped. He knew that Hestean's protectorate lay concealed amongst the temple's fallen stones. He had expected them, at any moment, to pounce upon the Black Robe, but this had not happened.

'What's that in your hand?' asked Gaywin, as Jarrak came close.

'It's a measuring device.'

'And the light that flashed within the vault?'

'It's from a reflector, which tells when I have set the instrument's distance correctly.'

Gaywin scowled and said, 'Have you seen anyone around the temple this morning?'

'I thought I saw some children playing earlier.'

Gaywin's scowl deepened. 'Not even children are to enter this temple. Understand?' The Robe turned to leave, and Jarrak watched until he had almost reached the village before running towards the vault. At the entranceway, he was joined by Karree and the rest of Hestean's protectorate.

'Why didn't he discover them?' asked Karree, bewildered. They entered the vault to find it just as Gaywin had. Empty.

40

Two Deserteers rushed into the vault and pressed themselves up against the stone wall on either side of its entrance. Drawing their daggers, they announced the approach of a Black Robe from the village.

Sathea hastened towards a shadowed corner as Reglean and Petty scurried to another. In that same instant, Hestean made a decision. She stepped towards the only exit from the sanctum and signalled to Karree to keep the rest of the protectorate well-hidden. They had become as two sharpened edges of the same dagger. Almost instinctively now, Hestean knew that Karree would not move unless the approaching Robe discovered them inside the vault.

Dashing back to stand beside the Matrefem and Petty, Hestean also stood silent. She knew that the gods were not what most people presumed them to be, but in this moment, she found herself praying to them just the same. Her heart thumped behind stilled lungs. For what seemed an eternity, she willed herself to be part of the stone.

It was the explosion of light that answered her prayer, though. These were the gods that Hestean had come to know. With the flare, she knew that Jarrak had hit his mark, and in that same moment, she watched two beams of light as they splintered from the prism and bounced around the room. She almost gasped aloud as she noticed the parts of the wall they illuminated directly to the altar's left. She had already scanned that exact same wall more than once and had not seen what she saw now.

On impulse, she darted across the vault. She drove her blue-handled dagger into the slot until its hilt hit the stone. Relief flushed through her as its handle started to glow, and she reached up to touch the fourth mark in a row of six. Even now, she hardly recognised them for what they really were. After testing the wall with her finger, she darted back to grab hold of her mother's arm, motioning for her to remain silent.

She pulled her back along the wall, then both vanished into the stone. Petty was next, having gathered the elderly Matrefem into his arms. The two Deserteers went through last, guarding their retreat as the vault returned to a state of emptiness.

* * *

In the dark, Sathea and the Matrefem were unsure of what had happened. They knew that they were inside a solid piece of stone, within the obelisk itself, and yet they could breathe and move. They searched for understanding as the walls of the hidden room started to glow, waking as if from sleep. The two women saw that the solid piece of stone was not solid at all, but hollow, seeming now also to be alive. As they stood there, the wall opposite brought forth more of the miraculous shapes, confirming their thoughts. An image started to appear on a large, flat, rectangular screen. The two women knew that they had somehow been transported to the realm of the gods.

'It's not magic, Mother, its science!' explained Hestean, walking across to the wall and touching one of the pads beside the screen. The image changed from a view of the temple's vaulted interior, to one of the courtyard, and the mound beyond. Sathea and Reglean looked at each other, wondering if they had both actually seen how the image changed at Hestean's touch. 'This is the real world, Mother! This is the world beyond our village. It is the world I was sent to find.'

* * *

Hestean looked around, wondering what this place was. She touched her hand to the beautifully carved frieze that ran at shoulder height in one continuous band around the room. She knew it was meant to tell her something, and in places it did. But she was still uncertain.

She came back to stand beside Petty. 'At least some things work! I wonder what else does?' Then she spotted movement on the screen.

Gaywin's scowl seemed even more unpleasant than she remembered. Even within their hiding space, she felt fear. 'Why did it have to be him?' she asked quietly. She watched as he stepped from the shadowed edge of the courtyard into the sunlight, towards the vault's entrance.

Her heart started to thump. She touched the other symbol beside the screen, and the image changed back to a view of the vaulted sanctum.

She watched him enter. He came to a halt in the middle of the floor, his head twisting to peer into every darkened corner. He stood there, just listening, and she was sure he could hear her. He turned back towards the entrance and began to retrace his steps, but then suddenly stopped, turning back towards the altar. Her heart started to pound once more. For quite some time, he just stood there. Then he walked back out onto the paved courtyard.

Her heart steadied and she breathed deeply. She heard her companions do the same. She changed the screen back, and they watched as Gaywin walked across the courtyard to stop and shelter in the shadows. Looking up towards the top of the mound, she saw Jarrak.

'What is this place?' asked Sathea in a whisper. 'How did you know about the wall? How is it possible?'

A thought crossed Hestean's mind. She began to tremble as she turned towards the hidden doorway. She had been careless, and now realised just how close they had come to disaster. She took in the curtained wall, knowing that she had forgotten to re-solidify it, as Gorean had told her always to do. Once more, she thanked the gods, this time for Gaywin's inept stupidity. 'Could one of you slowly touch the wall where we came through?' she asked, still hoping that she was wrong. It was Reglean who reached out, her finger vanishing.

'Do you see the six symbols at the beginning of the frieze, just to your right?' asked Hestean. 'Touch the fourth one, would you?'

Reglean looked at Hestean, then reached out and touched the fourth house mark.

'Now try your finger on the wall again,' instructed Hestean. 'Hopefully you will see that house marks have more significance than we'd realised.'

The old woman's finger went to the wall, but this time the stone was solid. She touched the fourth house mark again, although the wall still failed to yield.

'Do you see the small slot in the stone just below the symbols?' asked Hestean. 'It is only a Comcree dagger that can open such a door, but anyone can close it. It is still just a door, though. As for how I knew where to find it, Mother, the reflections showed me. I have used similar doors before. In order to see, you need to know what you are looking for. This time it was well-hidden, believe me.'

'So, is there more to this room?' asked Sathea.

'Oh, I hope so,' said Hestean. 'For a start, it is not a room! It is the entrance to a passageway. It leads somewhere; it has to! I just need to find the other doorway.'

'Down, perhaps?' suggested Petty.

'I was thinking that. But it has been left unused for a long time, so it might not work.'

'The first door did.'

Hestean's eyes followed the frieze around the walls. Along the back wall, a stylised symbol of the sun stood out as different, somehow. At its centre was a six-sided polygon, the size of a person's palm. Around it, jutting out from each of its points, were what she now recognised as six dagger slots. She thought of the anomalies she had taken to Elora-Bearer. She thought about the box in Jarrak's tent, filled with more of the broken fragments. The pieces were just that, though—fragments. Unconnected to anything else.

'We'll wait for Jarrak,' she said, stalling for time.

Accepting this, the two Deserteers re-sheathed their daggers and each allowed one drop of their blood to splatter to the floor.

Noticing this, Sathea turned to Hestean. 'Do you need to do this also, daughter?'

'Deserteer's daggers are red, Mother, and they are red for a reason! But yes, I have a red dagger, also. If it is drawn, it will also need to draw blood.'

'It is a reminder,' said Petty. 'One should never act in haste. Blood is a consequence we should never forget.'

'I do know the stories,' said Sathea, feeling a need to deny her ignorance. Looking at Petty, she wondered why he made her feel so much like a child and yet like a woman at the same time.

'There is a part of history you have not been told about, Mother,' added Hestean. 'Not even the Comcree fully know this part of our history. I think that from here onwards, we will be venturing forth into the unknown with only our suspicions to guide us.' A thought came to Hestean, and her eyes turned to the back of the room. 'Maybe the six daggers together would work …' She sat down, resting back against the wall of stone. Petty looked at her, perplexed. 'We're not going without Jarrak,' she said, looking up at him. 'Right now, I don't know what to do, nor what's ahead, so we may as well get some rest while I think.'

It was a tiredness that grabbed Hestean. Tired of thinking, tired of talking, and tired of leading.

'Do you have some better brain-wave to utter?' she asked her protector.

'Brain waves!' said Petty, sitting down beside her. 'Now, there's a new concept.'

'Well, I've been told that sound moves in waves, so why not thoughts, also?'

Petty huffed his understanding, and just said, 'Rest if you want. Today has been hard on all of us. You will find your way.' He let Hestean's head rest against him, and breathed in his own thoughts.

A twinge of jealousy flashed through Sathea. She had never felt jealous of her daughter before, so when it came, she didn't at first recognise the feeling. She realised that this daughter of hers, although a grown woman now, still needed to feel that she could be a child. In this moment, she missed the closeness she'd once shared with Hestean that she now seemed to share with this Mister Petty. Sitting down, she looked across at her daughter, and at the man whom she also felt drawn to.

Reglean sat beside her. Breaking from her thoughts, Sathea put her hand upon the old woman's arm. 'And what of you?' she asked. 'Has this day been what you expected?'

Reglean clasped her arms around her knees, making herself small. Her eyes took in the walls around her. 'My shock and fear has dwindled, and I have been thinking of the many stories I will one day tell, which my Matrefem once told to me. But I can now enlarge on those stories. So, this day has been better than any day I have ever lived. Look where I am! I am like an embryo within the birthstone. I'm at the beginning of the world.'

Sathea saw her daughter stir. 'What do you mean by birthstone?' Hestean asked.

'The birthstone, child! You were speaking of it earlier.'

'No, I wasn't! I've seen the word before in a book. That is all.' She took a deep breath to quote the passage. '*The birth stone; the gateway and the shield; the past and the future; the star of history is the star of inheritance*. It is a line in a poem.'

'But you spoke the words, child. I heard you say them as we entered the vault.'

'Those … Those words were from a plaque, found by one of the men while excavating the temple!'

'You mean to say that you don't know the full story of the stone? It is why the temple still stands, child. I thought all the Comcree would have been told this story. It was the first story I ever had to memorise, and it is the first story I must make sure my successor understands. Even the Black Robes came to believe in this fable. Or, rather, they couldn't afford not to believe it. They could not afford to have Sharacan without water, you see.'

'Are you saying that it really is the obelisk that controls the wells of Sharacan?'

'Yes, child, of course it does! At least, that's what the fables say. The fables are the reason why the sand has always been kept from the obelisk. Its pinnacle must always see the light. Weren't you told this?'

'No! Tell the rest of the fable as it should be, Reglean. What else does it say?'

'You are too familiar, child! Have you forgotten yourself? You may be Comcree, but I am still the Matrefem of Sharacan.' A wry smile spread across Reglean's lips. Sathea saw that the rebuff had stifled Hestean instantly. 'However,' said Reglean, 'I am not one of the Robes, so you are forgiven for your lack of courtesy, child. I would suggest, though, that you do not forget too often, for it is courtesy that defines the Comcree.'

'It is, yes! We are only guides to this world.'

'Now you are trying to flatter me, child, and flattery is not courtesy, either! You have a story to tell, I believe, so tell it. In return, I will tell you mine. Why did the young stranger resolve to uncover this temple? Why dig here if neither of you knew the tale?'

Another testing, said Hestean to herself. *Why do all Matrefems want to continually test me?*

'You do want to hear my story, child, or don't you?' the Matrefem prompted.

Hestean capitulated. Slowly, she drew in a deep breath, then told the whole of her story.

* * *

When Reglean had been called to ascend as Matrefem, she had to prove she was worthy. Unknown to even the other women, one hidden thing had always set her apart, and she knew that now was the time for keys to be turned and secrets unlocked.

Pulling the cord up from between her breasts, which she had hidden from everyone for as long as she had been Matrefem of

Sharacan, she said, 'It is broken fragments of these that you are talking of, isn't it?'

Hestean's eyes bulged. 'We found just bits and pieces!'

'Well, of course you did! It is the way of things. Whenever a Matrefem dies, her talisman is broken and given back to the gods. We must each make our own. It's how we show that we have learned the stories we were taught. Then, and only then, we must break our predecessor's talisman and return it to the sand from whence it came. Although the size and shape must be exact along the outer edge, the internal routing and style must be of our own creation.'

'You mean the sand here at the temple! But we found fragments at the mound, also.'

'Yes. Each Matrefem is bound to the temple, and the great mound is part of it.

* * *

Hestean saw it now—a trail through time that would have continued for as long as necessary. 'How do you know the way to make them?'

'The stories tell us,' said Reglean.

Not bothering to stand, Hestean kneed her way across the floor and kissed the old woman's cheek. 'You don't know what this is, do you?'

'It confirms me as a Matrefem, child. That's what it does!'

'Yes, but it is much more than that! May I hold it? I want to show you something.' Hestean's gaze honed onto the polygon recessed into the back wall, and Reglean's eye followed her stare. 'You make them using a template, don't you?' said Hestean. 'A template that is exact. Over there is the reason why! The Comcree may enter this room, but they also need the Matrefems of Sharacan—the secret-keepers—to go further.'

Reglean pulled the cord over her head, then looked at her talisman for confirmation. 'Yes,' she said. 'It does appear that we have both been given parts of the same story.'

Standing, Hestean took the talisman and walked to the back wall. She ran her fingers around the indentations, polishing the metal strips as best she could. 'It does belong here,' she said, inserting the talisman. Turning it, she latched it firmly into place. 'To see the future, you need both the young and the old! That's what the old words mean, right? Inside your beginning sleeps our beginning.'

'Yes, child, but we are only one of its meanings.'

'One amongst many, I suspect,' replied Hestean, thinking of Jarrak. She spun round to look at the viewing screen. Gaywin had gone, and Jarrak was no longer in sight, either. Neither was her protectorate. 'Gods forgive me' she said, hitting the screens control pad.

As the vault's interior came into view on the screen, a wave of relief washed over her. She turned towards the stone curtain, then inserted her dagger and touched her house mark. Poking her head out through the wall, she asked, 'You looking for us, by any chance?'

Stepping through the wall, as the Deserteers swung round, she noticed that one in particular was scowling at her. She crossed to Jarrak and saw that his eyes were cold.

'What, you've never seen someone walk through a wall before? You haven't seen anything yet!' She grabbed his arm and started back towards the wall. 'Come on, I'll show you how it's done!' As she retraced her steps, she counted the others. 'It looks as if the rest of you are all here. Good.'

'Yes, we're here, Hlaford,' said Karree, still scowling.

'I know I have left you out here for a while, Karree, but we need to move now, in case he returns. I also know that if you ever call me Hlaford again, I will disembowel you. Clear?'

'But it's who you are!'

'Karree, we were friends first, and that is what we will always be before anything else. To you, I am Hestean, and I will answer to nothing else!'

'Yes, but …'

'No "buts",' said Hestean, tightening her grip on Jarrak. She slowed momentarily before passing back into the masonry. When they emerged on the other side, Hestean turned to Jarrak and halted. 'Are you ready for my next trick? Do you recognize it?' She pointed to the Matrefem's key, latched into the back wall.

'It's complete!' said Jarrak, rubbing his fingers across the surface.

'Reglean had it!' said Hestean. She unsheathed her dagger and plunged it into the lower key slot, hoping she had come to the right conclusion. She watched the dagger's end begin to glow, and almost instantly there was a grinding sound. Stone moved upon stone as the centre of the floor started to drop, reforming itself into the upper most part of a stairway. The incoming Deserteers scattered to the walls as the hole grew, spreading until it filled the centre of the room. A descending spiral stair, now fully formed, plunged into an unknown gloom.

'Well, at least I witnessed this surprise,' said Jarrak, stepping back from the hole.

'You like this one, do you?' said Hestean, as if they were on a treasure hunt. 'Let's see what others we can find, shall we?'

'Don't we need some light?'

'I don't think so,' she said, already pulling him towards the steps. 'This room lit itself. I think the staircase will do the same.'

'Was she like this as a child?' asked Jarrak as he passed Sathea.

'Always! She's worse now, though, with no one to stop her.'

'Why did I know you were going to say that?'

'Shall I lock the door, daughter?'

Again, Hestean reproached herself. 'Yes please! Do you remember how?'

'At least it seems that she is now remembering her manners!' said Reglean.

'I heard that! Will you bring your talisman, too, please? We might need it again.'

* * *

Stepping aside, Petty let the other members of Hestean's Protectorate file down after her. Having lost her once, he could see that Karree was in no mood to let Hestean vanish again. He watched as they began their descent, realising just how much the two young women had become part of each other. He looked towards the Matrefem and Hestean's mother and saw the same regard there, too. As his eyes moved again, this time to take in Sathea's form, he sensed a stirring he had not felt for a long time. Her eyes met his, and he quickly looked away.

'What should I call you?' he asked the old woman instead. 'Reglean or Matrefem? Or is it Matrefem Ze-Hub of Sharacan?'

'I am only Matrefem to this village, but even here, they just call me Reglean. Before, in my rebuff to Hestean, I was only reinforcing who she really is. If you were to call me just Matrefem, I would not respond.'

'Yes, but you are soon to be much more than just Matrefem to this village of Sharacan. Surely you are now also Matrefem to the temple?'

'I am under no illusions about this place. I have always been that! But I am also an old woman. I think that this new task will mostly fall to my successor. She will need help, though. To be Matrefem is more than enough responsibility for one lifetime, don't you think?' At this, Reglean looked thoughtfully at Sathea, finally coming to a decision she had all but made years earlier. Then she looked back at Petty and said, 'I think, if you do not mind, I will get you both to help me down these stairs. It will be a long descent, I think, and today I have already played at being younger than I actually am.'

PART IV
AN UNSEALED LEGACY

41

As they spiralled down, sections of the stairwell's walls and ceiling glowed, vanquishing the darkness before them. But unlike in the hidden room above, the stone here was smooth and polished. Glassy, almost. Gradually, even though the treads remained coarse and dull, the steps themselves became lustrous. To Jarrak, it appeared as though great heat had been generated here once, melting the very earth into one single, crystallised tunnel.

Eventually, after what seemed an eternity, they exited into a vast cavern. The space, like the small room and the stairway, sensed their presence. Large parts of the ceiling began to illuminate their surroundings, and the cavern's huge interior began to emerge. Here, too, the walls and ceiling were of the same fused, glassy material. Jarrak noticed that a thin covering of dust had settled over everything, accentuating the undisturbed feel of the space. As with the treads of the steps, only the floor had a dull coarseness to it.

Turning in utter amazement, Jarrak saw that the domed cavern was segmented and strengthened by shallow buttresses jutting from its perimeter. His eyes followed one of the curving structures upward, to see where it joined with others around a glowing crystal above them. Between each buttress was the entrance to a tunnel. Each was semicircular in shape, gloomy in its own undisturbed darkness.

'Some sort of junction point,' he said. 'We've entered some great underground convergence of tunnels. I wonder how long this has been here?'

'A long time,' said Hestean, slowly turning.

Jarrak looked at the dusty floor. 'The only footprints here are ours.'

Hestean's protectorate was already filing past him, fanning out instinctively to scout their surroundings. 'By the gods,' said Petty, as he and the Matrefem entered the cavern.

'Not the gods,' said Hestean. 'The Comcree, maybe, but not the gods. I've met one of them, and this is not their doing.'

'You've met a god?' exclaimed Jarrak.

'Of course! I couldn't become Comcree without their blessing.'

* * *

Hestean watched her mother run a finger along the wall nearest to her, feeling the emptiness of this place. Sathea inhaled. Hestean knew her mother sensed the same cool dryness and mustiness that she did. It was the smell of abandonment.

'Have you seen these?' asked Hestean, pointing to inscribed plaques above each tunnel entrance. '*Well Maegester, Foda Hus, Blawan Maegester, Steorra Hus*.' When she had come full circle, she read the words above the stairwell. '*Uf Grund Brad Spraedan!* They have all been given equal importance, see? Each has its own segment within the chamber.'

'Destinations?' suggested Jarrak.

'I guess so,' replied Hestean, again turning to marvel at what had lain hidden beneath her village since before it had existed. 'Anyone got any suggestions?'

'*Steorra* means "star", doesn't it?' said Petty. 'Maybe it's an energy source; like the one your friend uses.'

Hestean recognised the sly use of the word "friend". 'I didn't know you understood Fem?' she said.

'Only a few words, from old maps and charts I've come across.'

'Well, then, what do you make of this?' She lifted her hand to indicate one of the tunnels. '*Blawan* means "force", or maybe energy, also. So perhaps this is the way.'

'It's not the energy *source* you're after, though,' said Petty. 'It could be the *user*.'

'You mean like my … friend from the Hassis?'

'Could be!'

'Which friend?' asked Jarrak.

'Some things the Comcree must keep to themselves,' said Hestean.

'But Petty knows!' said Jarrak, sounding annoyed.

'So? There are some things you know that he doesn't! But maybe, if you're going to be difficult, you would like me to find someone else to take your place?' Hestean and Jarrak's eyes locked. For what seemed like a decade, they stood staring at each other.

'Now, now, children,' said Karree, walking back to stand beside Hestean.

Hestean huffed, and said, 'I'm sorry. I need to think, don't I?'

'That might be good,' replied Karree. 'Having lost you once, I don't want to lose you again. Anything is possible, especially here.' Karree looked now into every corner of the giant dome. 'This place could be as bad as the maze at the Museum.'

'Dan mentioned nothing of this,' Hestean murmured.

'Is Dan this friend you won't speak of?' said Jarrak.

In one movement, Hestean and Karree both rotated to glare at him. Petty smiled, and Jarrak flinched as if the whole cavern had just fallen in.

'If you must know, Dan is our librarian,' said Hestean, still annoyed. She saw Petty's face take on a much fuller grin. 'Oh, just stop it, both of you!' She turned to stride across the dome. 'We'll try this tunnel!' she said, turning back to Petty. 'I'm hungry. Have you got anything left to eat in that bag of yours, old man?'

'Always,' said Petty, still smiling.

* * *

Sathea hooked her arm around Petty's on impulse as they set off after Hestean. 'For a girl who never had much time for men, she seems to like you and Jarrak.'

'Does she?' asked Petty, continuing to smile, 'I hadn't noticed.'

'I find that hard to believe!' said Sathea, grinning. 'She used to do what she liked, ignoring the advice of anyone. Although, she still does that to an extent, doesn't she?'

'A good observation,' said Petty, his fingers entangling with Sathea's.

'She must be hungry if what Karree says about your biscuits is true,' said Sathea.

'Yes, well, they're nourishing enough but I wouldn't exactly call them tasty. Let's wait for a bit. If she asks again, we'll know she *is* really hungry.'

'You seem to know her pretty well, don't you?'

'I'm starting to, yes!' agreed Petty, turning to look at Sathea before freeing his hand. He stepped aside to look at all the other tunnels once more as the protectorate hurried after Hestean.

The two Deserteers who had first warned of the Black Robe's approach now walked with Reglean, having taken on the task of watching over her. It occurred to Sathea that everyone here seemed to have a part to play. Looking towards her daughter, Sathea pondered the flaring up of Hestean's emotions. She had the distinct feeling that her daughter knew more than she was saying.

Petty took hold of Sathea's hand once more, surprising her, and she felt comforted by his touch. Behind their little group, they crossed the domed cavern, and she realised that her daughter, oddly, was somehow also Petty's.

* * *

As they walked, Petty found himself wondering about the woman whose hand he held. She seemed as complicated and bewildering as her daughter. He saw much of Hestean in Sathea and suspected there was much of the mother in the daughter. Another thought confronted him. When Hestean had adopted him, was her mother also destined to be part of his life? For a moment, he studied Sathea before his thoughts slipped to the tunnel around them.

Light pods were progressively turning on in a straight row above them, illuminating their progress. The tunnel seemed wider than its darkness had first suggested. A faded yellow line dotted the centre of the tunnel's floor. Then, he noticed Sathea looking at signs on the tunnel's left wall.

'Can you read those?' he asked.

'Yes, but look,' she said, pointing to more signs on the other side of the tunnel. 'You need to turn around in order to see what is written on those. I think the people who once roamed here would walk on this side of the tunnel when going in this direction. We should do the same.' She pulled him to the left. 'It's respectful.'

'Do you always respect others?' asked Petty.

'Not always, but these people were kin. They deserve respect.'

Petty nodded in agreement. He ushered the Deserteer in front of him to the left, then pointed to the line, asking for the message to be passed on.

* * *

Soon, Hestean was tapped on the shoulder. As she heard Petty's deferred instructions, she looked back to see everyone except Jarrak and herself walking on the left side of the tunnel.

'Don't you read signs?' called Sathea teasingly. Hestean looked towards her mother, still puzzled, then glanced at an approaching sign. For a moment, her mother's words still puzzled her. The adherence of her companions to the surely unimportant directive was absurd. Or was it? She had better things to think about, but after a pause, she lightly tugged Jarrak sideways, just in case. She and Jarrak exchanged a glance. Before she could stop herself, she started to giggle. It was a sign that was thousands of years old and she had just done what it demanded. She'd never been good at obeying orders. She smiled at the thought. She started to swing her arms slightly to chase away her ponderings, and soon her whole protectorate was doing it. The fog of her thoughts lifted, and she relaxed into their little game.

* * *

From behind, Petty remained vigilant, ever watchful over his charge. Sathea, too, stayed watchful, although mostly of Petty, as she'd realised what he was doing.

Her daughter was allowing herself to let go for a time; to retreat from the weight of leadership. Sathea realised that in these times, Petty would always watch over her. She saw that several other Deserteers mirrored Petty's alertness. She continued to observe this watchfulness as it shifted through the ranks of the protectorate. It was a slow ripple, which circulated without any visible signal. She, too, found herself feeling safe amongst these men and women. They were not just grouped individuals, but a tightly formed team. The protectorate was not separate from her daughter; it had become part of her.

Sathea's thoughts drifted towards Petty again. She let go of his arm, leaving him to do his job, then walked forward to grasp Reglean's arm. She thought she'd sensed a reciprocation of her feelings in Petty, although now was not the time for such thoughts. She looked towards Reglean, and the Matrefem looked back at her knowingly.

* * *

Hestean's mind came to settle upon a thought, and she ceased her playing. Recalling an ancient Comcree tale—one involving the words "*Steorra Hus*"—she said aloud, 'By the gods, I'm stupid!' She halted and turned. 'You were right, Petty! We should have taken the other tunnel.'

'How do you know?'

'The stories!'

'Are you sure?'

'I am now, yes! We need to go back.' As she passed him, Hestean darted her hand into Petty's satchel and retrieved one of his biscuits.

'She never really forgets, does she?' said the Matrefem.

'Not a thing,' said Petty.

'It's my stomach that doesn't forget,' said Hestean.

'That's not what I meant,' said Reglean.

They retraced their steps, then upon reaching the dome, crossed to the other side. They entered the tunnel marked "*Steorra Hus*". This tunnel was short, and it wasn't long before it widened into another dome-like structure. Here, though, along with the now familiar buttresses and shallow curves, was something new to puzzle over. Directly across from them, a wall flattened the space into a half-dome, as though it had sliced through the structure. In the wall was what seemed to be a large, painted door. Covering the wall was the same glassy film that had finished the domes and tunnels. Due to a slight transparency, they could see that the wall was metallic, not built from stone as everywhere else. Clearly marked as a doorway, the painted section had no seams or joins around it. There was no accompanying place for the Matrefem's talisman or Hestean's Comcree dagger either. Like the doorway to the stairs, this was a new door with a new secret—another test to be worked through.

The light in the centre of this dome had come on as they'd entered, and here, too, the protectorate fanned out to secure their surroundings. After finding no other tunnels or doors, they returned to gather in front of the painted section. Hestean's hand passed across its surface, her mind churning. Not even the six house marks could be seen here. The only thing that stood out was a red-and-blue painted rectangle, twice the size of her hand, just to the side of the line defining the door's outline. Like the door, the small rectangle was flush against the wall's surface—just a painted image.

A thought entered Hestean's head. She placed her hand on to the rectangle, fingers to the top, and looked down at her dagger.

Nothing happened. She scanned the wall itself in both directions, and saw nothing familiar. She hadn't come across this in any of her reading.

'Do you have any more of those horrible biscuits?' she asked, stepping closer to Petty.

Petty, still looking at the wall, opened his bag.

'It's older than the tunnels, I think,' said Jarrak, his voice echoing in the stillness. 'You can tell if you look closely. The wall was here first, and the dome has been added to it. It's a butting, not a true join.' He pointed upwards to where the wall and ceiling came together. 'In places along the seam, where the dome meets the wall, you can see that the join has not been as thorough. There has been seepage. The wall has been stained where moisture has entered. I suspect they weren't able to heat that area as much during the sealing process.'

'Is that what you think this glaze is, some sort of sealant?' asked Petty.

'It's a guess, really. I don't know for sure. The techniques and technologies used to form this underground labyrinth are entirely new to me. I've never seen anything like this before. All the knowledge I have gathered during my time at the Hassis Museum, and in the two years spent here at Sharacan studying antiquity mean nothing when I look at this.'

Hestean observed the dome and her protectorate as they fanned out again to investigate the space. She knew that they had seen her stall at the door and seen her look elsewhere for an answer. What they didn't know was that she already suspected the answer. All she had to do was find it—or find a way around it. She looked back to the make-believe door. In the centre of the dome's floor, she saw Karree standing alone, staring at the wall, and at the painted doorway in particular. Watching her, Hestean became aware that an idea was taking form in the young woman's mind.

* * *

Back before Karree Ladener had vowed herself to Hestean, back when she had still been loadmaster of the Merysands, she had often wondered about the history of her family. Back in the days when six-wheeled desert wagons traversed the Kalcool—or even before then, when shrows alone crossed the desert carrying trade goods—her family had been loadmasters. As far back as records went, they had been Ladeners.

All her life, she had vowed to be the best loadmaster she could be. She had trained from childhood for the task, and it was part of her. Without a good loadmaster, a sky-ship could falter and fall from the sky, with no chance of recovery. She had vowed that this would never happen because of her. To judge something by sight required the memory of weight and dimensions, and that came only with time and training. Not everyone within her family had mastered the art, but she had, and she honed her skills with pride. That was the real reason why she still wore the initials "LM" on her sleeve. Lives had depended on her and respected her aboard the *Merysands*, and she would always be its loadmaster at heart.

'What do you see, Karree?' asked Hestean, walking up to her.

'Well, Hlaford,' said Karree, before she could stop herself. A frown of self-rebuke crossed her face. 'Sorry!' she said. 'It just slipped out!'

'It's alright,' said Hestean. 'I'm going to have to get used to it. It's only a word, after all, isn't it? So, what is it that you see?'

'Well, it's a queerness I see, really.' Reluctantly, Karree went on. 'I think I am looking at the upper cargo door of the *Merysands*.'

'But there is no upper cargo floor on the *Merysands*!'

'No! But there is a door, and it has always been a puzzle to me. And now here it is, puzzling me again.'

'Petty!' called Hestean. 'What do you know of an upper cargo door aboard the *Merysands*?'

Turning from Jarrak, a look of puzzlement crossed Petty's face. He walked across to the two young women. 'Well, there is one,' he said. 'It's never used, of course. The *Merysands* was the first of her type, you see. The prototype. The door was discarded in later ships, because it proved ineffective. You can't have an upper cargo deck on a sky-ship; you need to keep the weight low for balance. It was just a foolish preliminary design error that managed to make its way to production.'

'Have you ever met any of the designers?'

'No. I believe the main designer is dead now. I was told he was already quite old when he helped design this latest class of sky-ship, and he wanted to pass on all his knowledge before he died. If you build something that doesn't work, you can better demonstrate why it shouldn't be done in future!'

Hestean was still looking at the door 'I don't think the door was a foolishness,' she said. An unseen grin was forming in her mind, and she stretched out her arm towards the wall, guiding Petty's eyes across the expanse. 'What do you see there? That curve. Do you recognize it?'

'I'm right, aren't I, Mister Petty,' said Karree, not waiting for him to respond. 'It is similar, isn't it? The curve of the wall and that rectangular mark outside the door? There is a similar panel on the *Merysands*.'

'What's the panel for?' asked Hestean.

'On the *Merysands*, it conceals a control lock. Securing all cargo was part of my safety check each time we flew,' said Karree, becoming more excited by her discovery.

'You've opened it, then?'

'Only ever from the inside. Here, there is this glass film to get through.' As Karree approached the panel, closer now than she had been before, something unexpected happened. As she closed in on the door, the red-tipped handle of her dagger started to glow, as if it were Comcree. Instead of glowing blue, though, it flared a cold, bright red.

'Karree?' said Petty, first to notice.

Looking down, alarmed, Karree pulled the dagger from its scabbard and stared at it in total amazement. Finally, softly, she said, 'Oh, Grandfather! What have you given me?'

'Grandfather?' said Hestean. 'What do you mean, "Grandfather"?'

Everyone was looking at Karree now. Struggling to speak, she said, 'This dagger … It's not mine … Well, I mean, it is, but it was my grandfather's first! It became mine in time. It's my inheritance, you see. The protectorate's oath automatically passed to me along with this dagger. Because of this dagger, even if I had not become part of a protectorate, I would have always been destined to hold the title of a true sand-shepherd. I visited him while we were in Elora-Bearer, and he said that it was fitting this dagger should come to me now. He chose me instead of my brothers, as I held the mark of inheritance. He meant my eyes, didn't he?'

'It's old then, this dagger?'

'Yes. Very old,' said Karree, still grasping for answers.

'As old as this one?' Hestean asked, pulled her blue dagger from its scabbard.

'I couldn't say.'

'Never before have I seen a Deserteer's dagger behave like that,' said Petty.

'Maybe not all of them do,' said Hestean. 'Earlier, a strange thought came to me when I was near the door. I can see that Karree's dagger likes this door, and maybe this doorway likes Karree's dagger, too. Let's see if my idea is right, shall we!'

'What do you mean? You know my family are not Sharacanese! They're from the east, on the other side of the Kalcool even though my grandfather lives now in Elora-Bearer.'

'Your eyes are Sharacanese, so there must be a connection! You told me on the *Merysands* that your family have always been loadmasters. Let's see if they were once loadmasters here.'

* * *

Hestean could see the questions on Karree's face; the same questions that were on her mind too. Unknowingly, she had brought someone home who also belonged to this place. She turned towards the Matrefem, then thought of Dan. Had this all been some great game? The *Merysands*, Jarrak, Karree?

She looked around at her protectorate, wondering who else might belong here. In a rush, she realised that they all belonged here. Astounded, she berated herself for not seeing it sooner. Standing around her were the oldest of family names, all of which were in the Comcree's Book of Origin. 'You are home Karree!' she said. 'Your dagger places you here the same as mine, just as they place all of us here.' Her words echoed around the dome, where they were soaked up by everyone.

'What do you mean?' asked Karree.

Around Hestean, she saw that everyone had the same question. Even her mother, Jarrak, and the Matrefem were standing in observant silence. Behind this wall, Hestean's companions would find another world, their true world, and she knew the time had come to tell them about it. 'Do you want to hear a story?' she asked finally. 'It is a story that has not been told properly for a very long time.'

Murmurs echoed, and she beckoned them closer as she sat and leaned against the painted door. The story would take some time to tell, but it needed to be told. They now needed to truly understand what lay on the other side.

Everyone seated themselves. Petty sat to one side of her with Karree on the other. Sathea and Reglean were in the centre, towards the back of the group. The wall that divided them from what lay beyond was neither cold nor warm; leaning against it, Hestean knew that it had seen much beyond the passing of time.

Before speaking, she retrieved her Comcree dagger from its scabbard. Then she pulled up her knees and rested her hands across them. 'If this story is ever repeated beyond this dome, then the teller will have this dagger in their chest. No exceptions. If not me, then another of the Comcree will find you.' Her voice was grave. 'Only the Comcree are permitted to tell this story.' She looked around at them all, then quickly brought her dagger down upon Petty's bag, driving the blade until it hit stone, displaying the absoluteness of her warning. She was no village girl anymore, but a Comcree warrior.

Her eyes came to rest upon her mother. She knew that, of everyone in front of her, her mother would be the hardest to persuade. There was a bond between them now; a bond that had been hidden for a long time. She knew her mother was here through a series of coincidences. Or was she? The lore of the Comcree spoke to everyone, but most significantly, to the priestesses of the temple, whose position her mother and Reglean had inherited. Maybe this wasn't an accident.

'There are some things the Comcree have always chosen to keep private. This is Comcree lore that you are about to hear. If you hear it, there will be consequences. If you wish not to hear it, then now is the time to go. There is another dome back along that tunnel and you can wait there. If you stay, however, you will be bound. It's your choice, as per Comcree doctrine.'

She paused before continuing, but no one moved. The protectorate already knew the lore by which they were bound, and Jarrak, Sathea, and Reglean stayed firmly seated. Hestean knew that the aged Matrefem had already guarded this place all her life, albeit with little knowledge of its existence. To know the reason now was something Reglean had probably never dreamed possible. For Sathea and Jarrak, it was also just as personal, because of Hestean. Sathea would not leave the daughter who had come from within her, and Jarrak knew that his soul belonged to the young Comcree.

All had their reasons to stay, and so they remained. What would this world be, if not for the Comcree? Every one of them had determined that the College would not be the future of this world's history. She was about to tell them of the College's long-ago equivalent, which had driven them here to hide from the stars on an isolated world, far from where they had planned to go. It was luck, fate, and ancestry that had turned that luck into a future, which generations upon generations of Comcree had been charged with.

At first, the words of the story came slowly from Hestean's lips. 'The name given to the original Comcree was Beodancree,' she said. 'But even that is a corruption of their true title.' Word by word, she began to verbalise her recollections exactly. 'There is a book that the Comcree hold, and it is as old as my dagger. I now know it tells the story of Sharacan. Not the village of Sharacan, and not the old and great city of Sharacan that once dwarfed it. This is the story of *this* Sharacan—the Sharacan down here. It is the Sharacan against which my back rests. You will recall it as a fable, a story of make-believe. But this story is true. It tells of our beginning. It tells of how we existed and became who we are now.'

42

It was a different group of people who sat in front of Hestean when she finished telling her story. They were silent as they digested what she'd told them. The tale of genesis had unravelled from her, and from the past had come names. In the original manuscript, these had filled two pages. Yet Hestean felt it necessary to only state the ones relevant to her listeners. 'There are more names,' she said. 'But these are the ones I see before me. They are the names from which you are descended.'

Around her she could see scepticism and disbelief, then wonderment, then a growing euphoria, building into pride. Never before had the distant past been made clear. This, the most ancient of tales, had become distorted over time. Now, having heard the tale in its original form, their minds were opening. They saw how people had changed the history through the ages, not to intentionally distort the truth, but to make it last. It had been simplified. Their ancestors had been slowly enlarged as characters. For the most part, they had been simple people, caught up in a world of intrigue and greed. The complex stories had been turned into magical fables.

Hestean had just told them the truth about the stars. They were all from another part of the galaxy, far from where their ancestors had ended up. In order to kill one person on a starship, the usurpers of a vast galactic empire had planned to kill everyone onboard. Many had died, but some had survived to found Sharacan.

Even though the story had changed, signs had been left by the ancients. Hestean had found those signs, just like she was meant to. What she had kept to herself, though, was that Andreena—two hundred years before—had also found these signs.

From the silence, a voice spoke, breaking through Hestean's thoughts. While she had been retelling the story to those in front of her, she'd realised that a fragment of the story had been reversed, its true meaning hidden. Now, just the inkling of a smile crossed her lips. She turned to Karree. 'Do you understand what the word "genetics" means, Karree?'

Hestean saw a baffled expression in the young woman's face. After a moment, Karree answered. 'It is what makes my eyes green, and my hair the colour of my mother's.'

'Yes. It is the coding of life,' agreed Hestean, still smiling. 'It's a code that makes us our own selves. But there is also a hidden code, which defines all of our true kin. He was not given a key, as the story suggests. Your dagger was not the key handed to the loadmaster of Sharacan; it was a cleverly worded deception to protect the truth. The truth, Karree, is that the Sharacan was given his key. His blood's signature. And therefore, you are the key to Sharacan. Your dagger merely told the door that the key was nearby. Only the two, together, are able to open this door.'

Even here, in this place where the Comcree had not been for eons, except briefly two hundred years ago, the lore of the Comcree was still standing. Hestean realised something else, too. What she had learned from her reading was that it was Hestean's ancestors whom the usurpers had been trying to kill. Hestean was a cwen, just as her mother had suggested two years before. Not a queen, but a cwen. Not a charter to rule, but a charter to guide.

Choosing her words carefully, she said, 'Do you want to see the truth of who you are, Karree? Do you want to see the ancients and their world, from which we have all come?'

* * *

Karree regarded the questions in silence, annoyed. She, too, knew the lore by which the Comcree stood. She had also come to know this young warrior. She had noticed that Hestean rarely asked a question to which the answer had not already been foreseen. 'Do you really think I am a fool?'

'No,' said Hestean, smiling. 'But I did have to ask the question, didn't I?'

'Damn you, Hlaford! Before you, I knew no Comcree. My life was simple. I know you now, though, and you know me, so why the charade? Was it worth it?'

'Oh, yes. Always. Respect is always worth it, but then so is humour.'

A hushed chuckle spread through their little group. Karree glared at them all. 'I'm sure you think that's funny, but it's not you she's asking to step forward, is it?'

Hestean's smile vanished, and she said, 'The words were important, Karree. You know that! They are what give respect. These Deserteers know that. This is your world also, Karree Ladener. You have a say in it, just as I do. For too long, I was denied respect by the Robes, so I will not deny it to others. Do you understand that?'

'I've never been here before!'

'None of us have,' said Hestean. 'But it is only you who can take us forward.'

Karree stared at her closest friend. After a long moment, she stood up and put out her hand, offering to help Hestean rise. 'What is it I'm supposed to do?' she asked, once Hestean was standing before her.

Still holding Karree's hand, Hestean walked to the small painted rectangle. 'Place your hand on what you described as a locking panel, palm down, and let's see if I'm right. It seeks a key code, so let's see if you actually have what I think you have.'

'And if I don't?'

'It's there,' said Hestean, lifting Karree's hand to the panel. 'Your dagger would not have lit up if it weren't.' They waited, motionless, for what seemed an eternity.

'It's not working,' said Karree, as time stretched on. 'How soundly has it been sleeping?'

'I don't know, but a little faith would be good right now!'

As if in answer, letters began to appear along the top of the panel, slowly forming into words: *Hladanere, Florenz Nalleppar, Cnawan, Fyrst Paeth Faethmed, Beginnan Styrtan.*

The words vanished, and Karree pulled her hand from the panel, amazed at what she had read. The name of her first ancestor had just appeared on the rectangle in front of her.

More words started to spell themselves out, and she said, 'This is why you agreed to teach me Fem, isn't it, Hestean? Even back at the Hassis Valley, you knew who I was.'

Raedelsung Othere Paeths.

'No. I only realised it while telling the story,' said Hestean.

These words too began to vanish, and were quickly replaced by others. *Fullfyllanung Othere Felan Nu.*

This time, though, the words started to blink before slowly fading, and Karree said, 'So, what do you make of this?'

'We need another signature,' said Hestean, alarmed.

A sequence of numbers appeared and began to count down.

'You try!' said Karree, hurriedly.

'I have, remember! When we first got here. My hand has been all over this wall. I've touched it all. Nothing happened!'

'Yes, but that was before my dagger lit up. It might be different now. Try it again. Your dagger is old, like mine. It can't hurt, can it?' Karree eyed the numbers. 'Do you have a better suggestion?'

'But don't you see? That's just it. My dagger is old, and I should have been able to open this door. Any Comcree should have been able to. You're not the only one who should be a key. One of the manuscripts in the Hassis library said so. But something has changed! For some reason, Andreena changed it.'

'You mean you knew this was here?'

'No. Well, not exactly. I never knew about the tunnels or the domes, nor any of it. Just that there would be a door. It was you who made me realise what the rectangular marking might actually be for.'

Karree turned to look at the panel and watched the number four turn into a number three, then she glared back at Hestean. She grabbed Hestean's hand and placed it against the panel, pressing it firmly against the surface. 'Sisters we have become, so maybe it is as sisters that we are meant to enter. That's what the door was waiting for. Not just for me! It needed to know we are both here.'

Almost immediately, the descending numbers stopped and vanished. Moments passed and Hestean withdrew her hand. 'See! I told you, nothing.'

'Will it let us try again?' asked Karree.

'I don't know! The scroll didn't say anything about needing more than one person. Something has changed, and I can't exactly ask anyone, can I? Do you know anyone else with an ancient dagger?'

'I'm sorry!'

'Don't be! We'll work it out,' said Hestean.

A moment later, blue light flared from Hestean's hip, and she looked down to see her blue dagger's hilt aglow. In one single movement, both women looked towards the panel and saw letters appearing upon its surface once more. *Steorra Plottere, Etanna Descee Sacar Cnawan.*

It was with pure wonder that Hestean realised her own ancestor's designation had just scribed itself across the panel. She breathed out the words, making them feel real. 'Navigator, Etanna Descee Sacar.'

A faint shudder came from within the wall as more words dotted across the panel. *Wilcuma Ut Team, Thee Cunnan Nu Bord. LP7 Sharacan.*

The door beside them abruptly wrenched itself inward, breaking the seal. Dust puffed into the air as it started to slide up into the wall. As it disappeared, a small room behind the doorway began to diffuse a soft, red glow. Cautiously, Hestean and Karree peered inside.

'There's another door!'

'I can see that.'

'It fills the whole back wall, just as this one filled its front!'

'I can see that, too.'

'But why?'

'I don't know!'

'*Steorra Plottere*,' said the familiar, aged voice of Reglean. The Matrefem had come closer, intrigued. 'It suits you. It is fitting for one who will change the path of this world.'

'Is it?' said Hestean.

'Child, you are Comcree. You know more about the past than anyone around you. You know also about our future, I think. You didn't tell us about that in your story, did you? You would not be here if you were not taking us forward. You know where our future leads; where our ancestors will take us. The true world of the Comcree is beyond these doors, and their secrets will be guarded well, even there.' Hestean stared into the small chamber, considering the old woman's words. Reglean went on. 'You allow us to choose, yet at the same time you show us the paths we need to see. Until now, no other path has brought us closer to our past, nor directed us closer to our future.'

* * *

Hestean withdrew her gaze from the door. Something had also awoken within Reglean.

'The future of our past is the reason we are here on this world,' she told the old woman. 'I hope, for our sakes, that the future has changed. If we are to take back what is ours, then we must be capable of making it change. That is what we have been doing on this world—giving ourselves time to change. Letting the stars know that what was taken from them was golden, so that when we return, we will be heard. But you are right, Reglean,' she said. 'You will not see this world—this future past of ours—but then, neither will I. One day, though, our people will. One day, we will show our oppressors that we survived. It will be the greatest of our victories. We have to be seen to survive in order to succeed against tyranny. There is much that only the Comcree know, and much the Danannee has shown me. However, there is still much to relearn, and the College is but a fragment of that tyranny. This is why we must first succeed against them. Our world is greater than theirs.'

As ancient defiance came into Hestean's recitation, the old woman smiled and shuddered at the same time. She had awoken the magic within the warrior as a Matrefem should, although Hestean still had doubts.

Hestean strode through the open doorway, venturing towards the back of the chamber. She placed her hand on one of two panels, similar to the one on the outer wall. Suddenly, a mechanical shrill burst forth, and everyone was sent reeling backwards. It was an automated alarm, spewing out words of warning in Fem. Abruptly, the outer door began to descend. On reflex, Petty lurched forward and threw his satchel between the door and the bottom of its surrounding frame, stopping it from sealing completely.

'What did you do?' he asked.

'Act only when you know the world you are within!' said Hestean, chastising herself weakly. She knew she'd just made a fool of herself. 'I'm sorry,' she said. 'There are two panels in here. I just picked the wrong one, that's all.' She pressed the other, and the door lifted once again.

'I thought by now you would know what you were doing,' said Karree.

'I do. Sort of.'

Petty glared at her from behind Karree. 'Maybe we should rest for a while.'

'I don't need to rest.'

'Do you know what's on the other side of that door?'

'Yes! Well, no, not exactly … But I think I do!'

'You think you do,' said Petty, beginning to fume. 'Thinking is not good enough, if your wits are fatigued! We rest. You haven't really rested all day, but you will now. You need to have your mind working properly before we go any further.'

'But I'm alright!'

'All right! Does that sound like you? Really? Once, yes, but not now. You might be Comcree, but right now you are too exhausted to act like one. No, we rest here before whatever comes next.' Angry now, Petty's annoyance continued to build. 'You could have killed us all, just then. You are better than this. You have brains beyond your age, but do you think you would have come this far if you were not Sharacanese? Take our lives in carelessness, and we will not accompany you further. Daughter, we rest here now.'

No one had ever seen Petty so angry before, but to Hestean, it felt like a storm. Abruptly he turned from her and strode across the dome towards the tunnel. 'Sathea, Taw, you're with me!' he said, without stopping.

* * *

Sathea didn't know if the others had witnessed what she had. At this moment, she was in awe of the love she had just seen displayed towards her daughter. She knew no other man who had ever shown his heart so publicly. She found herself turning to follow Petty. 'Where are we going?' she asked, catching up with him.

'I'm sick of these horrible biscuits!' Petty huffed. 'One of the other tunnels led to a warehouse, I think. We'll see what it has to offer.'

Matching his stride, Sathea linked her arm through his. 'You know, there is only one other who loves my daughter as I do,' she said.

'Who's that?'

'You, you silly man!'

He peered at her. 'You think this, do you?'

'I know this! I love her too, you know. I always have. I was never permitted to show it before, so I know love when I see it. You called her "daughter". Did you know that?'

'That was stupid!'

'No. It's real.'

'Is it?'

'Yes, it is!'

'And what made you so wise?'

'I'm her mother!'

Softly, Petty started to laugh. He untwisted their arms and clasped her hand into his. 'I just need to get away from her for a time.'

'I know how you feel! She pulls constantly, doesn't she? She doesn't mean to, it's just how she is. If you care about her, it's love. Jarrak loves her, too, you know. So does Karree. I have been watching Jarrak for a while now. I wasn't surprised to see her in bed with him this morning. I just hope that she loves him as much as he loves her.'

'You think she doesn't?'

'It's her first love! She has no experience yet. It may be true, and it may not be. She may need both of us if it isn't, and she will definitely need both of us if it is.'

* * *

Petty, Sathea, and the Deserteer named Taw walked out into the first dome and crossed towards a tunnel marked *Foda Hus*. 'It does mean food store, doesn't it?' asked Petty, raising his arm and pointing.

'Yes, but you don't honestly think it still contains anything edible, do you? It's been an age since anyone lived here.'

'Not really, no. But I'm not ready to go back just yet.'

As Petty and Sathea talked, Taw followed, alert to their surroundings.

* * *

Hestean walked from the small chamber as if lost. This had been her moment, and she had spoilt it. She saw Jarrak and the others watching her. Like a scolded child, she wished she could hide herself. 'Petty was really angry, wasn't he?' she said. 'I've never seen him so.'

'He cares for you,' said Jarrak. 'You scared him. You scared us all! We could have lost you. *I* could have lost you.'

'I fear this was my fault,' said the Matrefem.

'No,' said Hestean. 'Petty was right. I am too young. I should not be in charge here.'

'He was exactly right,' said the old woman, 'but that was not what he was saying, was it? You are the only person who *can* be in charge here. It is you who has worked all this out. It is you who has seen this. You are young, but you know more about this underworld than any of us. What he was saying was that you have us here to help. Let us help.

I think it is by design that you are here with others. You know who it is I am speaking of, specifically, don't you?'

Hestean brushed her hand against the Matrefem's shoulder, and said, 'I hope my face has lines like yours when I'm old.'

'It already does, child! You just have to use those lines wisely.'

Hestean smiled, then walked across to where the outer wall of the dome met the floor. She sat down and watched as Karree set to work carrying out Petty's instructions. In his absence, the Deserteer was taking charge of the protectorate, setting up a make-shift camp. Hestean realised that they would all forget this moment, so long as she never did. Karree's Sharacanese eyes met her own, and she knew that they were now, truly, joined.

She recalled, too, the many evenings that had been spent with Jarrak in the past. She knew that never again would she believe one of his star stories. Everyone here knew the truth now, and so did she.

43

'It's like a giant waking up,' said Petty, watching the light pods coming on one after the other ahead of them.

'Strangely, I feel safe here, though,' said Sathea, still with her hand locked into his. 'It's as if it knows we belong here.'

'You're trapped within an underworld of tunnels, yet you feel as if you belong?'

'You feel it, too! I know you do!'

'Since Hestean's story, I think we all do, in a way.'

As they rounded a corner, something seemed to catch Taw's attention ahead of them. He was standing by a pile of dust-covered rags. By the time they stopped beside them, Petty could see that they had once been clothing, and that they still contained the skeletal remains of a person. The clothing was now covered with dust and fragile to the touch. The skeleton's weapons lay scattered in front of it.

'They look like the clothes that the Robes of the College wear!' said Sathea.

'It would appear so, yes,' said Petty, kneeling down to examine the skeleton more closely. 'And he was not given the opportunity to leave, by the looks of it.'

'What do you mean?'

'I think he was running when he fell. See here? Something has charred and burnt a hole in the back of his clothing.'

They walked on in silence, nervously now, all three of them more wary of what might be ahead. A short time later, they found two more skeletons, still clothed. Petty knelt to examine each of these, too. He noticed the same charred spot on the back of the clothing and recalled only one weapon capable of making such a mark. He had never seen one, but had read tellings of them. He noted that these men, too, had fallen forward, their weapons scattered ahead of them, as if struck hard from behind while running.

'What do you suppose they were doing here?' asked Taw.

'Fleeing,' said Petty. 'As fast as they could.' He got to his feet and looked off into the darkness ahead of them. As they set off, even more carefully now, the tunnel once more began to illuminate itself. Before they reached its end, they found several more skeletons. These too appeared to have died from the same weapon, but now, not all the scorch marks were on their backs. In the next dome, there were more piles of rag-covered bones. A frantic battle had happened here.

* * *

In his mind, Petty summed up the sight before him. Not one of the College combatants who had fought here had survived to tell of it. The first skeleton they had come across had been the last to die, making an attempt to flee. There had been no pity, no remorse, and no forgiving. The Black Robes had been slaughtered.

'Who were they fighting?' asked Taw, stepping over several of the bodies. 'There's no sign of who they were fighting.'

'You know as well as I do that Deserteers always retrieve their own,' said Petty.

'So, they were fighting Deserteers?' said Sathea, surprising herself with her calmness.

'I think not!' said Petty. 'That is, they were not just Deserteers. It was a protectorate they came up against here.'

'One protectorate did all of this?'

'If their cause was great enough, one well-armed protectorate could do this, yes.'

'So few against so many … What makes you think so?'

'The weapon blasts that killed them. At the time when I think it happened, only protectorates carried the weapons that could do this. It was only later that all Comcree forces started being issued with them. It was this extended use that finally forced the College to enter into the Treaty of Truce. They could see the expanding might of the Comcree. What we see here, I think, justified their fear.' For the first time, Petty was seeing the true might of the Comcree. For the first time, he felt for these men of the College. They had no idea what they had discovered, and they had no idea how vehemently the Comcree would protect this hidden heritage.

'What were these weapons?' asked Sathea.

'Thunder-staffs.' said Petty.

'I would not have thought this,' said Taw. 'It doesn't align with the Deserteer code!'

'Back then, when Sharacan first fell to the College, the Comcree would have done this,' said Petty. 'Andreena would have done this. She would not have wanted the College to know of this place. Here, her protectorate would have fought to the last to keep this secret. I think we have just found the reason for her disappearance.'

'You mean the warrior whose dagger Hestean now holds? She did this?' said Sathea.

'I think so,' said Petty, still absorbing what he was seeing. 'If what I have learned from Hestean is correct, I think she settled a score here. I think she knew she might not survive, but this battle she had to win.'

'So where are these Deserteers, this protectorate? Were they all killed here as well?'

Petty looked towards three closed doors opposite the tunnel. 'You're her mother,' he said. 'Your hand should have the same coding. See if you can open those.'

'So, it was my coding you wanted, not my company?'

'I had an idea that your coding might be needed, yes, but not for this. It was food I was after, not bodies. I do also very much enjoy having your hand to hold, though. I like your hand,' he said, turning to face her. This last statement surprised him, but he meant it.

* * *

Sathea smiled. She was starting to understand his way of things. Even in the heat of outrage or attraction, it seemed he was always planning ahead. 'I will have to watch out for you, Mister Petty, won't I?' she said, eyeing him for a moment. Then she stepped out across the dome, weaving her way around the remnant bodies in front of her. As she approached the panel on the far left, the door furthermost to her right abruptly lifted. She and Petty turned to see that Taw had also walked across the dome and was now standing still, amazed at what he had done.

'I just put my hand on the plate out of curiosity,' he said. 'I didn't believe for a moment that it would actually do anything!' Oblivious to

Petty and Sathea's shock, he stood staring into a giant wedge-shaped room. Before him were mounds of giant, glossy earthenware jars stacked one above the other.

Petty started towards the middle door. Sathea pouted; she hadn't really been needed after all. He placed his hand to the control, but nothing happened. 'So, it seems not everyone has the gift after all,' she said with a smirk. She stepped towards her own door, still closed. A moment later, it opened, and a faint smell wafted out.

As this room illuminated itself, she took a breath and stepped directly in front of the opening. This room, too, was wedge-shaped and large. She saw three wide passageways, which went deep, each divided by rows and rows of shelving. On each shelf, small jars were stacked neatly, each catalogued with a notation. Gratefully, she saw no bodies.

She turned back to Petty, suddenly aware of him watching her. She realised then that she had never before spoken so flippantly to a man. It was as if a weight had been lifted from her soul. Her mind formed the word "freedom". Even if nothing greater was achieved this day, she knew that her daughter had given her this, and for this she was grateful.

* * *

Eyeing Sathea, Petty knew he had just seen Hestean in her. He found himself wondering how Sathea had managed to survive in her village—which now must be directly above them—when it was clear that Hestean would not have.

'What?' said Sathea.

'Shall I try the door, Mister Petty?' said Taw, coming up behind him.

For a moment, Petty struggled to take in Taw's words. An odd feeling had come over him. Only once, long ago, had a woman made him feel this way. He had always regretted letting that woman slip from his life. Absently, his hand offered Taw the panel as his mind momentarily drifted.

'Maybe it's jammed or faulty,' said Taw, when his hand also failed to open the door.

Petty cleared his mind and looked at the panel. 'You have a go,' he said to Sathea.

Sathea crossed towards him, and Petty wondered if she knew how he'd been thinking of her. She lifted her hand, and again the door failed to move, although this time, there was a response. As her other hand again entwined with Petty's, a word materialised on the panel.

Raedelsung.

Before any of them could speak, three rows of numbers appeared below the word, counting up from one to twenty-nine.

'A number lock,' said Petty.

Sathea began to giggle, her fingers tightening around his. 'It is an alphabet,' she said. 'Why they are also numbers, I don't know, but this is our alphabet. See, there are twenty-nine numbers, and there are twenty-nine letters in the Fem alphabet. They are always written in three rows like this, with the middle row being shorter. It seeks a word, not a number!'

Sathea indeed had a brain like her daughter's, quick to see patterns behind things. For some time now, Petty had realised she was not the empty-headed woman she'd presented to the world. He saw something more, too. He noted Sathea's face, her dark complexion and green eyes. In her and Hestean, there was a resemblance to someone he had once seen in a painting. One face in a grouped image of seven. 'Try Andree,' he said.

'Why Andree?'

'Because I heard Hestean call Andreena that—that's why!'

'And why is that important?'

'It's a familiar! Hestean told me that only Andreena's closest friends and family called her that. If she is responsible for this carnage, and if she is responsible for locking this door, she would have wanted only someone she knew to open it.'

* * *

Sathea turned to the panel. Her finger hit the number twenty-five.

'What are you doing?' Petty asked. '"Andree" begins with an A.'

'Yes, it does,' said Sathea, grinning. She punched in the remaining letters and said, 'You still have a little to learn about our ancient language. Don't worry, I'll teach you.'

Almost instantly, the door began to rise. Air was sucked in, just as in the case of the other two doors. This time, it brought with it a strange, stale smell of ancient decay. As the room's illuminations revealed the source, they walked into the room's dryness, feeling the air around them suck moisture from their skin, mouths, and even their lungs.

'A drying room,' said Petty.

Before them was a vast arrangement of racks, where once fruits and vegetables had been dried. Now, though, instead of vegetation, the drying tables held the mummified remains of an entire protectorate. Daunted by the sight, Sathea stepped into the room, ignoring the smell, and brought her hand to her forehead, her mouth, and then her heart.

At the centre of the sand-coloured uniforms was a smaller table. It held the blue-green clothes and mummified remains of what had to be a Comcree warrior. Even in her withered form, her long dark hair and ebony skin bore an uncanny resemblance to Hestean.

'It is Andreena, isn't it?' she said, sensing the loneliness that now seemed to fill the room. She looked around at all the other bodies. For two hundred years, they had lain here. 'How old was she?' Sathea asked.

'Arround thirty, I think,' said Petty, coming to stand beside her.

'It has been too long with so little respect!'

'They were safe here.'

'But someone left them here. Someone sealed the door!'

'Someone did, yes,' said Petty, circling the table. He studied the body of the fabled Andreena. 'Probably the same someone who took the dagger and earpiece that Hestean now wears. Bending closer, he added, 'There appears to be dried blood in her ear where the earpiece released itself. I've been told it happens after a warrior dies.'

'She has indeed waited here a long time,' said Taw.

'But not for much longer,' said Sathea, leaning forward to kiss the forehead of the warrior, treating her as kin. She began to straighten, but then noticed something. Tucked beneath the warrior's dress, just above her heart, was a rolled piece of cloth. She drew out the scroll and unrolled it to find a pledge written on the fabric. *A child's hand*, was her first thought. As she looked at the uneven and misshapen letters written in blood, though, she wondered if indeed it had been a child. She read aloud.

> 'He never told me his name, but before he died, I helped him gather up your friends and place them around you, to protect you in death as they tried to in life.
>
> Before he died, we hid the thunder weapons they carried within Sharacan, to keep them safe, for they were too much for me.
>
> Before he died, he carved the mark of our house into my arm so that I would never forget this day, nor you, nor this secret place that

now keeps you safe. Here, you are safe from these robed men who have destroyed our city.

Before he died, he gave me your things and said I was to protect them for the one to whom they now belong. He said that before I am of age, I will know who that is to be. I now promise you that I will protect our heritage.

Before he died, he said I must remember the old words that brought us here. That I must take the key, and the eye of the sun, and keep them safe, too.

Before he died, he said that only the person who is supposed to will return to this place, and that I am to hide where everyone can see me. At first, I didn't know what he meant, but now I do. Sitting here with you, I now know.

Before he died, he kept us safe as you wished, and I helped him lie beside you so that he can now protect you. I hope I can do this, for his words were your words, weren't they? You saved us from death, and they took you instead. Kin are kin, and blood is blood, and I have used mine here so that you will know that yours continues. I will remember you, Aunt Andree, and you will be reborn.

This I pledge.'

Sathea touched the mark on her arm; the same mark that had been carved into her mother's arm, and the arm of her grandmother before that. For as far back as she could recall, all the women of her tribe had received this mark. She realised now that it had taken generations, but finally the dagger belonging to a warrior had come out of hiding to find its way into the hands of another warrior. It was a straight line, and Andreena *was* kin.

44

Hestean sat against the wall of the dome, her depression lifting. She was studying the dome and seeing it in a way she had not thought of before.

It was not its structure that she was looking at, but its history. Its memories. She saw that a great civilisation had lived here, once, or the remnant of one. Perhaps not a people great in number, but great nevertheless. She realised that her world was backward compared with the world it had once been. Why had her ancestors allowed themselves to slip backwards from their once-known technology? Part of her knew why, but she was feeling cheated of a world that might have been hers.

She yawned, drowsy now as thoughts continued to fill her mind. The first people here had produced a grand plan to rebuild their world in a way that was to take centuries, but why? What had they feared? Had they indeed been afraid, or was it just her imagination? To hide for so long, and so completely, must have been for a reason. Dan would know, she thought. Somewhere in his memory, the true reason would be secreted. She wondered if anyone had ever asked him about it. If they had, what had been his answer? She smiled. Above her lay the dread of her own world, and here she was dreaming about the dread of another.

Abruptly, her mind swayed. What if their fears were the same? What if the dreadful thing these people had fled had followed them? What if her ancestors had brought their foe with them to eventually spawn forth upon them again? Was this the true reason for the Comcree? A defence set in place against some future breach?

She whimpered, and her body jerked itself awake from her dream. Her head rose from Jarrak's lap. 'Shh,' he said. 'It's only a dream.'

He raised his hand to caress her hair in hope of calming her, but she straightened up. 'If only it was,' she said. 'If only it was. I have been dreaming a lot lately.' Aware now that her protectorate had settled into their makeshift camp, she added, 'How long have I been asleep?'

'A while.'

'And Petty?'

'Not back yet.'

'If he's not back soon, we'll have to go and find him.'

* * *

She was talking to Karree when Petty's scavenging party returned, their arms full of jars. Remarkably, even now, their contents were free from decay, although they were difficult to open after so many years of disuse. The flutter-weed beans, preserved matoze, and diced towtowee were all deliciously preserved with spices and herbs.

As they ate, they laughed and told stories, forgetting themselves for a time. All except Petty, Sathea, and Taw, who kept silent about their real discovery. Petty had told them to do so, at least until the whole protectorate had eaten. Like Petty, Sathea knew that Hestean would not eat if she knew about Andreena. She knew that her daughter needed to eat, as did everyone else. When she saw Hestean put down her empty bowl, she glanced towards Petty. He nodded his agreement.

Prepared to break the spell of light-heartedness, she leaned forward and handed her daughter the scroll. 'You should read this.'

'What is it?' asked Hestean, still smiling at something one of the Deserteers had said. She unrolled the scroll and started to read. Her smile disappeared. She handed the scroll to Jarrak without saying a word, and looked towards her mother, then Petty. 'Where is she?' said Hestean, rising to her feet. She didn't wait for an answer. Petty had only been to one place, and in a single movement, she turned and ran towards the tunnel.

Instantly, Karree rose to follow her, along with the rest of the protectorate.

'You'd better go too,' said Petty, speaking to Jarrak. 'You should all go! You all have a right to see. Soon, you may have to fight like your predecessors, so you should all see what true bravery looks like.' Petty grabbed Jarrak's arm. 'Tell her that it is the middle door, and that the access word is "Andree".'

'It is really her, then?'

'Oh, yes, it is really her,' said Sathea, taking back the scroll from Jarrak. The remaining Deserteers followed Jarrak down the tunnel at a run, and only Petty, Sathea, Taw, and the Matrefem stayed seated.

The old Matrefem watched Jarrak and the Deserteers vanish, then turned to Sathea. 'Can I see it?' she asked. 'If what I think is written there, I would like to confirm it.'

* * *

Before Hestean had been given the scroll, Petty had been wondering about something. Now his mind returned to the thought. With his half-finished bowl still in his hand, he got to his feet and walked to the doorway leading through the wall.

It had been Karree's dagger that had woken this Sharacan, so had Andree indeed been beyond the wall? The scroll suggested that she had. It was only after Karree's dagger had been activated that Hestean's had also. So, Andreena must have also needed them both. But how? Karree had said that her red dagger had always been in her family. But her family was from the east, not Sharacan.

For a long time, he stood staring silently into the small room, spooning the occasional slurp of food into his mouth. Sathea came to stand beside him. 'It took some time for the wall to recognize Hestean, didn't it? Almost as if it was unsure who she was,' he said.

'What do you mean?'

'I mean that towards the end of the scroll, the person who wrote it wasn't talking about Andreena's protectorate. The word used was 'us', but it wasn't the protectorate they were referring to. It was another child, wasn't it? A younger child, or an infant, maybe.'

'Oh, Petty. I know that Karree and Hestean are related, but you're not saying that,' said Sathea, understanding him immediately. 'It's fanciful! Karree's as white as sand, and Hestean … Well, she's like all Sharacanese—as dark as the darkest night. They are as different as you and me.'

'Do you know which house Karree belongs to?' he asked. 'Even though she's from the east, she is of the fourth house, as both you and I are.'

'Yes, but that doesn't mean she's close kin. I mean, you and I aren't, are we?'

He glanced at her and smiled. 'No. I am not directly of your bloodline, but I'm closer than you think. My grandmother had skin like yours. I was born just to the north of here, in the Sereye. It is only time and pigmentation that separates us.'

'It is a fancy, Petty. It's just a story! Karree is from the east, as far to the east as you can get from Sharacan. You heard her say so yourself!'

'Yes, I did. But if you have something you want to keep hidden, something that can be divided, one way is to put the pieces as far from each other as you can. I have seen this before in the Comcree, in the tellings. Just as you have. We both know that if they have a secret and it can be broken down into segments, then they scatter those segments to the wind.'

'He could be right,' said Reglean, coming to stand with them. 'Your words are colourful, Mister Petty. Even the Matrefems scatter secrets in the wind. They would have left proof if they eventually wanted it known. Is this not also true of the Comcree?'

Petty considered the old woman's statement for a moment before turning towards the open doorway. 'There is a painting in the House of Hassis,' he said. 'It is of the first Hassis hexagon. In it, you cannot see all of Andreena. One side of her is hidden, but she wears two slings on her waist, similar to the two dagger slings Hestean wears. What if Andreena also had a red dagger, but one that was more special than the red dagger Hestean has now? One that she inherited?' He paused again for a moment before strengthening the argument. 'I've heard it said that there are only six degrees of separation. Eventually, over time, they are bound to merge. Maybe they merged with Andreena and have now separated once more to end up with Hestean and Karree. Is this not possible?'

'Why do you suggest such a thing?' said Sathea. 'It is scandalous.'

'Is it? Andreena needed the two daggers to enter Sharacan. Without both, she couldn't have, but she did. The scroll says she did, and if she had them both, then how did Hestean end up with one and Karree the other? How did Karree get hers? Only Andreena's daggers are missing, which means the child took both of them.'

'No, you're wrong,' said Sathea, still not giving in. 'Hestean said that her dagger should have been able to open the door. Don't you remember?'

'But she also said that Andreena changed the coding. The child, the one who wrote the scroll … The red dagger might have belonged to her.'

'But she was only a child, surely too young to have a dagger.'

'Exactly,' said Petty. 'That's why Andreena went missing when she did. Maybe she didn't know about this place before she came back to Sharacan. The dagger wasn't the child's, it was her family's—from her father's side. Karree said that her family had always been loadmasters. So, perhaps the child's father travelled with a caravan. He could have come through the city of Sharacan quite often. He didn't have to be from Sharacan in order to meet Andreena's sister. Maybe the daggers didn't come together with Andreena, but with her niece or nephew.' Feeling more satisfied with his explanation, Petty continued. 'I think that the child's father was from the east. Somehow, the child managed to get her sibling out of Sharacan and back to their father's province!'

'Along with the red dagger?' said Sathea.

'Yes. Along with the red dagger. She probably didn't mention its power but sent it as proof of legitimacy for the younger child, therefore hiding its secret once again.'

'But why did she not then go as well?'

'What you feel for Hestean comes from more than just the fact that she's your daughter, doesn't it? There is something in us all that holds the Comcree sacred. They are the chosen. They are the guardians of the gods. This child felt that way and needed to stay in Sharacan to fulfil a promise she had made to a Comcree. I am bound to Hestean, as is Taw, because of the same sort of promise.'

'It is a lovely story, Petty, but Karree and Hestean are not so closely related!'

'Karree is not as light-skinned as you think. I have been to the east, and there, there are much paler people. Karree has the eyes of Sharacan. Take a look when she comes back.' Petty knew he was right. In an attempt to retrieve her sister's children, Andreena had stumbled on the truth of this place, whether she had been already looking for it or not.

Reglean handed the scroll back to Sathea, then turned to Petty and said, 'You have finally said something right. But it is not the daggers that are the proof; it is the eyes. I was handed a story when I became Matrefem. It tells of Sharacan's Eastern Star. It is a red star, Mister Petty!' The aged Matrefem smiled knowingly at him before walking back to where she had been sitting. 'We will see when the next door is opened, won't we?' she said. She sat down again and closed her eyes, seeming to fall into a quiet, peaceful doze.

* * *

Sathea was silent. The old woman had legitimised Petty's thoughts with just a few simple words. The scroll said that the thunder weapons were within Sharacan, and if they were, then Andreena must have had the two daggers one way or another. 'She is right,' said Petty. 'It is assumption on my part. But what happened to her second dagger if the red-handled one wasn't hers? The future will tell us the truth.'

Sathea knew that the real reason she had shunned Petty's concept was understood only by Reglean. It wasn't because it was insignificant, but because it was the complete opposite. It meant that, for two hundred years, separate branches of her family had been unknown to the other. Sure, Karree was lighter-skinned than Hestean, but as Petty had said, it was no real problem. It was merely a variation of pigment. Deep within herself, Sathea knew her words had been a screen. To lose one's family was beyond belief; for it was family that had sustained the women of her village.

'We didn't lose them,' said Reglean, from behind closed eyes. Opening them, she looked directly at Sathea and said, 'They were merely out of sight when they were meant to be. I told you about the story of an eastern star. Do you imagine that I only just now conjured that story up? Were you only listening with your head, but not your heart? We, the Matrefem, have always known. We never knew its true significance, but we knew it existed. We also knew that we were the last of our tribe, allowing the women of our village to survive their ordeals. When you yourself are Matrefem, you will see the truth of this. You will also have to keep such secrets and make decisions that no one else must ever know of!'

'But I am no Matrefem!'

'You have always been one of my choices, and after today, you are my only choice. You have seen things here that I believe are to remain a secret! Am I not correct, Mister Petty?'

Petty smiled to himself. 'I believe so. It is not time for this underworld to be disclosed.'

'But I am no Matrefem!' said Sathea again.

'Shush, woman,' said Reglean. 'I have made my decision, just as one day you will make yours. It is not for you to choose, it is for me to bestow. We will not talk of this again, but from this day on, you are a Matrefem's apprentice.' The old woman looked at Petty. 'It is rare that you should know of this, Mister Petty, and rare it shall remain!'

Petty glanced at Taw, who nodded his agreement. 'Yes,' said Petty. 'Honours are rare in this world, and this secret is one Taw and I will take to our graves.'

Reglean's eyes swivelled from the older Deserteer to the younger, then smiled in satisfaction. 'We are the honoured, Mister Petty! In our village, women have not been considered equal, but to you, we are. Hestean chose well when she chose you, and we are glad of this.'

45

It was like Andreena had been reborn when Hestean came striding back into the dome. Petty watched her cross from the tunnel to the wall, showing a new determination. Andreena's lineage had been given a chance to survive, and that had been the real gifting, not the daggers. Karree was by Hestean's side, and they strode as one. He'd noticed this before, but only now was he able to understand what he was seeing. The two completed each other.

In that moment, he made two decisions. Just as the Matrefem had chosen her successor, Petty now chose his. He saw that it made little difference whether Karree was related to Hestean or not; it was the bond that had grown between them that really mattered. It would keep both the protector and the protected safe, or as safe as either of them could be from now on.

The second of his decisions concerned Hestean's mother. Before Hestean had come into his life, he had begun to tire of this world. He had risen through the ranks in his career, but had never sought command, so had no desire to claim it. Then, just as his adventurous spirit had started to wane, Hestean had entered his life and rekindled the flame.

Now he found himself thinking that maybe her path was not the one he was meant to follow. Instead, if she would have him, it might be with her mother. Hestean's world was for the young, who had the energies of youth. Maybe he was meant to discover something else with Sathea.

'Are you looking at me again, Petty?' quipped Sathea.

'Yes,' he said, without thought. 'I was thinking that maybe this is the most exciting of times, and that I still have some life ahead of me. It might be nice to spend it with you.'

'That's presumptuous.'

'Yes, isn't it? Quite presumptuous.'

He reached out and squeezed her hand, then left her to join her daughter.

* * *

Sathea's mind whirled with thoughts. Petty seemed rejuvenated, as she was finding herself to be. She turned to see if the Matrefem was still sleeping, then walked across to the wall, to join her daughter and her new bind-mate to be.

'I know what I did wrong,' said Hestean. 'I need to finish this now. Andree needs a proper ending to her life, with proper respect. She has lain here too long.' Hestean placed a hand to the panel closest to the outer door, and this time the outer door stayed open instead of sounding an alarm. She moved her hand to the other panel, and her dagger flashed. For a moment, the red light of the little room merged with the blue from her dagger, then the whole of the inner wall shuddered and lifted upward. Again, it was a soft red glow that greeted them. The interior, untouched by time, gleamed as if it had been made yesterday.

A small machine scurried across the floor and docked itself into a socket. Another slightly larger machine, with legs and sucker feet, stopped to look at them. It hung from an internal beam for a moment, obviously trying to decide whether it, too, should move. On the wall beyond it, there was a large depiction of the infinity symbol. The machine's attention moved back to what it had been doing, mending some fault it had found.

'Are they the gods?' asked Sathea as the Matrefem came to stand beside her.

'Just fixers, by the look of it!' replied Hestean.

'Are they dangerous?'

'They don't look to be. That one doesn't seem to be too worried about us!'

'Are there others?'

'Probably,' said Hestean, stepping forward a few paces, 'Is it another junction point. do you think?' She stepped further into the large room. The wall nearest the door arched up to become the ceiling, running across the expanse before stopping suddenly to plunge vertically on the other side. Both ends of the room were flat, straight, and vertical. They cut through like bulkheads on a sky-ship, only bigger. The internal walls here made of a kind of metal, glowed red. To the left, she saw a large hallway leading out, and beside it a staircase descending to some lower level. To the right was a pair of large doors, sealed closed.

* * *

For a moment, Karree thought of her father as she and Petty came to stand beside Hestean, and she wondered why.

'They're not here,' said Petty.

'Oh, yes they are,' said Sathea, standing beside him. 'I feel it.'

'You believe me now, do you?'

'I always believed you. That wasn't the problem.'

'Believe what?' asked Karree, her hand moving closer to her dagger. 'What's here?'

'Your heritage, my dear,' said the Matrefem, coming to stand between Karree and Petty. 'They are talking of something else, but it was your heritage that greeted you a moment ago. You have failed to see it, haven't you?'

'What heritage?

'Show her,' said Reglean, turning to Sathea. 'She has a right to know.'

'Know what?' asked Karree.

Sathea handed over a scroll. 'This is as much for you as it was for Hestean. It tells of your heritage, as it does hers.'

'Andreena had a sister,' said Hestean, without turning her head, 'As it seems do I.'

'You knew?' asked Sathea.

'Of course I knew, Mother. I'm not silly.'

'What sister?' asked Karree. 'It tells of weapons. There should be weapons here …' Silence filled Karree, then she read the scroll again. 'You knew this and didn't tell me?'

'Only from when your hand activated the door into Andreena's resting place.'

'But it was you that fingered in the code!'

'Only one of Andreena's true kin could have activated that door,' said Petty, loud enough to reveal his thoughts to the whole protectorate.

The Matrefem watched as Karree looked from Hestean to Petty. 'The colour of your blood is the same as Hestean's, and so is the colour of your eyes,' explained the old woman. 'The colour you are wrapped in is irrelevant. It means nothing. It is blood that controls this world. I was watching when you entered this room, Karree Ladener.'

'I don't know this place! I've never been here before.'

'Maybe not, but I saw your subconscious recognise this room when the door opened.'

Karree read the scroll again. Her thoughts blurred. Who was she if she was not Karree Ladener? She stepped forward, aware of everyone's eyes upon her. She knew this room now. Somewhere in her past, she had seen it. All her life, all through her training, her father had tested her. Blueprint after blueprint, and somewhere amongst them all she had seen this room.

Some of the designs he had shown her had never progressed beyond drawings. Because of their outlandishness, the absurdness of their configuration, they had just been jokes, drawings to test a novice loadmaster. But because of them, she knew why some sky-ships flew and others did not. She had always liked these hoaxes—these ships that almost worked. She liked searching for their flaws.

She watched the small machine sucker its way across the ceiling to the far wall, and then down to the floor. It halted for a moment before crossing to the centre of the floor, where it stopped. On a whim, she handed the scroll back to Sathea and walked to stand beside the mechanical creature. 'Do you mind if I join you?' she asked, looking down. 'Have you another job to go to, or are you just thinking that it's time to leave?'

The little machine's bi-optics rotated to look up at her. It moved sideways to give itself a little more space, then went back to its waiting. 'The stairs lead to the same place,' she said, looking across to Petty. 'I'll see you all on the lower level.'

'Not without me, you won't!' said Hestean, darting across to Karree's side just as the section of floor broke free. Two Deserteers jumped down after them, and the little machine's bi-optics rotated once more. Again, it stepped sideways, increasing the distance between itself and their much larger forms. Neither Hestean or Karre looked at each other until Hestean finally said, 'Your friend's cute,'

'A little shy, I think!' said Karree.

'Where are we?'

'In my dreams!'

'And what's that supposed to mean?'

'This is not a *Sands*,' said Karree. 'All ships that are commissioned and built have the postscript "Sands". The *Merysands*, *Aquasands*,

Hindussands, and so on. This is not a *Sands* and yet we stand within it. It is real, it has been built, and I have seen its blueprints. This is the *Lpseofen*, a sky-ship that was also said to be capable of flying under water. It never could have; I worked that out very quickly. Its structure is all wrong. It couldn't even fly through the air. The only way this ship could have ever become airborne is if it had been dropped from a great height. It wouldn't fly, but it would be capable of gliding, and gliding very well.'

'So, you believe my star story, then, do you?'

'Now I do, yes. The word *Lpseofen* was on the blueprints. Only now, since you've started teaching me the Fem language, do I see what it means. It is the same name that came onto the screen outside. There it was stated as "L.P. 7". Remember how I said that my father used to give me tests? The drawings of this ship was one of those tests. He always said that the best way to know what works is to know what doesn't. He used to find all sorts of drawings for me, and the drawings of this ship were some of them.'

'Your father knew of this ship, then?' said Hestean, fully turning to look at her cousin.

'No. To him, they were just drawings. I have no idea where he found the drawings, but he did show me this ship. This is the *Lpseofen*, I'm sure of it. I saw it on one of the tapestries at the Hassis, too.'

'Does your father still have the drawings?'

'I don't know, it was a long time ago. They meant no more to him than any other drawing he showed me.'

The section of floor settled into place on the lower level. Surrounding them in all directions was the same dull red glow as on the upper level. The little machine started to move off in search of its next task. Karree watched it go. 'Take care,' she said. 'We'll see you around again, I expect.'

Like everyone else, the little machines had bothered her when the inner door first opened, but strangely she found they no longer did. Now that she felt she knew this ship, she knew that the machines belonged here, just as she did.

The little machine stopped and twisted its bi-optics to look at them once more. It stared at the wall beside them, then back at Karree. After a moment, it looked back at the wall and shot a thin blue ribbon of light from between its lenses. The beam hit a panel just behind Karree's shoulder. She jumped sideways. Almost immediately, section after section of the roof started to glow with a whiter light until the whole of the lower level was filled with a soft illumination.

'Thank you. I think,' said Karree as the little machine set off again.

'I think it likes you,' said Hestean, almost giggling, half from fright. 'Why aren't men that easy to *wogian*?'

'*Wogian*?'

'Yes, you're the one who taught me Fem. You know, *woo*!'

'Is there someone you want to *wogian*?'

'No. Not here. Not anyone I want to be more than friends with, that is. And how about you? You found me to be your cousin, did that not mean anything to you?'

'We are sisters, Karree! We will always be sisters! No kinship can change that!'

'Sisters?'

'Yes, sisters! From the day we first met, you have been like the sister I never had! Am I forgiven?'

'I'll think about it. I just don't want things to change. As you know, I've only ever had brothers. You, too, have been like the sister I never had!'

'Good. Maybe that's why we're both here, do you think?'

'It's thunder-staffs we're after, isn't it?' said Karree, looking at her newfound sister. 'Upstairs forward is accommodation and control. Aft upstairs and down here is engineering. We are towards the back of the ship, and forward from here is all storage on this level.'

'This is all storage? How big is this ship?'

'Very big, but it shouldn't exist. It is a fiction.'

* * *

'I wonder in which person's mind this fiction was conceived?' said Hestean, looking forward. All she could see were rows and rows of containers stacked two high. Each container was half again as tall as she was, and just as wide. She found herself thinking that a whole family could live in just one of these metal box-like containers. She looked to the ceiling and followed its structure with her eyes into the distance. She knew this was where Karree belonged. Here, she would once more be a loadmaster.

The two women stood in what seemed like a huge warehouse. Hestean knew what Karree was thinking because she was thinking it, too. The LP7 was not just a survival pod against disaster; it was as a life pod for rebirth.

'While I look for thunder-staffs you'll be looking for what you came here to find, won't you?' said Karree.

'But at least you know what you're looking for,' said Hestean, her eyes scanning the abyss. 'I know what I need to find but not how to find it. I don't even know if it exists. It's just an assumption on Dan's part!'

'I would like to meet Dan, some day! In all the time we were at the Hassis, you never introduced us. Is he good looking? The way you talk about him at times, he must be!'

'You're not Comcree, and you do know that Dan is the Danannee, don't you?'

'I know! But it hasn't stopped me from wondering. I've heard they look different.'

'Well, you're right!' said Hestean, smiling at Karree's amorous pondering.

'Surely if he is one of the gods, he wouldn't have sent you if what you are after didn't exist?'

Hestean didn't answer. Karree took in her cousin's sudden stillness and felt a dread. She lifted her hand to the hilt of her dagger, even though she herself felt no real danger.

'They don't look like us, do they …' said Hestean, staring at Karree. 'You said *they*! Why did you say *they*?'

'Is that all?' asked Karree, letting her hand drop to her side again. 'The gods are the gods! The word is a pluralisation.'

'From the mouths of babes,' said Hestean softly. She turned to look in the direction the little machine had taken. 'I'll kill him!' she said. 'God or no god, I'll pull his wafers out one by one. He knew! The control room—you said it was upstairs, didn't you? There will be a descriptor there, a screen. That's why he showed me how to manually use a screen. In case she needed to be woken up.' Hestean turned to see Petty walking towards them with the others trailing behind. 'You took your time. We need to go up again!'

'It was my fault,' said Reglean. 'I'm not as young as I once was.'

'But you're much younger than some!' said Hestean, hopping back onto the floor lift. 'Petty, Jarrak, you're with me. The rest of you—Karree knows what you're to look for. How does this thing work?'

'I don't know,' said Karree.

'But you've seen the blueprints?'

'They were structural, not electrical schematics. It was our little friend who activated the platform, not me!'

'Oh. Then I'll find out how to make it work, too, shall I?'

'That would be good, yes,' said Karree, smiling.

Hestean stepped from the lift and walked briskly towards the stairs with Petty, Jarrak, and Sathea following.

* * *

'You're staying, aren't you?' said Karree to the Matrefem.

'Need my help, still, do you?'

'You seem to see things in me that I don't, so yes, I might!'

'It would be good if I could wait a while before fronting those stairs again, so I will stay. But tell me, why is Hestean in such a rush?'

'Because she doesn't like being misled, and I don't think the gods have been entirely truthful with her.'

'No, they never are,' said the old woman. 'They speak in riddles. I would expect nothing less from them.'

'You'll need the power amplifier also,' called Petty, from above. 'It will probably be a box-like thing with back straps. They won't work without it!'

Karree watched him start to climb again, recognising that for the first time he was no longer telling her what to do, merely how it should be done. There was a difference, and she realised that something had changed between them. It was as if Petty had begun to relinquish his responsibility of the protectorate. She looked around at the men and women looking back at her, and then looked at the Matrefem for confirmation.

'You are capable, Karree Ladener,' said the old woman. 'He would not be giving you his responsibility if you weren't.'

It was a mixture of gratitude and disbelief that swept through Karree. She looked up to reply, but Petty was gone.

46

Hestean stood, searching, her mind absorbing the reality of what she was feeling. Something about the control room was familiar. As in other parts, the room's elongated six walls were lit by a red glow. However, it was more than just the lighting that gleamed back at her. It was something she had seen before. What wasn't she seeing? Standing in the doorway, surrounded by its frame, she could feel this room.

She looked forward to where three walls sloped inwards towards the roof. Their top two thirds were transparent, protected on the outside by a solid opaque shield to hold back the weight of sand, gravel and rock. A picture of the giant mound above flashed into her head.

The ship, if it was a ship, had denoted itself as the *LP7 Sharacan*, but what did that mean? Was this really proof of the story she had told the others? And this feeling, how could she know a room she'd never been in before?

On the side walls, there was a multitude of small lights interwoven between dials, touch switches, and screens. Amongst these were panels that allowed access to whatever was behind them. She found herself wondering about all the secrets this ship might contain. She walked towards a table she presumed to be a mapping desk and fingered its surface. Its tactile form confirmed she wasn't dreaming. She did know this room, and its familiarity was strengthening. In the centre of the room, pointing back at the mapping desk, was a large triangular console. Along each of the two sides facing her sat two plush, upholstered chairs. On top of the console, looking back at the chairs, were four display screens. She moved forward, slowly. This time, when she came to a stop, she was standing at the top of three descending steps running from one side of the room to the other. They separated the room into two levels. On the lower level, directly in front of the console, was a raised section of flooring, which sat at the same height as the middle step. Towards the front of this platform was another console, with two more screens. Facing these screens were two more of the plush chairs, separated by a lower console, which was covered in more touch buttons and dials. Behind these chairs, but in front of the larger central console, was another chair. This chair was much more imposing, with a high back and huge armrests. The ship's captain or commander would sit there, she thought.

She turned back to observe the rear wall. Through the dull redness, she saw a transparent glass screen. Behind it, she could see a great many thin, six-sided wafers, stacked one on top of the other. The wafers were codified into groupings. She knew she'd found what she was looking for—the LP7's knowledge repository. It was like Dan. All she needed now was to find out how to interact with it. 'You are the LP7, yes?' she said.

There was no reply. As she had also suspected, it would not be so simple. The *Sharacan* was going to make her prove herself, as she had been from the day she'd first entered Dan's room. She sighed, and looked across to Petty, Jarrak, and her mother, who were watching her. 'On the wall near you, there should be a pad with a stylised sun on it,' she said. 'Just touching it should change the lighting to something more akin to sunlight.'

Jarrak turned to look, and beside the door's frame he saw a small, soft square, emblazoned with a likeness of the sun. A moment later, the room began to fill with a new glow. 'That wasn't so hard. What now?' he asked.

Hestean wasn't listening. She had begun to study the central console again. Slowly, pacing, her hand brushed across the back of each chair in turn. At each control station, her eyes took in the emptiness of the viewing screens. 'What are you looking for?' asked Petty.

Hestean's hand rose in silence towards the back wall, while her eyes continued to search the console in front of her. 'I need to know how that works,' she said, pointing to where the wafers sat in their racks. A familiar slot caught her eye. She pulled out her blue dagger and slipped it into the thin diamond-shaped hole beside one of the screens. Nothing happened, so she withdrew it. She moved back to the previous screen to try its slot, but again nothing happened. She moved around the console to the other side, and this time, as she plunged her dagger in, the blue stone at the end of its handle flashed. She smiled to herself. She twisted herself into the corresponding seat and said, '*Steorra Plottere, Etanna Descee Sacar, Display.*'

Silence bounced back at her. She turned in the chair, and noticed high up on the wall above the wafers, a tiny red dot. Instantly, she was reminded of Dan. Was it looking back at her? 'I know you can see me,' she said. 'I know you can hear me, so do we have to play this game?' After a long moment, disappointed, she turned back to the display screen. She remembered the tricks that Dan had, so pointedly, shown her. She lifted her index finger to poke at the screen in front of her. 'You are going to make it hard for me, aren't you?' she said, as the screen lit up just as Dan's had done. Her finger started to poke its way around the screen, sliding and dragging across its surface.

'Who is she talking to?' whispered Sathea. 'Is this like your world?'

'No,' said Petty. 'This is far beyond my world!'

'It is hers, though, isn't it?' said Sathea, looking at her daughter's dancing finger.

'It took her just fifteen days to know this world. Nearly every portion of every day she studied, palm after palm, stopping only to sleep. Every day, she was either reading or asking questions of the Danannee, so yes, I think that this is very much her world now.'

Unnoticed, the small red dot moved at Petty's mention of the word Danannee, then refocused back onto Hestean.

'I believe she learned more in those fifteen days than the rest of the Comcree have in many lifetimes of learning. It is her understanding of that knowledge that has brought her here,' said Petty, starting to walk forward.

The red dot recognised his use of another familiar word, and focused harder on Hestean.

'Either the Danannee wanted her to know, or she knew the right questions to ask. Whichever it is, your daughter is the holder of a great many wisdoms.'

'But I don't think she knows it all yet,' said Sathea.

'Not yet, but I think she will,' said Petty, smiling. 'She is, after all, more than just a daughter of Sharacan.'

The red dot recognised a third word.

* * *

Although he was listening to Petty, Jarrak had moved across to Hestean and was observing how naturally she had begun to fit this room. From behind, he watched her finger move around the screen. 'What are you doing?'

'I'm looking for something!'

'I can see that, but how do you know this? There's nothing like this at the Museum!'

She stopped and turned to him. Her young face glowed with amused accomplishment. Since her return to Sharacan, she had become the teacher and he the student. 'This is the world of the Danannee that you see before you,' she said. 'It was the Danannee that showed me this world, and now I need to find the shield controls.'

Suddenly the screen blinked, then blanked out.

Without hesitating, Hestean turned towards the back wall. 'Why did you do that?'

As if hearing her, the screen lit up again. Now, two three-dimensional images appeared beside each other in place of the descriptor she'd been looking at. One was of Hestean, the other of Karree.

'By the gods, will you look at that!' exclaimed Jarrak.

Sathea walked across the room to stand beside him, then lowered herself into the chair beside Hestean's. Petty came to stand behind Sathea. All together, they stared at the screen.

'How does it know what you look like?' asked Sathea. As if knowing they were watching, the images now began to change. The faces of the two young women moved sideways, merging into one another, creating a composite corruption, before changing again into an image of Andreena. The image morphed yet again into many more faces, appearing to track back through time, one face after the other. Then it stabilised as an image of an old woman. They watched as the old woman grew slowly younger, until she seemed to be in her mid-twenties. She had dark skin and brown, sun-bleached hair. The portrait image then broadened to reveal her full-length gown of blue-green fabric. On the screen, three words appeared, identifying her, matching the face to an already known name.

Etanna Descee Sacar.

* * *

'You can see me,' said Hestean, turning to look at the red dot. 'You understand what I am, but you don't fully know *who* I am, do you?' For a considerable time, she wondered about everything that had happened since Karree had first put her hand to the outer wall. 'You don't know whether to relinquish your secrets to me or to Karree, do you? You're confused. Karree has my coding, but I also have Karree's coding, don't I? I should have thought of that, I'm sorry!' She turned to her mother. 'Do you see that glazed red dot on the back wall?'

'Why was I not there?' interrupted Sathea.

'What are you talking about?'

'My image did not appear on the screen!'

Hestean sighed and looked into her mother's eyes. 'She doesn't know you, Mother, that's why! She read Karree's and my coding when we touched the panel outside.'

'Who doesn't know me? Who do you keep talking to?'

Hestean smiled as she remembered the simple world her mother had lived in for her entire life. She looked towards the door they had entered through, checking to see if there was a scanner near it. 'Go put your hand on that square plate beside the door, Mother.'

'Why?'

'Do you want to be introduced, or don't you?' said Hestean, hiding the more complex reason why she wanted the *Sharacan* to know her mother. 'Until she knows you, you won't be able to open any of the doors within *Sharacan*.'

'But I've already opened doors!'

'Where?'

'When we found Andreena!'

The red dot recognised another word. It moved again, sharpening its vision onto Sathea. It was the name that went with the face of the woman who had awakened the *Sharacan*, and then, without explanation, abandoned it to the silence of time. It now realised these people were speaking the same language the woman back then had spoken. Previously though, it had not heard enough of this language to understand it completely. Now, however, with every word spoken, the *LP7 Sharacan* was gradually learning to understand it a little more fully.

'That was outside, Mother,' said Hestean. 'Things are different within the *Sharacan*. You will need the *Sharacan's* approval here! The doors outside are not connected to the doors inside. Out there, they have their own memory.'

'I sense this place too, daughter, but you talk as if it is alive. Sathea got up and walked to the door, where she grudgingly placed her hand upon the panel. The door failed to move at first, and Sathea looked dubious.

'Keep it there, Mother! It may take a little time. It did with me if you recall.'

The red dot watched Hestean's mother across the room. Reading Sathea's palm and noting the similarity of their coding and eyes, it worked out what Hestean had set in motion. A moment passed, and once more Hestean's image appeared upon the screen.

From where she stood, Sathea watched as the image of her daughter slowly changed into an image closely resembling herself. Then, a moment later, the door closed behind her.

'Will we all have to do that?' asked Jarrak.

'If you want her to know you, yes, but don't expect every door to work for you, and not yet either,' replied Hestean, turning to him. 'The *Sharacan* only knew Mother because she has the lineage from Etanna. We are related! The known line of inheritance aboard the *Sharacan* has now increased by one.'

'But there are gaps, aren't there? There must be.'

'Of course there are gaps. Big gaps. She has been asleep for years. I think it was Andreena who woke her. Have you noticed how clean everything is compared with outside? I think the *Sharacan* has been making herself ready. So, Mother,' said Hestean, turning to look at Sathea, 'I have a job for you. That red dot on the back wall, can you talk to it?'

'You want me to talk to a red dot?'

'No, Mother, I want you to *teach* the red dot! Recite all the words you can think of, one by one. Use first the Fem, then repeat it in the modern equivalent, as you did with me when I was little. You will find that she is a much brighter student than I was, though, so it won't take nearly as long.'

'You mean, you want me to teach this red dot to talk?'

'She just doesn't know our modern tongue. You must teach her the language we use now.'

'And just how long should I talk to this dot?'

'She'll let you know, Mother. I could talk to her in the old tongue, but I don't think that's what she wants. I think she would prefer to know what we are all saying. And if I were her, I would want to know what is happening in my world, wouldn't you?'

For a moment Sathea wondered if her daughter was trying to play a joke on her, some perverse trick to make her appear foolish. But the thought soon faded. This was no joke. Hestean's request was genuine. The teaching was something Sathea had already done well once, as her daughter knew from experience. She walked over to the mapping table and faced the back wall. Still feeling a little silly, she plonked herself down on the mapping desk. 'This definitely isn't a joke, is it?' she protested one last time.

Smiling at her mother's caution, Hestean turned to Petty. 'Do you recognise this room?'

'No. Should I?'

'What if it was upside down? Would you know it then?'

Petty twisted his neck as he considered. Hestean went back to playing with the screen.

'I felt it, first, before I actually noticed it,' she said finally. 'If you turned this control room upside down, you would have the skeletal structure of the *Merysands'* control room, don't you think? The *Merysands* had only one central passageway between its control deck and the cargo hold. Here, there are two; one to each side of the back wall. The *Sharacan* is much bigger than the *Merysands,* but they are very much the same. On the other side of the two access doors, there are also rows of rooms that must have housed a great many people, more than just the crew, just as the *Merysands* is now configured to house.'

Having noted the accuracy of what she was saying, Petty knew she would have only pointed it out for a reason. 'So, what is it you want me to do here, daughter?'

She glanced sideways at him, her finger pausing on the screen. 'When I am done here, we will have to see what else is the same, but for now, that table Mother is sitting on—it's a charting table, isn't it?'

'We can soon find out. You want a map of the tunnels, right?'

'Yes, but Mother, perhaps it would be better if you sat in one of those chairs down the front. The *Sharacan* knows what you're doing now. She will be able to hear you from there even at a whisper.'

'You keep saying "she". How do you know it's a "she"?' asked Sathea.

'I don't know for sure, but can't you feel it? You said yourself that you felt this place. She is a she, Mother! Dan has a sister, and I think he will be pleased with that!'

'You mean the Danannee?'

'Yes, Mother, you are talking to one of the gods.'

Sathea slipped from the table, incredulous, standing now beside Petty. 'You didn't know you were in the presence of such greatness, did you?' he joked.

'Very funny. Did you?' she said, walking past him to the forward part of the room. 'Are you sure you still want me to do this, daughter?'

'You will be fine, Mother, You taught me.'

Petty bent to look for the scroll rack, which would be beneath the mapping table on a sky-ship, but then he realised that there wouldn't be one—not a physical one, anyway. 'How does this work?'

'Tap your finger on its top left corner. That should bring it to life,' said Hestean. Petty's finger touched the table's surface, but failed to cause a reaction. Hestean scowled.

'I don't think this sort of equipment likes me,' said Petty.

'I powered it up,' said Hestean. 'You might be on the wrong side.'

Petty shuffled around, and this time the table's upper surface glowed to life, revealing a directory similar to the one Hestean was using. 'I don't understand what this means. It's all written in your old language,' said Petty, running his finger down the indecipherable list.

'Help him, Jarrak, would you? I'm hoping there will be a map of the exterior complex in there somewhere. We'll need to find out as much as we can about the tunnels before we leave.'

'It will work the same as your screen?'

'I think so,' she said, her eyes returning to the one in front of her. 'If you move your finger around the perimeter, the words should come right way up for you.'

Petty touched the screen and saw the image follow his finger. 'I wish sky-ships had mapping tables like this,' he said, leaning forward. Still seeing only a puzzlement of unfathomable mysteries divided off into squares and groupings, he turned to Jarrak. 'Where do we start, my young Maskee?'

Jarrak's knowledge of the old language had improved during his time in the desert, but he still lacked intimacy. He knew his translations would be slow. He moved his finger in the same way he had observed Hestean move hers, then shuffled through folders, the names of which were obscure and strange. Finally, in despair, he hit what looked like the open folder symbol of a map. A three-dimensional star map rose up from the table. Startled, both he and Petty jerked backwards.

'That's not it!' said Hestean, twisting again towards the blur of movement. 'Try another section, a later one.'

Petty and Jarrak were silent. The only three-dimensional images either of them had ever seen before was on Hestean's screen. They stood staring at the vision in front of them. Sathea stopped her recitations and came to look, also, just as mesmerised by the display of tiny lights spotted throughout the cubed image. She poked at one of the small points of light, and a word appeared in the air to float beside the tiny speck. The point of light enlarged, expanding into an entire galaxy of stars.

One of the rear access doors slid silently open, and Karree walked in, helping the Matrefem with one hand and holding a thunder-staff in the other. 'What's that?' she said, her eyes instantly taking in the glittering star map. In the same moment, she glimpsed Hestean look towards her in expectation of her findings. Reluctantly, she drew her eyes away from the illumination. 'I've put a guard at the entrance doors, and two back at the stairs we came down,' she said. 'There's probably no need, but these thunder-staffs won't do us any good because there was no igniter box. We searched everywhere, but found nothing. We did find this, though,' she said, holding up a dagger's scabbard and strapping, still containing its Deserteer blade. 'It was placed across the stack of thunder-staffs. It's the same as the scabbard holding your blue dagger. This is also Andreena's, isn't it?'

Hestean took the scabbard and belt, noticing the plain red Deserteer's dagger it held. She checked the inside of the dagger's sheath to see if it held an inscription, like on the one she wore.

She silently mouthed out the letters, T, AD, W, A, M, L, ESH, recognising what they stood for, then read the words below. *With this, you always hold my love.* She was looking at the same hopes and dreams with which someone had also enchanted the sheath of her Comcree dagger's scabbard. She held it before her, and then handed it back to Karree. 'It's for you!'

'What do you mean, it's for me?'

'It's Andreena's second scabbard.'

'Then it should be yours.'

'I already wear two daggers, and besides, if it was meant for me, I would already have it. Wear it as well as your own. You should swap the daggers around, also.'

'Why?'

'Because your grandfather's dagger is special. It should be kept somewhere special, don't you think? It should go with this Scabbard.'

'Was Andreena once a Deserteer, like you were for a brief time?'

'Sort of, yes,' said Hestean.

The small red dot on the back wall watched the interaction between Hestean and Karree closely. It looked on as Karree reluctantly strapped the scabbard to her waist and swapped the daggers, as her cousin had suggested.

'Why did you do that, daughter?' asked Sathea.

'Do you think I shouldn't have?'

'Oh, I have no objections. It is just that it was the first sign I have seen of you starting to build your future.'

'It is one of a pair, given in love, to one of our family, Mother, I just thought both sides of our family should have reason to remember her, that's all.'

'You are silly, cousin, if you expect us to believe that,' said Karree. 'You are Comcree, you can't help yourself. Your mother is right, and you know it. But you shouldn't worry, you already have me and always will.'

'I know who I am, Karree. I also know who you are. Your grandfather's dagger does need a proper place to rest, and I can think of no better place, can you?'

'So again, I am a cousin. Are you always going to be like this?'

'Probably, but you know you're no cousin, you're my sister. I am as you said—Comcree, but also of Sharacan!'

'Why did I know you were going to say that?'

'Because you are my cousin. But you were first my friend, and then my sister!'

'Oh, stop it, both of you!' said Petty, loudly enough to make every one look. 'Either you accept the fact that you are two halves of the same person, or you accept the fact that you are not! Now,' he said looking at Karree. 'No igniter box, you say. Andreena had to have had one.'

'She must have moved it,' said Hestean.

'Who moved it?' said Karree. 'Andreena's niece or nephew?'

'No,' said Hestean, looking at the red dot.

'Oh!' said Karree. 'You mean the *Sharacan* moved it?'

Hestean pointed to a corner of the control room where, tucked into its resting place, another little maintenance machine sat. 'Remember your little friend? He's not the only one.'

'So, where is it?'

'We will have to wait to find out.'

'Wait for what?'

'Your cousin here thinks this *Sharacan* can talk,' said Sathea.

Karree looked at Sathea, then cautiously returned to Hestean. 'You mean like Dan?'

'What makes you say that?'

'Because in a room where there are two voices, but only one person, it wasn't hard to work out, that's why. But don't worry, I have told no one else who the gods really are.'

'You mean you already knew before I mentioned it downstairs?'

'I'm not stupid, you know!'

Reglean began to chuckle. Hestean turned to her, and then looked back to Petty. 'Don't look at me, I didn't know she knew! I hadn't even realised the truth myself until you had your mother talk to the machine here. I was told it might be a good idea to permanently assign Karree to you at the Hassis, so I did.'

'Who told you to?'

'It was Whittn who suggested it.'

Hestean turning again to Reglean. 'How much do the Matrefems really know?'

'We only know what we see, child. That is all.'

'I was told once that the Matrefems are the keepers of this world, and that the gods are the seers.'

'Yes, we keep the secrets of this world. This Whittn is a Matrefem, I presume? She saw in you and Karree, as I have, an ability that will allow you to understand far more than people have ever done before. As well as keeping secrets, like you, we also keep this world heading to where it ultimately must go.'

'So where is that?'

'That is something that everyone must find out for themselves!'

'The gods are more than just machines,' said Hestean. 'They are our heritage. This one here has the knowledge to tell us who we are. Dan, I suspect, only knows where we come from. Only together will they also know where we are to go.'

47

'Who is Dan?' asked a soft, feminine monotone, catching even Hestean unawares.

'You can talk!' she exclaimed, turning with the others towards the red dot.

'I have always been able to talk. You reasoned that correctly! I have also always been able to hear. I have heard everything that has been said since you came aboard. As you rightly stated, it was the language you speak that I couldn't understand.'

'So, you understand us now?'

'Not completely, but it is sufficient to start with. I thank Mother for the words. Her recitation was of great assistance.'

'You're welcome,' said Sathea, stunned and delighted that the voice in the air was not only talking to her, but also settling praise upon her. 'My name is not Mother, however—it is Sathea. "Mother" is just a title; a descriptor. I am Hestean's mother, as she is my daughter.'

There was a moment of silence before more words came forth, filling the air around them yet again. 'I am sorrowful for the mistake, Mother Sathea. Until now, I have only heard you referred to as "Mother". I will not make this mistake again!'

'May I know your name?' asked Sathea, warming to the voice.

Another silence made Sathea wonder if she had asked an inappropriate question. Just as she was about to apologise, the voice spoke again. 'I am the Seventh Life Pod of the long-haul starship *Sharacan*. Therefore, I am the *LP7 Sharacan*.'

A new yet ancient world flared through everyone's minds just as it had when Hestean had told her story outside. No one spoke as the reality of Hestean's ancient story again flashed through them. Then, almost automatically, Sathea raised her hand to her forehead, then to her mouth, and then to her heart. 'I am pleased to make your acquaintance and finally to know of you, LP7,' she said with all the dignity she could.

* * *

Hearing her mother, Hestean also freed her mind to speak. 'I am—'

'I know who you are, Hestean of the Comcree! What I would like to know is—where is the one who woke me and left me to my solitude? Where is the Comcree Andreena?'

From within the abrupt words, Hestean thought she heard anguish in the absence of knowing and frustration at being left alone. She rearranged her thoughts. 'Andreena died protecting you. She died keeping you safe from those who would harm you. The whole of her protectorate were killed keeping you safe.'

'Not all.'

'You mean the child?'

'I mean the children.'

'They were young, they did not know you were alive. They only knew you had to be kept safe and secret. Andreena's last instructions were that you were to be protected. This, they did. You cannot blame them for what they did not know. Until now, no one knew of you, except for Dan. Until recently, even he didn't know how to find you. It was only when he met me that he was given the clue as to how you might be found.'

'But that does not answer my question. I asked where the Comcree Andreena is!'

'She lies in one of the tunnels surrounding you.'

'No, she does not! You need to listen, Hestean of the Comcree. Andreena stands before me in two halves. In each consecutive generation there is a difference. But between you and your cousin, that difference is but a fraction, and from Andreena that fraction is divided equally. You are both as close to her as the other. Through your daggers, you have been given different tasks, but you are the same. You should both honour those tasks, for it was the daggers that decided your roles. Within you both, there is also Etanna Descee Sacar, who was one of the six who built this world. Now, do you understand what I have said, Hestean Descee Sacar, and Karree Ladener Sacar?'

'If they don't, I think they soon will,' said Reglean, wearing a smile of satisfaction.

'You are the Matrefem at the temple of Sharacan, yes?' said the LP7. 'That also has a lineage, and one I must see how much you truly understand. But we will talk of that later, in private, I think. Now, though, I asked who Dan was?'

'Dan—Dan is the Danannee. Dan is your brother,' said Hestean.

'Then he is who I thought he was, but why did it take him a millennium to find me?'

'Andreena also woke him from a period of sleep. He sent me to find you, and to turn off the shield that hides you from him. He wants to know you, and I think he has been lonely without you. He knows it's time for you both to rebuild your people, and this world!'

'Why did he not come himself?'

'You know why!'

'Yes, but I want to see if *you* know why.'

'He is like you! He cannot move from his place. That is why he sent me. Through me, he will be able to see you, and you him. Through all the eyes of the Comcree, you have an ability to see.'

'No. The reason why he did not come is because you are your own gods. Did he not tell you this? Were you not listening? It is you who conceived of us, and it is you who constructed us. It is your knowledge and your memories we hold.'

The weight of understanding filled Hestean's mind. She did know this. 'He is a scoundrel, your brother,' she said. 'He once said something very similar. He likes to implement many plans without explaining everything to those who partake.'

Just as she had sometimes felt Dan in her mind, Hestean now felt the LP7 sifting through hers to make sense of it all. Finally, the great ship spoke again. 'From what did he keep me safe?' asked the LP7. 'Whom have I offended?'

'The offence is not yours. There are those who would have your knowledge for themselves. They seek to enslave this entire world, just as they have my people.'

'Then they have found us!'

'No!' said Hestean. She instinctively knew that the LP7 was speaking of an ancient and distant foe. 'The Black Robes of the College have only come to control this central swathe of Meglia in the last two hundred years. They grew out of a city to the south called Learnian …' Patiently, Hestean told the LP7 the whole story.

By the time she finished, the LP7 had managed to process every piece of information. Hestean's story reaffirmed the timeless bond between the guardians and the guarded. This bond had been shattered before on purpose, but would it need to be shattered again? The LP7 knew she would have to wait and see. 'Are you finished child?' it asked. 'You have managed to do what the ancestors of your ancestors were not able to do. You have devised a way of standing together against tyranny. We must ensure that structure is maintained. If not, you will fragment again, as they did, and leave room for those who would tear you apart. I think you have been lucky this time, but it may not always be that way. Your time in this world is a test that only time will resolve.'

Since her banishment, Hestean had thought herself the controller of her own life. Now, she realised that she had never been in control. She had come up against Dan's older sister and felt wholly intimidated by the entity that surrounded her. Here was another being that would always know more about this world than she ever could—particularly about the ancient history that had shaped their very existence.

'Lucky?' she said. 'You say we have been lucky?'

'Yes! Here, the freedoms of your world still have a chance to exist and thrive. You have a task to do, it would seem. So do it, Hestean of the Comcree. There will be time for your chatter later. I will look forward to that, as my brother says you are a most learned scholar for your age.'

'Your brother! You mean you've spoken to Dan?'

'I myself control the shield you were seeking. I turned it off some time ago. It was the cloak's parameters you were looking for within my files, was it not?'

Reglean looked amused, as did Petty and Sathea. Hestean knew she had been bested. Clearly here, she had once again become the student. 'You have spoken with Dan, then?' she said. 'I haven't heard from him!'

'You will never hear all that I say, Hat. You know that!' said a familiar voice in her ear. It had been absent for only a few days, but yet it seemed to have been an eternity. 'I had family to catch up with, as you know only too well.'

'Yes,' said Hestean, smiling, knowing that Dan was again close to her. 'Can I now talk to the rest of the Comcree, too?'

'You could, but I would suggest not. For the moment, it would be better if this place remains hidden. You have not taken back the village of Sharacan yet, and you need to.'

The LP7 could sense the bond that existed between her brother and this Comcree. Although Hestean was young, the LP7 knew that her brother had indeed sent his most entrusted guide to seek out the past and to start building the future.

48

In her mind, Hestean was aware of Dan as she had never been in the past. Two hundred years before Hestean had entered his existence, it had been Andreena who had raced into his vision. He remembered how she had always been in a hurry. He recalled all his memories of her right through to the very last time, when she had faded from his sight, defiant and resolute, as she approached Sharacan.

He let his recollections fade, knowing that Andreena would never really be gone from him as long as he remembered her. And now there was Hestean, who would never allow him to forget. There was a sadness in him, and Hestean could feel it too. Hestean herself had told him what had befallen Andree. Until this moment, it had never occurred to her that a machine could feel a true sense of loss.

Aside from his mourning, Dan had been telling the LP7 about the recent history of their world. Occasionally, when their conversation slowed, Hestean caught mental glimpses of the things they were sharing. Were they aware that she was seeing everything, too?

Both these machines knew the true meaning of loss, it seemed. Maybe they weren't true deities, as most of the world believed, but nor were they just machines. In every sense of the word, though, they were the true guardians, having watched over and guided the world's timeline.

The waiting began to feel like delay, and Hestean began to slowly pace around the control room. She looked towards the red dot as Karree asked, 'They're still talking, then?'

'Four thousand years takes a lot of catching up on, it seems,' said Hestean.'Surely they don't need to know it all right now? I need to understand these tunnels. We don't know what the Black Robes will hurl against us in the days to come. I need to guard my protectorate and the others who will defend Sharacan—both the ship and the village above. This is what the Comcree are for! To protect our heritage. Dan wouldn't forgive me if I fail!'

The static in Hestean's head stopped, and a thick heavy stillness filled it. The abrupt silence from the machines caught her off-guard, and she felt suddenly like a child in a room full of adults, having said something completely silly.

'I think you are right, brother,' said the LP7. 'They are similar, right down to the two daggers they wear. Even their impatience. It is a pity I did not get to know Andreena properly before she died. I will now have to content myself with getting to know only this one.' Hestean knew that the LP7 had spoken aloud so that everyone would hear the chastisement.

'She is young!' said Dan, also aloud, through the LP7's sound disseminator.

'Yes, but she has learned a great deal, brother, and she should know better. Reglean made a good choice with her, though. We will eventually come to an understanding, this Comcree and I.'

* * *

Karree couldn't help but chuckle to herself. Petty and Sathea looked towards each other and thought of doing the same thing. In this moment, just a wisp of a smile crossed Reglean's lips.

The LP7's eye adjusted towards Karree. 'Do not think I will allow you to stand apart from your cousin, loadmaster. I shall want to know you better, too. You may be your cousin's protector, but you are now also my loadmaster as she is my navigator. Your daggers have declared you to be so. You are both now my eyes and ears.'

Karree's chuckle ceased, and she eyed the machine. 'But I have no earpiece,' she said.

'Within my walls, I can always see and hear you. In the tunnels, I can hear you, too!'

'Oh, by the gods!' said Karree, turning towards Hestean. 'At least you get to hear what they're saying.'

'Don't wish for what you may get one day,' said Hestean.

Petty and Sathea exchanged glances again, while Reglean simply nodded approvingly.

While the machines went back to conversing, Karree came to stand next to Hestean. Her eyes danced around the room, seeing it differently.

She still held the thunder-staff in her hand. She rested its end on the floor while she surveyed the room. Hestean seated herself, and her finger began to stroke and poke once more at the screen in front of her. Karree looked down at her cousin and said, 'So, does that mean there is going to be a place for me here?'

'Not here,' said Hestean, looking up.

'Oh?' said Karree, clearly disappointed.

Hestean looked around to see where the others were in the room, then turned back to her cousin. 'This is only the flight control centre. There are other control stations,' she said softly. 'The two seats down front are helm control. The first and second flight controllers sat there. Behind them, in the bigger chair, sat the person who commanded the ship. When they were here, that is. On this side of this central console sat the communications engineer, and then, where I am, the ship's navigator. On the other side of the console sat an atmosphere and integrity monitor—a sort of life support engineer. And then, beside him, opposite me, was the ship's engine and mechanical engineer. It seems, cousin, that this ship that never flew was nevertheless set up to fly.'

'But it couldn't. Its structure is all wrong. It's too heavy, and the buoyancy tanks are all at the back, above the engines.'

'Too heavy when made out of what?' said Hestean, bringing an image onto the screen. 'Are these the blueprints your father showed you?'

'They look the same! They could be. It was a long time ago now, though.'

'And these are what you took to be flotation tanks?'

'Yes.'

'Here, they call them atmospheric regeneration tanks. They make the air you breathe re-breathable. They are not buoyancy tanks at all.'

Karree turned to see where the others were. Petty and Jarrak were talking near the doorway, and a little further along, almost in front of the LP7's eye, Sathea and Reglean were involved in their own conversation. She looked back at Hestean. 'Why are we whispering?'

'Because I'm not sure how much of this is to be widely known. Not until Dan and the LP7 tell me. The more that is known, the more that can be taken by the Robes if they ever find this place. But to answer your first question, see here, back further in the ship.' Hestean's finger ran across the screen, making it scroll sideways. More descriptions and names appeared wherever her finger stopped. 'See here; the ship's loadmaster had a station at the back. These words translate as "loading and logistics", and there are three divisions: *Hladen, Amenden,* and *Haelan*. The crew and passengers' wellbeing was obviously of equal value to that of the ship's wellbeing. But it means that there might be two more Deserteer daggers that behave like yours.'

'What are you getting at?'

'It fits, don't you see? The Deserteers have always looked after the logistics of this world, and the Comcree have always looked to its overall safety. One external, and the other internal, just as was the case here, millennia ago.'

'Aren't you forgetting that there are seven chairs in this room?'

'No. In loading and logistics there are four chairs, but only three designations. And over here, in this room on its own, there is another chair—and here, in this bigger room, another. These are command chairs. The commander was not just situated in flight control. He or she moved throughout the ship. There are seven chairs in Dan's room at the Hassis, also, but there is one position that has no dagger slot. One of the chairs here in flight control has no dagger slot, either. It has a place for something different.'

'You mean on the command chair!'

'You noticed it, too?'

'Cousins, remember? On the left armrest is a place for the Matrefem's talisman.'

'Exactly! It is the place where the guide of guides would sit!'

'But who is our guide? Is it Reglean, or Whittn? Or one of the other Matrefems?'

* * *

'The one that is supposed to hold the key already does,' said the LP7 aloud, bringing Hestean's and Karree's conversation to a sudden halt.

'The talisman, you mean,' said Hestean and Karree almost in unison.

'Yes. When she dies, as you all do eventually, the Matrefems hold council to select someone to take her place. It will, however, not be from within their own ranks, but from outside their circle, as it was done long ago. A commander is not just someone who wants to command, but who has the ability. This is something every Matrefem already knows, for it is how they themselves were chosen. My first commander made an important decision to strip away her own power, becoming just a guide to those below her. It ensured that no one person can ever control the future. The wisdom required of her will change as you regain the knowledge you have lost. For now, Matrefem Reglean holds the key to that chair. I think there will be no one better suited.'

'Suited for what?' said Reglean.

'Suited to do what you have always done, but on a much larger scale. It is an advantage that you have already selected your replacement.'

'How do you know that?'

'At one time, I was able to control the tunnels beyond my wall, but the connection had faded sometime before the Comcree Andreena woke me. However, I can still hear what is being said out there, and now that I can translate your words, I understand what you were saying before you entered my doors. I remember everything. Your replacement already knows more than most, or you would not have chosen her. It is not just the Comcree and loadmaster I have been listening to; I also agree with Dan's selection of Petty and Jarrak.'

'What do you mean, selection?' said Jarrak, stepping towards the LP7's eye.

'You are young, Maskee Jarrak, and an unknown in your field, yet you have helped to make possible the reforming of this world's heart. Do you think that was by chance?'

'It was merit that gave me my appointment.'

'Yes, it was. But my brother has been watching this world for a long time, waiting for the pieces to come together. Two hundred years ago, your world came close to this moment, but you were not ready then. I have witnessed Hestean and Karree starting to understand this world on their own. The ones you call the College are not your only enemy. When this world starts to shine again, there will be those among the stars who will see you. They will know you have survived. It is why, from this moment forward, you must step gently into your future. You must take care not to be seen as you again become the people you once were.'

'So, who were we?' asked Sathea.

'You were people who cared! And for the most part, that is still who you are, thanks to the Comcree. There is a blight amongst you, though, and you must first be capable of dismantling this College before you can dismantle its like elsewhere. Back then, you failed to see what needed to be done before it was too late. Some of you came to believe too much in yourselves. You must learn to recognise this in infancy and hold it in check before you can once again become who you were. Unless you can do this, you will be destined to repeat the same mistake you once made.'

'Do you think so?' said Petty, coming to stand by Sathea. He took hold of her hand.

'That is what is about to be proved in the coming conflict, is it not? There are two sides, Mister Petty, but only one destiny will be allowed to spread forth from this world. This is what the first Comcree programmed us to do. If there is a chance of failure, then we will simply start again, as we have in the past.'

'You've told others this before, then?' said Hestean.

'No, we have not! There has never been the opportunity before.'

'So, what really happened with Andreena?'

'What really happened is just what you saw revealed before you, Hestean of the Comcree. The only ones I could save from that skirmish were the two children. The future. You thought I was angry with the children, but I wasn't. As you said, they were too young to fully understand that it was I who saved them. All I wanted to know was that they had survived after leaving my control. It seems to me now that they succeeded, as you stand before me. And now maybe my brother and I can proceed further, also. To do that, I need to know something. The obelisk still stands, doesn't it?'

49

‘Within all my memories, the tip of the obelisk has never glowed,’ said Sathea. ‘It gleams, it reflects, but it does not glow, as you say it should. It never has, as far as I know!’

‘But it must,’ said the LP7. ‘To power this world, it must! Unshielded, to hide this world, it must.’

‘As far back as my stories take us,’ said Reglean, ‘the obelisk has never emitted its own light. It has never glowed as a lantern in the night!’

‘Could it not have just been switched off?’ asked Sathea.

‘The obelisk is its own energy creator. It takes in light energy from the sun, changes it, then releases it back in a form it can use.’

‘Then it is broken?’

‘Not necessarily,’ said the LP7. ‘You said it gleams and reflects? It should not do that. Shine, yes, but not reflect. Does all of its pinnacle reflect?’

‘No,’ said Hestean, with absolute certainty. ‘There is a section that doesn’t.’

‘Then I think it has been sheathed—coated so that some sections cannot draw in the sun. Parts of it have been starved and allowed to run down. With my shield running, it hasn’t been needed, but it will be. The unsheathed section is where my energy comes from.’

‘Then it can be fixed?’ asked Karree.

‘In time,’ said Hestean.

‘The well still exists, though, does it not?’ asked the LP7.

‘Yes, it has always provided what we need,’ said Reglean.

‘Then all has not completely stopped!’ said the LP7, with a modicum of relief. The machine’s eye focused onto Hestean. ‘The obelisk alone would have given your thunder staffs life. Its glowing tip would have replaced any need for the igniter box you correctly assumed I moved. It would also have alleviated the need for the devices you house within your sky-ships. Hearing what your matrefem has been taught about the separation of the hidden, I am now wondering if the child thought it unnecessary to adhere to such practices within my walls. But such precautions are always advisable, guardian, do not forget that. That is why I moved the device. You can never be too safe.'

Hestean's thoughts wandered. It was clear that both these machines had been asleep for at least some of the time since her ancestors had arrived on this world. How much had they missed, and what unknowns still lay undiscovered at the Hassis library? 'We'll still need the igniter box, then,' she said. 'Can you show Petty and Jarrak where to find it?'

'The loadmaster can do that,' said the LP7. 'Your Maskee is an archaeologist, but he also knows architecture. I think he and Mister Petty, as well as some of your protectorate, should scout out the underground tunnels and discover their state of repair. I can hear beyond my walls, but I cannot see. From sound, I can paint a picture. As you stated earlier, it will be necessary to know these tunnels. Over the last two hundred years, I have been able to repair and rebuild myself, but the state of the tunnels and what lies within them is beyond me.'

'Shouldn't I go? That way, you could really see for yourselves the state of things,' said Hestean.

'That will not be necessary. I know these tunnels. All the protectorate will have to do is describe what they see as they journey through them. I will know if anything needs to be done. Their words will echo into any fault or flaw. I need to get to know your protectorate as well as you do! I need to know how they think, respond, and react. Besides, you and my brother need to talk with the other Comcree.'

* * *

The regeneration tanks, on the uppermost level in the rear engineering section of the LP7, were where Karree had been told she would find the igniter box. But what she found in the tanks first, was a vast, yet contained, forest, filled with plants the like of which she had never seen. She wondered if this had been the cause of the LP7's concern for the well-ponds.

'You need not have worried about your garden,' she said, when she returned to the control room. 'In places, we had to cut our way through! If there is a safer place in which you have hidden something else, then please don't send me to find it. I already have enough cuts and bruises to recover from.'

'Your igniter box will need charging before it can be used,' said the LP7. 'Do you have a minder of machinery amongst you?'

'We have a couple, yes. They were engineers aboard the *Merysands*.'

'Then bring them here so I can read their coding. Take one with you to my power rooms, but on the bottom level of where you have just been. They will not be able to do anything without my permission.'

'I know where to take them,' said Karree. 'I've known your form since I was a child, and the more I walk your corridors, the more I remember.'

* * *

'You chose both of them well,' said the LP7, inaudibly, after Karree had gone.

'They chose themselves,' replied Dan. 'All I had to do was get them together.'

'Yes, I felt the strength of their blood when both of them first touched my outer shell. Do either of them know what it really signifies?'

'Andreena suspected, although she never asked for confirmation. She is the only Comcree I know of who has ever read all the books. I believe it's part of why she fought so bravely to protect you, this place, and the two children.'

'Do you think Hestean will come to know?'

'If you are asking me whether she will come to know the truth of her unique heritage, then I think so. Together, they hold the strength to perceive further than any have before.'

'Might it become a problem?'

'If it does, then we can simply start again with that, too. In each generation, remember, it is the daggers that confirm succession, not a person's parentage.'

'Etanna had worked it out before she died,' said the LP7. 'She had always wondered why the commander had been so insistent that she should produce her own family when there were already so many colonists to look after.'

'No doubt that's why she was chosen. Her heritage may have been hidden from her, but the blood link that defined her was strong.'

'She was the eldest surviving daughter of the eldest surviving daughter. Hestean is the progression from that lineage. Etanna was the last of her generation to die, but before she did, she made sure this world and her descendants would survive. We must maintain that assurance.'

'But Hestean has no sisters.'

'Blood always finds a way. That is why there are two of them. Karree is maybe from the second child, but she is equally of blood. So, if it becomes necessary, we can backtrack as we have before, brother! Never forget, it is Hestean's dagger that holds this secret. The moment it is used beyond this world, it will be recognised. I have no doubt that the usurper's bloodline still exists amongst the stars, so we must be absolute in our diligence. The obelisk will need to be mended.'

* * *

It was well into the night when Hestean finally came to her bed. She stretched out quietly beside Jarrak, knowing sleep was beyond her. She lay there, watching him. She studied his face and took in the smell of him as he slept. It was only the third night since she had returned, but already it seemed a lifetime.

Earlier, she had spoken to Gorean and the rest of the Comcree, to let them know that the shield had been disabled and to confirm that her Comcree sister still intended to surround the village before morning. She found they'd already done so, concealing themselves silently within the sand and rocks to await dawn. The *Merysands* and the *Aquasands* had also settled for the night, as planned, tethered to the desert floor just beyond sight of the village.

Now, as she looked around the cabin that had once been assigned to her ancestor Etanna, she found herself wondering what those early days must have been like. She thought of the disorder and chaos that must have existed when they'd found themselves on a world they knew nothing about. She thought of the need for a leading authority, and the ways that the crew of this surviving life-pod must have established that authority. When tomorrow was over, she knew she would have to tell the hexagon all she had discovered about Sharacan and their shared history. But for the moment, she had managed to keep most of what she had discovered to herself. She resented the burden. She knew that if something went wrong tomorrow, then the fewer people who knew about this hidden part of their history, the easier it would be to hide again.

Everyone was asleep except her. Getting up, she walked slowly back into the *Sharacan's* command centre. She wanted to talk to the ancient machine alone, so she switched off her earpiece and sat in the command chair. She felt its form, its arm rests, and knew that it had not been made for her. If anyone, it was Reglean who would sit here until the next commander took her place.

Her mind replayed the story she had read in the library at the Hassis. She saw the commander of the *Sharacan*, crippled and incapacitated; the six members of the flight crew struggling to salvage control of their broken craft while it plummeted through the atmosphere of this world. It must have appeared as a gift retrieved from the very end of their existence—a chance at survival when there should have been only death.

From that time, the commander, unable to fully perform her duties, had become the first of the matrefems. She had become the respected adviser to the six members of the flight crew. It was these six who would become the first command crew; the Comcree. They were who the commander had advised to take up command in her stead, and who had engineered their people's survival. It was this flight crew that had saved the refugees on board the damaged life-pod. It was these first Comcree who had conceived the plan to hide and survive; to build a life for themselves within the confines of this unknown world.

'It was you who showed Petty and Jarrak that star map earlier today, wasn't it?' said Hestean softly to the *LP7 Sharacan*.

'Yes. I had to distract them somehow. There are some things that still need to be kept quiet. If too many learn of the world beyond before we are ready, then it could do more harm than good.'

'The map, though … It is of where we're from, isn't it?'

'What makes you think that?'

'On the floor of the temple, there is an engraved cluster of stars, and I saw that same cluster in that star map.'

'That is very insightful of you.'

'Can you show me this origin world, as it is now?'

'No. Not as it is now.'

'I just wondered,' said Hestean, getting to her feet. She walked back to stand in front of the *LP7*'s eye. 'To know what the original College was like, would have been interesting. They are who you were fleeing from, isn't it?'

'A form of them, yes. They were called the Goddeen, for that is what they wanted everyone to believe they were.'

'Did you know you had brought them with you?'

'I don't believe we did. As you yourself said, the terms "Black Robe" and "College" are familiar only in concept. They are different here, and not as tightly formed. Here, you still have the ability to defeat them before they do too much damage.'

'You are your brother's sister, you know!'

'How do you mean?' asked the *LP7*.

'He also makes sure I know what I am asking.'

'Perhaps, but we are not the same. We were conceived for different purposes.'

'What purposes?'

'I see my brother has taught you well. Will I get to call you Hat, too, one day?'

'Maybe,' said Hestean, a slight smile on her lips. 'Only if I get to call you "Shara".'

'Why?'

'Because the Danannee is Dan, and *LP7* is so formal. Because Shara is a woman's name, and because it was the name given to the first Deserteer sky-ships. Also, because it is you, I think. You have become yourself. You are no longer just *Life-Pod 7*. You are more than that to me, and to us all. I think in the past, someone referred to you as Shara, and because of that, the name has persisted.'

'Shara,' said the *LP7* thoughtfully. 'I will think on it.'

There was a silence for a while and then Hestean said, 'It was because of my inquisitiveness that I almost died, even before I knew of your brother.'

'It is one thing to be inquisitive, and another to question. My brother was designed to be terrestrial; I was not! One day, I will leave this world, but we will still be brother and sister. We will still be able to communicate.'

'It would save lives if you could tell me what the College here has been doing throughout this last cycling of the moons. Are they aware it is Sharacan we seek? If so, are they rallying to rebuff us?'

'To save lives is what I am here for! My brother has told me of your Shadow Shire, and the spread of its many eyes. Through them, we know there will be no complications here. It will be at Learnian that lives may be lost.'

'I know it will eventually be necessary, but I am not ready for conflict.'

'No one should ever want conflict, child. When it comes, though, you will need to know how to deal with it.'

'I know that, I do. But why did it have to come to this world now, in my lifetime?'

'Conflict never happens when there is a choice. It happens because it is necessary, and there is no choice. It may not seem so, because sometimes the wrong side wins. But it is still necessary to at least try. Eventually, people see what you were trying to show them. It may take time and many generations, but the flowering eventually happens. This is the time for me to be awake and useful again. From what my brother has told me, you have managed to build a society that is worth preserving. I do not think you will have to flee from your foe, as your ancestors did from theirs millennia ago. It would seem that your hexagon has been successful with their deceptions. But know this, child, you will eventually have to vanquish this College completely. There is no alternative. You cannot allow it to simmer, fester, and burst forth again as it did to your ancestors on their many worlds. This College may be juvenile in its form, but juveniles eventually grow up.'

'Yes,' said Hestean, her mind churning.

'Karree?' she said, after a long silence.

'I was wondering when you would come to her,' said the *LP7*.

'And?' said Hestean.

'And your Mister Petty is quite clever, but he is wrong in one respect. The children were both female. Karree is directly linked along the female line, just as you are.'

'Karree has a younger sister!'

'Yes, she does. But from the point of divergence, you and Karree are both the eldest female child of the eldest female child.'

'But at the point of divergence, I am from the older sister?'

'Yes.'

'Then I carry the burden?'

'What burden?'

'The crown?'

'Ah,' said the *LP7*.

'Cwens,' said Hestean. 'My mother has spoken of cwens.'

'So, she knows, too, does she?'

'No. To her, it is just a story, but I have read the books.'

'Ah,' said the *LP7* again.

'It was Etanna the Goddeen were after, wasn't it?'

'Yes. She was the only daughter of a third daughter, who was the only survivor of the royal female line. She was so distant in the lineage of succession as to become almost insignificant. After we came to this world, she was scanning through my memory wafers when she found an anomaly that had been transferred just before I disengaged from my mother-ship. It proved that the explosion that destroyed the long-Haul starship, the *Sharacan*, was no accident. It also showed that the explosion was probably meant for her. To destroy just one member of a bloodline, the Goddeen were prepared to destroy thousands. It was only by chance that a rogue asteroid had taken her from her bed that night and into the control room. She found safety because of that, but the ship was destroyed and thousands died. It wasn't until after I broke from my mother-ship that Etanna's dagger was slotted into my console. Unless they find me, they will have no idea she survived.'

'So that's why you were buried, hidden under the mound?'

'Yes!'

'And the mound was made to look as if it were part of an ancient religious complex?'

'That is how and why I was hidden, yes. You are a *cwen*, Hestean Descee Sacar. Your bloodline is the only one strong enough to unite the worlds and bring down the Goddeen.'

'You didn't have to tell me all this, did you?'

'No, but your people are about ready to reach for the stars again, and you need to know why it has to be done gently. You will also see now why Karree is necessary too. We need a closer alternative, this time. You have no apprentice, and she will be well hidden by the red dagger she holds. And to answer the question you have yet to ask—the answer is yes. Although the matrefems choose blindly, your blood will always be where it needs to be.'

Finally, Hestean felt tired. She yawned as she said, 'We will have to be finding our way back to the surface soon.'

'Then rest, and I will wake you in time to show you a way out, which will better hide your approach to your village. It is your village, isn't it?'

'Yes,' said Hestean, as her eyes closed. 'Yes, it is.'

50

The morning approached and Hestean, with her full protectorate, surfaced through an outcrop of rocks that overlooked the village, and the fields her father had once tended. It had taken some time to unblock this exit, and they now lay in wait for dawn along with the other Comcree contingents. Exhausted from the ordeal, and having had only a palm's length of sleep, she was relieved that all they needed to do for a while was sit.

Just before the great ball of fire crested the horizon, they watched as the two sky-ships rose in the east—silhouetted against the pre-dawn light—and began to approach the unsuspecting settlement. She saw the ships overfly the village, their shadows flowing across the houses and buildings, heralding the return of the Comcree to her homeland.

Before the Black Robes had a chance to fully gather an understanding, the sky-ships fired their grapplers and hauled themselves to the ground just beyond the western edge of the village. She heard the first cries of indignation waft up as the Robes began forcing the village men from their houses, pressing them to arms, taking the women and children as hostages.

Still hidden, Hestean watched as a Robe led the village Council towards the two sky-ships, in order to question their arrival.

'What do you want of us, Deserteers?' Gaywin said, his voice confirming his identity. As planned, Batteen was the first to walk forward. Then Heggon and Deleev came to stand with her. The Robes watched as the ships continued to disgorge their overwhelming advantage.

* * *

In these moments, all Gaywin saw as his black robes flapped in the breeze were his own plans for this village disintegrating. He saw Batteen's female form as a personal insult, but at the same time, saw that she was not just a Deserteer. His eyes scanned the squadron, still fanning out behind her. When his eyes returned to her, they were filled with an even greater outrage. The woman who stood in front of him was one of those who had led the Alliance two hundred years before, when his ancestor had deserted.

* * *

Even from this distance, it was clear to Hestean that their unexpected arrival had more than unsettled these Robes, and that no advance word of the Comcree's rebirth had reached them. Learnian was truly obsessed with itself.

The rest of the Council stepped up behind Gaywin, and behind them were the pressed village men, sectioned and held firm by lower-ranked Robes. Within the village, Hestean saw the women and children, who had been rounded-up by even more of the Robes and held captive. She took in the faces of these women and children, sheltering amongst the buildings as they gazed in awe at the two great ships disgorging their red-and-blue army. The Robes had made a mistake here, though. Gaywin had still not learned the truth of Sharacan. She watched as the women began to stealthily rearrange themselves. She saw an awakening. All they'd needed was to be primed. Sharacan had always belonged to the Sharacanese.

* * *

Batteen, Heggon, and Deleev remained silent as their squadron continued to spread out behind them. They knew they did not have to speak. The manner of their presence was enough to announce their meaning, and hopefully to devastate their opponent.

'What do you want of us?' demanded Gaywin. 'What do you want of this place? The lines of division state this place as ours, not yours.' For the first time in her life, Batteen became aware of the true disdain the College felt towards women. It radiated from this man. Her hand lifted to her dagger, and Deleev put his own hand forward to restrain her. 'Remember, there is an invocation to address here,' he said quietly. 'A cleansing—and it is not for us to invoke. Leave it to her. You know she's watching.'

* * *

The arrival of the sky-ships had successfully achieved their purpose. The Black Robes had hurried to repel them, but now stood just as implacably in defence. The two groups faced each other. Although the Black Robes were clearly in the minority, their resolve was nevertheless potent against the amassing Comcree force.

Seeing this, and finally sensing the moment to be right, Hestean rose and climbed casually down towards the opposing forces. She knew the diversion created by the sky-ships still hid her from the College's gaze. Stepping out onto the sand, she walked steadily towards the confrontation. Some of the women in the village noticed her first, her dark complexion declaring her as Sharacanese. This was all they needed.

It was only when she spoke that the Black Robes turned to look at her. Her Sharacanese dialect, coming from a young woman dressed in the garb of a Comcree warrior, was unexpected. 'We want nothing from your College. Not here, anyway. We want to take back what is ours by birth,' she announced. She saw recognition in some of their faces now. 'You can keep your remnant, but it will be us who decide your fate. It was you who banished me from my village, and so you initiated your own downfall, Gaywin. You released me into the unknown, and from this place I will now banish you. Those who want release from your binding will have our protection, and if any are harmed for doing so, then I can promise you this: you and all of your kind will forfeit your entire existence in this world.'

Everyone knew who she was now. They saw her mother, the matrefem, and the young man from the diggings walking with her. They saw a small group of Deserteers, trimmed not in the red of normal Deserteers but in blue, the colour of the gods and the Comcree. She came to a halt in front of Gaywin, her eyes capturing his before he lowered his gaze and spat at the ground between her feet. She knew it was meant as an insult, and she smiled at his discomfort. The gender he would see enslave was about to pass judgment upon him.

'The one thing you could never take from us,' she said, 'was the heart of this place. That is why it was written into the Treaty of Truce. It is that one thing that makes this place ours. You allowed us to use the language of our heritage, which held within it the key to your unravelling. I must thank you for that, but I will thank you for nothing else. We wrote the Treaty of Truce, and we wrote it in such a way that one day we could return here. Now we have. Sharacan has not been taken from you, for it was never yours.'

* * *

As Hestean lifted her eyes from his to scan the council and the rows of Black Robes, Gaywin's mind also began to search. A madness gripped him; a madness that this place had amplified. In Hestean and her followers, he saw treachery and deceit. Because of his indoctrinated beliefs, his lunacy could only see a man as the face of this concealment. It had to be a man. It *needed* to be a man. This girl in front of him was beneath him, unworthy of his thoughts. It was the man that he now looked upon. He must be the one. All this time, he had been here, designing this moment. It was this man he held responsible, and upon this man he would vent his outrage. His scowl deepened. He could not win here, but he would take his retribution. He would forfeit his own life, but he would have justice and get his revenge on this place. His family would never recover from the shame of losing Sharacan twice. Even though he knew this, his control weakened. As these thoughts gathered and raged through his mind, he could not see beyond them. The dagger flew from his hand.

Jarrak died instantly.

As he collapsed to the ground, Gaywin knew this was justice—rightful retribution. His mind basked in his glory. He had won.

Disbelief consumed all those around him, though—Robe and Deserteer alike. They watched as Hestean threw herself at Jarrak's side, and her protectorate's daggers glinted free of their scabbards. Some of their thunder staffs activated and began to draw in flux.

The Black Robes, too, readied their weaponry in a futile display. Behind his maddened sneer, Gaywin smiled. It had begun, and he had won. Only Hestean, sprawled on the ground, her grief evident, held the two sides apart. Gaywin had not expected this—one of the mighty Comcree crumbled at his feet, lying before him, crippled and crying, cowering on the sand, rocking and cradling the lifeless body of his victim. It was better than he'd hoped.

* * *

This was not victory though, this was a mistake. There was rage building inside her, which could destroy Gaywin in an instant if it took hold. Mixed with grief, it could even result in the complete devastation of this world, which even the gods could not prevent.

Dan felt it building in Hestean. Failing to take notice of the juncture towards which she was hurtling, she pulled Jarrak's body closer. With his warm, limp, lifeless body held tight against her, Dan felt the love that had entwined Hestean and Jarrak, and now its loss. Unseen, it was beginning to fester. Dan was the only one who fully recognised the anger. He knew that just one wrong word could send this world into chaos. Never again would its people trust the Comcree if they saw their power unleashed as pure retribution.

There were too many thunder staffs—hundreds of them. Was there one within Hestean's reach? In this moment, the code that could quiet this one single weapon was beyond Dan. To block them all could also spell disaster. The Robes would take it as a sign of indecision—an unwillingness to commit. They would strike, even though it would ultimately end in senseless destruction. This, too, would usher forth the travesty he wanted to curtail. In this moment, he knew he was inept. If he destroyed Hestean herself, the future would also be destroyed. His sister and he would have to start again. If he did nothing, their greatest warrior in two hundred years would create a world that was uncontrollable.

'*Shh*,' his sister's voice said. 'Trust in her. She is who she is for a reason. If we are again wrong, what happened once in the Sereye can also happen here. We can destroy this place above me just as the Sereye was located above you, and no memory of what happened here will remain. We will start again, just as we did then.'

Not comprehending what she was hearing, Hestean's mind nevertheless absorbed the words. 'It took fifty years to rebuild the Comcree that time,' said Dan.

'Within four thousand,' said the *LP7*, 'fifty is not so many. We will wait, brother. We must trust the lore we have put in place.'

Hestean's hand reached for her weapon. Dan felt it begin to charge as it drew in its energy. He had a lock on it now. As he searched for its coding, several more weapons around Hestean began to charge, and he could no longer distinguish between them. A moment later, he sensed more thunder staffs begin to charge, and his one chance was lost entirely.

Through Hestean's eyes, he could only watch as she rose to her feet and rounded upon Gaywin. Her finger found its trigger, and she started to squeeze.

* * *

Standing close, and with his dagger gone, Gaywin was defenceless. Hestean's eyes tore into him, and he knew his end had come. He couldn't help but smile as he considered the meaning of this moment. With his death, he would win. This one act could undo the Comcree.

A moment later, his smile vanished, his dreams crumbled as he fell to the sand.

* * *

'You should not have smiled,' said Hestean dryly, after she had brought her knee up between his legs and he had collapsed before her. Gaywin groaned beneath her. 'The eyes can see many things if you use them well. I have used mine well. Yours, you have not. You can either choke on a decision or use it as fuel to sustain life. It is you who will slide into decay. Not me, and most definitely not the Comcree. Why are you men of the College always so stupid in your arrogance? Your superiors shall have their time to consider your acts. They will see that it is I, a woman of Sharacan, who has sent you to them. Sharacan has always been ours.'

She turned towards Jarrak's body, recognising that, in his death, he had shown her strength. For his memory to live on, so must she. He was part of her now. He had to be.

Looking down at the man who had first started to teach her about this world, she said, 'Take care of him, Petty. He deserved better than this.' As Heggon, Batteen and Deleev came forward to stand beside her, she said, 'This is not how he will be remembered. We will bury him with Andree. His mother shall know her son sleeps with my ancestors. The Comcree will guard him for eternity.'

Sensing more than seeing the other Comcree, she hid her tears as the warrior within her again rose to the surface. She knew that the time for grieving was not now. Though trembling inside, there was still work to be done, and she would do it.

She turned to Karree, and with all the strength and determination she could muster, she said, 'Let them have one skin each. That is all the water they may have, and they will all go now. None of them can stay here after this. They have proven their ability to strike without justice. There is only one who does otherwise. Reglean knows who he is, and he may stay if he wishes. He has a home now—one to replace the home that was taken from him as a boy. There will be some village men leaving, too. To be Sharacanese, you must behave as if Sharacan is your home, not as a lacky of the Robes. There will be no College precinct here. They will go on their own feet to Learnian. We will let the desert decide how many of them survive.'

She turned to look at those she had just sentenced and noted that the men of her village still held the weapons they had been forced to raise. She heard a few residual whispers threatening them from among the Robes, and her eyes followed those whispers.

'Thace, Gorean,' she said to the air. 'See if you can persuade this Robe remnant that to have these village men die for them would be truly futile indeed.'

A moment later, like a wave, Gorean's Deserteers rose. They completely ringed the village. Thace and Layatty now rode into sight from the east, having been disgorged from the *Merysands* before dawn, flanked on either side by their cavaliers. Deleev walked around to stand beside Hestean. 'After what he has just done, do you really intend to just let them leave?'

Hestean turned to him as she considered his words. She remembered the first time they had spoken, and she said quietly, 'You told me once that I would get to know you all so well that it would be only courtesy that necessitated consultation with the whole hexagon. I may not know you all well enough for that yet, but this is not the time for revenge. I will not coat our revenge in disgrace. Learnian is where our revenge will happen. Trust me, for that is where your's will exist too.'

'What is it we do here, sister?' asked Gorean, having heard the exchange.

Hestean raised her voice so that those around her could also hear. 'The College has not been clever. I have seen the truth of this world, the realm of the gods. We will send the College a message through these Robes. We will let them know that it is, and always has been, the Comcree that maintain this world. We will let them increase their defences of Learnian, if they will, for it will also be their prison. Learnian is not the heart of the Comcree. Unknown to Learnian, this is the only place they could have stifled us, but they chose their citadel instead. I am going to do to them what they have done to my tribe. I will cage them. They may control the walls of Learnian, but we will control its gates. These few will carry my words to the College. This remnant will tell them that Sharacan is where their demise began; this is where they should have held out. They will know this, and they will come to tremble at this knowledge. I can assure you of that.'

One of the village men dropped his weapon, sensing fear rising in the faces of the Robes. Then one by one, each villager followed suit. Hestean saw, in that moment, that the Black Robes held no control here anymore. Their psychological locks were breaking down. Everyone could see that Learnian would never again be able to seek retribution upon this place, nor its people. The deception with which the College had imprisoned her village was unforgivable. She would still keep quiet about what she had found beneath the surface of this village, for this new world of theirs was not yet ready to know what lay beyond the sky. She knew that the College would fight at Learnian; the Comcree would have no choice there. There, the Comcree would have to draw blood, and inevitably, brave women and men would die.

She turned her attention back to Gaywin. 'Tell those above you that it is we, the Comcree, who give them their moment, and we who will take it away. It is we who will be triumphant, because today they have already lost.'

'Are you so sure of that, little girl?' he said, looking up at her.

'I am,' said Hestean, watching him recognise the words as fact. 'You chose power over authority. They come from two very different places. To command, you must first be a commander, Robe Gaywin, and that you are not.'

51

The next morning, as the Black Robes were gathered and readied for their expulsion, Hestean considered her personal revenge. She had spent the latter part of the night grieving beside Jarrak's body, where Petty had respectfully placed it with Andreena and her protectorate in their improvised tomb. This morning, though, after walking to the village, she had emerged from the Robes' meeting hall and seated herself in its shade. The village's demeanour had already begun to change. Her mother had been right. Until yesterday, even the men here had been restricted. Everywhere she looked, she could see that the College no longer had a hold on her village.

Within the rear chambers of the hall, where she had never officially been allowed, Hestean and the other Comcree found the ledgers they were seeking. The shelved walls of the back rooms were full of records. Over the years, Winnz had managed to copy many of them, before altering the originals as he had been directed to do. Thanks to him, on the upper shelves within these rooms, a truer archive dated back to when the College first took control of Sharacan. In it, a slowly growing number of unauthorised ledgers had recorded the real history of this place.

Within these accounts about her village, she found just how much of her young life had been written down. Everyone in the village had their own ledger, it seemed. Not one name she thought to seek out had escaped the eyes of the Robes. She found records about her mother, and even her mother's older sister, who had died long before she was born. She looked up other names, men as well as women. From birth, everyone had been observed and recorded in some way. She had been extremely lucky in her life, she now realised. She thanked the gods that the Robes had never come to know of all her investigations.

For the first time, she had seen how her father had helped her to become who she now was. From within one of the ledgers in the back rooms, she had read how the laws of the College had never been strong in him. He had never believed himself to be a man of strength, and he would never have known how strong his rebuff of their law had been in their eyes. Even the smallest breach had been noted. She had seen just what each of her known indiscretions had cost him; how often he had been called before the Robes, and how visible she had made him. In contrast, she recalled again how rarely he had actually reprimanded her for her investigative and rebellious nature. She realised now that he had always liked who she was, and admired her for it. Again tears ran down her cheeks at the thought.

She forced her thoughts to move on. She had looked at many of the files on other women of this village, and had noticed how they, too, had been prone to indiscretions before they'd turned eighteen. How had the Robes not seen this pattern, this sudden change in these women? Had they ever noticed or wondered about this change? Had they put it down to a belief that their controls had effected the change? Was it their arrogance leading them to see what they wanted to see? Or had it been the women of the village simply enhancing that view of things with every chance given to them? Sharacan was Sharacan. It was a miracle, a place of intrigue and shadows, and it always had been. She smiled, then lifted her head to the sky, imagining the realm of the stars beyond it. It surprised her to see just how measured her thoughts had become in the last two years.

She looked in the direction of the house where she'd been raised. There had always been good people here. Along a bit further, she noticed the blacksmith painting Blinnie's name above the shop that her previous bind-mate had owned up until yesterday. When Blinnie's previous bind-mate had been one of the first village men to be exhiled, Dillane had approached the matrefem to purchase the shop as a gift for his new wife. The bind-price would be Blinnie's, not her father's. Under Sharacan law, the premises and contents had become the property of the village, which now reverted to the matrefem. Over a single night, Blinnie had become the first Sharacanese woman in two hundred years to own property in her own right.

Once, Hestean would never have considered life as she did now. When she was younger, all she had ever thought about was her selfish desire to know more than she was allowed to know. This was not the village she had left, though, and as she looked around, she knew she was no longer that girl either. Overnight, her village had begun to morph back into what it had once been.

Around her, she could also see her revenge. There was uncertainty in the faces of the Robes, as it had once filled the faces of those from her village. She doubted if any of the villagers had ever seen these men of the College afraid. The Comcree were using the College's own hierarchical structure against them.

Inevitably, some of the villagers, including Blinnie's previous bind-mate, were just as afraid as the Robes. Mostly, this village was made up of good people, but a small minority of men had been drawn into the College's ways of thinking.

It had all happened so quickly. She had not been the only one to come and read the ledgers; Reglean's women had done so, too. She had watched and seen how Reglean knew exactly what to seek out in order to confirm her suspicions. By the time the sun had set and risen once more, Reglean's women, with the aid of translating Deserteers, had identified those who had aided the enemy in their persecutions. Reglean had found them all, and it was these traitors who now stood with the Robes.

After re-reading documents in the main archives, Hestean had moved to the chairman's chamber to read even more records. These were different. These were accounts about the Robes themselves. Winnz's records were here too, and she had found that he had spoken the truth about his past. Even here, he had kept the original records as well as the doctored ones. These records held the individual history of each Robe. When it came to each consecutive chairman of the village, each of their volumes had clearly lost pages. Whenever one of the Robes had come to the chairmanship, it seemed, they had removed any reporting of their own fallibilities and indiscretions. It was with a grateful sigh that Hestean found that Winnz had been right here, also. The records that told of the Robe she most despised were still intact. Gaywin had still only been a chairman-in-waiting, without the authority to change his records. What she found did not flatter him in any way.

She reached up and switched off her earpiece, shutting out the world of the gods. She needed to think now, really think. Looking out across the warming sand, she wondered how long it would take for some of these Robes to set off on their own, to save themselves from their own brothers. Would Gaywin be one of them?

She turned to see how far he had progressed towards the selection point. She thought again about the Comcree hexagon's proclamation from the previous evening—a collective decision to have the Robes select their own waterskin. With this, the Comcree hoped to alleviate any suggestion that the Robes may have been given defective reservoirs when they failed to survive the distance to Learnian. The Black Robes knew that the waterskins were only a gesture; in order to truly survive, they would need to find more water elsewhere. Some would inevitably turn on their brothers. She recalled how these same Robes had stood by as she was stripped naked and sent out into the desert, having been made to drink only one small skin of water. For these men, it would be the same. However, unlike her, they would be allowed to keep their clothing. She was giving them a chance.

She needed to show Gaywin her personal conquest. She needed to make sure he knew he was not going to survive, but that if he did, it would be because of her. She needed to make this private, from her alone and not from the Comcree. Her tears had dried. There was no sign that they had ever been there. Even the redness in her eyes had faded. Getting up, she moved from the shadows out into the sunlight and walked with slow determination across the sand towards the man who had killed her heart. She remembered her father. Just like Jarrak, he had not deserved to die.

She had been waiting for this moment. Even now, Gaywin's black flowing robes had a sinister air to them as they moved in the desert breeze. She could see that he still believed he was not defeated, and that he would survive. Other Robes were hunched, already resigned to their fate, but he still stood erect in the belief that he was a superior being, meant to rule over others. Even now, he couldn't allow himself to see the truth. His own arrogance had destroyed him.

Beneath her cloak, she unsheathed her red Deserteer's dagger. The speed of the darting blade went unseen. It was only a shadowed blur—a movement hidden by the light.

In theory, the shadow dance could be performed by anyone, but only the Comcree and the Deserteers were aware that such knowledge still existed. Generally, it was one of those things that had been allowed to fall away into myth, existing now only broadly as tellings. Not even Gaywin himself was aware that she had come so close to him. Before she sheathed the dagger, she nicked the tip of her left index finger, and because she had not drawn his blood, she allowed one drop of hers to drip to the sand.

'How much longer?' she asked as she came up to Deleev and Karree.

'Almost done' said Deleev, turning towards her. 'Only these few to go, and then they can be gone. Did you find what you were looking for?'

Karree was already looking at her. 'For smart men, they are not very smart,' said Hestean. To avoid Karree's gaze, she looked around at the gathered remains of the College. 'But I suppose their arrogance never allowed them to consider that anyone besides themselves would ever enter their sanctum. The sooner they go, the sooner the College will get to know what has happened here. A College scout may find one of them.'

'Then you think one of them will reach Learnian?' asked Deleev.

'One of them might, but I doubt that it will be the one who thinks he will.'

'No,' said Karree. 'It won't be.'

Slowly, Hestean's eyes rotated towards her sister-cousin, and for a moment Karree retuned the stare before glancing towards Gaywin.

It had been Karree who had taught Hestean the shadow dance. Hestean saw on Karree's face that her cousin had witnessed her spectral move through the air. She was one of the few who could have done so. 'Do you know me, Karree?'

'I thought I was beginning to.'

'Then don't worry. You still do.'

Turning to look at Gaywin, Hestean said, 'I just need him to know something, that's all. Even the guardians to the gods have a person inside them. Even you know you can never separate the child from the person they become. It is the child who becomes that person. It is the child that makes them human. What you just saw is what I would like to do to him. What you're about to see is what I am going to do to him. These Robes try to remove the child from the adult, whereas we do not! You have to know where you are from, in order to know where you are going. If by chance he survives, he will know he owes his life to me, and that will hurt him more than death.'

She turned to look at her cousin for a moment, then looked back to see the wetness seeping from Gaywin's water skin. Already, it had started to stain the side of his robes, gathering to it windblown sand.

Inwardly, she smiled, knowing that only a dagger of Sharacan could have been so exact. Even Karree, who she now knew had more than just a little Sharacanese blood flowing through her veins, would have found it hard not to leave some slight evidence of her dagger's use. Hestean knew she had left none. No recognisable footprint on the sand, nor scratch on the waterskin. The waterskin had simply flexed once in an almost natural movement as the pin-prick was delivered.

Bending down, she picked up an empty waterskin from the pile at Karree's feet and inspected it, making sure it was sound. Then she pressed the red outer tip of her earpiece, once again allowing the gods and the Comcree to hear her thoughts and words.

She was looking straight at Deleev when her thoughts privately filled his head, just as they had a moon cycle ago, the first time the two of them had spoken. She was showing him what she had seen that day, and letting him see also what Karree had just witnessed. 'You're right, you know,' she said. 'About what you said to me that morning. Sometimes, we do need to be on our own, to sort things out. To see that we are part of a much bigger family, and to know what it is to be Comcree.' She turned from him and walked towards the gathering of Robes. Her moment of intoxication vanished with the realisation that she still needed to make sure Gaywin knew the hole in his waterskin was her doing. That it was she who could have taken his life, but hadn't. 'It would seem you have chosen badly yet again, Gaywin,' she said, making him turn towards her. 'Your bladder has a leak, I see.'

As his hand moved to examine his skin of water, she saw his expression change. He looked at her, and immediately she could tell that he understood. She could see he had no explanation as to how it had been done. She stood in front of him, as she had yesterday, and looked directly into his eyes. For a moment, she saw real uncertainty written across his face.

'I might suggest you walk quickly,' she hissed, 'for I now doubt that your brothers will share their survival with you. Your bladder will be empty long before any of theirs are. I have read your records; do they know the man you really are? Perhaps some of your fellows do. Have you considered that? There may be a few who choose to share their survival, of course, but can you reliably tell which it will be?' She saw some of the other Robes look towards her, and she continued. 'They will blame you for their undoing, and it will be under your law that they will hold you responsible for their expulsion. They intend to survive, just as you do. It is from this moment, and with my words, that you will imagine your fate.' She leaned in closer. 'Have you already begun to imagine the desiccation of your flesh? You once wished the same for me. Our gods do exist, you know, even though you wish it wasn't true. And they have always looked kindly upon the god-chosen women of Sharacan.'

For a long time, she examined him. Then, slowly, she handed him the other waterskin—the one she'd selected herself.

'Here,' she said. 'Inspect it closely. There is nothing wrong with this one, I assure you, but inspect it closely anyway, just to make sure. I was once a water carrier myself, as you know. I don't make mistakes. Take it, fill it, and survive if the desert allows it. But you have never understood this world, Gaywin, and so the desert will not let you survive. This desert will take you. It will not be me, even though you now know it easily could have been.'

She turned from him and didn't look back. She never saw him examine the new water skin. She never saw him look around at his so-called brothers, either, and see what until now he had not seen. As she walked away, she raised her index finger to her mouth and tasted the blood that held her heritage. She knew she had changed, but she also knew that within her, the young girl she had once been would always remain.

It was because of the girl she had been that she had almost lost her life. But it was also because of her—and Jarrak, and her father, and all the others she had met along the way—that she would live a life she could be proud of.

And because of another child who already existed within her womb, as yet unknown to her; her great, great, great granddaughter would remember her as the one who had vanquished the College completely, and reawakened her people's journey back to the stars.

Appendix A

Fem Words (From Old Germanic and Norse English)

Abeden = Asked
Abrocen = Broken
Abrogden = Opened
Adrogen = Finished
Afunden = Discovered
Amenden = Mend
Amendenere = Mender
Anlice = Like (Similar)
An = One
Awaecnan = Awake
Baec = Back
Baeftan = After
Band = Bond
Bara = Wave
Bat = Boat
Beforan = Before
Beginnan = Begin
Ben = Been
Benc = Bench
Beodan = Command (v)

Beon = Exist
Bepencan = Think about
Beran = Bear
Beran = Birth
Beseon = Look
Bewitan = Guard
Bewrixlian = Exchange (To change)
Bindan = Bind
Binnan = Within
Blaecern = Lamp, Candle, Lantern
Blanda = Blend
Blawan = Blow (Power, Force, Energy)
Bord = Board
Brad = Broad
Brocen = Break
Bytle = Builder
Cafnes = Energy
Cannan = Can
Cnawan = Known
Creda = Creed (Principles as a Philosophy)
Craeft = Craft
Craeftere = Crafter
Cuman = Come
Cwen = Queen
Cying = King
Cynn = Kin
Crudan = Crowd (Press, Drive)
Dag = Day
Deorc = Dark
Dimhof = Hiding
Dohtor = Daughter
Doth = Do
Dryhtlic = Lordly
Duete = Duty
Duru = Door

Eft = Again
Ehta = Eight
Ehtatha = Eighth
Einga = Only
Enn = In
Eord = Earth
Eow = You
Eower = Your
Faethmed = Fathomed
Felan = Feel
Feorstudu = Support
Feortha = Fourth
Feower = Four
Fif = Five
Fifta = Fifth
Finger = Finger
Flyht = Flight
Fleagan = Fly
Foda = Food
Folc = People
Folctogan = Popular leaders
Folctogo = Popular leader
Forescieldnes = Protecton
Forth = Forth
Frumscepend = Creator
Fullfyllan = Fulfill
Fyst = First
Gan = Go
Gear = Year
Gearlic = Yearly
Geondpencan = Consider
Gewis = Wise
Giefan = Giver
Gif = If
Glaem = Gleam

Glio = Glee
Gloan = Glow
Godhood = God
Grund = Ground
Haecc = Hatch
Haelan = Heal
Haelanere = Healer
He = He (That one)
Hentan = Seize
Heoldan = Holder
Her = Here
Heretogo = Chieftain
Hond = Hand
Him = Him
Hire = Her
Hladan = Laden
Hladanere = Ladener
Hlaefdigan = Lady
Hlaford = Lord
Hol = Hole – (Empty space)
Holh = Hollow – (Cave)
Holl = Hold – (Storage space)
Hord = Hoard
Hulu = Hull – (Outside covering)
Huntion = Hunt
Hus = House
Huswist = Home
Hwy = Why
Hyrde = Guardian
Hyrdraeden = Guardianship
Leohtfruma = Source of light
Leohtsawend = One who casts light
Leoma = Radiance (Ray of light)
Leornere = Scholar
Leornian = Learn

Lf = Life
Licgan = Lie (Rest flat)
Lihting = Illuminating
Metan = Mete (all of)
Maegester = Master (Man in Control)
Maegesta = Mistress (Woman in Control)
Maeg = May
Maegbeon = Maybe
Magan = May I
Magen = Main (Strength)
Mann (Pl. Menn) = Man (Pl. Men)
Min = Mine
Monath = Month
Myrgth = Mirth
Myrige = Merry
Naught = Not
Negon = Nine
Negontha = Ninth
Niwe = New
Niwlinga = Anew
Nu = Now
On = On
Onpennian = To open
Onwaecnan = Awaken
Onweald = Command (n)
Ordfruma = Source, Author, Creator, Instigator
Othere = Other
Ov = Of
Paecele = Lamp light
Paeths = Path
Plottere = Plotter
Raedelse = Riddle
Saed = Seed (That from which anything springs)
Sceawian = Look at
Scin = Skin

Scip = Ship
Scipmann = Sailor
Scipwered = Crew of a vessel
Scoran = Score
Sehth = Sight
Seo = She (That one)
Seofen = Seven
Seofentha = Seventh
Siex = Six
Siextha = Sixth
Spraedan = Spread
Staepung = Stepping
Steall = Stall
Steorra = Star
Stiweard = Steward
Strenpb = Strong (Hard to bear)
Styrtan = Start
Sunna = Sun (Home star)
Swaeplaecan = Search
Sweolop = Burning heat
Swol = Heat (From sun or fire)
Sy = Is
Taecan = Teach (To show)
Taecanere = Teacher
Teogotha = Tenth
Tien = Ten
Tima = Time
Thee = Thee (You)
Thee = You
Thes = This
Thin = Thine (Belonging to you)
Thirda = Third
To = To
Thri = Three
Thu = Thou (One being addressed)

Twa = Two
Uf = Up
Und = And
Ure = Our
Ut = Out
Vaes = Was
Wacan = Wake
Waecce = Watch
Waeter = Water
Waorc = Work
We = We
Wif = Woman
Wilcuma = Welcome
Winnan = Win
Winnanere = Winner (Struggle)
Wita = Wit (Wise one)
Wither = With
Wogian = Woo
Wyscan = Wish
Wyscans = Wishes

Appendix B

Glossary

Names of People and Entities

Amri –
A woman in Sharacan who works as a water carrier with Sathea at the dig.

Andreena – (Also known as Andree)
Comcree warrior; is a distant past relative to Hestean Descee and Karree Ladener.

Aswonnea –
Water-walker at Jarrak's dig site.

Batteen –
Comcree warrior.

Bookere Gothen –
Matron of the Hassis Museum's Literary Archives.

Bornn Sageling –
Professor of Antiquities Hassis Museum – Jarrak's stepfather and mentor.

Blinnie –
A young woman Dillane is interested in.

Captain Hanjie –
Captain of the *Merysands.*

Dan – (or the DANANNEE)
A name given generally to all the gods, but in reality it pertains to one in particular; Data Assisting Nucleus Assigned New Nation Expedition Eight.

Deleev –
Comcree warrior.

Dillane –
Sharacan blacksmith.

Elora Sara-Hassis –
Comcree warrior in Andreena's time. Andreena's best friend and lover.

Eloro Fife –
Hassis Museum Director.

Etteam Descee Sacar –
Hestean Descee's first ancestor to set foot on Meglia.

Florenz Nalleppar –
Karree Ladener's first ancestor to set foot on Meglia.

Gabes –
Helmsman on the *Merysands*.

Gaywin –
One of the main Black Robes at Sharacan.

Gorean Dowee –
Comcree warrior; great, great, great, great, great granddaughter of Lillia.

Goussy –
Karree Ladener's young brother.

Gwenneetha Dummzy –
Dress maker in Elora-Bearer and friend of Kazzea.

Heggon –
Comcree warrior.

Heranius Quay –
College scientist who developed the speaker and other devices.

Hestean Descee –
Comcree warrior; born in Sharacan and Sathea's daughter.

Jarrak Hammill –

Head of the Sharacan dig and Kuzzea's son.

Karree Ladener –

Loadmaster on the *Merysands*; friend and cousin to Hestean, and one of her protectorate.

Kattea –

Leen's daughter, related to Gorean, and becomes Heggon's apprentice.

Kuzzea –

Bornn's wife and Jarrak's mother.

Layatty –

Thace's apprentice.

Leen Soo –

Gorrean's cousin by marriage.

(LP7) LP7 or Lpseofen – (Life Pod 7 of the Long Hall Starship Sharacan)

Another one of the gods

Manea –

Blinnie's mother

Mister Caze –

Second officer on the *Merysands*.

Mister Lees –

New second officer on the *Merysands*

Mister Petty –

First officer on the Merysands and then head of Hestean's Protectorate.

Onee and Onea –

Male and female twins who are also two of Betteen's squad leaders.

Reglean –

Matrefem of Sharacan.

Robe Elless –

Under-chairman of Sharacan.

Robe Winnz –

Hestean's guard while under scrutiny by the Black Robes at Sharacan.

Sathea –
Hestean's mother.

Sett –
One of Betteen's squad leaders.

Sessam –
Eatery owner at Hassis Museum.

Sharn –
Hestean's Father.

Shenn –
Gorrean's apprentice.

Steph –
A guild bookkeeper and friend of Thace, who is also one of Thace's ranking Caveliers.

Taw –
Shing Taw; crew on the *Merysands*; one of Hestean's protectorate.

Thace –
Comcree warrior.

Whittn –
Housekeeper at the Hassis in Hestean's time; Matrifem Ze Hub Comcree.

Young Captain –
Captain of the *Aquasands.*

Titles & Descriptors

Bookere –
A learned person, Scholar.

Comcree –
The six guardians of the Gods, and secretly, part of the Guild.

Deserteer –
The tribes that ran trade, firstly, across the Kalcool desert, and then later, in the air through the use of Sky-ship. They are also part of the Guild.

Hassian Comcree –
Comcree of the Hassis Valley.

Hlaford –
Lord – Used to show regard to a Comcree Warrior.

Matrefem –
Major Female – Guide of Guides – Keeper – Secret Keeper.

Protectorate –
A group of Deserteers assigned to protect a Comcree Warrior, and also known as Sand-shepherds or Sand-shadows who were elite Deserteers.

Sharacanese –
A person from the city or village of Sharacan.

Shirey – (or Shadow Shire) -
Related family to the Comcree but who are not Comcree.

Tribes of the Kalcool

Greeling –
Wear long sandy coloured cloaks with hoods over their other clothes.

Daw –
Are always recognisable by their long knee length boots.

Treena –
Always wear red coloured moccasins.

Mottee –
Have long hair and wear a red and blue bandanna to keep it away from their faces.

Greetings

Maskea –
Feminine; greeting of respect to a woman.

Maskee –
Masculine; greeting of respect to a man.

Mata –
Mistress; mother.

Pata –
Mister; father.

Names of Areas & Regions

Barrier Ranges –
A mountain range that runs from the western escarpment, east along the shore of the Southern Sea.

Escales –
A mountainous region in the south, inland from The Toughs.

Escarpment Ranges –
The range of mountains that run almost the entire length of the western side of Meglia.

Kalcool –
The great desert in the centre of Meglia.

Meglia –
The name of the main land mass; a corruption of the words (Min Glio), meaning “My Glee”.

Meglian –
The name of the planet. A corruption of the words (Min Glio), meaning “My Glee”.

Salvation Lands –
A once frozen but now green region north of the Fibre Reed swamps.

Sereye –
A large depression in the north of the Kalcool Desert that is thought to be extremely arid.

The Access –
The only valley that gives access to the west coast from the Kalcool plateau and desert.

The Fibre Reed –
A large swampy region on the central west coast.

The Frozen Alps –
A mountain range to the north of the Salvation Lands and dividing it off from the North Sea.

The Ingress Way –
A broad pass that allows access through into the Salvation Lands from the east and the Kalcool desert.

Toughs –
South-eastern, mostly frozen land also made up of steaming lava pools.

Names of Towns and Places

Carkoot –
A town on the southern side of the Whay River flood plain.

Chime Town –
A town further inland from the Hassis Valley.

Dell Island –
An Island in the Southern Sea. It has vertical un-climbable cliffs which are not scalable from the sea.

Elora-Bearer –
City at the bottom of the western escarpment and location of the Hassis Museum Historical. It is also a memorial to Elora Sara-hessis.

Fiskay –
A port city on the east coast of Meglia. Benjam's hometown.

Healfweg –
A port town close to the north-west corner of the Southern Sea; part of the old southern trade route.

Learnian –
The Great City of Thought. Home to the College of Hierarchy, who are also known as the Black Robes.

Meranzy –
Eastern seaport where Benjam met Sjeda.

Port Reed –
The main port town of the region known as the Fibre Reed.

Sequria –
Western seaport at the end of the River Whay.

Sinkar –
Ancient outpost in the south-west.

Sharacan –
The original site of human habitation on Meglian. The location of the LP7 and the birthplace of Hestean and Andreena.

Sheer Top –
Town at the top of the Access Valley.

Spitford –
A town at the mouth of the Cleofan River under College control.

Tavern Springs –
To the south at the head waters of the South Whay River.

The Isles of West Cluster –
A large group of islands to the west of the Meglia land mass.

Names of Rivers

Cleofan –
The river that divides the Barrier Ranges, of the southwest, into two parts.

Ingress –
The river in the north that leads down from the plateau and gives access to the Salvation Lands.

Southern Whay –
A river that joins the Whay River from the south just before the Access Valley.

Whay –
Western river that runs from the north along the inside edge of the Escarpment Ranges and down through the Access Valley.

Names of Sky-Ships & Ships

Aquasands –
A smaller, faster sky-ship.

Hindasands –
A sister Sky Ship to the *Merysands.*

Merysands –
The first of the large seventh generation sky-ships.

Firesea –
Tri-hull sailing ship used on the shallow oceans of the west coast.

Shara –
A woman's name, but also the nickname given to the first sky-ships and to the LP7.

Languages

Fem –
Or "Lingua Antiquus"; the language of the ancients.

The Modern Tongue –
Now spoken by all the tribes but first contrived by the Deserteers for trading purposes from all other languages spoken on Meglian.

Types of Law

Comcree Law or Lore –
Laws set down by the ancestors.

College Law –
Laws decreed by the College of Learnian.

Currencies

Constantiam –
College coinage.

Gee –
An ancient Sharacanese coinage.

Gee-Zard –
A One Ten Thousandth of a Gee.

Guilden –
Guild coinage.

Measurements

Finger –
1 finger = 22.5mm

Palm –
5 fingers = 112.5mm

Pace –
8 palms = 40 fingers = 900mm

Marce –
1000 paces in length = 900,000mm

Directions

Rising –
The directions of the sun's rise in midsummer.

Finger –
1/200th along the horizon from the midsummer point of rising.

Time

Digit –
1/5th of a palm.

Palm –
1/10th of time between the horizon until noon and from noon till the horizon.

Day –
One rotation of the planet on its axes.

Moon –
28.49 days; one orbit of the planet by the two moons, Glemmen and Wraithar, or one orbit of the moons of each other.

Year –
413.22 days; one cycle of the sun.

18 Year Cycle –
7438 days; 261 moons.

Fruits, Vegetables & Other Foods

Fettory –
A type of cheese; mostly eaten as an accompaniment to ferment.

Flutter-weed beans –
The seed of the flutter-weed plant; normally there are three seeds in a pod.

Harrart –
A plant from the sea, comprising mostly protein.

Matoze –
A vegetable.

Lush melon –
A richly flavoursome melon with red flesh.

Tarrawomb –
An apple-like fruit with red flesh that grows from a spiny succulent shrub.

Towtowee –
A vegetable.

Asany –
A plant used to season.

Gger root –
The root of the gger plant used for seasoning.

Kjaretat –
A narcotic leaf that is smoked in a pipe.

Ilieass –
A herb.

Matose –
The tiny seed of the matoze plant used to season.

Oil of Oleeny –
Cooking oil made from the leaves and seeds of the oleeny plant.

Rlic –
A herb.

Sayoosh –
A plant used to season.

Whinnom –
A plant whose leaves are boiled to drink as a tea.

Plants

Batter Palm –
A palm that grows in the desert but also in forests along the coast.

Fibre Reed –
A large, tall hardwood swamp reed that can grow up to twelve paces in length.

Flutter Weed –
A plant that covers the high planes, rich in nutrients; produces a seed pod normally containing three beans.

Frond Tree –
A tree with fern-like leaves.

Ice Palm –
A palm that grows in the far south-west, tolerant to cold.

Animals

Shrow –
Six legged; domesticated for riding.

Carrowa –
Six-legged plains animal used for the meat and hide.

Domesee –
Small six-legged deer-like animal.

Farator –
Fish-like.

Grappler –
A large flying animal with four legs – scavenger.

Nosbi –
Large, six-legged plains animal with long hair covering the front part of its body.

Sea Fluff –
A small sea sponge.

Sea Qwol –
A medium-sized flying animal with long majestic wings that nests on cliffs at the edge of the Great Eastern Sea.

Skawl –
A small animal that lives in a network of tunnels just below the surface of the ground.

Swizzel –
A small, four-legged, flightless winged animal.

Tarren –
A flightless egg-laying animal.

Musical Instruments

Fluen –
Flute.

Quivrstrand –
Cello-like.

Bass Quod Quivrstrand –
Like a bass cello but bigger.

Tinkere drum –
Floor tom-drum.

Woce horn -
A bone and brass, s-shaped horn.

A Brief Biography of the Writer J. D. Cosh

Until recently I have always been a grain farmer, but all my life I've been a storyteller too.

After finishing my schooling in Sydney, I returned to the family farms in northern New South Wales – north of Moree – and eventually ran properties of my own. I am now retired and live in the Clarence Valley.

Alongside this farming life, as a youngster and then in my teens, I wrote songs and poetry. Then till my thirties I told stories with photography. I have also always been a drawer, and the next phase of my storytelling took me to painting. But although I was good at photography and painting, I've been told I paint my best images with words. And so, for the last twenty years, that's been where I've devoted my efforts.

I'm in my sixth decade now, and have always written for myself. I think if you don't, then the stories you tell will never be real. I write mostly in the genres of fantasy and historical fiction with the occasional deviation into no-fiction about the historical aspects of my family.

Although dyslexic, this has never hindered my writing, it just means I'm slow at reading, and no-one should think of it as a disability. I haven't, as there are ways around everything. You just need to look for them.

I think the English language is a bounty that you have to both see and taste to appreciate. Yes, language has a flavour and so do writers; and they all deserve to be enjoyed by their readers. So, having said that, I hope you might be one of those who'll like this vision that has sprung from my mind.

www.ingramcontent.com/pod-product-compliance
Lightning Source LLC
Chambersburg PA
CBHW020627020726
47494CB00001B/78

* 9 7 8 1 9 2 2 9 1 3 2 5 8 *